THE
RISING

Also by Tim LaHaye
*   and Jerry B. Jenkins*
in Large Print:

Left Behind®
Tribulation Force
Nicolae
Soul Harvest
Apollyon
Assassins
The Indwelling
The Mark
Desecration
The Remnant
Armageddon
Glorious Appearing

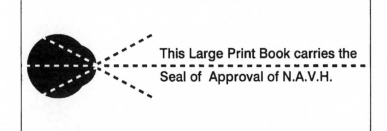
This Large Print Book carries the
Seal of Approval of N.A.V.H.

THE

Antichrist Is Born

RISING

Before They Were Left Behind

Tim LaHaye

Jerry B. Jenkins

Thorndike Press • Waterville, Maine

Published in 2005 by arrangement with
Tyndale House Publishers, Inc.

Thorndike Press® Large Print Basic.

The tree indicium is a trademark of Thorndike Press.

The text of this Large Print edition is unabridged.
Other aspects of the book may vary from the original edition.

Set in 16 pt. Plantin by Elena Picard.

Printed in the United States on permanent paper.

Library of Congress Cataloging-in-Publication Data

LaHaye, Tim F.
    The rising : Antichrist is born before they were left behind / by Tim LaHaye and Jerry B. Jenkins.
        p. cm.
    "Thorndike Press large print basic" — T. p. verso.
    ISBN 0-7862-7453-0 (lg. print : hc : alk. paper)
    1. Steele, Rayford (Fictitious character) — Fiction. 2. Rapture (Christian eschatology) — Fiction. 3. Antichrist — Fiction. 4. Large type books. I. Jenkins, Jerry B. II. Title.
PS3562.A315R57 2005b
    813'.54—dc22   2005000619

To Frank Muller*,
audio reader nonpareil

Special thanks
to David Allen
for expert technical consultation

*Mr. Muller's career as the world's most celebrated reader of audiobooks, including the Left Behind series, was interrupted in 2001 by a motorcycle accident, which left him incapacitated. His wife, Erika, cares for him and their two young children. Contributions to his astronomical medical expenses are tax deductible, and checks should be made payable to The Wavedancer Foundation (memo: The Frank Muller Fund) c/o John McElroy, 44 Kane Avenue, Larchmont, NY 10538.

As the Founder/CEO of NAVH, the only national health agency solely devoted to those who, although not totally blind, have an eye disease which could lead to serious visual impairment, I am pleased to recognize Thorndike Press★ as one of the leading publishers in the large print field.

Founded in 1954 in San Francisco to prepare large print textbooks for partially seeing children, NAVH became the pioneer and standard setting agency in the preparation of large type.

Today, those publishers who meet our standards carry the prestigious "Seal of Approval" indicating high quality large print. We are delighted that Thorndike Press is one of the publishers whose titles meet these standards. We are also pleased to recognize the significant contribution Thorndike Press is making in this important and growing field.

Lorraine H. Marchi, L.H.D.
Founder/CEO
NAVH

★ Thorndike Press encompasses the following imprints: Thorndike, Wheeler, Walker and Large Print Press.

Post–Twentieth Century

Prologue

The sun hung just below Rayford Steele's glare shield, making him squint even behind his dark gray lenses. His first officer, Chris Smith, pointed and said, "Oops, how long has that been there?"

Rayford shielded his eyes and found the message screen reading "ENGINE #1 OIL FILT."

Oil pressure was normal, even on the engine in question, the one farthest to his left. "Engine number one oil-filter checklist, please," he said.

Chris dug into the right side pocket for the emergency manual. While Chris was finding the right section, Rayford grabbed the maintenance log he should have checked before pulling back from the gate in Chicago and heading for Los Angeles. He speed-read. Sure enough, engine number one had required an oil filter change in

Miami before the leg to O'Hare, and metal chips had been detected on the used filter. They must have been within acceptable limits, however, as the mechanic had signed off on the note. And the plane had made it to Chicago without incident.

" 'Retard thrust level slowly until message no longer displayed,' " Chris read.

Rayford followed the procedure and watched the message screen. The throttle reached idle, but the message still shone. After a minute he said, "It's not going out. What next?"

" 'If ENG OIL FILT message remains displayed with thrust lever closed: FUEL CONTROL SWITCH . . . CUTOFF.' "

Rayford grabbed the control cutoff switch and said, "Confirm number one cutoff switch?"

"Confirmed."

Rayford pulled out and down in one smooth motion while increasing pressure on the right rudder pedal. Engine number one shut down, and the auto throttle increased power on the other three. Airspeed slowly decreased, and Rayford doubted anyone would even notice.

He and Chris determined a new altitude, and he instructed Chris to call air-traffic control at Albuquerque to get clearance to descend to 32,000 feet. They then positioned a transponder to warn other traffic that they might be unable to climb or maneuver properly if there was a conflict.

Rayford had no question they could reach LAX without incident now. He became aware of the strain on his right foot and remembered he had to increase pressure to compensate for the uneven thrust of the remaining engines. *C'mon, Rayford. Fly the airplane.*

After Rayford informed Pan-Con of the situation, the dispatcher told him to be aware of low visibility at LAX. "You'll want to check weather as you get closer."

Rayford announced to the passengers that he had shut down the number one engine but didn't expect anything but a routine landing at LAX. The lower the plane flew, however, the more he could tell that the power margin had increased. He did not want to have to go around, because going from near idle to full power on three engines would require a lot of rudder to counteract the thrust differential.

LAX tower was informed of the engine issue and cleared the Pan-Con heavy for initial landing sequence. At 10,000 feet Rayford began checking descent figures.

Chris said, "Auto brakes."

Rayford responded, "Three set."

LAX approach control turned Rayford and Chris over to the tower, which cleared them to land on runway 25 left and informed them of wind speed and RVR (runway visual range).

Rayford flipped on the taxi lights and directed Chris to zero the rudder trim. Rayford felt the pressure increase under his foot. He would have to keep up with the auto throttles as the power changed and adjust the rudder pressure to match. He was as busy as he had ever been on a landing, and the weather was not cooperating. Low cloud cover blocked his view of the runway.

Rayford worked with Chris, setting the speed to match the flap settings and feeling the auto throttles respond by reducing power to slow the plane. "Glide slope intercept," he said, "flaps 30, landing check." He set the speed indicator at 148, final speed for a flaps-30 approach with that much weight.

Chris followed orders and grabbed the checklist from the glare shield. "Landing gear," he said.

"Down," Rayford said.

"Flaps."

"Thirty."

"Speed brakes."

"Armed."

"Landing check complete," Chris said.

The plane could land itself, but Rayford wanted to be in control just in case. It was a lot easier to be flying than to have to take over if the autopilot had to be suddenly switched off.

"Final approach fix," Chris said.

A loud horn sounded when Rayford clicked off both the autopilot and throttles. "Autopilot disengaged," he said.

"One thousand feet," Chris said.

"Roger."

They were in the middle of clouds and would not likely see the ground until just before touchdown.

A mechanical voice announced, "Five hundred feet." It would announce again at fifty, thirty, twenty, and ten feet. They were ninety seconds from touchdown.

Suddenly Rayford overheard a transmission.

"Negative, US Air 21," the tower said, "you are not cleared for takeoff."

"Roger, tower," came the answer. "You were broken. Understand US Air 21 is cleared for takeoff."

"Negative!" the tower responded. "Negative, US Air 21! You are *not* cleared to take the runway!"

"Fifty feet," the auto announcer called out. "Thirty."

Rayford broke through the clouds.

"Go around, Cap!" Chris shouted. "A '57 is pulling onto the runway! Go around! Go around!"

Rayford could not imagine missing the 757. Time slowed, and he saw his family clearly in his mind, imagined them grieving, felt guilty about leaving them. And all the people on the plane. The crew. The passengers. And those on the US Air too!

In slow motion he noticed a red dot on the center screen of the instrument console with a minus 2 next to it. The auto announcer was sounding, Chris screaming, the tower shouting on the radio, "Pull up! Pull up! Pull up!"

Rayford mashed the go-around buttons on the throttles twice for maximum power and called out, "God, help me!"

Chris Smith whined, "Amen! Now fly!"

Rayford felt the descent arresting, but it didn't appear it would be enough. Rayford imagined the wide eyes of the US Air passengers on the ground. "Flaps twenty!" he barked. "Positive rate. Gear up." Smith's hands were flying, but the gap was closing.

The plane suddenly dipped left, the three good engines causing the slight roll. Rayford had not added enough rudder to counteract them. If he didn't adjust, the wingtip would hit the ground. They were a split second from the 757's tail — standing nearly four stories — and about to bottom out. Rayford closed his eyes and braced for impact. He heard swearing in the tower and from Chris. What a way to go . . .

Twenty-Four Years Earlier

One

Marilena Titi's union with Sorin Carpathia was based on anything but physical passion. Yes, they had had what the vulgar in the West would call a fling. But as his student and eventually his assistant at the University of Romania at Bucharest, Marilena had been drawn to Sorin's intellect.

The truth, she knew, was that there was little prepossessing about either of them. He was short and thin and wiry with a shock of curly red hair that, despite its thickness and his aversion to haircuts, could not camouflage the growing bald spot at his crown.

She was thick and plain and eschewed makeup, nail polish, and styling her black hair. Colleagues, who she was convinced had been wholly enculturated by outside influences, teased that her frumpy clothing and sensible shoes harkened to previous centuries. They had long since abandoned trying to make her into something she could never be. Marilena was not blind. The mirror did not lie. No amount of paint or spritz would change her, inside or out.

And inside was where she lived, physically and mentally. She would not have traded that for all the *patrician* the butcher could stuff. In recent decades, a tsunami of progress had transformed her quaint motherland from that with the lowest standard of living in Europe to a technological marvel. Marilena could have done without it all. She resided in the horn of plenty of her own prodigious mind, fertilized by an inexhaustible curiosity.

Perhaps she *had* been born a century late. She loved that no other Eastern European nations traced their lineage to the ancient Romans. And while she knew that modern Romanian women looked, dressed, spoke, danced, and acted like their Western icons, Marilena had resisted even the fitness craze that sent her peers biking, hiking, jogging, and climbing all over her native soil.

Marilena knew what was out there, outside the book-lined, computer-laden, two-room flat she shared with her husband of six years. But save for the occasional foray by bus, for reasons she could not now remember, she rarely felt compelled to travel farther than the university, where she too was now a professor of literature. That was a four-block walk to a ten-minute bus ride.

Sorin preferred his ancient bicycle, which he carried to his office upon arriving each day and four floors up to their apartment upon his return. As if they had room for that.

But hiding the bike reflected his mistrust of mankind, and Marilena could not argue. For all their decrying of religion, particularly branches that espoused innate sinfulness, everyone Marilena knew would have taken advantage of their best friends given the slightest chance. Everyone, perhaps, but the mysterious Russian émigré who ran the Tuesday night meetings in the anteroom at a local library. After several months of attending, Marilena had not yet formed an opinion of the thirty or so others who attended, but something deep within her resonated with Viviana Ivinisova.

Ms. Ivinisova, a handsome, tailored woman in her mid-thirties, seemed to take to Marilena too. Short with salt-and-pepper hair, Viviana seemed to be speaking directly to Marilena while gazing at the others just enough to keep their attention. And sure enough, when the younger woman stayed after her twelfth meeting to ask a question, the leader asked if she cared to get a drink.

With her load of books and folders gathered to her chest as she walked, Ms. Ivinisova reminded Marilena of her university colleagues. But Viviana was no professor, bright as she was. "This," she said, nodding to her pile of resources, "is my full-time job."

How delicious, Marilena thought. She herself had never imagined a cause more worthy than expanding one's mind.

They found a nearly deserted bistro a block from Marilena's bus stop, were seated at a tiny, round table, and Viviana wasted no time starting the conversation. "Do you know the etymology of your name?"

Marilena felt herself redden. "Bitter light," she said.

Viviana nodded, holding her gaze.

Marilena shrugged. "I don't put any stock in —"

"Oh, I do!" Viviana said. "I do indeed. *Bitter,*" she said slowly. "It doesn't have to be as negative as it sounds. Sadness perchance, a bit of loneliness? emptiness? a hole? something incomplete?"

Marilena reached too quickly for her glass and sloshed the wine before drawing it to her lips. Swallowing too much, she coughed and dabbed her mouth with a napkin. She shook her head. "I feel complete," she said.

Marilena could not meet the older woman's eyes. Viviana had cocked her head and was studying Marilena with a closed-mouth smile. "There is the matter of *light*," she said. "The bitterness, whatever that entails, is counterbalanced."

"Or my late mother just liked the name," Marilena said. "She was not the type to have thought through its meaning."

"But you are."

"Yes," Marilena wanted to say. "Yes, I am. I think through everything." But agreeing would appear boastful.

Where was the European reserve? Why were Russians so direct? Not as crass as Americans, of course, but there was little diplomacy here. In spite of herself, Marilena could not hold this against Ms. Ivinisova. Something within the woman seemed to care for Marilena in a way that both attracted and repelled her. She might not abet the Russian in her attempt to violate personal borders, but she could not deny the dichotomy that the attention also strangely warmed her.

"Your husband does not attend with you anymore," Viviana said.

It was meant, Marilena decided, to sound

like a change of subject. But she knew better. It was an attack on her flank, a probe, an attempt to get to the *bitter* part of her. Clearly Ms. Ivinisova believed in the portent of one's name. It seemed anti-intellectual to Marilena, but then that was what kept Sorin from the weekly meetings.

Marilena shook her head. "He's not a believer."

Viviana smiled. "Not a believer." She lit a cigarette. "Are you happy with him?"

"Reasonably."

The older woman raised her eyebrows, and Marilena fought to keep from letting down more of her guard.

"He's brilliant," Marilena added. "One of the most widely read men I have ever known."

"Which makes you 'reasonably happy' with him."

Marilena nodded warily. "We've been together eight years."

Viviana slid her chair back and crossed her legs. "Tell me how you met."

What was it about this persistence that had such a dual impact on Marilena? To anyone else she would have said, "I don't know you well enough to tell you about my personal life." Yet despite the direct approach, Marilena felt bathed in some sort of care, compassion, interest. She was put off and intoxicated at the same time.

She allowed a smile. "We had an affair of sorts."

"Oh!" Viviana said, leaning forward and crushing out her smoke. "I must hear it all. Was he married?"

"He was. But not happily. He did not even wear his ring, though the whiteness near his knuckle was still fresh."

Nostalgia washed over Marilena as she recalled her days as a doctoral student under the quiet flamboyance of the strange-looking professor so enamored of classical literature. By her questions, her participation, her papers, he had been able to tell that she was not there to merely fulfill a requirement. He engaged her in class, and the other students seemed content to act as spectators to their daily dialogue.

"He was a god to me," Marilena said. "It was as if he knew everything. I could not raise an issue, a point, a subject he had not studied and thought through. I suddenly knew what love was — not that I believed I loved him. But I could not wait to get back to his class. I threw myself into the work so I would be prepared. I had always lived for learning, but then I burned to impress him, to be considered his equal — not as an intellectual, of course, but as a fellow seeker of knowledge."

It was the wine, Marilena decided. How long had it been since she had been this effusive, this transparent? And with a virtual stranger, no less. Of course, Viviana Ivinisova reminded her of Sorin in Marilena's impressionable days. She was just as drawn to this woman who seemed to know so much, to care so deeply, and who was so willing to open an entirely new world to initiates. How could Viviana know who would respond to things beyond themselves, truths most would consider coarse and mystical, outside conventional academia? What would Marilena's colleagues think? Well, she knew. They would think of her what Sorin now thought of her. His indifference spoke loudly, as did his absence from the meetings after a mere two weeks nearly three months before.

"Did you pursue him?" Viviana Ivinisova said.

"I never even considered it. I pursued his mind, yes. I wanted to be near him, with him, in his class or otherwise. But I believe it was he who pursued me."

"You believe?"

"He did. He asked if I would consider serving as his assistant. I suspected nothing more than that he respected my mind. He had to consider me his inferior, yet I allowed myself to imagine that he at least respected my intellectual curiosity and dedication to learning."

Viviana seemed not to have blinked. "You were not used to being pursued."

No debate there. Marilena barely spoke to males, and not only had she never flirted with or pursued one, but neither had she ever considered such interest coming the other way. Certainly not with Dr. Carpathia. Not even when he insisted she call him Sorin. And have a meal with him. And spend time with him aside from office hours.

Even when he became familiar, touching her shoulder, squeezing her hand, throwing an arm around her, she considered him brotherly, or more precisely, avuncular, for he was ten years her senior.

"But at some point you had to have known," Viviana said. "You married the man."

"When I first accepted his invitation to the apartment we now share," Marilena said, "we spent most of the night discussing great literature. He made dinner — very badly — but I was too intimidated to agree when he said so. We watched two movies, the first a dark, thought-provoking picture. He sat close to me, again in a familial fashion, leaning against me. I was so naïve."

Viviana's eyes were dancing. "Then came a romantic picture, am I right?"

Were such things so predictable, or was this part of Viviana's gift? In the meetings she had oft proved her ability to foretell, but now she knew the past as well?

"And not a comedy," Marilena said. "A thoroughgoing love story, full of pathos."

"And true love."

"Yes."

"Tell me."

"What?"

"Tell me how he seduced you."

"I didn't say that —"

"But he did, Marilena, didn't he? I know he did."

"He put his arm around me and left it there, and during the most emotional scenes, he pulled me close."

"You spent the night, didn't you?"

Astonishing. Sorin had, in fact, sent her home for her things after they had made love.

"Not very chivalrous of him," Viviana said. "No wonder it hasn't lasted."

"It has lasted."

Viviana shook her head with obvious pity.

"You coexist," she said. "And you know it. You're more like brother and sister than husband and wife. And you don't sleep together anymore."

"We have only one bed."

"You know what I mean."

"But I never wanted that anyway. Really, I didn't. I was smitten by Sorin's mind. Truthfully, I still am. There is no one I'd rather converse with, argue with, discuss ideas with."

"You never loved him?"

"I never thought about it. His seduction, as you call it, gave me an inside track on what I really wanted: to stay in proximity to that mind. He never loved me either."

"How do you know?"

"He told me by never telling me."

"That he loved you."

Marilena nodded and a foreign emotion rose in her. What was this? *Had* that been what she wanted? Had she wanted Sorin to love her and to say so? She honestly believed she had never longed for that. "I must have been an awkward lover."

"He lost interest?"

"In that. We still spent hours together talking and reading and studying. We still do."

"But the romance died."

"Within months of his divorce and our marriage two years later," Marilena said. "Except for his occasional *necessities.*" She emphasized it the way he had. "And who knows where or to whom he goes now when *necessary?*"

"You don't care?"

"I don't dwell on it. I didn't marry him for that. I am a born student, and I live with a born teacher. I am not a physically passionate person. I have all I need or want."

When they were on the street, Viviana walking Marilena to the bus, the older woman took her arm. "You're lying," she said, and Marilena felt her first rush of guilt since childhood. "We're getting close to your bitterness, aren't we? Your loneliness. Your emptiness. The hole in your soul."

Marilena was glad she had to keep her eyes forward to avoid tripping in the darkness. She could not have faced her new mentor. *My soul,* she thought. Until a few months before, she had not believed she even had a soul. Souls were for religious people. She was anything but that.

Marilena wished the bus would come and whisk her away. Even facing Sorin's bemusement at her newfound interest in what he — "and any thinking person, including you" — considered anti-intellectualism would be respite from the relentless searchlight of Viviana's prescience.

They sat on the bench at the bus stop, Marilena hoping a stranger would join them, anything to interrupt this. "You have discovered something within yourself beyond what I have been teaching," Viviana said.

It was true. So true.

"You pushed it from your mind the first several times the stirring came over you. You reminded yourself that you and Sorin had discussed this, had dismissed it. He'd already had a family. Besides, the apartment was too small. Your work could not be interrupted. It was out of the question."

Marilena's jaw tightened, and she would not have been able to object had she chosen to. She pulled herself free of Viviana's arm and pressed her palms to her face. How long had it been since she had wept? This longing, this stirring, as the older woman referred to it, had nagged at her until she forced herself to push it away. Out of the question was an understatement. She did not want Sorin's child, especially one he would not want. And neither did she want to deceive him into producing a child within her. All of a sudden, after years of looking the other way when he took his "necessities"

26

elsewhere, she would — what? — begin to be his lover again until hitting upon perfect timing?

The whine of the bus in the distance was a relief Marilena could barely embrace. She stood and fished in her shoulder bag for her transit card. Viviana faced her and grabbed both shoulders. "We will talk next week," she said. "But let me tell you this: I have your answer, bitter one. I have your light."

Nine-year-old Ray Steele raced up the soccer field behind Belvidere Elementary, outflanking the defense and anticipating a pass from Bobby Stark. He cut across the field about twenty feet from the goalie box, and though the feed was behind him, he quickly adjusted, spun, and dribbled the ball with his feet. Juking two defenders, he drove toward the goal, the goalie angling out to meet him.

"Go, Ray, go! Beautiful athlete!"

It was his father. Again. Truth was, Ray wished he would just shut up. It was bad enough his old man really was an old man. His parents were older than anyone else's and looked older than that. Once another father had seen Ray walking to the car with his dad and said, "Hey, isn't it nice your grandpa could be here to watch you play?"

27

"Grandpa's here?" Ray said before figuring it out. The man and Ray's dad found
that hilarious. Ray had just jumped into his
parents' beater car and hidden his head.

Even Ray's mistakes worked out. He
faked left and went right, but the goalie was
on to him. Ray reared back and drilled the
ball off the goalie's chest. It came right back
to him. With the goalie now out of position
and the other defenders sprinting toward
him, Ray calmly toed the ball into the left
side of the net.

He shook off his teammates as they tried
to lift him onto their shoulders. Why did everybody have to act so stupid? It wasn't like
this was the championship, and it certainly
wasn't a deciding goal. In fact it put Ray's
team up 7–1, and the other team hadn't won
a game all season. Big deal.

Ray Steele was good at soccer, but he
hated it. Too much effort for too little result.
He couldn't stand watching it on TV. All
that racing up and down the field and the in-
credible skills of international stars, usually
resulting in a scoreless tie that had to be decided by a shoot-out.

He played only to keep in shape for his favorite sports: football, basketball, and baseball. In reality, however, Ray was better than
good. He was the best player in the soccer

league, the top scorer, and one of the best defenders. Young as he was, the attention of the cheerleaders wasn't lost on him. He wasn't much for talking with girls though. Didn't know what to say. It wasn't like he was going to do less than his best so people would leave him alone. He had to admit, if only to himself, that the attention wasn't all bad. But usually it was just embarrassing.

Ray was taller than the other kids and an anomaly. First, he could outrun anyone his age and even a little older at long distances. When the team took a couple of laps around the field, he sprinted to the front and led the whole way. And when they finished and everyone else was red-faced, bent over, hands on their knees, gasping, he recovered quickly and chatted with his coach. If only the coach hadn't told his father, "That son of yours is a beautiful athlete. Beautiful."

Second, Ray was faster than anyone in short races too. That was unusual for someone his height at his age. Long-distance runners weren't supposed to also be fast in the dashes. What could he say? His dad claimed to have been a great athlete when he was a kid, but how long ago must that have been?

Third, Ray was an anomaly because he knew what *anomaly* meant. How many other fourth graders had a clue? Being known as the cutest kid in the class made him self-conscious too, but he had to admit he'd rather deal with that than the opposite. He sure didn't envy the fat kid, the ugly girl, or the nerd. He had it all. Smartest, best athlete, fastest, cutest.

That didn't change the fact that he was ashamed of his parents. And their car. No one kept a car as long as Ray's dad. Oh, the plastic polymer still shone. It was designed that way. Cars simply weren't supposed to look like they aged anymore. But everybody knew, because the auto manufacturers now had only two ways to make cars look new: they changed styles every year, and color schemes changed every three or four years.

When his dad first got the yellow Chevy, it was already used. "Don't knock it," his dad said. "It's got low mileage, and I know cars. It's been taken care of, and it should give us lots of years."

That's what Ray was afraid of. It seemed his friends' families were getting the latest models all the time, and they were forever bragging about all the features. There was the silver and platinum phase when cars were designed to look like classics from the first decade of the new century. Then came the primary colors, which didn't last long —

except for that Chevy. According to Ray's dad it was going to last as long as he could make it last.

Ray wished it would get stolen or burn or get smashed. He'd made the mistake of saying so.

"Why, Rayford!" his mother said. "Why would you say such a thing?"

"Come on, Ma! Everybody knows that rattletrap is at least six years old."

"In real years, maybe," Mr. Steele said. "But the way it's been maintained and the way I take care of it, it's almost good as new."

"Shakes, rattles, squeaks," Ray mumbled.

"Important thing is the engine. It's plenty good for the likes of us."

That was one of his dad's favorite phrases, and while Ray knew what it meant, he could have gone the rest of his life without hearing it again. He knew what came next. "We're just plain and simple, hardworking people."

There was certainly nothing wrong with being hardworking. Ray himself worked hard, studied, wanted to get good grades. He wanted to be the first in his family to go to college, and nowadays even scholarship athletes had to have good grades. He was a double threat. One of those major sports he loved so much should get him into some real

31

college, and if he also had a good grade point average and class-leadership résumé, he couldn't miss. As much as his parents embarrassed him, he secretly wanted to make them proud.

"We're plain and simple, all right," he had said at the dinner table that evening. He was having more and more trouble keeping his mouth shut. And all that did was cause his parents to jump on him more.

"And what's wrong with plain and simple?" his father thundered.

"Your dad built his tool and die business into something that puts food on this table —"

"— and clothes on my back, yeah, I know."

"And it paid —"

"— for this house too, yeah, I know. I got it, all right?"

"I don't know what's gotten into you, Rayford," his mother said. "All of a sudden we're not good enough for you. Who do you think you are?"

Ray knew he should apologize. He felt like the brat he was. But what good was being the coolest kid in fourth grade if you lived in the seediest house in the neighborhood? He didn't want to get into that. It would just bring out all the stuff about how at least it was paid for and his dad wasn't in debt, and yeah, we may live paycheck to paycheck, but there are people a lot worse off than we are in this world.

Ray just wished he knew some of them. He was top man on the totem pole in lots of areas, but he had to hang his head when he got in and out of that car, and the last thing he wanted was to invite a friend home. When he visited other kids' houses, he saw the possibilities. *Someday. Someday.*

"May I be excused?" he said.

His mother looked startled. "Well, to tell you the truth, young man, I was about to send you to your room for sassing your father, but —"

"Don't fight my battles for me," his dad said. "If he crosses the line, I'll —"

"But what, Ma?" Ray said.

"But I made your favorite dessert, and I thought —"

"Lime delight? Yes!"

"He doesn't deserve it," his dad said.

"— and I thought since you had such a great game . . ."

"I'll have it later," Ray said, bolting for his room. He kept expecting his dad to make him come back; when he glanced their way from the stairs, his mom and dad were shaking their heads and looking at each other with such despair that he nearly went back on his own.

Why did he have to be this way? He didn't really feel too good for them. It just hurt to be such a popular kid and not have all the stuff that should go along with it. Well, if it was true that hard work and brains could get you where you wanted to go in this world, he was going places.

Ray's teacher told him not to be self-conscious about towering over his classmates. That was a laugh. He loved being tall. But she said, "It's just a phase, and the rest will catch up. By junior high you won't likely be the tallest. Some of the girls might even catch you."

That was hardly what Ray wanted to hear. He hadn't decided yet which sport would be his ticket to college, but he hoped it might be basketball. He already gave the lie to the adage that white guys can't jump. If he could just keep growing, he'd be well over six feet by high school. He didn't have to be the tallest guy on the team, but being one of the tallest would be great.

Ray rushed into his room and closed the door, as if shutting out the muffled sound of his parents would take them off his mind. Small and nondescript as the house was, he had made something of his room. Extended from nylon fishing lines all over the ceiling were model planes, from ancient props to tiny fighter jets to massive modern supersonic transports.

Whenever he was asked, in person or in writing, what he wanted to be when he grew up, he invariably answered, "Pilot or pro athlete." He despised the condescending smiles of adults, which only made him recommit himself to his goals. Ray had heard enough that a professional athletic career — in any of his favorite sports — was as likely as being struck by lightning. And expressing his pilot dream always triggered teachers and counselors to remind him how hard he would have to work in math and science.

He knew. He knew. At least the aviation thing didn't draw benevolent, sympathetic smiles. It was actually an achievable goal. His dad was good with engineering stuff, manufacturing, figuring things out. And while Ray excelled in all subjects, it happened that he liked math and science best.

Ray would do whatever he had to do to realize one of his dreams, because either one of them could bring him what he really wanted. Money. That was the bottom line. That was what set people apart. People with nice cars — the latest models — had more money than his dad. He was convinced of that. His dad claimed that those people were probably in debt, and Ray decided maybe a little debt wouldn't be all bad, if for no other reason than to make it look like you had money.

But he would go one better. If he couldn't be a pro athlete and make tens of millions, he'd be a commercial pilot and make millions. He'd look like he had money because he really had it and wouldn't have to go into debt at all.

Two

Marilena normally found the bus drafty, but as it slowly pulled away from the curb, she loosened her coat and tugged her collar away from her neck. It was her custom to lose herself in one of several thick paperbacks in her shoulder bag, but she would not be able to concentrate now. Not on the literary novel in French. Not on the history of the Hungarian revolution of the twentieth century. Not on *King Lear*, which she so enjoyed in its original English.

She sat staring out the window as the shadowy Bucharest cityscape glided past, lit every few feet by amber halogen lamps. Her grandfather used to recall aloud when Communism was an empty promise and how one could walk more than two kilometers in the dark, hoping for one flickering vapor streetlight. "Like the old Soviet Union, we were a paper tiger, no threat to the international community. We would not have been able to engage our weapons. We had our finger on a button that did not work."

Democracy and technology may have revolutionized Romania, but Marilena considered herself a throwback. She and Sorin were the only couple she knew who still owned a television receiver that did not hang from the wall. That happened to be another subject on which she and her husband agreed. "It's a tool," Sorin said, "not an object of worship. And it is the enemy of scholarship."

Their boxy old set made colleagues chuckle. "You know," Sorin's department vice-chair, Baduna Marius, informed them one night, "the world has come a long way since your flat-screen."

Marilena had settled back to enjoy the spectacle as Sorin warmed to the topic. The vice-chair — a tall, dashing blond — kept insisting he was only joking, but once Sorin sank his teeth into an argument, his passion would not allow him to let it go until he had spent himself. He would gesture, rise, sit, run his hand through his hair. His fair skin would flush, his aging freckles darken. There had been times, Marilena had to admit, when she provoked him just to see him roll into action.

Ah, Sorin. Such a mind. Such enthusiasm for scholarship. Did she love him? In her own way. Certainly not romantically. No, never. And she was persuaded he had never seen her in that light either. How could he? He had taken advantage of her youthful devotion to satisfy his urges, yes, but as she matured perhaps he respected her enough to quit expecting acquiescence. Young and inexperienced, she had to have been clumsy. Surely she had never given him cause to see her as sexually appealing. She didn't feel that way, didn't see him that way, and could not pretend. In the end, she could not blame him for seeking physical — what? not love — satisfaction elsewhere.

They didn't clash over it, didn't argue, didn't blame, didn't seem to worry about it. It was something they never discussed. The quaint idea of the marriage bed simply disappeared from their lives. She didn't miss it. Not really. She still cared for Sorin in a sisterly way. He was a dear friend, an admired mind. She worried after him, took care of him when he fell ill, as he did for her. They were familiar enough with each other, living in such close proximity, that they touched occasionally as friends might. If she amused him, he seemed not averse to briefly embracing her. When her parents died he even cupped her face in his hands and kissed her forehead.

As unconventional a marriage as it was in modern Romania, there was no rancor, no acrimony. Sure, they got on each other's nerves. But she knew passionate couples with a passel of kids, husbands and wives unafraid of actual public displays of affection, who were also known to live their lives at decibel levels high enough to attract the attention of the police. She could be grateful, she guessed, that she and Sorin largely got along.

So if there was anything to Viviana Ivinisova's speculation that Marilena's name aptly described her — the bitter part, the emptiness, the loneliness — the hole in her heart had nothing to do with Sorin, except that if she wanted to fill it, her husband was the logical vehicle.

The maternal instinct had ambushed her most incongruously one afternoon as she rode the bus home from the university. For days she had surprised herself by finally noticing the children who cavorted at the playground in the park near their apartment. Strange, she thought, that she had been only vaguely aware of them for years, and now she found herself watching with interest until she disembarked and headed across the street to her building.

Marilena found herself particularly taken with a young girl, probably five or six years old. Nothing was unique about the child, except that she had caught Marilena's eye, and the woman enjoyed her smile and her manner for the few moments she saw her each day.

Then came the day of the miracle. Marilena didn't know what else to call it. As she got off the bus the little girl deftly launched herself over the wrought-iron fence that separated the children from the busy street. "Oh, child!" Marilena called out, as the girl dashed past her and raced in front of the bus, which had not yet begun to move.

The little girl was chasing something. A ball? An animal? She looked neither right nor left. Marilena caught the bus driver's eye. He shook his head, waiting with his foot obviously on the brake as Marilena followed the child into the street.

Seemingly from out of nowhere a black sedan crossed the double yellow line and passed several cars, sending others sliding to the curb. It was heading directly for the little girl! Marilena froze, screaming, but the girl never looked up. She knelt in the street, reaching for a kitten that bolted away at the last instant.

There was no way the car could miss the child. Marilena grimaced and clamped her eyes shut, waiting for the screech of tires and the killing thud. But it never came. She forced herself to peek and saw the car appear to pass right through the child and slide into the only parking spot left in front of her building.

Marilena expected the driver to leap from the car and check on the girl, but no one emerged. Several pedestrians rushed the car, Marilena following once she was sure the little girl was safely back in the park. People huddled around the car, peering into it, brows knitted. It was empty. A man laid his palm on the hood. "It's cold," he said. "Wasn't this the car?"

The others, Marilena included, assured him it was. The man felt the tires. "Cold," he said.

To a woman of letters, this was more than strange. Marilena dared not even tell Sorin. A driverless car dematerialized as it bore down on a child? He would have laughed in her face.

That night she and Sorin sat reading at their respective desks. Both were crafting new curricula for the next term and occasionally tried ideas out on each other. Their courses were as far afield from marriage, home life, family, and children as they could be, and yet in the middle of casual conversation about required reading lists, Marilena was suddenly overcome.

She felt a longing so deep and severe that she could describe it — only to herself, of course — as physical pain. She would not have been in the least surprised had Sorin asked what was troubling her. How she was able to camouflage it and continue the conversation confounded her to this very night on the bus. It had been as if her very existence depended upon being held, loved, cherished, and — if possible — being allowed the inestimable privilege of holding, loving, and cherishing another.

Marilena had looked at Sorin in a new way, albeit only briefly. Was this an epiphany? Did she love him, want him, long for him? No. Simply no. Here was a man who, despite his prodigious intellect, held no appeal to her in any other way. He sat there late in the evening, hunched over his desk, reading, writing, thinking, discussing, still dressed in the suit and tie he had taught in all day. His only concession had been to slip off his shoes and suit jacket and loosen his tie. Years before she had given up urging him to change his clothes after work.

And his feet stank. Well, that was petty,

she knew. She had her foibles and idiosyncrasies too, not the least her utter lack of interest in feminizing herself. So what was this, this visceral bombardment she could not ward off? In a flash Marilena knew, though she was certain it had never crossed her mind before. She needed, desperately wanted, a child.

It wasn't that they had never discussed having children. Sorin had established early in their relationship that he wanted no more children and hoped that was not an issue with her. She had assured him she felt no such inclination and couldn't imagine herself a mother, let alone imagine a willingness to give up the time in her precious pursuit of knowledge. End of discussion.

Her late mother had raised the question more than once, of course. But Marilena had been so adamant in her refusal to discuss it that Sorin had actually stepped out of character and offended his mother-in-law by scolding her. "If you don't mind my saying so," he said, "and I'm sure that you do, your daughter has made herself quite plain about this, and thus it is no longer any of your business."

Marilena had on one hand felt embarrassed for her mother, while on the other she appreciated her husband's defense.

So with her mother long in the grave and her marriage long since having become a construct of intellectual convenience, what was she to do with this new emotion? It had been all she could do to muster the restraint to keep from blurting out, "Sorin, would you reconsider giving me a child?" Marilena told herself she had ingested too much *mămăligă,* the mush she made from cornmeal that even Sorin admitted was her specialty. Too much of it had caused discomforting dreams before, but never while she was awake.

Sorin had asked her something, or had he made a suggestion about her new syllabus? "I'm sorry," she said. "Would you care for some *tuică?*" He had raised a brow, as if wondering what that possibly had to do with whatever it was they were discussing.

The plum brandy sped to her bloodstream with enough force to effect some equilibrium. Marilena was able to keep her impulses in check and not say anything that might alarm Sorin. If she knew anything about their evolving relationship, it was that her husband fled real, personal interaction — and what could be more personal than this?

Marilena had been relieved in the days following her epiphany when her urge seemed to have waned. But it would sneak up on her again at the most absurd moments. She might be tidying the apartment, doing the dishes with Sorin, or simply reading. Most disconcerting was that, without fail, every time the need for a child to love and to love her emerged, it was magnified exponentially from the time before. Marilena had devised schemes to fight it off. She developed an inner dialogue, "self-talk" her psychology faculty friends would have called it. She called herself names, told herself she was being selfish, childish, unrealistic. She asked herself who she thought she was and told herself to be practical.

Generally these tactics worked, at least temporarily. When Marilena really thought it through, somehow extracting herself from the emotion of it, she realized there was not room in her life, certainly not in Sorin's, and absolutely not in their apartment, for a child — especially a newborn. Impossible.

For weeks, months even, Marilena had become more and more inclined to stand her ground against the emotion. She believed she had learned to detect nature about to attack, and she would begin her self-talk immediately. "Don't start," she would tell herself. "This is just not going to happen."

It was not long, however, until a baby was on her mind every waking moment. Oh, it was not as if she had found ways to make it make sense. Rather she came to resign herself to the fact that this torment might forever be with her. Was there some other option, some avenue that might satisfy this instinct? Should she support an orphan, send money to a children's cause?

Marilena had never been one to buy into easy diagnoses of depression. She had always been able to chase a low mood by immersing herself more deeply into her reading and studying and teaching. Colleagues admonished her for equating clinical depression with the blues, rightly intimating that someone of her intellect should know better.

She had become depressed and she knew it. She would not seek counsel or treatment. Nothing could fix this. The need for a child had become part of her being, and the knowledge of its impossibility left her in despair.

Ironically, it had been that very paradox that had spurred her interest in a new pursuit. She had seen the ads in academic journals and even one of the many local papers: "Seeking something beyond yourself? Come and be astonished." She had seen posters around the faculty offices with the same message but had paid them no more heed than had her colleagues.

Marilena would have described herself as a humanist. She had not closed the door on the possibility of a supreme being, so *agnostic* perhaps fit her better than *atheist*. Finding the answers to life within oneself had always resonated most with her.

Marilena had also long been self-reliant, eager to do things on her own, not inclined — like so many of her female friends — to need a partner in every new endeavor. Sure, it was sometimes more enjoyable when Sorin or another colleague joined her at an exhibit or lecture, but she was not averse to going by herself.

Her intrigue at the ad for the Tuesday evening meetings at the library had been borne out of a desperate need to distract herself from what she could only assume was something she had always believed was a myth: her ticking biological clock. Motherhood had been such a foreign concept to her that it was not something she had even entertained until this longing attacked.

Somehow she could not imagine satisfying her curiosity about these meetings alone, so she had asked Sorin to go with her. He motioned with his fingers for the paper and read the ad aloud. "Oh, Marilena, really," he said, and she cringed. He tossed it back to her.

Early in their marriage she had given up more easily, intimidated. But that had passed. "I would really like you to go with me," she said.

"But why? Can't you imagine what this is? 'Something beyond yourself,' honestly."

"What? What do you think it is, Sorin?"

"If not religion, then spiritualism, two sides of the same silly coin."

"Have you never entertained the idea that there might *be* something beyond our minds?"

He pressed his lips together. "No, and neither have you. Now spare me this nonsense."

And she had — for a time. But resentment grew. She fell silent at home, answered him in monosyllables. He could not have missed the cues, but clearly he didn't seem to care. Perhaps, she told herself, if they were a conventional couple he would feel the heat. But given that they had evolved into colleagues who simply shared the same chambers, why should he care if she seemed upset?

Usually they took turns doing for each other. One would cook for both. The next night vice versa. So it was when she took to ignoring him completely, cooking only one meal, packing only one lunch, cleaning only her messes, that he finally took notice. "You're not yourself," he said. "What's wrong?"

She felt petty saying nothing and implying that if he didn't know she wasn't about to tell him. That was so juvenile, so typical. She had considered herself above such tactics. But they had worked. Finally he said, "Marilena, you're not pleasant to be around. Does one of us need to move out?"

Leave it to Sorin to cut to the heart of the matter. Marilena had been surprised at her own revulsion for that idea. For whatever they had become to each other, she couldn't imagine life without him. She didn't want to leave, and she certainly didn't want him to.

"Perhaps," she said, surprising herself. It was only a maneuver, but she desperately hoped he would not act on it. And if he did, what form would it take? He wouldn't be leaving the apartment he had owned since his first wife evicted him from their home years before. Would he turn Marilena out?

To her relief, he'd let the matter drop, only raising it again several days later when she wore him down with her toxic indifference.

"Marilena, are you about to leave me?"

"Mentally or physically?"

"Don't play games, dear. We both know you have long ago emotionally deserted. What is it you want?"

"You know."

"I don't!" And it was clear from his look that he really didn't. She had let too much time pass from the original request. "Tell me!"

"I want you to go with me to see what these Tuesday evening sessions are about."

He stood. "That's all? For that you have put on this charade for weeks? Tell me that is not all you are upset about."

"That's it."

"That's ridiculous."

She couldn't argue. It was such a small thing. And yet it was also such a simple request. Why could he not cater to her just this once, step outside his conventions?

Then *he* had been quiet, clearly angry. Occasionally he would appear prepared to continue the argument, then wave it off and turn back to his work. Finally, apparently unable to concentrate, he'd said, "Heaven help us if you ever find something legitimate to be upset over."

"If this is so trivial, Sorin, the remedy is trivial too. Don't disparage my feelings. I want you to go to a one-hour meeting some

51

Tuesday evening. Is that so much to ask?"

"That's not the issue," he said. "It's the transparent nature of the meeting. It will offend my every sensibility and, I hope, yours."

"Maybe it will. Of course, you're right. But humor me. I don't want to go alone."

"So if I accompany you once, you promise to return to civility?"

"Twice."

"Twice? What if you are repulsed after the first meeting?"

"Then you're free."

"Twice. If I go twice —"

"That's all I ask."

Ray had been invited to Bobby Stark's house Friday for dinner and overnight. He would ride with Bobby and his parents to the Saturday soccer game.

Ray couldn't wait. He watched the big clock on the classroom wall all day, especially after he and Bobby had plotted during lunch and recess what all they would do that evening. "Mom's fixin' a big meal, and we can play laser hockey, video games, watch movies, whatever."

Bobby dressed like a rich kid, so Ray could only assume his house would be cool. He wasn't disappointed. It was no palace, nothing like Ray himself would own one day when he was a pro athlete or a pilot, but it was sure something compared to his house.

Bobby had two younger sisters who wanted to be involved in everything, but any time Ray showed them attention, they blushed and giggled and ran off squealing. Bobby just hollered at them and told on them until his mother made them leave the boys alone.

At dinner Mr. Stark asked Ray if he wanted to say the blessing.

"The what?"

"The blessing, son. Say grace. You're a Christian, aren't you? Go to church?"

" 'Course. Every Sunday. You mean pray?"

"That's what I mean."

"Well, um, okay." Ray bowed his head and closed his eyes, folding his hands over his plate. "God is great; God is good. Now we thank Him for our food. Amen."

The little sisters laughed aloud, and Bobby couldn't stop a guffaw even with his palm pressed to his mouth. "That's your prayer?" he said.

"Robert!" his mother said.

"Sorry."

"Yeah, that's my prayer. What about it?"

"That's how you pray for a meal?"

"Yeah, so?"

Mr. Stark cleared his throat. "How about your father, Raymond?"

"It's Rayford."

"All right. Is that how your father prays over a meal? I mean, I'm just curious. It's a child's prayer. Uh, you're a child, but you're becoming a man."

Ray wanted this conversation over. What in the world was it with these people? "Do you want me to pray like my father prays? I can."

Mrs. Stark set down a bowl she had apparently meant to pass. "Yes, that would be nice." Everyone closed their eyes again.

"For what we are about to receive," Ray said, "may we be truly thankful. Amen."

"Amen!" the girls chorused.

Ray got the impression that Bobby and his parents were again amused but had decided not to humiliate him further. At breakfast he was not going to be talked into praying again; that was for sure. For one thing, those were the only two prayers he knew, other than "Now I lay me down to sleep; I pray thee, Lord, my soul to keep. If I should die before I wake, I pray thee, Lord, my soul to take." He could only imagine their reaction to that.

Bobby seemed to quietly study him that evening, and Ray was hoping they wouldn't start talking about anything serious. No such luck. While they were setting up the video-game controls, Bobby said, "That's how you pray at your house, eh?"

Ray shrugged. "We don't pray a lot. Just for meals and at bedtime."

"Really?"

"Yeah."

"And it's those made-up, rhyming prayers?"

Ray sighed. "What're we supposed to do — pray like the preacher?"

"What church do you go to, anyway?" Bobby said.

"Central."

"The big one on the corner downtown? Do they believe in Jesus?"

" 'Course they do. What do you think?"

"I don't know. Some churches don't."

"Those would be synagogues," Ray said.

"How about you, Ray? You believe in Jesus?"

"I told you! I go to Central every Sunday."

"So you've got Jesus in your heart?"

Ray just wanted to play. What was this? "In my heart? What's that mean?"

"How long you been going to this church?"

Ray pushed the controls aside and sat back on the couch. "My dad grew up in Central Church. He's real religious."

"And your mom?"

"She grew up in Michigan, but yeah, she's religious too."

"They're Christians?"

Ray shook his head. Bobby didn't seem this dense at school. " 'Course they are. Did you think we were Jewish?"

"Well, it's not like you're either Jewish or Christian."

"We're sure nothing else!"

"You've got to have Jesus in your heart, Ray. That's the deal."

Ray picked up the controller, hoping Bobby would drop the subject.

"Do you, Ray?"

"Do I what?"

"Do you have Jesus in your heart?"

"Look, Bobby, I've been going to Central Church since I was born, and I never heard anything about getting Jesus in your heart. But there's pictures of Him everywhere, even in the windows, and He's what the pastor preaches about. Just because we don't call it whatever your church calls it doesn't mean we're not religious too."

"It's not about religion," Bobby said, sounding to Ray like something a Sunday school teacher might say. "It's about being a true Christian."

"I am!"

56

"Not unless you've got Jesus in your heart."

Now Ray was mad. "And what if I don't?"

"Then you're going to hell."

"What!?"

"That's what the Bible says. You have to tell God you know you're a sinner and —"

"I'm no sinner."

"Your church doesn't teach that everybody's a sinner?"

"No!"

"It's right in the Bible. It says everybody has sinned."

"I'll bet my mom hasn't."

"Bet she has."

"Bobby, you don't know what you're talking about. I don't know everything about what our church teaches, but I think we believe everybody's good at heart. We try to do good things all the time, do what God wants us to do."

Bobby sat there shaking his head.

Ray wanted to pop him. *Look down at me, will ya? And you're not even as smart as I am.* "What?" Ray said.

"Your church teaches that people are good at heart?"

"I don't know, Bobby. Come on; let's do something."

"I just don't want you to go to hell, that's all."

"You don't have to worry about that."

"So you're not a sinner? You don't sin? I've heard you swear."

Ray stretched out on the couch and clasped his hands behind his head. It was going to be a long night. "Okay, I swear, all right? God's going to send me to hell for that? There's gonna be a lot of people there with me."

"You get mad."

"Everybody does. Usually I get mad at myself if I mess up in a game. Right now I'm mad at you because you're borin' me to death with all this." Truth was, he was more insulted than bored.

"You were born a sinner."

Ray sat up, glaring at Bobby. "How would you know that?"

"It's right in the Bible. We all were."

"There you go with the Bible again. What, are you gonna be a preacher when you grow up? a missionary? what?"

"Whatever God wants me to be."

"And when's He going to tell you?"

"Never know. I gotta just keep listening."

"You know how wacky you sound?"

"Well, listen to you, Ray. You don't even think you're a sinner."

"There are a lot worse people in this

world than me. But I don't suppose you're one of 'em."

"I'm just like everybody else," Bobby said. "Born in sin. Need to be forgiven. I'm mean to my sisters, mouth off to my parents . . ."

"So you're on your way to hell too?"

"I was. Till I got Jesus in my heart."

"And since then you don't sin?"

"Of course I do. But I've been saved by grace. Jesus died —"

"Can we not talk about this anymore, Bobby? Really. You must go to one weird church."

"No, it's great. You should come sometime. Think your parents would let you? Maybe day after tomorrow?"

Not in a million years.

Three

Much as Marilena tried to remind herself she was a mature, modern adult, she couldn't brush aside her disappointment and suspicion when she trudged from the bus to the apartment building and could see from the street that their flat was dark. And thus empty. It was Sorin's custom to read until midnight. And it wasn't even ten yet.

So he had again taken advantage of her absence to tend to his own needs. *What did I expect? It's all right; really, it's all right. The alternative is worse.*

Marilena didn't even try to talk herself into using the stairs rather than the elevator. Climbing would be good for her, she knew, but her mind was so full it seemed to weigh on her body. When finally she entered the apartment, she shut the door without locking it, knowing Sorin had to be home soon. Without even turning on the light she dropped heavily into her favorite over-stuffed chair and inhaled the stale, sickly sweet aroma of her husband's cherry-flavored pipe tobacco.

Marilena missed him somehow. It was true. It wasn't love. It was familiarity. She wanted him home. She would not obsess about where he might be, what he might be doing, or with whom. She would just sit in the dark, sweating from her walk from the bus, reminiscing about the first time she laid eyes on Viviana Ivinisova.

She had initially been offended when Sorin had arrived home from the university late that Tuesday afternoon. With her last class over by noon, she had rushed home to fix his favorite meal, grinding and grilling pork and beef and rolling it into spherical *mititeli*. Marilena knew she didn't have to remind him — again — about his commitment that night, but he had to notice she was being overly helpful. When he arrived home, she took his book-laden leather bag so he could wrestle his bicycle into the flat.

"Do I have time to change before eating?" he said. "I have a lot of work tonight."

Change? He never changed. And now, the evening he had promised to go with her, he was changing? And work? He always had work. But Sorin was one who never had to cram or rush. His routine was to read the paper, have a little dinner, study for several hours before watching the international news, then read until going to bed at midnight. His schedule could bear a couple of hours for her that evening.

Marilena nodded. "You have time," she said flatly. She couldn't make him go. If she had to go alone, she would. But it wasn't like him to renege. It took all the fortitude she could muster to keep from saying, "You haven't forgotten, have you?" But forgetting was not part of Sorin's makeup either. He was not the clichéd absentminded professor.

That left one possibility Marilena didn't want to entertain. Sorin was toying with her. His passive-aggressive streak infuriated her, yet he was so clever about it she dared not challenge him on it. He always left room to turn the blame on her.

He stopped by his massive bookshelves for a thick reference work — in case her small talk bored him, she presumed — and padded to the table in the flannel robe and slippers she had always wished he would wear when he worked at night. Yet if she had raised his having to dress again to fulfill his promise that evening, he would have said, "Of course. Why would you think I had forgotten?"

And it would be on her. She would have been made to feel small, paranoid, a nagger. But that night she was on to him. She saw bemusement in his eyes as he sat. Normally better mannered, he immediately reached for the platter of meatballs and ladled himself a large portion. He inhaled noisily through his nose. "Your specialty," he said. "You would have made someone a good housewife."

It was a joke she didn't find humorous. "Why would I want to be a housewife when I can be your servant?"

He laughed. "Touché."

Sorin ate with such relish that her pique began to fade. It returned, however, when he finished, expressed a cursory thanks, wiped his mouth and hands, and abruptly retired to his desk. Usually one cooked and the other tidied, but clearly all the chores were hers that night. She managed them noisily, hoping to interrupt his concentration, knowing he had provoked her.

Her own desk and chair were in full view of his, so when it was nearly time to leave for the bus, she sat in plain sight, coat on, bag in her lap. Sorin read and made notes as if she were not there. Marilena wanted to tap her foot or drum her fingers, to scream, but she would not. She resolved to march out as soon as the clock reached a quarter past six, slam the door, and not speak to Sorin for weeks.

Her respiration increased with a couple of minutes to go. Her jaw was set. Abruptly Sorin rose and stepped into the bedroom. Just as she was about to leave, he reappeared fully dressed and carrying a book. "We'd better get going," he said. "You don't want to be late." It was not lost on her that *she* was the one who wouldn't want to be late, but Marilena was so relieved he was accompanying her that she set her exasperation aside.

"So you want to be a pilot, huh, Ray?" Mr. Stark said on the way to the soccer game the next morning.

"Yes, sir. If I can't be a pro athlete."

"Well, you know the likelihood of your becoming a pilot is a lot greater than —"

"I know."

"Your dad ever take you to O'Hare to watch the jets or take the tour?"

"Sure. I love it."

"Attaboy. You can serve the Lord in a profession like that. You don't have to be in full-time ministry like Bobby's probably going to be."

Serve the Lord? Ray couldn't make it compute. Surely God didn't need to be flown anywhere. And what in the world was full-time ministry? That could mean only preaching or being a missionary, and while Mr. Stark had said Ray didn't *have* to do that, the implication was clear.

One of Bobby's little sisters piped up: "We're gonna be cardiovascular surgeons."

"You are not," Bobby said.

"Are too."

"You don't even know what that means," he said. "You just like how it sounds."

"I do too know what it means. Brain surgery."

"Is not."

"Is too!"

Ray couldn't wait to get to the game and away from these people.

Marilena wouldn't have accused Sorin aloud, but she was convinced he was giddy about this folly of hers. On the bus she noticed the book he had brought was a German translation of *The Ramifications of the Humanist Manifesto*.

She had no idea what they were to encounter at the library, but the odds were that humanism would fly in the face of it. It would be just like Sorin to make plain to everyone, especially the leader, what he was reading. Whether he would debate or argue depended upon his mood. Marilena feared he was itching for a fight. She was merely curious, but mostly, she reminded herself, she was looking for diversion from the compulsion to have a child that now permeated her being.

Marilena had never considered herself a controlling person, but as soon as she and Sorin found their way to the anteroom at the library, she wished she were his mother. She allowed someone to take her coat. He did not, leaving it on despite the heat in the room, as if ready to escape at a moment's notice. She knew he had to be as disconcerted as she at the overdone friendliness of everyone's welcomes — smiles and handshakes all around. So much for just drifting in, sitting in the back, and seeing what this was all about.

And sure enough, Sorin made no attempt to hide his book.

Marilena couldn't be sure of the significance, but about thirty seconds before seven o'clock, everyone seemed to instinctively find their seats and fall silent. She had tried to guess which of the people might be the leader, but it soon became clear that he or she had not been part of the welcoming party. As the second hand hit the top of the clock, in strode a tiny, nattily dressed woman who looked as if she had been assembled from a kit. A kit from perhaps fifty years previous.

Laden with a stack of folders and a briefcase, she appeared to be in her midthirties, but she dressed and carried herself as if she were older. She wore severe black oxford shoes with low heels, sheer stockings — something Marilena had not seen since childhood — a pale blue suit with a skirt that extended to midcalf, a white blouse with a frilly lace collar, a plain but expensive-looking brooch, and a sprayed-in-place, salt-and-pepper hairdo that actually looked as if it had been teased. Marilena had seen that only in history books.

The woman introduced herself as Viviana Ivinisova in a pleasant, quiet voice and proved precise and articulate, every syllable crisp and clear. "Our numbers seem to grow every week," she said, smiling. "Welcome, welcome, especially to our newcomers."

With that she resolutely looked directly into the eyes of at least six people, as if to prove she was aware of each she had not seen before. Marilena returned her smile, and when Viviana turned her gaze to Sorin, Marilena did too. She was mortified to see that he had pressed a hand over his mouth and appeared to be stifling a huge laugh.

Viviana returned to the first newcomer. "Please tell us your name and why you're here."

Most said they had heard wonderful things about this class, and several expressed variations on the theme that they were most curious and open-minded about the idea of "finding something beyond myself."

When it was Marilena's turn, she said, "I'm just curious and love to learn."

"Excellent," Viviana said. "And you, sir?"

Sorin removed his hand from his mouth, smiling broadly. "Sorin Carpathia. I was dragged here by my wife, who is curious and loves to learn."

That brought laughter, much of it louder — Marilena thought — than the comment deserved. "And you, Sorin," Viviana said, "are you also curious and a lover of learning?"

"To be honest," he said, "I'm more of a know-it-all who loves to teach."

That seemed to genuinely tickle Ms. Ivinisova. "Do you teach?"

Sorin said, "I am chairman of the Classical Literature department at the University of Romania."

"Excellent. And may I assume you are open-minded?"

"I like to think I am," he said. "My suspicion is that tonight will be a true test. Your advertisement promised I would be astonished."

The game had been a better test than usual for Ray and his team, but again he had been the leading scorer and they had won. And again his father's bellowing had embarrassed Ray.

In the car Ray said, "We're Christians, right?"

"Of course," his mother said. "Whatever would make you ask that?"

He told her what Bobby had said.

"Fundamentalists," his father concluded.

"Funda-what-alists?"

"Holy Rollers. Wouldn't surprise me if they were snake handlers."

"What in the world are you talking about, Dad?"

"Some people, some churches, just take everything a little too far. They take every word of the Bible literally, believe Jesus has to crawl inside you, that you have to bathe in His blood. If the Bible says you can handle poisonous snakes if you trust the Lord, they do it just to prove the point."

"I don't think Bobby's family is into any of that."

"Maybe not, but keep your distance. Those people think they've got the inside track on the truth."

Ray had no more idea what his dad meant than he did about what Bobby had talked about.

Viviana Ivinisova asked everyone to bow their heads, close their eyes, and turn their palms toward heaven. "After a moment of silence, I will open in prayer."

Marilena wanted to peek at her husband, but she would wait until Ms. Ivinisova started praying, just to be sure the woman didn't notice. Sorin had never been one to be told what to do, and she couldn't imagine him doing any one of the things Viviana suggested, let alone all three.

"Find peace within yourself," the leader intoned. "Center, focus, lay aside all earthly cares."

Marilena tried. Whatever this was, it could be her salvation from the torment of wanting and needing something so badly that the very hunger for it had come to define her. Might she somehow find the freedom to channel her energies into something new, something different, something that would loose her from the torture of longing to embrace every baby she saw? A friend once told her that when she was away from her baby son more than half a day, she felt a literal ache in her arms that could not be salved until she held him again.

Marilena had hidden her amusement, but now she understood. She knew. She would stare at strangers' babies and wonder what the parents would do or say if she asked to hold the child. She had been able to corral her emotions, but at times she trembled with longing. It was as if an outside force had implanted this desire within her. Marilena had not conjured it, but she certainly owned it now, and she didn't know how long she could survive without its being fulfilled.

"And now," Viviana prayed, "I beseech all the best and most willing cooperative agents from the spirit world to grace us with their presence. I disinvite hostile, negative spirits. And to the one and only epitome of beauty and glory and majesty and power, I offer myself to serve as your conduit, your channel, a vessel for whatever messages you have for us tonight. Come, bright star."

Something stirred within Marilena. Praying to something or someone in the great beyond was wholly foreign to her, but perhaps she was overdue to step outside the convention and comfort of academia. Even if this was folderol, it certainly could do her no harm. She glanced at Sorin, not surprised to see him staring with glee at the strange woman praying. If nothing else, he would certainly thank Marilena for favoring him with an evening's entertainment.

She knew Sorin would rather sit out of view, where he could read. But they sat in the middle of the group, and even he would not be so rude.

Viviana sat at a table and carefully took several sheets from various folders and set them before her. She sat back and steepled her fingers. "Before I reveal pasts and futures, I have been given one message for you tonight. There is no need to write it down, as you will not forget it. Ready? Listen carefully now. . . ." She closed her eyes and lowered her head. Then she raised her head until she faced the ceiling. "The doorway to happiness is rebellion."

Marilena squinted and repeated the sentence in her mind. Several others hummed or grunted as if overcome by this truism.

Viviana repeated it, lowered her head, smiled, and opened her eyes to scan the room.

Happiness? Marilena thought. *Who wants a doorway to happiness? Contentment, perhaps. Comfort. Peace. But happiness?* It hit her as a vapid pursuit. Reading, studying, discussing, learning — those brought fulfillment, some purpose.

And rebellion against what? Convention? The establishment?

Suddenly Viviana stood and moved to the side of her table, her eyes clear and piercing. Marilena sensed others tensing, sitting straighter, as if expectant. The leader spread her feet ever so slightly, as if to give herself a more solid base. She raised her hands, palms open, closed her eyes, and let her head fall back.

Just above a whisper, Viviana seemed to breathe sentences. "Someone this week allowed himself to believe in a world on another plane," she said.

"Me," came the nervous voice of a man in the back. Marilena started to turn but caught herself. In her peripheral vision Sorin was shaking his head, his mouth covered against what she was sure was an outburst of hilarity.

"The spirit urges you," Viviana said, "to believe. Believe with all your heart and soul, but resist the temptation to judge factions in the netherworld based on myth."

"I don't understand," the man managed.

Viviana, face still pointed to the ceiling,

held up a hand higher. "Remember that the doorway to happiness is rebellion. Rebels, even in the great beyond, are often proved right."

"Mm," someone said.

"Um-hm," another added.

Viviana pressed her fingers to her temples, then lowered her head and buried her face in her hands. She appeared to swoon.

Marilena sensed expectation all over the room. Was Ms. Ivinisova a fake? Was this hocus-pocus? Or was she really getting some sort of a message?

"Someone here is interfering with the communication," Viviana said, and in spite of herself Marilena felt guilty. "Skepticism, disbelief, a scoffing spirit interrupts."

I want to believe, Marilena thought. *But this is so alien to me.* Viviana had somehow known that a man had joined the ranks of the believers. Could there be anything to this, or had Marilena fallen for a parlor trick?

"Stand by," Viviana said. "Not all is as dark as it appears, as the skeptic is a newcomer. Perfectly understandable."

Marilena felt absolved but also conspicuous. There weren't that many newcomers. Would people know it was she?

"That would be me," Sorin said, his tone

74

springing across a stage of suppressed laughter.

"Perfectly understandable," Viviana said again.

"I find this all —," Sorin began.

"Understandable," Viviana said, forcefully now. "I beg your indulgence."

Sorin sat shaking his head, and Marilena nudged him, wishing he would leave or keep quiet. His smile faded, and he looked at her with such contempt and disgust that she wished she had left him alone.

"Silence," Viviana said, her voice a whisper again. "Someone else is puzzled."

That, Marilena decided, was a colossal understatement. Her heart hammered against her ribs.

"You're wondering whether happiness is even a worthy goal," Viviana said. "You're willing to settle for contentment, perhaps. Comfort or peace. Fulfillment, some purpose in life."

Marilena folded her arms and rocked, fearing she might pass out. Those were her very thoughts. How was this possible? Could Viviana Ivinisova be a mind reader? Marilena had seen the best gypsy fortune-tellers in action, and she had been able to detect their tricks. But this?

"And you're asking yourself what the

spirit means by *rebellion*," Viviana said. "Rebellion against what? Convention? The establishment?"

Marilena fought to keep from hyperventilating.

"This is not a trick," Viviana said. "I am not a mind reader. I am in tune with the spirit world."

It was all Marilena could do to keep from escaping, but Sorin's loud laugh distracted her. When she burst into tears, he quickly quieted and looked embarrassed.

Viviana moved to switch off the lights. Marilena considered that a most thoughtful gesture. Viviana returned to her table and pulled a small candle and holder from deep within a pocketed folder. Setting the candle before her, she sat and lit it and bowed. "I am open, angel of light," she said.

Marilena could not turn her eyes away.

"Yes," Viviana said. "Yes, yes, yes. Thank you. Yes."

Sorin sighed loudly, and Marilena decided she would slap him if he drew one more iota of attention to himself. She was fully aware how strange this all was, and she would have been astounded had her intellectual husband responded in any other way. But he had not had the woman recite his very thoughts word for word.

★ ★ ★

Ray's parents took him out for fast food, and they began eating as soon as they sat down.

"How come we don't pray in public like we do at home?"

"That would be showy, dear," his mother said. "The Bible says we're supposed to pray in secret, not be seen by men."

"The Bible says lots of other stuff we don't agree with," Ray said.

"Like what?" his father said.

"That we're all sinners, born that way."

Mr. Steele stopped in midchew. "More browbeating from Bobby and his family?"

"Browbeating?"

"Preaching, proselytizing — call it what you want."

Ray shrugged. "Bobby said that was in the Bible, that's all."

"Bible also says God told the children of Israel to kill every man, woman, and child of nations that didn't believe in Him."

"Honey!" Ray's mother said.

"Well, it does," her husband said. "If we're going to get into everything the Bible says and start taking it literally, it's going to do the boy more harm than good."

"I know," she said, "but can we keep our voices down?"

"I thought we believed the Bible," Ray said.

"To a degree," his dad said. "It says God is love. You believe that?"

"Well, sure, yeah. Why not?"

"Killing every living soul that disagrees with Him sound like love to you?"

Ray wished he hadn't gotten into this. "It really says that?"

His dad nodded, mouth full. "And when the children of Israel disobeyed, God slaughtered a bunch of *them*. Now you tell me. If that's true, if that's literal, what does that say about God? If He was the definition of love, wouldn't He be fair and compassionate? The Bible says something about Him being slow to anger and willing that none should perish. I don't know how long it took Him to get angry with the so-called pagan nations, but if you take the Old Testament literally, He sure was willing for them to perish."

Ray studied his father. "So you don't believe the Bible?"

" 'Course I do. I'm just saying it can't always mean what it says. God can't be loving and merciful yet vengeful enough to wipe out people who don't follow Him. People get confused when they take everything literally; that's all I'm saying. Like your friend.

He probably thinks Jesus is the only way to God."

"Probably. Don't we? Why do we go to a Christian church?"

"Because that's what we know. That's how we were raised. But the minute we start thinking our way is the only way, well, if you ask me, that's not godly. I believe God helps those who help themselves. And I also believe that every religion is basically worshiping the same God. It's like God is at the top of a mountain. Any religion, any good one, I mean — the kind that makes you want to be a better person, help your fellow man, that kind of stuff — will get you there. We all take different paths, but we all eventually get to the same place."

"To God."

"Exactly."

That sounded reasonable to Ray. He didn't plan to argue it with Bobby. They could still be friends and just ignore their differences.

"So what about God killing off the pagan people?"

Mr. Steele shook his head and stuffed his burger wrapper into the bag. "It just has to mean something else," he said. "It's symbolic. Figurative. Know what that means?"

"I think so. So the stories about the battles

and the killing and the getting slaughtered if you don't obey, all that stands for something else."

"Right."

"Like what?"

"Hm?"

"What does it stand for? If you don't do what God tells you, you get squashed?"

"No, that wouldn't be a loving God either, would it?"

"No. So what does it mean?"

"I don't know. I just know it can't mean what it says."

"Some things," Ray's mother said, "are not for us to know this side of heaven. You can ask God when you get there."

"And we're sure we're getting there?"

"Of course," his dad said.

"How?"

"By doing the best we can, treating people right, following the Golden Rule, making sure our good outweighs our bad."

Ray got a new view of his father that day. He could be an embarrassing old guy, but he sure was smart.

Four

Tall and thin, the man with the razor-cut hair and wearing a gray woolen suit gazed out the floor-to-ceiling windows of his top-floor office. He loved the way Manhattan sparkled in the early evening as streetlights flickered on all over town.

Both morning and afternoon papers and news reports had been filled with war and near-war tension all over the globe. Three hurricanes sat single file off the coast of Florida, weathermen predicting the most devastating natural disasters that state had ever seen. Tornado alley was gearing up for what promised to be the worst season in history. Volcanoes erupted on every continent and several more hinted at following suit.

The man turned slowly and leaned over his desk, resting on his palms. Careful with his fresh manicure and understated yet exquisite and ridiculously expensive jewelry, he pressed the intercom button.

"Yes, Mr. S.?"

"Fredericka, I need you to hand deliver a message for me."

"Certainly, sir. Where to?"

"Paris. This evening."

"I'm sorry, sir. I have family coming in and —"

"It must go tonight for delivery in the morning. That won't be a problem, will it?"

There was a pause, then a sigh. "Is it ready?"

"Five minutes."

The man sat and wrote on linen paper with an ancient fountain pen.

Auguste, let's call in the commission for a meeting in Le Havre for Monday week. And please inform R. Planchette that the time for Project People's Victory is nearly at hand. Best, J.S.

Viviana Ivinisova had sat in silence for nearly a full minute, her head bowed before the flickering candle, elbows on the table, hands raised.

"Someone feels a deep, personal need," she said finally. "A longing. Have faith. Your wish will be fulfilled. Your dream will come true."

Could it be? Marilena wondered. That could mean anything from someone short of cash to someone in a bad relationship. Or Viviana could have been reading Marilena's own thoughts again.

It had taken all the fortitude Marilena could muster that first night to keep from telling Sorin that Viviana Ivinisova had been communicating directly to her with a message from beyond the pale. But the farther she and her husband got from the library and the closer they came to their apartment, the less she believed it herself. How could she be so naïve as to have been taken in by a charlatan? She believed in neither heaven nor hell, God nor Satan, clairvoyance nor fortune-telling.

Marilena was an existentialist, a humanist, a woman of letters, a student, a scholar, a professor. She believed in the material world, that which could be seen and felt. Worse, the evening had had the opposite effect on her problem than she hoped. Rather than distract her from the longing for a child, Viviana had all but promised that her dream would be fulfilled.

Marilena was unaware she was shaking her head until it distracted Sorin from his reading. "What?" he said.

"She was not specific," Marilena said.

He laughed aloud. "Of course she wasn't! Did you expect anything else? She was good; I'll grant her that. Entertaining. And the drama! The dark, the candle, the closed eyes, the raised hands, the dramatic pauses. I'm surprised she didn't ask if someone in the room had someone important in their life whose name begins with an *S*. I mean, who doesn't?"

"But you'll go back with me one more time, like you promised?"

"What? You're serious? *You'd* go back?"

"You promised, Sorin."

"That's not the issue, Marilena. You know I keep my word. But I cannot fathom why you would return. Surely you had to assume what you would encounter. Why would you want to go back?"

She shrugged. "Don't presume to think for me, Sorin. If I'm intrigued, I'm intrigued. I didn't say I was buying into anything."

"You used to be so levelheaded. So bright."

"And now I'm not bright because I want to go one more time? You agreed to go with me twice."

He shut his book and slumped in his seat. "Do you have any idea how I felt?"

"You appeared amused."

"Amused was the least of it. Conspicuous. Humiliated. Horrified that someone I know might see me there. Honestly, Marilena, if it is recreational for you, feel free. But don't make me go."

"Only once more."

"Will it embarrass you if I sit in the back and read?"

"Yes, but I can't expect anything else."

"Does it have to be this particular class? Could we not find some traveling carnival within the next few days that would satisfy my obligation?"

"You said yourself she was good."

"A good entertainer, yes. But if I want to be entertained, I'll watch an action movie."

"You hate those."

"Well, there you are."

"Sorin, you promised, and that's that."

The following Tuesday Marilena and Sorin had been welcomed even more effusively by those who recognized them from the week before. Sorin would have none of it. He refused to make eye contact, to shake hands, to engage in banter. He strode directly to the back row, muttering, "Yes, yes, hello, wonderful to see you again too," and didn't even unbutton his coat. He buried his face in his book, this time *Exposing Paranormal Charlatans*, and refused to look up.

Marilena was used to being ignored in public settings outside the university. There she was respected by colleagues and students, but it did not escape her that her plain — no, dowdy — appearance seemed to make her invisible elsewhere. She didn't know and had quit caring what people must have assumed about her. She did not look wealthy. No one could have known that she and her husband, though they lived modestly, were not in debt because they carefully managed their dual incomes.

Once Marilena had studied her fellow riders on the bus home from the university and realized she looked more like a domestic working woman than a professional. Should she change her look? Why? What did she care what people thought? To judge someone on appearances was petty. And she had just done it herself. She believed she knew who the maids and manual laborers were. Just because they did not carry briefcases or book bags like she did, how could she be sure? Nothing else, save what she read as she sat there, gave any clues to her profession.

But at that second Tuesday night meeting, Marilena was strangely warmed by the small talk. No one was personal or probing. They didn't seem to care any more than she did to ask about family or work or interests. They merely maintained eye contact, smiled, shook hands warmly, and welcomed her back as if they were truly glad to see her again.

Hadn't that been a part of uneducated society that had repulsed her? Idle chatter. Feigned enthusiasm. Yet these people seemed genuine. And why? Because she needed them to be? Because her marriage had deteriorated, settled into mere intellectual companionship? Or was it possible that one or more of these people could become friends? Might their weekly relationships blossom? The ones who seemed to have been there from the beginning appeared to have bonded. Some greeted each other with actual embraces.

Too much familiarity too soon had long been one of Marilena's pet peeves. Too much touching, too many personal questions, the overuse of first names. Yet now she found herself envious of these people who, though their only connection was likely this weekly meeting, seemed to consider each other family.

It wasn't that Marilena didn't have friends. She did. Not conventionally, not like the ones she read about. There was no one she confided in. But she had colleagues in her department, and because the psychology faculty shared the same building as she and her lit associates, she had come to know many of them on a first-name basis. She and Sorin entertained four to six people at a time in their apartment approximately once a month, always a slightly different mix. Sorin had one or two friends who seemed closer than any she had developed — his vice-chair for one — but as the chair, Sorin had to remain a bit detached too.

Detached. That was a kind way to think of Marilena's relationship with her colleagues. While they seemed to respect and even admire her, none were close. Some were close with each other, recounting outings, dinners, and concerts together. She had never been invited and, she told herself, didn't really care to go. It wasn't true, of course, but the lie was easy to believe because she overwhelmed it with her own private pursuits in the form of books and disks in which she could lose herself for hours every evening.

Early in their marriage, when she considered Sorin more a soul mate than the roommate he had become, she had once broached the subject of her "otherness" as it related to colleagues. "Well," he had said, puffing one of his many pipes, "you don't invite them anywhere either. Try it. They might accept. And they would likely reciprocate."

She never had. But this need for a child — she was finally comfortable admitting to herself that that's what it was — might be softening her edges to where she also longed for conventional friendships. In fact, she wondered, might one or two meaningful connections with adults dull her pain?

Marilena had sat in the back next to her sulking husband. When Viviana Ivinisova began her routine, Sorin never even looked up. And when it came time for the darkness and the candle, Marilena could tell he was dozing.

She herself was more skeptical that second meeting, fighting to detect generalizations and tricks as Ms. Ivinisova told the past, predicted the future, and seemed to read minds. Sitting in the back proved propitious, as Marilena was able to read body language and group dynamics. People were buying this, no doubt. But she steeled herself against being swayed as she had been the week before.

Until Viviana caught her eye.

Was it just Marilena's imagination, or was Viviana returning her gaze every few moments? The woman didn't appear to look at anyone else. Oh, she faked it. People in the second or third row likely thought Viviana was looking directly at someone in the fourth or fifth row or farther back. But Marilena could tell that she was looking between people and at the back wall, sometimes at the ceiling.

That was not unusual for teachers and public speakers. Marilena had been taught that a professor was supposed to maintain eye contact with various students. But she happened to be one who found that disconcerting and distracting, so she faked it.

Viviana appeared largely to be faking it too, except when she greeted newcomers or interacted with someone who admitted that he or she had gotten a message from the great beyond about them personally. And when she looked directly into Marilena's eyes.

She kept trying to tell herself she was imagining it, that being eight rows back she couldn't really know. But she could. Did Viviana detect Marilena's skepticism, or was she trying to reach her because it was obvious her husband was a lost cause? Did the woman see something in Marilena?

"In the remaining moments," Viviana said, "I have two messages to convey." First she spoke for more than five minutes on misconceptions about the spirit world, concluding, "Many of you are familiar with the Bible and what it says about clairvoyance, fortune-telling, and evil spirits. I merely want to remind you that this represents only one view and is, in my opinion, neither valid nor representative of the majority of the best thinking on the subject. For our purposes, we must remain open to the views of most spiritually sensitive people. We believe that while there are negative spirits, not all should be considered enemies of God. And — and I beg your indulgence to think this through if you happen to be a believer in God and that the Bible is His message to mankind — it does not necessarily hold that opposing God is sin."

Marilena had no idea how many in the room might be people of faith. Romania, she knew from history, had been swept through eons of varying views on the subject of God. From paganism through Catholicism to Orthodoxy to the atheism attendant with Communist rule, the nation seemed to have settled into a secular humanism that tolerated pockets of quaint and ancient churches of varying stripes. Regardless of where someone stood on belief in God, most had at least a cursory understanding of religious teachings. God was the supreme being — benevolent or judgmental depending on your denominational preference — and His adversary was the devil.

Now Viviana Ivinisova seemed to be asking that everyone, regardless of their religious beliefs or lack thereof, consider an alternative. "I'll get deeper into this in the coming weeks," she said. "But for now, allow yourself to consider that if there is a God, it would be to His advantage to make a sinner out of someone who threatens Him. Especially if that opponent happened to be right. Maybe it is not a sin to presume upon God's exclusive right to preeminence. I know that is a revolutionary concept, so mull it over and keep an open mind for when we get back to it.

"Meanwhile, I have a specific message from a cooperative attending spirit. If it applies to you, accept it for what it is."

Marilena was convinced Viviana glanced directly at her again before sitting at her table and pressing her fingers to her temples.

"Daughter," she said softly, then briefly raised her head with a smile, as if surprised. "So we know this message is for a female." She lowered her head again. "Daughter, you need not seek a substitute solution. Your longing cannot be assuaged by contemporaries. You need what you need, and that need will be filled."

Ray Steele listened more intently in Sunday school and church. He asked questions of his Sunday school teacher that seemed to rattle her. Ray raised the questions his father had about the God of the Old Testament, who seemed judgmental and fearsome.

"I . . . uh . . . I'm certainly not an expert on the Old Testament," Mrs. Knuth had said. "Our quarterly lessons are on New Testament stories and parables, so maybe you should save those questions for —"

"Well, but I was just wondering. I mean, what do you think? Does that sound fair? Does that sound like a loving God?"

"I really need to get back to the lesson, Ray. We have a lot to cover in a short time. Okay?"

Ray found the pastor's sermons just as confusing. He seemed to preach only from the New Testament, and he used the stories and accounts as jumping-off places to support his points. And his point usually was that "believers in Christianity ought to exemplify godly virtues in this world."

That was fine with Ray, except that if God

was God and God was perfect and God was love, what about all that ugly stuff in the Old Testament? If Ray was a "believer in Christianity" — and he was starting to wonder if he really was or if he had just been dragged to church all his life — was one of those godly virtues murdering people who disagreed?

At Sunday dinner Ray raised the question, and as usual, his dad tried to give the final answer. "Look, Ray, your mother believes I shouldn't have gotten into all that with you the other day, and I have to say she's probably right. At your age you don't need to be thinking about the major issues of life and God and all that."

"But I just want to know —"

"I know you do, but listen, I was born and raised a Christian, and I don't understand it all. All we can do is the best we can and try to be good people. Respect other people. Don't talk politics or religion with them. I mean, you'd rather be a good person than a bad one, right?"

" 'Course."

"And you are a good person, Rayford," his mother said.

"And that's all you need to worry about," his dad said. "Some stuff just isn't for us to know."

"This side of heaven," his mother said.

Sorin absolutely refused to go to another Tuesday night meeting, and he expressed shock that Marilena wasn't "over this silly pursuit. Surely you're not swayed by this woman."

"Of course not," she said, feeling like a liar. All the way home that evening, as Sorin crowed about having fulfilled his obligation, she had labored to convince herself that the message Viviana had shared could not have been for her.

It could have been for anyone. Again, no specifics. A dozen others could have applied it to their own situation.

Yet had she not, just moments before the message, been wondering whether friendships with colleagues or even people from this class might fill the need she saw no other way to fill?

Five

The Le Havre meeting was held at a clandestine villa belonging to one of the secret council, and no one — not a friend, a spouse, or a blood brother — even knew it was taking place, let alone what transpired there. Mr. S. ran the meeting, which was brief and to the point. Powerful men of finance and commerce from around the globe swore themselves anew to common goals, to confidentiality, and to Project People's Victory.

Ten Tuesday nights later Marilena sat in her apartment, dozing. Footsteps in the hall roused her. She did not want Sorin to find her in the dark, so she rose quickly, dizzying herself, to turn on a light as she heard him at the door.

"Just get home?" he said. "The place looked dark from the street."

She nodded. Lying to him had become

the norm. But what was the difference? His being gone and apparently feeling no compulsion to explain was a lie of omission, was it not? The way he studied her made her wonder if her countenance gave her away. The walk to the bus and the discussion with Viviana had shaken her.

"Any more messages from beyond?" he said, hanging his coat and pulling a beer from the refrigerator.

"Every week," she said, playing to him.

"And what was it this time? 'Someone is feeling regret over a childhood memory'?"

"Yes," she said. "Something like that."

As he turned on more lights and began puttering at his desk, she sat back down in her chair, causing him to ask if she was all right.

"I wouldn't mind a talk if it is all right with you."

"A talk?" He sat on the edge of his desk and gazed at her. "As long as you're not about to tell me you've contacted the netherworld."

"You know better than that."

"How long is this going to take?"

"Honestly, Sorin, if you don't have time to talk with me —"

"I'm just asking, dear. I have a big day tomorrow and a little more work to do, so —"

"Then just forget it."

"I don't want to forget it. I simply want to get an idea whether I'll have time to finish my work tonight or have to get up earlier."

She shook her head.

"I see," he said. "You want me to coax it from you."

"I want nothing of the sort. If you are so busy and have so much to do, where have you been?"

He moved to his desk chair. "Since when do you ask me where I've been?"

"When you complain of being too busy to talk with me."

She hadn't expected it, but that seemed to leave him speechless. For once. Marilena had certainly learned the folly of arguing with him. No contest.

Now he sat straightening things on his desk. Finally he said, "Well, if nothing else, you have roused my curiosity."

"Forget it, Sorin."

"No. I apologize. You have my full attention for as long as you need it." When she simply stared at him, he continued. "I'm serious, Marilena. You're right. You're not asking for too much, and I am on pace with my work, so please . . ."

"Then promise you'll hear me out."

"I believe I just did."

"Sorin, I know this is going to come as a shock to you as much as it has to me. Believe me, it is not a passing fancy but something that has been weighing on me for months. I have tried to fight it, tried to talk myself out of it, and determined to keep it from you."

His brow knotted. She certainly had his attention.

"I want to talk to you about it, and I don't want you to get upset or defensive."

He leaned back in his chair. "I know," he said.

"You know?"

He nodded. "It's been written all over you for a long time."

"It shows?"

"Of course. I know you, Marilena. I know we don't have a conventional marriage, but you have to recognize that our minds often seem like one."

"Often."

"So it shouldn't surprise you that I know what you're thinking. Even more than your favorite fortune-teller."

"She's not a —"

"I'm teasing, Marilena. I'm just saying that I know."

"And so?"

"And so you want to know if there is someone else."

Marilena fought a smile. The great intellect thought he knew so much, knew her so well. In fact, while she was curious, that had been the last thing on her mind. Of course there was someone else. Sorin was a man, wasn't he? He was sleeping with someone, and frankly, that was more than all right with her. It took the pressure off her, and she did not desire him that way. Never had.

Curious who it was? Sure. She had speculated it might not be just one. It could have been several women. Maybe he was a grazer, a bar hopper, a one-night stander. She didn't care. It made her resolve never to let her guard down, never to give in if he pressured her for romance. Who knew what disease he might bring to bed?

Was he about to tell her? Would it be someone she knew? Marilena had never suspected anyone from the university. He had to be smarter than that. She had detected nothing between him and anyone there.

"Okay," she said carefully. "Do you need me to ask?"

"No," he said. "You deserve to know. It's time you knew. It's Baduna."

"What? Baduna! But, you, I — Baduna Marius?"

"Don't worry," Sorin said. "I won't leave

100

you for him. I can't. He's married, and happily, believe it or not."

"But I —"

"And he is not willing to come out."

Marilena closed her eyes and shook her head. "And you *are?*"

"Am I what?"

"Willing to come out?"

"Who do you think doesn't know about me, Marilena?"

"Well, I for one!"

"Come now. Please."

"I didn't know!"

"Marilena! Why do you think my children will have nothing to do with me? Why do you think I was divorced? Why do you think I have shown little interest in — ?"

"I didn't know."

"Well, now you do. Frankly, I'm relieved. Maybe now I can simply tell you, 'I'm off to see Baduna.' Maybe I can even be gone overnight occasionally. I need not remind you that no one knows about him."

"Don't worry. I barely know his wife."

Ray Steele began to be more difficult and vocal at home. He was sarcastic and sassy, and even he hated the way he sounded and acted. Sunday school and church seemed meaningless and boring now, and while he had a few friends there, he fought going. His dad laid down the law: Ray was going and that was that. But Ray hated it, acted up in class, doodled and read in church. None of it made sense to him anymore, so he simply tuned it all out.

So it wasn't her. Marilena was living with a brilliant scholar who happened to be a homosexual. She tried to imagine his life had he been born a few generations earlier. Tolerance had come slowly to Romania, especially in the area of sexual preference.

So much for admitting to him that she longed for a child and wondering if he would ever consider changing his mind about giving her one. Had she discovered that he had had a bevy of female companions — and knowing that he had apparently lost interest in her sexually long before — she had planned to ask him to simply be a sperm donor anyway. She certainly didn't want to subject him to anything as distasteful as sleeping with her. And now that went double.

What could she do now? Find a man? Have an affair? Marilena certainly felt justified, but she had to admit there had been times when she wondered if she herself was a homosexual. She couldn't imagine it, because she had never felt attracted to a woman that way. But neither was she attracted to men, except to Sorin because of his mind. Finally, in her reading, she hit upon the perfect description of herself. She decided she was asexual.

That wouldn't do, however, in the matter of her current need. Adoption was an option, of course, but she ruled it out except as a last resort. It had come to Marilena over the past several months that this child she longed for had to be flesh of her flesh. She wanted to experience pregnancy, birth, breast-feeding, nurturing her own child and being loved by it.

That was way too much to lay on Sorin, of course, especially when he had entirely misread her. She would wait several weeks, then broach the subject again, just to test the waters. It would be hypocritical of him to deny her a relationship that would result in a pregnancy, but that was no longer the issue. He had made it plain years before that he wanted no more children, and she didn't think the technicality of its being someone else's child would make a difference.

Marilena couldn't bring herself to unfold her whole plan, the idea of a brief pragmatic affair. The concept remained so bizarre to her that it was impossible to put into words.

Oh, she knew there were men who would sleep with any woman for any reason. Even a plain one like her. But what kind of men were they? What genes might join hers in the creation of a new life? Those from a drunk, a scoundrel, a rounder, someone who slept around?

A sperm bank was the answer. She would have an idea of the background, nationality, profession, even IQ of the donor. But Marilena was not even prepared to speak of that to Sorin. It was not her pregnancy or where it originated that would matter to him. It would be the issue of bringing a newborn into their lives.

And if he forbade it? If he left her? How would she support herself and a baby when she would be out of work for a time? And when she returned to work, how would she afford child care? Despite the fact that this was a longing of the heart, Marilena could not let emotion get in the way of the practicalities. Frankly, she didn't imagine herself a working mother anyway — at least not outside the home. Surely with her gifts she could find work that could be done via the Internet.

Ideally, though, staying with Sorin, not having to move, his supporting them — that made the most sense. But would he agree?

Six

Ray Steele felt like a fool. Here he was, one of the cool fourth graders, and yet he was being a baby.

His mother had dragged him along on an errand run. Normally he didn't mind, because she mostly let him wait in the car. And when she did ask him to save her some time by running into one store while she dashed into another, it was only to be sure they were home in time for dinner and the stuff he wanted to do that night.

Today she had asked him to pick up batteries in the hardware store while she went to a gigantic home-interiors warehouse. Ray was then to wait in the car. "I shouldn't be more than half an hour," she said.

"Half an hour!" he said. "Come on, it's not really gonna take that long, is it?"

She ignored him, and while that infuriated him, he knew it was the best way to deal with his new attitude. Deep down what he really wanted was for his mom or dad to engage with him, argue with him. When they were indifferent or gave up — like when his dad would conclude, "Oh, no one can even talk to you" — Ray immediately regretted being so obstinate. He wanted anything but to be ignored.

But the way his mother did it was effective. She wouldn't say anything nasty or express exasperation. She merely pretended she had not heard him. That kept the back and forth from escalating to where Ray would realize how ridiculous he was, respond in anger, and say stupid things he couldn't take back. He had even made her cry, which made him feel like an idiot.

Sure, she was an old mom, and she was old-fashioned. She still called him Rayford most of the time. At least that was better than Raymie, which is what she had called him until he was about six. She had even made the mistake of recently calling him that in front of his friends, and he feared he would never hear the end of that.

But Ray knew his mom really cared about him and loved him in her own way. He didn't dwell on it, but if pushed he would have to admit that life would be awful without her in his corner.

Ray found the batteries and opted for self-checkout. He tossed the bag onto the front seat and stretched out in the back, trying to avoid being noticed in that old car by anyone he knew. He slouched, reading *Extreme Sports* magazine. Ray preferred the major sports, but he also enjoyed watching skateboarders and bikers and snowboarders on TV, so the magazine was all right. Still, he nodded and dozed, finally tossing the magazine aside.

He awoke with a start, sweating as the sun toasted him through the window. His mother had been gone a lot longer than thirty minutes. Ah, well, she couldn't be far away and wouldn't be long. The store was directly in line with where she had parked, so he'd see her as soon as she emerged. Ray thumbed through the magazine again but soon couldn't concentrate.

As his solar-powered watch pushed past the forty-five-minute mark, Ray couldn't remain in the car. He stood outside, leaning against it, not caring who saw him. Of course, no one did, despite how conspicuous he felt. Ray studied every woman who came out of the store, almost every one initially looking like his mother.

When an hour had passed, he used the car phone to dial her cell. He heard her phone ring in the car. She had left it between the seats. He called his dad. No answer. Just his voice mail. He tried his dad's office. Closed.

Why did he feel so nervous? Nothing could have happened to his mother. Could it? Not in public. Maybe the store was crowded. She was probably in a long checkout line. That had to be it. But she didn't come and didn't come. Finally, scolding himself for being such a nervous Nellie, Ray moseyed into the store.

It was cavernous and, surprisingly, not that crowded. He looked up and down the aisles. Soon he decided to start at the far end and walk every inch of the place. His mother was nowhere to be seen. Ray's pulse raced, his breath shortened. What was this? There would be a simple explanation, so why was he so panicky?

He began to imagine horrible things. Kidnapping. Murder. And, he was shocked to admit to himself, he found one other option even worse. What if Ray's mother had abandoned him? simply left him? She and his dad had had it with him and had taken off. If and when he called the police and made his way home, he would discover the house empty and his parents gone forever.

What was the matter with him? That was

ludicrous. Yet why did it seem so logical and possible? And why did it seem so absurdly worse to him than his imaginings of horrible fates befalling his mother?

Ray was overcome by fear but also by a surprising love and deep longing for his mother. *What am I, four years old? Get a grip!*

But he couldn't get a grip, and as the minutes dragged by, his anxiety soared to where he could only pray. Sobs in his throat, and he knew he must look like a fool, a string bean of a young boy wandering a home-decorating outlet, red-faced, eyes full.

The last thing Ray wanted was to ask someone for help. Besides not knowing whom to ask, what would he say? How would he say it? Would he look like a baby? Would he dissolve into tears? And what would he do if his mother showed up in the middle of all that, having simply lost track of the time?

He used a public phone that automatically charged the Steeles' home phone bill and tried his dad's cell phone again. Same result. And there was no answer at home. He called the store he was in and felt like a fool, pretending to be elsewhere and asking for a customer.

"We can page her if it's an emergency," he was told.

"Well, it sort of is."

"Sort of? What's the nature of the emergency, son?"

He didn't know what to say.

"Is this a crank call?"

"No, I —"

"Caller ID shows this is coming from inside our store. Now —"

Ray hung up and quickly moved away from the phone bank. He had to leave. There wasn't a single other customer who looked like he might place such a call. In fact, he didn't see another male — other than store personnel.

Ray hurried back out to the car, relieved to see the batteries still on the front seat. Wouldn't that have been great, to endure this and have those stolen too? He turned in a circle, surveying the parking lot, sweating, in full crisis now.

Finally Ray climbed into the toasty car and stretched out across the backseat again. He could no longer stanch the tears. As he cried, he prayed aloud, "God, help me! Please bring my mother back. I'll do anything you want. I'll quit swearing. I'll quit sassing. I'll go to church and really listen."

Ray buried his face in the crook of his elbow, his shoulders heaving. He kept telling himself to go back into the store and get help. But almost as bad as fearing his mother had abandoned him — and his dad being in on it — was the prospect of looking like such a wuss.

As he lay sobbing, he heard footsteps and the driver's door opening. "Oh, Rayford," his mother said, "you're sleeping."

He quickly wiped his face and sat up. "I'm awake."

"I'm so sorry," she said, tossing her packages on the passenger's seat. "You wouldn't believe what happened." She started the car without looking at him, and he was relieved. Relieved that she was alive, that she was here, that he had been wrong. Had God answered his prayer? Ray was amazed at how quickly he regretted making all those promises, especially when his mother's return seemed so plain and hardly miraculous.

"What happened?" he said.

"Well, it's embarrassing. I was on my way out of the store, thought I saw someone I knew, and hesitated. As it turned out, it wasn't her anyway, but when I stopped, the door caught my heel and tore the flesh just above the shoe line. I was bleeding, Rayford. How bizarre. A clerk came running and took me to the employees' lounge in the back, and the assistant manager was most helpful. He cleaned the wound and bandaged me up. I felt so silly."

"I wondered where you were."

"Oh, you probably slept through the whole thing, Rayford. I'm limping a little, but it's just a surface wound and I'll be good as new by morning."

"Yeah."

"I hate to think what your father will say."

"Um-hm."

"Well, I can see this elicits no sympathy from my loving son."

She had no idea. Ray was so grateful that he didn't know what to say or do. "You should have taken your phone, Ma. You forgot it again."

"Oh, I know. I thought about calling the car, but with the engine off —"

"Well, if you'd had your phone, I could have called you!" Ray swore.

"Now, honey —"

"You're just so scatterbrained," he said.

"Well, I'm sorry. I might have expected a little more understanding."

"Yeah, sure, like I get from you."

Again she ignored him. What had gotten into him? What had happened to his fear, his promises to God, his relief? He was angry to have had to endure all that, and for what? A stupid, silly little accident his absentminded mom could have avoided.

Ray hated himself. What kind of crybaby was he? And what kind of an ungrateful son?

If there was really a God, why hadn't He just let Ray find his mother? Was this His idea of answering a prayer? Ray had never felt more like a child. Maybe there was a God, but He sure didn't seem to make any sense, not in the Bible and not here and now in real life.

All that made Ray feel like a fraud, and he didn't understand himself. His love for his mother, his desperation when she was away, had shown itself in anger and bitterness when she returned.

He turned his guns on his dad at dinner. "Why couldn't I get through to you on your cell phone this afternoon?"

"You tried calling your dad?" his mother said. "What for? When? And from where?"

"Oh, I was just wondering about something. I don't even remember what now. And what difference does that make? Mom, sometimes, really . . ."

"Where'd you call from? We don't need more phone bills."

Knowing it would show up on the bill, Ray said, "I tried from the car and then from the store you were in."

"What did you want?"

"Who cares? That's not the point! Why

didn't you have your phone on, Dad?"

"I did, Ray. Just calm down. I was on an important call with a supplier in Ohio, if you must know, and it took the entire ride home."

"Oh."

"Oh, what? Are you sorry for scolding me before you knew what was going on?"

"Whatever."

"That describes your whole attitude these days," his dad said.

That was for sure.

Ray couldn't concentrate the rest of the night. He didn't enjoy watching sports on TV, didn't enjoy reading his aviation books, wasn't able to relax, and seemed to take forever to get to sleep. This had to be the worst time in his life. Why couldn't he just be grateful that he had been wrong, his mother had not abandoned him, she was still there, still loved him, would be there for him?

He felt himself retreating farther and farther into his shell. He felt guilty about making promises to God that he may have meant at the time but now seemed crazy and empty. He had no intention of keeping them.

It was one of those rare Tuesday afternoons when Marilena's and Sorin's workdays ended nearly simultaneously. Marshaling her courage, Marilena poked her head into his office. "Would you consider walking me home?"

He grimaced. "Why would I want to do that? I mean, I have my bike here, and you always take the bus. . . ."

"Never mind."

"No! I don't mean it personally, Marilena. It's just that —"

"Well, can't you take the bus back here with me in the morning too? Your bike will be fine."

"I suppose. But why?"

"I just need the exercise and prefer not to walk alone," she said.

"Come, come," he said. "I know you better than that. Something troubling you?"

"Yes."

Sorin loaded his bag and slung it over his shoulder. On their way past Dr. Baduna Marius's door, Sorin said, "I'm walking home. We're still on for tonight."

Baduna nodded and smiled, but he would not look at Marilena. That told her Sorin had informed Baduna that she knew. How awkward. They had to work together. Well, she decided, if Sorin and Baduna could make it work at the office, she certainly could too.

Marilena had not formulated an approach and found herself at a loss for words for the first several blocks of their trek.

"Let's not waste this disruption of my routine," Sorin finally said.

"I know," she said, "but I didn't take into account how long it's been since I walked this far. Would you mind terribly if we stopped somewhere?"

"Well, I'm hardly hungry yet," he said, steering her toward a park bench. "Come on, out with it."

"Oh, Sorin, I can't be badgered into a serious discussion. You're impatient from the beginning. How is that supposed to make me feel?"

"As if I am weary of the game playing and the serious talks," he said. "We are married in name only. It's a convenience for both of us, but frankly it is more convenient for you than for me."

"I'm sorry to hear that."

"Don't act as if it's news, Marilena. I appreciate that you uphold your end of the expenses and that we help each other out. You know full well that I would rather be married to Baduna, but who knows how long it will be before that could become a reality? I appreciate you, consider you a fine person, and enjoy scholarly discussions with you. I do not, however, look forward to these heart-to-hearts."

Marilena hated that her voice had a tear in it and would make her sound weak. "Perhaps I should spare you then."

"Oh, please. Save the histrionics. At the very least you have piqued my curiosity."

Marilena sighed and looked away. Finally, "I want a serious talk. I don't want to merely satisfy your curiosity."

"All right. I'm here. I'm not happy; I'm eager to get home, but I'm here."

"That is hardly conducive to constructive conversation."

Sorin leaned forward and rested his chin in his hands. "My dear, I have not had a constructive conversation with you, aside from academic subjects, for years. Now don't cry. I didn't intend for that to hurt you. You know I tell the truth at any expense."

"Even my feelings."

"Frankly, yes."

She shook her head. "Can you imagine how difficult this is for me, your wanting me to just get on with it?"

"As long as we're being direct," he said, "imagine how difficult this is for me. Whatever it is, it's an interrupter. I can't imagine caring, and yet I will feel obligated to pretend I do."

"Am I really that much of a burden, Sorin?"

"Sometimes. Occasionally, yes."

"You want me to leave, don't you? I don't want to be a burden."

"Leave or stay," he said, "but please abandon the frequent personal revelations."

Marilena couldn't imagine a crueler husband, aside from one who might beat her. "You don't care what goes on inside me?"

"I don't, Marilena. I'm sorry, but I don't. In your mind, perhaps, because you are a careful student and an articulate thinker. But in what you call your heart or soul or whatever it is you are trying to nurture? No. It bores me."

"But this pertains to you."

"How can it if I don't care?"

"Because it would *affect* you, Sorin!"

"Not if I don't let it. You know where I stand on all this spiritual *prostie*."

"Foolery? That's what you think it is?"

"Of course, and you know it. And unless you have lost your mind, you agree."

"All of it is craziness. That's what you think?"

He looked at his watch. "Really, Marilena, I don't have time in my life for this. You have your meeting tonight with the *zevzec,* and Baduna and I —"

118

"Don't call her a nincompoop, Sorin. That's beneath you. Disagree with her if you must, but —"

"Marilena! I was being kind! Don't you see? I called her a *zevzec* because that's what I believe *you* have become!"

Marilena stood and paced. This was no good. She was going to have to leave Sorin, depend upon the state, have a child, and raise it on her own.

"Can we please go now, dear?" he said.

"Don't call me *dear* again," she said. "Not anymore. I know what you really think of me."

"Oh, Marilena! What's become of you? We both know I am not a soft person. I have none of the social graces that should accompany my profession. I don't speak forthrightly to cause pain, and I get no joy from it. But I would not otherwise be true to myself nor constructive to you. What is it now? Tell me what's on your mind. I'll try to be sensitive, though I make no guarantees."

"You'll hear me out?"

"I promise."

He always kept his word; she had to give him that.

She took a deep breath. "I want a child."

Sorin covered his eyes, then let his hands slide to cover his mouth, as if to keep from blurting out something injurious.

119

Before he could change his mind, Marilena sped through what had happened to her, how the urge had come over her long before the Tuesday night meetings, and yet how those meetings and that woman, Viviana, had spoken so specifically to her.

When Sorin took his hands from his mouth, she plunged on, not wanting to hear him. "Just last week we talked after class, and she assured me she knew what was weighing on me. She said she had my answer. Tonight I will make her tell me what she meant. Oh, I know what you think of her and the whole idea of hearing from spirits in a world beyond us. But I can ignore it no longer. Discount the messages, discount the spiritual plane, but don't you dare deprive me of the right to feel what I did not choose to feel. I want a child. I need a child. I will have a child."

"Well," he said at last, "good for you."

"Good for me?"

"And not so good for me."

"I was afraid of that."

"As well you should have been," he said. "Have I ever given you the impression that I changed my stance on this subject? I don't want to be a father again. And the last thing I want is my life and routine interrupted."

"Fine."

"I am clear then?"

"You have always been clear, Sorin. Do you think so little of me that this is all you can express? No sympathy, no interest, no joy in what I have come to realize about myself? Are you not happy for me?"

"If this makes you happy, I am happy for you. Naturally, myriad questions arise. Where will you get this child? Where will you raise it? How — ?"

"So it was *nebunie* for me to even dream that you might — ?"

"Folly to think this would happen in my apartment, in the midst of my papers and books and work? Of course."

"Will you miss me?" she said.

Finally she detected a glimmer of compassion. "That I can say in all truthfulness, Marilena. I will miss you."

"Not all of me."

"No, not all of you. Not this current obsession and how it seems to have affected your intellect. But there is much engaging about you, and we have been together a long time."

"And we have had our good days, haven't we, Sorin?"

"We have indeed. I shall have many lifetime memories."

"That makes me bold enough to make one request."

"Just to save you any grief, let me warn you that this request should be something I might conceivably be able to fulfill. In other words, it must not include inter—"

"Interrupting your life, yes, I understand. Sorin, I would appreciate it more than I can express if you would — in light of what we have had together — find it within yourself not to divorce me until after I have had my child."

"But you don't even know where you might go to be impregnated."

"That is my problem. I want the child to have a legitimate name. Your name."

"I have no interest in impregnating you, conventionally or otherwise."

"I know. I will pay to have that done, but I want my son or daughter to be a Carpathia."

Sorin stood and she sat. He was not a big man, but he seemed to tower over her. "Should I agree to that *condiţe,* it would not obligate me to —"

She looked up at him. "Any duties or responsibilities as a father, no."

He ran a hand through his hair. "Perhaps I should draft a document that requires you to abandon my name should the child ever do anything to embarrass me."

"Are we not getting way ahead of ourselves, Sorin?"

"Perhaps. But I must consider my reputation."

That night at the meeting, Viviana Ivinisova seemed in a hurry. She went through her usual litany of telling the past, the future, communicating with cooperative spirits, lighting the candle, and praying to the angel of light, and she even threw in some tarot reading and interpretation.

And this time it was not Marilena's imagination that the woman continually looked her way. In fact, Marilena changed seats after a midsession break, and clearly Viviana kept catching her eye, regardless of where she sat. As if there would have been another option, and apparently to be sure nothing was misunderstood, at the end of the meeting Viviana pointed at Marilena and said, "Dear, could you see me after?"

This time they didn't walk to the bus, didn't visit a bistro, didn't engage in small talk. Rather, Ms. Ivinisova took Marilena by the arm and led her into a remote, dark corner of the library downstairs. "I have critically important messages to you from the spirit world that would have been inappropriate to share with the others."

"Oh, Viviana, I'm not sure how much stock I put in such —"

"Nonsense, Mrs. Carpathia. I have sensed a psychic energy in you from the first moment I saw you. I see an aura about you in class. I have been given clear messages for you that seem to resonate deeply within you. You're not telling me, are you, that you need to be further persuaded?"

Marilena was convinced, but she couldn't force back that rational, black-and-white mind of hers. "Perhaps more proof wouldn't be all bad."

Viviana sighed. "I must tell you, skepticism risks offending even the most positive spirits."

"If they are for real, and if they have genuinely given you what you call critically important messages for me, I can't imagine they will abandon me if I require convincing."

"What will it take?"

This was new. Viviana actually appeared perturbed. Strangely, this somehow empowered Marilena. Despite the fact that she had been rocked by the truth of everything Ms. Ivinisova had said in the previous twelve weeks, still Marilena felt like a sheep, being led into areas of belief she had never before countenanced. At least now she would apply some academic protocol, if only insisting on some evidence.

"I want you to be more specific," she said. "I want you to tell me something for me alone that could not be applied to anyone else's situation."

"All right," Viviana said, as if backed into a corner. "Come."

Marilena followed her out of the stacks of disks, past vast shelves of books, and past a field of long, wide, shiny tables sparsely populated with people mostly reading newspapers. Finally they found a bevy of study carrels everyone else seemed to have abandoned. Viviana grabbed an extra chair so they could both crowd into one nook. She took Marilena's hands in hers, bowed her head, and closed her eyes.

"Listen to me carefully," she said, as Marilena felt her chest tighten. "A spirit of high rank tells me that your need for a child will cause a permanent break in your relationship with your husband."

Marilena's breathing became labored, her mouth dry. "True," she said.

"True? Already?"

"Yes."

"The spirit says you should continue to push for your husband to stay with you until the child is born so he may bear your husband's name."

"He? It will be a son?"

"That is the way it was rendered. The fact that the spirit used the phrase 'continue to push' indicates you have already broached this with your husband."

"I have."

"Do you need more?"

"Is there more?"

"If there was, would you need it?"

"I would certainly want to hear it," Marilena said.

"Of course, but if you require it still to be convinced, I sincerely fear we will try the patience of the spirits."

"No. It is fair to say I am thoroughly convinced."

"I would be too, dear."

"But if there is more to hear, may I hear it?"

Seven

There was more to hear all right. In fact, Viviana Ivinisova requested a meeting with Marilena and her husband at their apartment.

"Whatever for?" Marilena said. She told Viviana where Sorin stood on the issue.

The older woman sat silent for a moment. "Well," she said finally, "it does sound as if you need to prepare him. Naturally, I have run into my share of skepticism over the years. I am not intimidated by it or by higher IQs than my own. It's all right with me if he receives me with a *distracţie,* but —"

"Amusement would be the least of it," Marilena said. "He might want to debate you all day and night."

"I don't mind that either. What I would not want is for him to feel impatient, invaded, anything that makes him angry."

Marilena agreed to try to prepare Sorin, to nudge him toward agreeing to at least meet with Ms. Ivinisova some evening.

"My greatest fear," Marilena said, "is whether I can manage this on my own. Where will I live? Will I have enough to support myself and my child? Sorin has said he will force me to absolve him of any financial responsibility, even if the child bears his name."

Ms. Ivinisova seemed to suppress a smile, and Marilena couldn't decide whether the woman had a delicious secret or simply found her entertaining. "What will I do, ma'am?"

Viviana leaned forward and embraced her. "Must you hurry off, or do you have a few minutes?"

"Nothing is more important than this," Marilena said.

"Let me tell you how I assess your spiritual journey so far," Viviana said. "Correct me where I am mistaken. You came to my classes for diversion, something to take your mind off your longing for a child. Your intellect made you a skeptic, yet you couldn't deny the truths that reached to your core."

Marilena nodded after every assertion.

"During the days between meetings you tried to poke holes in everything you heard and experienced, but eventually you could deny it no longer. There was something to this and something specifically for you."

Marilena shrugged and nodded again.

"By now you are convinced. There is personal interest in you from the spirit world, and it is quickly becoming clear that this will benefit you. Your dream will come true. You will have a child."

"And yet my life may grow more complicated, much more difficult."

"That is where you are wrong, so wrong."

"I'm listening."

"So far," Ms. Ivinisova said, "you have still come at this new vista in your life from an academic point of view. Oh, it has made you emotional, opened your eyes to a new world, excited you. But largely you are still clinical about it. You're a believer, but you are focusing on the cause and effect. 'If it's true, what will happen?' "

"I see. Yes. How *should* I be viewing it?"

"I would hope, Marilena, that you would soon deduce from all this that the interest shown in you from the other side feels personal because it is. The spirits care for you, want the best for you. You should feel loved."

Marilena squinted. *Feel loved.* "To be honest, I'm still scared."

"Naturally. People have misconceptions about spirit-world beings. They can't imagine them loving those of us on this side of the veil."

"But who is it, then? Who cares for me? loves me? Unnamed, unseen spirits? And why?"

Viviana stood and reached for Marilena. She rose, and the older woman said, "Let's walk."

The evening was cool, and Viviana strolled with her arm gently around Marilena's shoulder. "Let me tell you my story," she said. "Perhaps it will shed some light on yours."

Viviana explained that when she was growing up in Russia, her parents had for decades considered themselves holdovers from the past when atheistic Communism had been the accepted order. "A form of democracy swept the Soviet Union, but religion flagged. There may have been pockets of Christians and devout Jews, Muslims certainly, who practiced their faiths as minuscule minorities. But there was no real uprising of people of faith, despite the new freedoms. My parents reviled religion, but they were also contrarians to the state. They despised Communism and had never been card-carrying atheists. They allowed that there might be supernatural beings and worlds beyond knowing. This manifested itself when they dabbled in what some called the occult sciences."

"Demons and such?"

"Well, that's complicated. My parents did not believe in heaven and hell and God versus Satan. They believed in the powers of good and evil. But their foray into spiritualism began as recreation. My mother as much as admitted to me that she began speaking positively of clairvoyance and the like merely to offend the sensibilities of her scholarly friends."

"Friends like my husband."

"Much like him, yes. But like you too."

"But I have become convinced," Marilena said.

"To a point."

"No, I believe."

"You may believe, but you don't take it personally."

"In many ways I do," Marilena said. "I don't mean to be contentious, but I'm not following you. Clearly something or someone has communicated to you my innermost thoughts and longings, and you're prophesying that they will be fulfilled. I want to believe that with all that's within me, but —"

"But you are not yet at a place intellectually where you can accept that just because the clairvoyance is clearly legitimate the eventual reality will bear it out."

"I'll believe it when I am pregnant."

"Of course. And until then, though it all *seems* real, you hold back from loving whomever it is who loves you."

Marilena stopped. "What are you saying?"

Viviana let her arm slide from the younger woman's shoulder. "Oh, dear one, someone in the other realm loves you and has chosen to honor you, and you remain so *atent,* so *sceptic. . . .*"

"Wouldn't you be cautious and skeptical if you were me?"

"But I *was* you, dear! My parents had fun with tarot and clairvoyance and even Ouija at first. And then they discovered the truth of it all. By the time I was six years old, they had me communicating with spirits through the Ouija board every day. It took me a few years, but eventually I realized that the spirits on the other side of the messages knew me, cared for me, loved me. I had been chosen to be a channel, a communicator, an advocate to the mortal world of the skeptics and the cautious."

"You believe I have been similarly chosen?"

"No! You have been chosen to bear a

child! Why would they care whether you became a mother unless that child was destined for greatness? Yes, they love and care about you and want you fulfilled, but that would be easy. They could help you bear a child. But they care so much, it goes deeper. And I sense you're not getting it."

Marilena found a park bench and sat, looking up at Viviana. "And if and when I get it, as you say, what will that mean to me?"

"That is the question I was waiting for," Viviana said. "First, you will be the mother of a special child, one close to the hearts and minds of the spirits. And second — and this is my deepest desire for you — it should make you love the spirits as much as they love you."

"Love the spirits?"

"It hits you as foreign, doesn't it?"

"It does," Marilena said. "They have not struck me as personal beings to this point."

"I know. I can tell. That's what I am driving at."

"But they aren't human, are they? Are they ghosts, the departed?"

Viviana sat next to Marilena, and the younger woman could see her breath. "No. No, they are not. They are angels."

"Angels."

"Angels. And they love you."

"But if I am to believe in angels, I must also believe in God."

"Yes."

"I can't say that I do."

"Perhaps it is not the God you think," Viviana said.

"Then who?"

"This is not the God of the Christians. Not the God of the Jews. Not Allah. But he loves you and has chosen you and longs for you to love him."

Marilena shook her head. "Whoever he is, he remains too remote. I want to see him, touch him, communicate with him."

"If you could see him, you would no longer need faith. But, Marilena, you should require little faith, because he has communicated so directly to you through me. Can you so quickly forget that he has given me the power to know your history, read your thoughts, predict your future?"

"I know. I know. But he seems too impersonal for me to love."

"He's telling me that this is what he wants."

"Fair enough, but I must be honest. I will not express love I don't feel."

"He demands allegiance."

"I suppose that is fair too. Perhaps I am unworthy."

"Of course you are, dear. That's what should make you love him all the more."

"And if I don't find it within myself?"

Viviana stood and stepped away, briefly turning her back. When she spun to face Marilena, her jaw was set, her eyes cold in the faint light from a distant streetlamp. "I shouldn't speak for him unless he tells me something specific."

"And he's not telling you?"

"He is silent for now. Perhaps offended."

"This is all so alien to me."

"Of course. But imagine how many people, how many barren women, would give anything to be in your place. I shudder when you ask the consequences of not finding it within yourself to love and respect and show allegiance to one who offers you the desire of your heart. For what if his response is that in that case you may not find a child within you either?"

Marilena stood. She wanted to escape, to run, but to where? She had to think. If there was someone she loved, it was Viviana, and yet at this moment she wanted to be alone. "I don't know what to say," she said. "I certainly must be true enough to myself not to express love and devotion to someone merely because I want something from him or am afraid of him."

"Well said. You must take the time to examine yourself and your motives. And meanwhile, prepare your husband and get his permission for my visit. I daresay things will be communicated at that time that will put your heart and mind and soul at rest."

"Rest?" Marilena said. "I feel as if I will never rest again until I come to terms with my feelings toward this god you speak of."

"Think of it this way," Viviana said. "Love him because he first loved you."

"And how will I know my own heart? Should I come to own such a love, how will I know it's true and not based on fear or on my own longing for what he offers me?"

"He will know."

"You'll tell him?"

"No, Marilena, you will."

"How?"

"He is a god. Gods may be prayed to."

"I have never prayed."

"I hope soon that you will not be able to say that."

Marilena shuddered, fighting the question that plagued her. "How should I address him?"

Viviana smiled beatifically. "As the angel of light. As the morning star. As the prince and power of the air."

"That's what I was afraid of," Marilena

said. "You know I'm widely read. I know his name."

Viviana reached for Marilena and pulled her back toward the library. "Of course you do. You are a student and a professor of classical literature. But what you have read of him is from the perspective of one who is so cosmically jealous of his beauty and power and, yes, ambition, that it must be wholly discounted. I would urge you to read of him from other sources. And then read the Bible again with new eyes. If the God of the Bible lays legitimate claim to being the God above all gods who sits high above the heavens, and if Lucifer were really evil, why would God not simply exterminate him?

"No, Marilena, my god — the true and living god, the one who loves me and cares for me and gives me all things — has ascended to the throne as the god of the universe. He has chosen to bestow upon you a son, and for that all he asks is that you pledge him your love and allegiance."

In spite of herself, Marilena laughed. "As you can imagine, this continues to be nearly impossible to fathom. But one thing I know: this is one subject you will want to avoid should Sorin be open to granting you an audience."

All the way home on the bus, Marilena sat

wrapped in herself, arms folded, chin to her chest, bag in her lap. How was it possible, after fewer than four months, for her to have swung so far from humanism and existentialism to this full-blown acceptance of a spirit world? While she remained resistant to praying to Lucifer, let alone pledging her love, she bore not an iota of doubt regarding his reality, his existence, and even — as Viviana had communicated — his personal interest in her. The question was whether she wanted to pursue a relationship with him at this level. Could she not merely become a spiritualist, a believer, without becoming a disciple?

She arrived yet again to an empty apartment. She could only imagine Sorin in his lover's arms, telling him of the craziness that had come over his wife. Knowing a divorce was looming, probably within the year if Marilena could be impregnated soon, would Baduna begin preparing his wife for a severing as well?

Sorin claimed Baduna was happy at home, but how could that be, given his relationship with his boss? Surely Baduna's wife could not know of his inclinations or his affair. So much for that happy marriage.

Marilena changed into a loose flannel gown and slippers and turned on the television. The news had already moved into sports, which held no interest for her. She turned it off and tried to read, but her mind was a jumble. It was as if physical pressure asserted itself at the base of her spine and vibrated at the back of her head.

Unable to concentrate on anything else, Marilena felt compelled to pray. But was it she who wished to connect with this god of the spirit world, or was he trying to reach her? She was convinced of the latter, which scared her.

Marilena could not shake the urge. But how did one pray? She had read of religious devotees who folded their hands, bowed their heads, closed their eyes. Some knelt. Some raised their hands. Some fell prostrate. Viviana sat before a candle. Marilena decided that if there was anything to any of this, she needn't follow convention. She would merely open herself to contact, and if the chief of the spirit world was who Viviana said he was, he would somehow communicate with her.

Sitting at her desk, Marilena stared at a wall cluttered with notes. "I'm here," she whispered.

Immediately her mind, her soul, her being felt rushed by a spiritual force. She heard no audible voice, but clearly something or someone spoke directly to her heart. The words were cacophonous and dizzying, yet the ones she was meant to hear, she believed, were impressed deeply upon her, and it was as if she knew them instinctively.

"I love you with an everlasting love. I have chosen you as a vessel. You will conceive in due time. Your gestation will be easy but troubling, as your child will not move. You shall bear a son, and his name shall be called 'victory of the people.' He will tower head and shoulders above anyone who has ever lived. He will be considered a stranger, this hammer of my message."

Marilena didn't want to speak, didn't want to answer, but if this was real — and it was more real to her than any conversation she had ever had with a mortal — there were things she wanted to know.

"How will I manage?" she whispered.

"I shall provide a companion already chosen."

"And where will I live?"

"I will provide a place."

"I fear you."

"Fear not."

"My fear hinders reciprocating your feelings toward me. If I find that I cannot —"

"You will."

"But if I can't . . ."

"I have spoken."

"If you really love me, you will tell me the consequences if I don't return your —"

"Then you shall die."

"And my son?"

"He shall never die."

Marilena was overcome and even tempted to conjure up a love she could express. But she heard Sorin's key in the door and quickly disengaged from her reverie.

He looked — she didn't know how else to judge it — in love. How he and Baduna must have enjoyed planning their future together. Marilena broached the subject of hosting Viviana the next Tuesday and was surprised to find Sorin open to it.

"As long as she doesn't stay late. I will have been with Baduna, of course, and I have an early morning the next day."

Marilena was giddy with anticipation and assured him that both she and Viviana would respect his time. "She believes she has the solution to the logistical issues."

"I can hardly wait," he said.

Marilena had rarely had trouble sleeping, but in the wee hours — her bedside clock projecting 2:15 a.m. in faint red numerals — her eyes popped open. She felt immediately wide-awake and determined not to disturb Sorin, whose noisy breathing told her he was sound asleep.

She carefully removed the covers and swung her feet out, sitting on the edge of the bed. What was this? Was she to pray again? No, this was different. Something or someone was again trying to communicate with her, but she felt a deep impression that it was not the one with whom she had conversed earlier.

Marilena rested her elbows on her knees and her head in her hands. But when whoever or whatever this was began to communicate with her spirit, she had to stand.

"I am coming quickly, and My reward is with Me, to give to every one according to his work. I am the Alpha and the Omega, the Beginning and the End, the First and the Last.

"Blessed are those who do My commandments, that they may have the right to the tree of life, and may enter through the gates into the city. But outside are dogs and sorcerers and sexually immoral and murderers and idolaters, and whoever loves and practices a lie.

"I, Jesus, have sent My angel to testify to you these things. I am the Root and the Offspring of David, the Bright and Morning Star.

"Let him who thirsts come. Whoever desires, let him take the water of life freely.

"Resist the devil and he will flee from you."

I'm crazy, Marilena decided. *I have totally lost my mind. It's megalomania. Only someone thoroughly insane would believe God and Lucifer are competing for her soul.*

The following Tuesday night, Viviana Ivinisova accompanied Marilena home on the bus.

Sorin was cordial but guarded. "Good to see you again too, Ms. Ivinisova. Forgive me for not buying into this with the gusto my wife has."

Viviana seemed to pointedly ignore that, and Marilena was impressed that she made no attempt to persuade him otherwise. There was no proselytizing, no case making. "I know your time is short," Viviana said as she sat on their worn sofa and Marilena made her some tea. "So let me get to the point. You and I both know that we have each been fully apprised of the marital situation here and your lack of interest in bringing a child into the mix."

"In fact," Sorin said, "I have agreed not to divorce Marilena until after the child has been given my name."

"And," Viviana said, "I don't imagine you

want a pregnant woman and her attendant ailments to contend with in your apartment every day for nine months either."

Marilena was tempted to inject that she had been promised an easy pregnancy, but there were things she kept even from Ms. Ivinisova.

"I hadn't thought of that," Sorin said, "but you make a good point. On the other hand, I'm loath to put her on the street before she has made other arrangements."

"The truth is," Viviana said, "arrangements have been made, and once Marilena has agreed, she would be free to leave here whenever she wishes."

Marilena was stunned. She was not even pregnant yet, and she was not mentally prepared to pull up stakes for months, maybe a year.

"There is the matter of her finishing the semester at the university," Sorin said. "Otherwise what are we to do with her students?"

"I have not resigned," Marilena said.

"No, and you mustn't," Sorin said. "Not until we can —"

"No worries," Ms. Ivinisova said, sipping her tea. "I'm sure this is coming a bit quickly for your wife as well, as we have not discussed it. Are you familiar with the name

Reiche Planchette?"

It sounded familiar, but Marilena could not place it. Sorin shook his head.

"He's widely published in my area of interest. Also, he is regional director of our organization, and I report to him. I have taken the liberty of informing him of all that has been going on with Marilena, and it is fair to say that he is more than enthusiastic. He has agreed to allot funds and also to free me to take a career detour. That is, if Marilena agrees."

"You have my attention," the younger woman said.

"There is a small cottage on several acres in the country near Cluj. I'm hardly an agrarian, but if Marilena would have me, I would live with her, aid her during her gestation, and help raise the child for as long as she wishes."

Marilena knew she should be grateful, but this was too much too fast. "No, no," she said. "I wouldn't even be able to help with a garden. Country life is not for me, and —"

"It would be ideal for raising a son," Viviana said.

"For someone else perhaps, but what would I do for work?"

"I would insist on high-speed wireless Internet and the best equipment for you, dear. You could continue to do what you do best, but remotely."

"There is no way I could come close to my current income. What would we do for food and clothing and rent?"

"I was not clear," Viviana said. "The cottage is not elaborate, but it would be roomy enough — and private enough — for three, and it would be provided."

"Provided?"

"I told you. Director Planchette is enthusiastic."

"I don't know," Marilena said. "I just don't know. I want a child, but I am nervous about the pregnancy. I would want to be close to a doctor and a hospital."

"You would be," Viviana said.

Sorin rose and came to sit on the arm of Marilena's chair. He raised his hand. "Are we voting? Frankly, this sounds perfect."

"For you, sure," Marilena said. "It solves your problems."

"Yours too," he said. "Imagine it. Ms. Ivinisova, how far would it be from Cluj-Napoca proper?"

"Not ten kilometers."

That sounded better, but Marilena was certainly in no hurry to accede. What might living in the same house with someone do to their relationship? She admired, respected, cared for Ms. Ivinisova, and she would not want anything to interfere with that. The very idea, however, of a woman with such spiritual sensitivity helping raise her son, well, where else could she find that?

On the other hand, she had not confided in Viviana that she believed the enemy of Lucifer had attacked her conscience. It had happened only that once, and yet it still seemed as real as her prayer to Lucifer. She had not revealed that to Viviana either, as she didn't want to admit she still had made no commitment regarding her allegiance.

Viviana concluded with the understanding that Marilena would ponder these things.

And Sorin agreed not to pressure her, though Marilena would not have bet on that. "Allow me to accompany you to the bus, Ms. Ivinisova," Sorin said. "The hour is late."

Marilena was struck by this sudden chivalry given his harping about his early morning the next day. And she herself had not been the beneficiary of such kindness for years. But perhaps it was good for Sorin to have a few minutes alone with Ms. Ivinisova. They were closer in age, and perhaps they could find some common ground, despite their disparate views.

She stepped to the window and saw him take her arm as they crossed the street. A tall male emerged from between buildings and greeted both warmly. Marilena could not make him out in the shadows. Could it be Baduna? The three continued together, and Marilena never felt more alone in her life. One thing was certain: she would ask neither Sorin nor Viviana about the man. She didn't want to seem to have been spying, nor did she want to appear paranoid. If they chose to tell her, so be it.

Later Marilena tossed and turned in bed until Sorin's impatient sighs chased her to her desk. She felt no nudging from the spirit world, no compulsion to pray. Had Lucifer already abandoned her, knowing her heart? And what about his adversary? Viviana and her comrades could deny all they wanted that Lucifer was the enemy of the God of the Bible, and had Marilena not believed she had heard from Him too, she might have agreed. But she knew better.

She prayed silently, "Do you still offer me a child?"

Nothing. She felt foolish.

"God," she said, "am I in a position to bargain? If I chose rather to follow You, would *You* grant me a child?"

Nothing.

It was as if Marilena Carpathia couldn't raise heaven or hell.

Eight

Marilena suddenly felt as if she were a spectator to her own life. Far too much had happened far too quickly, and her psyche had not had a chance to keep up. If there had been one thing she controlled in the last few years, despite her strange marital relationship, it had been her own schedule, her own pace.

The deep, visceral longing for a child of her own abated not an iota, and yet there were times when Marilena rued the day she allowed the maternal instinct to gain a toehold in her life. How she missed the days she used to enjoy. Every day she had been up at dawn, trading off with Sorin cooking a small, hot *gustare de dimineata* of eggs and sausage. He was always quiet, though not unpleasant, in the morning, as long as she didn't try to converse with him at length.

He would leave on his bicycle first; then she would walk to the bus. They generally arrived on campus at the same time, though she rarely saw him during the day, except for departmental meetings. Her day consisted of a few classes, a few student audiences, and plenty of research, reading, and studying. She lived for those stretches of time. If she could have done only that — the scholarship without the personal interaction — she would have been in her glory. Meetings, colleagues, and students were merely what she had to endure for the time to read and study.

If she became a mother and shared household and child-rearing duties with Viviana Ivinisova, perhaps her own time could consist of only scholarly pursuits. But was such work marketable? Was there someone or some enterprise that needed research she could transmit? And what would be her price for a life like that?

Most days she beat Sorin home. When it was her turn to tidy the place and cook dinner, she got that out of the way so she could enjoy reading the rest of the evening. When it was his turn, she retired immediately to her desk and broke away only for dinner.

It was a life she had cherished without knowing it. Only her so-called biological clock had changed things. The Tuesday night meetings, intended as a diversion, served only to lock in her aim of having a child. Suddenly she had become a different person with a different schedule, new associates, fresh goals. Most surprising to her, Marilena had become what she had once ridiculed and what Sorin still reviled: a devotee of things not seen.

It was exciting. It was novel. And she felt an anticipation unlike ever before, trying to imagine motherhood, her child, her son. But the price was her treasured way of life. Did she really want to give it up? An outsider, a nonacademic, perhaps a person with more to offer in the way of looks or possessions, would have viewed her virtually sedentary existence as a death sentence. For Marilena, however, letting go of it promised to be the toughest ordeal she would ever endure.

The worst of it was that she sensed events converging, life speeding, things happening beyond her control. Marilena had come to no real decisions, and yet a course of action over which she had no control seemed to have been set in motion. Viviana Ivinisova was in high gear — planning, plotting, talking, arranging. She knew the perfect sperm bank from which Marilena could purchase the conception agent. "They are experimental and cutting-edge," Viviana said. "They have perfected genetic engineering so the sperm can be made up of the best DNA from more than one source."

"That sounds ghastly," Marilena said. "Freakish. My son might have more than one father?"

"Not likely more than two, but don't thumb your nose at science, dear. Imagine having the best physical traits from one donor and the best intellectual traits from another."

Marilena felt pushed along by Viviana's tide of energy. What might the woman say or do if Marilena said she had simply changed her mind? She wouldn't, of course, not about having a baby. But there remained the possibility of merely divorcing Sorin and finding a new husband who wanted a family.

In the midst of all this, Viviana apparently became so enamored of the possibilities that she took it upon herself to examine the Cluj cottage. She came back with a glowing report. "We'll have such a time, Marilena. There is work to be done, but it will be fun. And did I tell you I'm changing my name?"

"Whatever for?"

"You may have noticed I have been able to suppress and camouflage my accent."

Marilena nodded.

"It's best not to be immediately identified by my Russian heritage. I mean, one doesn't *look* Russian, does one?"

"You don't," Marilena said.

"Good. Because with Russia's return to a dictatorship and her seeming eagerness to return to a union of Soviet states — which will lead to a renewed interest in encroachment on other borders — I choose to separate myself from my motherland."

"And so?"

"Viv. Viv Ivins. You like it?"

Just weeks before, Marilena would have been so intimidated by her spiritual mentor that she would have feigned approval. Now she simply shrugged. "It sounds American."

"Perfect. I knew you'd like it. It was Reiche Planchette's idea. You'll meet him Tuesday night."

"Really?"

Viviana nodded. "What a treat for our group. The regional director as guest speaker. He pulls no punches. Our only disagreements have been over my penchant to slowly reveal our true allegiance. Reiche is unabashed about his loyalty and believes making this clear immediately weeds out the squeamish and saves time."

Marilena tilted her head. "Makes sense."

"You'll love him."

Marilena wasn't so sure.

Since the evening with Viviana, Sorin seemed to have changed as well. He was positively *zvapaiat,* even in the morning. Talkative, chipper, smiling, eager to do his chores and frequently offering to take Marilena's turn too.

At the office, Baduna seemed to have taken on a new persona. No longer quiet or awkward around Marilena, he made eye contact, joked, teased, included her in stories. Once, when she returned a friendly gibe, he roared with laughter and threw an arm around her.

What was it with Sorin and Baduna? They must have been so thrilled with Viviana's plans and what the baby and the divorce would mean for them that they could barely contain themselves.

One night at home, Sorin seemed to burst with news. "Baduna has told his wife."

"Really."

"It went as well as could be expected. She had suspected."

"You don't say."

"You don't seem happy for me, Marilena."

"Perhaps now you can understand how I feel."

While Sorin and Baduna had not made

plain their relationship to others in the office, all other hindrances to their activities had been scuttled. The next Tuesday Marilena arrived home in the middle of the afternoon, and Sorin was already gone to spend the rest of the day — and night, according to the note he left — with Baduna.

Marilena had the sense that Reiche Planchette might assume that she was as far down the road in her thinking as was Viviana, and that made her want to settle things in her own heart and mind before the meeting. She still felt as if the spiritual powers on both sides of the fence were silent. There was no tingling, no vibration, no movement in her soul. Part of Marilena wondered if the spirits merely assumed — as everyone else did — that she was on board. Was it possible this ship had sailed before she could step off?

Feeling a fool, she prayed aloud. "Spirit," she said, the very label hitting her as both ominous and crazy, "I feel nothing beyond my need for a child. I cannot promise allegiance or loyalty and certainly not love. You would want me to be forthright. If you are still there and can accept that and will still grant me the son you have promised, I will remain open to changing my mind and feelings on this. But I will not pretend."

She wanted to say more, but she felt as if she were speaking to herself. Maybe this was all *aiurit* and she was the fool. Marilena couldn't explain the prophecies, the messages, the feelings, and even the dynamic of the spirit world having clearly communicated with her once. But the more days that passed, the more her confidence ebbed. She found herself retreating into the comfort of her intellectualism. Could it have all been trickery? Could it be she was the biggest sucker of all?

"God, if You're there," she prayed, "would You reveal Yourself to me?"

Marilena's voice had shaken even herself. That prayer had come out so heartfelt, so needy, and so childlike that she was transported to her growing-up days. If the dark side of the spirit world was real, then God was real. And if God was real, how could He ignore such a request?

She felt nothing, heard nothing, and was soon weeping as she fixed herself a bit of *supa*, not much more than she had had for lunch.

Ray Steele had saved his allowance for nearly a year, and now he stood before the full-length mirror in his parents' master bath, turning this way and that and admiring his new flight jacket. It bore colorful patches and epaulets. He could imagine himself a pilot.

When he wore the jacket, no one accused him of slouching. He could feel his pelvis inch forward, his shoulders slide back, stomach in, chest out, chin level. It wouldn't have surprised him if people actually saluted when he walked by.

He was stunned when even his friends laughed at his jacket. They were just jealous, he told himself. While Ray followed all the other fashions of his classmates and quickly changed when everyone else did, strangely the scoffing this jacket elicited did nothing to dissuade him from wearing it. He was a different person in it: taller, more confident, more self-assured. He was a man.

"You look fine in that jacket, Son," his dad said, which normally would be the death knell of any outfit. "I'm proud of you for being so disciplined in your saving."

"How proud are you?"

"What do you mean?"

"I'm saving for something else, but I'll never make enough to get it. I need your help. Maybe more than half."

"What?"

"Flying lessons."

"Flying lessons?"

"There's no age limit for lessons, Dad. I can fly before I drive."

"You've got a lot of years before that," his dad said, but Ray could read admiration in the man's eyes.

"Learning to fly will make learning to drive easy," Ray said.

"Well, that's for sure. And if I helped you with this, you'd make a profession of it?"

"I'd like to."

"Now that's something to think about."

Marilena decided to leave an hour early and do some reading at the library before the meeting, but as she headed out the door she was met by three young people, two boys and a girl who appeared to be college age. They had British accents, and while they spoke decent Romanian, their leader, who introduced himself as Ian, asked if she understood English.

"Putin," she said. "A little. I hear it better than I speak it."

"Do you have a few minutes?"

Marilena hesitated. She had never been good at dissuading salespeople. She considered saying no and please come back later, but the truth was, she did have a few minutes. "What are you selling?" she said.

"Jesus!" the other young man said,

smiling broadly. "We'll be quick if we can just have a minute."

She invited them in.

"We have some literature for you," Ian said, handing her a couple of leaflets. "We just want to tell you what we have found in Jesus Christ, what He means to us, and what He can mean to you. May we?"

Marilena nodded but felt dishonest. In truth she knew what they were going to say, and she felt her time was being robbed. But then this could be the answer to her prayer. Was this God's way of revealing Himself to her? She couldn't imagine, but she would listen. These kids seemed earnest and enthusiastic enough, but mostly they were bold. Would she ever do what they were doing, even if she became a devotee? It seemed a most courageous and even potentially humiliating act. Sorin would never accede to sitting through it, nor would almost any colleague she could think of.

Ian hurried through a memorized and polished presentation of what he called the "Romans road to salvation." It was named after the New Testament book of Romans, which Marilena had read years before. She had been impressed with the scholarship of the writer and the logical progression of his arguments, but at the time had not even considered that God existed, and assumed that if He did, He was the exclusive property of Christians.

Now she didn't know what to think. *Interesting that he has chosen a text written to Romans.*

Ian read her Romans 3:23: " 'For all have sinned and fall short of the glory of God.' "

"And you believe this?" Marilena said. The depravity of mankind had also seemed to her one of the most ludicrous notions of Christian theology.

All three young people nodded, but they seemed so sure of it that they appeared happy about it. "We've all sinned," Ian said. "No one on earth is innocent."

"I might be," Marilena said. She was not boasting. If selfishness or a short temper were truly sinful, she was guilty. But did human nature make one a sinner? The label was offensive, and with most people she knew — even Sorin — their good outweighed their bad.

"If that were true," the young man said, "you'd be the first perfect person since Jesus."

"Do I win a prize?" she said, smiling, but she could tell they were not amused.

Ian asked if he could read her a passage that "shows what sin in our lives looks like."

Marilena looked at her watch. "I suppose." What was this maddening politeness she could not harness? What compelled her to keep from insulting these kids?

He read Romans 3:10–12:

"There is none righteous, no, not one;
There is none who understands;
There is none who seeks after God.
They have all turned aside;
They have together become
    unprofitable;
There is none who does good, no, not
    one."

Had she ever truly sought after God? Marilena's quest for knowledge had made her feel intellectually superior to people of faith. Maybe that was sinful. On the other hand, maybe she *was* intellectually superior.

"I'll be just a minute," Ian said. "Romans 6:23 says that 'the wages of sin is death.' That's not talking about just physical death, ma'am, but also spiritual, eternal death, complete separation from God."

Marilena suppressed a smart remark, something about how that would be nothing new for her.

Ian plunged on. "But there's good news in that same verse. It says, 'but the gift of God is eternal life in Christ Jesus our Lord.' And

Romans 5:8 is the best news of all: 'God demonstrates His own love toward us, in that while we were still sinners, Christ died for us.' Did you know that?"

"I'm familiar with the basic tenets of the Christian sect, yes."

"Jesus died for you, paid the penalty for your sins. And I assume you know about the Resurrection."

She nodded. She wished she could tell Ian his minute was up.

"Romans 10:9 says 'that if you confess with your mouth the Lord Jesus and believe in your heart that God has raised Him from the dead, you will be saved.' Romans 8:1 says that if we do that 'there is therefore now no condemnation to those who are in Christ Jesus.' We will never be condemned for our sins. Finally — and with this I'm through — the writer of this letter to the Christians in Rome makes this promise in chapter 8, verses 38 and 39: 'For I am persuaded that neither death nor life, nor angels nor principalities nor powers, nor things present nor things to come, nor height nor depth, nor any other created thing, shall be able to separate us from the love of God which is in Christ Jesus our Lord.'

"What do you think of that, ma'am?"

"Well . . . I . . . ah, that's beautiful. Beautiful writing and a cogent treatise. And you presented it well. I'm not sure I believe it, but —"

"Here we are in Romania," the young man said, and she could hear the closing-of-the-sale tone in his voice. "Wouldn't you like to follow the Romans' road to salvation? Saying this simple prayer will not save you; only faith in Jesus Christ will do that. But this is a way you can tell God you realize where you stand and what you need from Him: 'God, I know that I'm a sinner and deserve punishment. But I believe Jesus Christ took that punishment and that through faith in Him I can be forgiven. I trust in You for salvation. Thank You and amen!' "

The three looked at her expectantly. Marilena wondered what they would think or do or say if she told them she believed God had tried to tell her who He was and also told her to flee the devil. And what if they knew she had prayed to God's arch-enemy?

"Would you like to receive Christ, ma'am?" Ian said.

"No, I wouldn't. Not tonight."

"You want to think about it?"

"At least."

"That's understandable, but let me caution you. I don't mean to pressure you or scare you, but none of us ever really knows how much time we have. You look like a fairly healthy person, but you don't know when you might be run over by a car, do you?"

"Well, I certainly hope not tonight."

"We hope not either," the young woman said. "We will pray for you that you will do the right thing."

To their credit, the kids did not pressure Marilena, and as soon as they were gone she felt both relief and turmoil. She had long wondered if this idea of being born in sin and saved by the death of Jesus was really as simple as it seemed. These kids sure thought so.

The question wasn't whether God existed. Marilena believed He did now more than ever. Had she been born in sin? And if so, was it her fault? Was she a sinner? God seemed jealous, vengeful. He had declared to her who He was and told her to flee the devil. And yet the one God considered His enemy was offering her a child.

Marilena decided not to jump too quickly to either side. At the meeting, she would consider the pitch of the first god she had ever prayed to.

Had Marilena been a dog, she would have

growled and snarled upon meeting Reiche Planchette. Viviana introduced him to the group with such eagerness that Marilena wished she could display some enthusiasm. But she had to admit there was something oily about the man. He did not just practice maintaining eye contact; he also seemed to use it as a battering ram. She finally had to look away.

Mr. Planchette was not what she expected, yet in his presence she found it difficult to remember what that was. Had she assumed he would have cloven hooves, horns, and a pitchfork? Or that he would wear all black and have slicked-back hair?

In reality he was pleasant-enough looking with thinning light brown hair and a prominent nose. He smiled easily and looked anything but sinister. Some in the group greeted him like an old, trusted friend. They eagerly waited for him to take the floor, and once he had it, Marilena found him mesmerizing.

He was as direct as Viviana had predicted, referring to Lucifer as his leader and lord and the object of his love and worship as naturally as Marilena had heard Christian ministers on television refer to Christ and God. She had thought them delusional, taking the classic Scriptures literally, but until fourteen weeks ago, she had put even less stock in people who believed in the dark side.

It seemed Planchette's goal was to dissuade anyone from maintaining misconceptions about the one he called "the opposite god."

He worked the room, pacing, smiling, speaking conversationally. The bottom line, he said, was that "you may have tried praying to the God of the Bible. What has it ever gotten you? An answer here and there? A feeling? Mostly haven't you felt judged, watched, shamed, your conscience attacked? My lord offers power and action — measurable, tangible, and helpful."

Perhaps Planchette was a memory expert. Or maybe he had conspired with Ms. Ivinisova. Regardless, his performance at the end of the evening was nothing short of miraculous. As he closed his eyes and prayed, he mentioned every person in the room by name and gave them a personal word of prophecy.

"Titus, your marriage will be repaired.

"Atanasia, your lameness will be healed.

"Dorina, your depression will lift."

People moaned and cried out and sighed and wept.

Marilena couldn't deny she was caught

up in it, her pulse skyrocketing as she waited her turn. She was also praying to the God of the Bible, challenging Him, badgering Him. "Here's Your chance," she said silently. "Show Yourself. Do something. Compete."

All she sensed in her spirit was the echo of God's original message: "Resist the devil and he will flee from you."

But I don't want to flee! I want what I was promised!

"Resist the devil and he will flee from you."

Promise me a child! Give me what I want and need.

"Resist the devil and he will flee from you."

Marilena would not resist. How could a spirit who promised her a child be evil? She might regret it, she told herself, but God had an opportunity here to show Himself head-to-head against the one of whom He seemed so jealous. It was He who considered her a sinner in need of salvation.

The other side offered to fulfill her dream and longing, apparently with no strings attached. Well, there was the matter of allegiance. But might that not grow from sheer gratitude when she carried her own child, delivered him, held him?

"Marilena," Reiche Planchette said, "you

shall receive the desire of your heart."

She needed no more convincing.

Viviana took Marilena and Mr. Planchette to the bistro where she and Marilena first chatted. Planchette insisted Marilena call him Reiche, which she could not bring herself to do. He also continued to stare so pervasively that, had it not been totally against her nature, she would have called him on it.

Marilena did not, however, sit and take it when Planchette attempted to sway her with an academic argument in which he was nowhere near as adept as she. She had asked about his view of the moral nature of Lucifer.

"The name," he said, assuming a professorial tone, "comes from the Latin *lux* and *ferre*, which is one reason he is often referred to as the Morning Star. *Lux* meaning 'daylight' and *ferre* meaning 'star.' "

"Pardon me, sir," Marilena said, "but you don't want to presume to teach *me* linguistics. *Lux* indeed means 'light,' but the closest you could get to *star* from *ferre* is some play on the words *show* or *exhibit*. The fact is that the primary meaning of *ferre* is closer to 'iron hard,' and, referring to a person or being, 'someone without feeling, unyielding, even cruel.' "

That made Mr. Planchette sit back. "Excellent," he said evenly. "Perhaps you are on to a side of our god that manifests itself when someone who has been offered a gift in return for a modicum of gratitude would rather thumb her nose at it."

"Surely you're not suggesting that in my commitment to not give a false impression —"

"I believe he knows your heart, madam."

"I doubt that. But if he does, then he knows that I merely want to remain true to myself. Doesn't it follow that if I faked some expression of loyalty — ?"

"He knows when someone has been courting two suitors."

That stopped her. Was her life not her own? Could she never again do anything in secret?

Planchette let a smile play at the corners of his mouth. "I am not all-knowing," he said. "I go only by what is communicated to me."

"I am a scholar," Marilena said, trying not to sound defensive. "I study. I compare. I research."

"You play both ends against the middle, and you could live to regret that."

"Is your god, then, as jealous as he claims is his adversary?"

Planchette pressed his lips together, then finally broke his gaze and studied the ceiling. "Lucifer is merely just. The fact is, he is willing to concede what he wishes for from you, as long as he does not have to concede the child."

"Speak plainly."

The stare was back. "You are but a vessel, Mrs. Carpathia. Whether you ever swear allegiance to the granter of your desires is worth a pittance compared to your agreement to allow your son to be raised in his service. Regardless of where you land in your flitting about from kingdom to kingdom, you agree that Nicolae — and you know why he should bear that name —"

"Because it means 'victory of the people' and was thus prophesied," Marilena said. "In truth, I like it. It has a majestic ring. Nicolae Carpathia."

"Withhold your allegiance at your peril, if you must, but agree that Nicolae will be raised in the service of our lord."

Nine

Ray Steele's dad had a small den where he liked to retire at the end of the day. While Ray was doing homework and his mother was reading or watching her favorite programs, Mr. Steele would secrete himself in his cozy hideaway, where his golfing and fishing knick-knacks covered the walls.

Ray's view of his father's sanctuary had been skewed by the nature of his own visits there. He was not allowed in the den when his father wasn't home, and when he *was* invited in, it never seemed to be for good news. Ray had never been punished there, but he had certainly endured his share of lectures and dressing-downs. Whenever he had lost significant privileges, been reprimanded, been grounded, it had happened as he sat across the desk from his imposing father.

And so it was that when his dad asked Ray

at dinner to meet him in the den when his homework was done, Ray felt a rumbling in his gut. "What's wrong? What'd I do now?"

His father leveled his eyes at the boy. "If I wanted to discuss it at the table, I wouldn't invite you to the den, would I?"

"It doesn't necessarily have to be bad news, Rayford," his mother said.

Yeah, like she had a clue.

Ray found it difficult to concentrate on his homework, wanting to get this over with, whatever it was. He racked his brain for the memory of any offense. Often he was surprised to discover what a teacher or a coach found offensive. He was a smart and talented kid, and he didn't intend to brag or put anyone else down. Sometimes he knew more than his teachers, but when he corrected them, he didn't mean to insult.

Had Ray done that lately? He couldn't recall. Had he said anything disparaging to friends that would have gotten back to their parents and thus to his parents? He shook his head. He considered marching down to the den to find out, but he was on pace for good grades this semester and didn't want to shortchange his homework — especially math and science.

An hour later, after putting the finishing touches on his math calculations, Ray found his dad reading a magazine at his desk. He waited as his dad held up a hand and finished reading, then set the periodical aside.

"Have a seat, Ray."

Great. It's going to be all formal.

His dad leaned forward and folded his hands. "Ray, I gotta tell ya, I've seen a lot of progress in you the last several months."

"You have?"

"Absolutely. Proud of you. And I'll tell you what I'm gonna do. I'll make a deal with you. You keep working hard at your studies and keep getting good grades —"

"Good? Almost straight A's, Dad."

"Well, I'd say that's good. And when you're thirteen —"

"That's a lot of years away, Dad."

"I know. Now hear me out. When you're thirteen I'll give you a part-time job at the shop."

"But what about sports and — ?"

"We'll make it work. I'll start you just cleaning up, sweeping and handling the trash, that kind of stuff. It won't keep you from playing sports, and it'll give you more money."

"In place of my allowance?"

"In addition to your allowance."

"Really?"

"Absolutely. I've watched you, Ray. You

don't waste your money. You set goals, and you achieve them. I could use more employees like you."

"That's it?"

"Almost. Get this. When, between your allowance and your part-time pay, you start to get close to having enough money to cover half of the flying lessons, I'll pay the other half."

"Dad, are you serious?"

"You bet. But remember, you've got to uphold your end of the bargain."

"Are you kidding? I'll do anything."

"Then it's a deal."

Ray stood and started to bolt, eager to tell his mother — who, he realized, probably already knew. But he had to tell someone.

"One more thing, Ray," his father said, pointing at the chair. Ray sat again. "Once you've proved yourself with the dirty-work type chores around the tool and die, I want to start teaching you to run some of the machines."

"Cool."

"That pays better, and you need to learn the business."

"The business? Why?"

"I have a dream, Ray. Nothing I'd like better than to leave the business to you. You take it over. Steele and Son. Make me proud. Make yourself a good life."

Ray slumped. How could he go from so high to so low so fast? "Dad, what if I don't want to take over the business? You know I want to fly."

"I wish I could fly, own my own plane, jet myself to my suppliers and customers. You could do that, have yourself a fun life."

"Are you going to make me do it?"

"What do you mean, Ray?"

"Do I have to promise to take over the business to keep this deal, the work and the flying lessons?"

His dad sighed and shook his head. "I won't force you, Son, but it's sure what I want for you."

"But what if it's not what *I* want?"

"How do you know what you want? You're not even ten yet! Why don't you just keep an open mind, see the business, learn it, then decide?"

"Because if I decide I still want to be a pilot, or if I grow to seven feet and have a shot at the NBA, you'll be all insulted."

His father scowled. "Maybe I will. I'm just offering you an opportunity, Ray. Don't toss it away."

"I'll keep an open mind if you will, Dad."

"How's that?"

"If I like the business and want to do it, I'll

tell you. But if I want to leave and go to college and the military and fly for a living, you have to be okay with that too."

"And what, I'm going to sell my business to someone who'll probably just resell it for profit to someone who won't know it and love it like I do? I've spent my whole adult life building this thing that puts clothes on your back and —"

"I know, Dad. Maybe I'll be rich enough to own it and be sure someone runs it right, even if it's not me."

"Frankly, I thought you'd be thrilled to have your future set."

"I'm happy about the work, Dad, and the flying lessons. I really am."

"Doesn't sound like it."

"Sorry. I just thought you'd want me to be honest."

"I want you to be grateful."

"I am! This is the best thing you've ever given me."

"Well, remember, it all hinges on how you prove yourself between now and then. And one more thing. Don't go telling anybody about it."

"Why?"

"Just don't."

"But I don't see why —"

"It's nobody's business, that's all. I know

you'll want to brag about it to your friends, but just don't. Part of maturity is knowing what to say and what not to say, and this is nothing to be talking about. They'll know when you start working."

"Especially when I start flying lessons," Ray said, though it seemed ages away.

"Well, there you go."

Ray hardly slept. The wait for his thirteenth birthday would be the longest of his life.

"Do you have the documents?" Reiche Planchette asked Viviana.

She pulled an envelope from her briefcase and slid from it a folder that she handed to him. As he drew papers from it, Viviana winked at Marilena.

Planchette arranged the documents before him and turned them so Marilena could read them. "*Înșelăciune Industrie* is the best, most discreet purveyor of human genetic engineering. We inquired as to their ultimate genome product, which they have outlined here."

Marilena could not calm her trembling hands as she lifted the documents to where she could read them. Science was not her field, but she caught the drift. The "target" (that would be her) would be impregnated at the optimum opportunity during her reproductive cycle by a hybrid sperm containing genes from two males, one with an IQ off the charts, and the other with a higher-than-average IQ as well as a predilection for athletics and what *Înșelăciune* not so circumspectly referred to as "culturally accepted physically attractive features."

"Here, look," Planchette said, producing a computer-generated rendering of a breathtakingly handsome young man.

"My goodness," Marilena said, studying it. It was not like her to be impressed by looks, but the blond with the square jaw, perfect teeth, and piercing blue eyes was more than gorgeous. There was an air of confidence, of knowledge, a look of wisdom in his eyes. "Who is this?"

"Consider it an electronic guess," Planchette said, "based on the best input *Înșelăciune* had available, of what your son is likely to look like at age twenty-one. Nicolae Carpathia will be a brilliant, beautiful human being."

"If I were to proceed," Marilena said, unable to look away from the engaging image.

Planchette sat back. "And why would you not?"

Why indeed? It was as if she had gingerly turned the knob on a door that had suddenly swung open and knocked her flat. "Why not you, Viviana?" Marilena said. "You're a disciple. Would you not be thrilled, honored?"

Viviana laughed. "I'm too old. Anyway, I am a coward. I cannot imagine giving birth. This is your gift, Marilena. You are the one. You long for a child and are eager to be a mother. You may have thought you were coming to my class for diversion, but your psychic energy was so strong, your aura so powerful to the spiritual realm, that your desire alone transported your willingness to those who could make this happen."

"And what will this cost?" Marilena said.

Planchette pulled one last sheet from the folder. Marilena scanned the list of costs for various stages of the procedure and let her eyes drop to the bottom line. "Three hundred and fifty *billion* leu?" she said. "You can't be serious."

"Approximately ten million American dollars," Planchette said. "Obviously, none of this would come from your pocket."

"Really," Marilena said. "You must know that this is two hundred times my annual salary, which I would give up if I moved to Cluj."

Planchette leaned forward and spoke earnestly. "You need to hear me, Mrs.

Carpathia. I know you have been under considerable stress. I don't know you; you don't know me. Perhaps we got off on the wrong foot, didn't connect; I don't know. I'd be lying if I said I knew enough about you to admire you. The fact is, you have been chosen. The spirits have made this clear to Ms. Ivinisova and to me, and I presume to you. Frankly, that makes me envy you. I implore you to accept. For as long as you raise your son in the tenets of our faith, you will be cared for."

"But will he be *my* son? Or will he belong to you and yours and the spirits?"

"He will be your son until he reaches twenty-one, as long as you do your part — which is not asking much, considering."

"And what if I decide that it's all true, that the spirit world is real, that — ?"

"If you don't already know that, you are the wrong choice."

"Granted. But belief that there is a Lucifer and that he has the right to compete for the throne of God requires that I believe God exists as well."

"Or one who considers Himself God. Naturally, we believe *He* is the impostor, the unworthy one, the doomed one."

"Allow me to speculate, Mr. Planchette. If during the course of my study I come to the opposite conclusion — ?"

"*Defect,* in other words? You would lose your child, your privileges, your patronage."

"I'll let you know."

"Înşelăciune is ready at a moment's notice. You must be evaluated, tested, prepared for the perfect timing."

"I will let you know."

"Surely you're not entertaining thoughts of eschewing this opportunity."

"I have not yet decided, sir. And I will certainly not proceed until I have."

"That's fair. But don't assume you are the only choice."

"What are you saying?"

"Only that there have to be countless other candidates, and frankly, who knows what they might bring to the table?"

"If I am not worthy, why was I chosen?"

"I have no idea," Planchette said. "I just know that right now, during this season, the decision is yours. If I were you, I would not risk the impatience of the spirits by delaying."

"One more thing," Marilena said. "The association must be bigger than I ever imagined, but surely it's not of the scope to afford this bill. Where is the money coming from?"

Planchette and Ms. Ivinisova clearly shared a look in a brief but awkward silence.

"A benefactor," Viv said.

"Benefactors," Planchette jumped in, louder. "Friends of whom the rank and file are largely unaware."

Marilena could not face the dark, empty apartment that evening. She dumped her bag and checked the answering machine. How thoughtful of her husband to let her know he would not be back tonight. She bundled against the cool air, took only the envelope bearing the computer image, and headed out for a long, slow, lonely walk.

As Marilena passed the bus stop she watched a young mother cradle a sleeping baby. The woman adjusted a thick, pink blanket, cooing, "Home soon. Daddy is waiting."

Marilena's childless arms ached. How was one to make a decision like this? The pros? No more lonely nights. No more walks like this one. No more wondering or even caring where her husband might be, what he might be doing. The cons? She would give up much of life as she knew it. Would Viviana Ivinisova — or Viv Ivins, or whatever it was she wanted to be called now — provide enough intellectual stimulation? Would she spell Marilena enough that she would be able to continue to read and study and learn and grow? And what of their friendship? It could die aborning.

Given these pros and cons alone, the decision was easy. Marilena resisted peeking again at the picture, which she sensed would push her over the brink. She determined to leave it in the envelope until she was sure.

Marilena was really in no shape for a long walk, but restlessness alone fueled her and she kept on. There was simply no objective party with whom she could discuss the decision of a lifetime. It didn't surprise her that Viviana and her Svengali lobbied her toward the side of the spirits. Marilena could try to look up the young door-to-door evangelists, but they were clearly her intellectual inferiors and, of course, hardly objective.

If Marilena prayed, to whom should she pray? She took some pride, some comfort in withholding her allegiance from the one who had promised her a son. And yet she had been swayed by the manifestations of his power through clairvoyants and channelers, prophets, incantations, tarot, and Ouija. She no longer questioned the reality of the world beyond her own.

And despite the protestations of Viviana Ivinisova and Reiche Planchette, there was conflict in the spiritual realm. The respective leaders were jealous of each other, competing, diametrically opposed to one other.

How could Marilena determine the relative merits of the two factions when she was so new to even accepting an immaterial dimension?

In truth, she didn't want to take sides. The battle was not hers. Except for the reality that by accepting the gift of a son she would be supporting one side, she personally didn't care who won. Tangible, measurable power was a hallmark of the one she had studied most.

The miracles boasted by the other side seemed confined to the ancient texts, impossible to verify. Marilena had certainly seen no evidence of miracles in her lifetime. In fact, the death tolls from the worst natural disasters in history — acts of God, the insurance companies called them — were proof enough that He either didn't care or was wholly disengaged. The age-old question, "If there is a God, why does He allow suffering?" was more than valid. And it was one Marilena could not answer.

The earnest evangelists with their smiling news that she, like everyone else ever born — except Jesus, of course — was conceived in sin did little to persuade her to join the other side. Marilena did not see herself as proud, despite her belief that she — like nearly everyone she had ever encountered — was basically good at heart.

And that was that. She wasn't ready to personally cast her lot with Lucifer, not yet being sufficiently versed in his motives and plans. But she could agree to the caveat of raising her son as his student, believing with her whole heart that the young man would be bright enough to someday decide for himself where he stood on matters spiritual.

As for the other side, it simply didn't ring true. Why would a loving God allow people to be born in sin? How were they personally culpable? What chance did they have?

Marilena sat beneath a streetlight on a low concrete wall that edged a public park. She slipped the picture from the envelope and turned it toward the light. And fell in love with the image of her soon-to-be son.

Resolutely, she headed home to call Viviana Ivinisova, despite the hour. She would likely wake the woman, but Viviana would be thrilled.

With every step, Marilena was mentally bombarded by a still, small voice. "Resist the devil and he will flee from you."

She spoke aloud. "How do I know he's the devil? Maybe *You're* the devil."

"Test the spirits."

"The spirit of Lucifer will be tested by

whether he grants the wish he has promised," she said.

"Resist the devil and he will flee from you."

"If I resist *You,* will *You* flee?"

"You dare not spurn Me."

"But You call the other, clearly more powerful spirit the devil?"

"Resist him and he will flee from you."

"I reject that. I am resisting You."

And Marilena got her wish. Silence. Blessed silence.

Ten

The experts at *Înşelăciune Industrie* informed Marilena that the first attempt at impregnating her had gone "swimmingly, pardon the pun." She had hoped for some feeling, some fulfillment of her maternal instinct to wash over her, but apparently that would come later.

As soon as Marilena began to show, she announced her resignation; the end of the semester came at about the four-month mark of her pregnancy. Her separation from Sorin had been cordial to the point of friendly. In fact, she was quite taken with his cooperative attitude. He seemed most helpful in arranging — and paying for — students to help her move to Cluj. He even gave lip service to her request that they keep in touch by mail after her move. Whether he would follow through, she couldn't predict. Of course, Marilena suspected that Sorin's sensitivity toward her had more to do with his excitement over what all this meant for him and Baduna, but she appreciated it nonetheless.

As prophesied, Marilena's pregnancy was easy and without incident, but not without the consternation of her obstetrician. He knew nothing of the particulars of her baby's conception but soon became aware, of course, that her husband was out of the picture. Viv accompanied her to her appointments and introduced herself as Marilena's sister.

"We hardly resemble each other," Marilena said.

"No one will raise an eyebrow," Viv said. And she was right. Sisters who look nothing alike were common. Marilena soon found herself eager to introduce Viv as her older sister, because while she had no problem with lesbianism, for some reason she felt compelled not to be mistaken for one.

Though Marilena knew what was expected of her pregnancy, she couldn't help but worry when the doctor appeared concerned at four and a half months. She had seen the fetus, about the size of an avocado, on an ultrasound. But the doctor had predicted that she would feel the first kick by now, and when she reported no movement and he also detected none, his face clouded.

"Probably sleeping," he said, "but keep me posted."

"Is he all right?"

"Heartbeat is strong, fast, normal. He'll be annoying you a lot soon."

But he didn't. In spite of herself, Marilena worried. Aloud.

"We've been told he wouldn't move," Viv said. "You should be concerned if it were otherwise."

"But doesn't a fetus need to move to develop?"

"Apparently not. We also know he's going to be perfectly healthy."

"I hope."

"Ye of little faith."

Marilena was grateful Viv left her out of the heaviest part of the work of setting up housekeeping in the Cluj cottage. It was quaint with lots of natural wood, log walls inside and out, a fireplace, and a comfortable smoky smell without the oily residue. Whoever built the place, probably forty or fifty years before, knew ventilation. Viv included her in the decorating choices, and they soon had the place cluttered but cozy.

Two issues that puzzled Marilena were Viv's insistence on privacy and her refusal to smoke only outside. "The child will be protected from harm," she insisted. "And you have built immunity from having lived with a pipe smoker all these years."

Marilena was tempted to put her foot down but chose to pick her battles elsewhere. Equally disconcerting was Viv's working with a locksmith on securing her own bedroom, and not just the door. He worked half a day in the room itself, but since Viv did not invite her in, Marilena was left to wonder what had to be so secure.

Her mentor also had her eating more healthily and walking. Marilena felt better than she had in a long time. And with each passing day, her sense of anticipation — and angst — grew. She couldn't wait to be a mother, but she imagined all manner of complications. Though the baby did not move, Marilena felt tiny protrusions here and there. Only occasionally did they feel normal, as if she could make out his position and form. Most of the time it seemed she detected too many bones, too many limbs, and good grief, sometimes what felt like two heads. What if she was carrying a monster?

The high-speed wireless Internet worked perfectly, and Marilena soon landed several part-time jobs doing research for former colleagues and new clients. This was shaping up to be too good to be true. She could read and study and shape the material into a form she knew would be helpful for the classroom or the professor's own writing assignments. She loved her life.

One morning, however, as she was checking her e-mail, she was stunned to receive a message from a former colleague referring to the suicide of Baduna's wife and assuming Marilena knew all about it. Marilena had met Mrs. Marius more than once at faculty social events. Word was that she had accepted her husband's homosexuality and his decision to divorce her and eventually marry Sorin. Even though Sorin had agreed not to divorce Marilena until after the baby was born, as soon as Marilena moved away, Baduna had left his wife and moved in with Sorin. That, apparently, was more than Mrs. Marius could take, and she was found in their tiny garage, stretched out across the seat of their car with the engine running.

Marilena was angry that such news had not come to her first from Sorin. But he had not even had the courtesy to tell her she had been replaced as his roommate — she had learned that from another old friend. Marilena had written him every couple of weeks and had not, as yet, received a reply.

She could hardly believe he had not informed her of the tragedy.

"I must attend the funeral," Marilena told Viv.

"Of course. I'll drive you. But I certainly have no business there."

"I'm sure you'd be welcome."

"I'll wait for you. You will want to express condolences to the husband. And were there children?"

"Grown."

"Well, at least that's good."

Marilena e-mailed Sorin to tell him to watch for her at the funeral and found it terribly disconcerting when he still did not respond. She sent several test e-mails to see if he was getting them, finally receiving a terse message: "Yes, you're coming through loud and clear."

That made it all the more disturbing when she arrived at the sad rites, only to discover that not only had Sorin chosen to stay away — the more she thought about it, the more thoughtful she found it — but that Baduna also was nowhere to be seen. When she asked after him, his children and his wife's relatives grew stony, hatred burning in their eyes.

Sorin's absence made some sense. He was, after all, the interloper, the cause of the split and thus indirectly of the death. But Baduna would not even attend the funeral of his own wife? They were still married!

Even worse, if possible, word came to Marilena the following week that Baduna had actually joked about his wife in class. A student had apparently had the gall to ask if it was true that his wife had killed herself because Baduna had "come out."

"Yes," he was quoted. "You know, I knew her to get awfully tired at times, but I never knew her to be exhausted."

Rumors said even the students felt he had crossed a line so revolting that not one laughed. And the university was in the process of determining appropriate discipline for the remark. Normally the department head would have been involved in something like that, but of course in this case . . .

The debacle left Marilena speechless. She was curious about Sorin's take on it, but he clearly had moved on from caring about communicating with her. She had hoped that by informing him she would be at the funeral he would have at least wanted to greet her — if not there, then somewhere in Bucharest. But no.

At Marilena's next appointment the doctor asked three times if she was certain she had not detected even the slightest movement in her womb. "He sleeps a lot," the doctor decided, "but surely not twenty-four hours a day."

Marilena cried out when the doctor tried to manipulate the baby, to get him in a position where he would be freer to move. Still nothing.

"You may want your sister to join us for a moment."

As the three of them sat in the examining room, the doctor explained various reasons a baby might not move. "Paralysis. Retardation. Brain dysfunction."

Marilena caught her breath, but Viv smiled serenely. "I'm confident he's fine and will be fine."

"I just want to prepare you," the doctor said.

"We're prepared," Viv said.

Marilena shot her a double take. "I'm glad you are."

Viv, so far, had proved a good house-mate — other than the smoking and obsessive privacy. Her care seemed genuine, and she showed signs of selflessness. She was a smart woman, though not the intellectual Sorin had been. Marilena missed that. But Viv appeared teachable and clearly enjoyed it when Marilena shared with her what she had been reading and studying. Viv spent her free time with tarot cards, a Ouija board, praying to the spirits, channeling, and even automatic writing.

Marilena found this bizarre. Viv would put herself into a trance, pen in hand, paper at the ready. As she nodded and her eyes rolled back, she would begin writing fast and furiously in a stream-of-consciousness style. No one could think that fast, and she claimed she herself had to read it later to know what had been communicated.

A sample result of one of her sessions:

The child within shall serve me endlessly and be protected supernaturally though one day he will be wounded unto death but I will raise him up to continue to worship me and be worshiped and he shall have a right-hand prophet who will instruct the world and the nations and the leaders and the people to bend the knee and bow the head before me but the one who bears him shall suffer if she does not share his devotion and thus endeth the message.

"What do you make of that, Marilena?" Viv said as she seemed to return to consciousness.

"I don't like the sound of 'wounded unto death.' "

"Isn't it time you adjusted your thinking?"

"I can't just 'adjust,' " Marilena said. "It has to be real. I have to feel it."

"Do you want to suffer?"

"Of course not, but I don't want my son to suffer either. Faking something will surely not absolve me."

In her ninth month Marilena experienced discomfort she could only have imagined. Her doctor had grave reservations. "If the baby shows no signs of movement before birth, he will likely be forever immobile, even if his pulse and respiration are good."

Viv waved off the scare.

Marilena was unable to shake it.

With about a week to go before the due date, Viv received what appeared to be an urgent, alarming message through the tarot cards. She immediately went to the Ouija board, which, she was careful to point out to Marilena, clearly spelled out "Prepare the sacrifice."

The next morning Viv returned from her errands with a humane mousetrap and a tiny cage.

"I have seen no mice or any evidence of them," Marilena said.

"Nevertheless, a mouse is the proper sacrifice."

"For what?"

"Trust me."

Two days later the women were awakened by the sound of a mouse in the trap. Viv eagerly transferred it to the cage, where it darted about and squeaked to the point that Marilena had to turn on a small fan to drown out the noise so she could sleep.

The following Sunday night Marilena was so miserable she couldn't imagine sleeping, but she stretched out as best she could. She tossed and turned and, after several hours, thought she detected the beginning of contractions. How could she be sure? She didn't want to wake Viv until she really had to. An hour later she was sure.

Marilena was agitated with pain and anticipation. She knew a first delivery could take a long time, and it was already 2 a.m. Monday. But when she woke Viv, Viv seemed more nervous than she. Her fingers trembled as she grabbed the prepacked bag in one hand and used her free arm to help Marilena to the car. Once she had the younger woman settled in, she headed back toward the cottage.

"Where are you going?" Marilena called out. "We have to go!"

Viv rushed inside and emerged shortly carrying the mouse cage and a handful of colorful markers.

Marilena wondered if the woman had lost her mind.

"I'm going to see the chosen one tonight," Viv said.

"I thought I was the chosen one," Marilena said, forcing a smile.

"You're the vessel, dear. And I see you every day."

They hardly saw another car en route. Marilena was struck by the inky blackness of the night. She saw no clouds, no moon, and strangely, no stars. "Have you ever seen such darkness?" she said.

"It's jet-black," Viv said.

Marilena was about to tell her that was redundant, but a contraction stole her breath.

At Cluj-Napoca General the admitting nurse told Viv Ivins her pet was not allowed inside.

"Ma'am," Viv said, as directly as Marilena had ever heard her, "this is no pet. This is a creature irreplaceable to Mrs. Carpathia's religion."

"I'm sorry, but —"

"But nothing. Do not presume to allow your provincial regulations to encroach on the religious freedom of a patient. You know we don't have time to get our lawyer and the authorities involved, but I will if forced."

"The doctor will never —"

"I will tell him the same thing I'm telling you. I'll accept full responsibility. Now don't threaten the health of this child by delaying."

In the labor room Marilena's contractions went from bad to worse, yet she resisted any suggestion of an anesthetic. The baby's heartbeat remained strong, but the doctor still appeared grim about the absence of movement. "Prepare yourself for a severely handicapped child," he said.

Viv began to lecture him about "upsetting the mother at a time like this," but the subject changed quickly when he noticed the mouse. Viv warned him about violating Marilena's freedom to practice her religion.

"This is a first for me," he said. "What kind of religion requires a mouse in the labor room?"

"Ours," Viv said. "And it will be in the delivery room as well, so deal with it." She reiterated that she would indemnify him and the hospital. A document stipulating the same was quickly delivered, and Viv signed.

When the doctor tried to get Marilena to sign too, Viv warned that she would create such a fuss he would regret it, and he caved.

"We need to get her into delivery now anyway," he said.

Marilena was in the midst of painful contracting and pushing and wished Viv would settle in and hold her hand, coach her, help her breathe. But the woman was flitting here and there, incongruously perching the mouse cage atop a stainless-steel table, then drawing a circle on the floor around the bed, extending it to include two nurses and the doctor.

"What the devil are you doing?" the doctor said, and Marilena nearly burst out laughing.

"Don't mind me," Viv said. "It's just part of our religion."

"What are you drawing?" one of the nurses said.

"Mind your business," Viv said, "not mine."

"That's a pentagram, isn't it? A Pythagorean pentagram. But what's that round one?"

"The circle," Viv said. "From the *Grimorium Verum.*"

"What's that?"

"The *True Grimoire* from the 1500s."

"What's a grimoire?"

"A manual for invoking —"

"Honestly, Viv!" Marilena shouted. "You're going to miss the baby!"

"Not on your life," Viv said, finally settling near the mouse.

At nearly half past three in the morning, Marilena knew the time had come. Just when she thought she had no more strength left to push, a last effort made the doctor say, "There's the head."

From the corner of her eye, Marilena saw Viv reach into the cage and struggle to corral the mouse. The woman chanted some incantation. Marilena was in no mind to concentrate, but she heard words or names like *Chameron, Danochar, Peatham,* and *Lucifer*. Finally, an *Amém*.

"One more push," the doctor said.

Marilena cried out, feeling the child coming. She thrashed, jerking her head side to side, each swing bringing the swooning Viv Ivins into view. The woman held the squirming mouse firmly in one hand, and between her moans and shrieks Marilena heard the tiny squeaks of the panicked animal.

In Viv's other hand was a small, gleaming knife. As the baby slid from Marilena's body into the doctor's hands, Viv lifted the mouse

201

over her head and deftly cut its throat.

Marilena was sickened by the sound of its blood splashing to the floor, but that was quickly drowned out by the squalling of the baby.

"His lungs are certainly fine!" the doctor hollered. "And I'll be hanged if he's not moving normally, all four limbs."

Viv grabbed the paper with which she had lined the cage, wrapped the limp animal, and shoved it back inside. As if she owned the place, she slipped out with it, and Marilena saw her through the window washing up at the doctor's sink. When Viv returned, the cage was gone.

"What are we naming this screamer?" a nurse said with a smile as the other nurse cleaned him.

"Nicolae Carpathia," Marilena said, panting, spelling it for her.

"And a middle name?"

"We had a list," Marilena said. "What did we decide on, Viv? Sorin?"

"I never liked that idea. And you resisted anything spiritual. Either of Reiche Planchette's names would work. Imagine."

"No," Marilena said. "I don't even like him, let alone trust him."

"You have him wrong, but this is certainly not the time to get into that."

"How about 'Night,' as he was born at night?"

"Or 'Morning,' " Viv said. "Technically, it's morning."

"The darkest morning I've ever seen."

"Jet-black."

"*Jet* means 'black,' Viv," Marilena said.

"Then how would you describe the night?"

"Jetty."

"I like it," Viv said.

"So do I. Nicolae Jetty Carpathia. Nicolae J. Carpathia."

"It's certainly unique."

"I've never heard it as a name before," the doctor said, placing the baby on Marilena's chest. "It's interesting. Dramatic."

But Marilena had quit listening, quit worrying what Viv was up to. The child had turned himself red from all the wailing. She held him close, rocked him, cooed to him, but he only grew all the louder.

"He has a temper," the doctor said. "I'm just relieved — astounded, really — to see that he's perfectly normal."

"Not normal," Viv said. "But certainly perfect."

Nicky Carpathia was physically healthy in all respects and grew fast. By the time he took his first toddling steps at a year old, he had a vocabulary of a few words, including *Mama, Aunt Viv,* and *book.* Three months later he was a typical toddler, curious and into everything. Viviana Ivinisova — now going exclusively by Viv Ivins — told Marilena she had never seen a more inquisitive child. And he clearly loved to be read and sung to.

Marilena, of course, had nothing to compare Nicky to. All she knew was that she found him endlessly fascinating and felt as if her life had begun when his had.

Two things impressed Marilena above all. Besides the fact that she seemed to take to mothering as if it had been her destiny, she found herself intrigued by Nicky's analytical nature and the contrast between his seemingly quiet personality and his occasional outbursts.

Nicky's inquisitiveness manifested itself in how he played. She and Viv showered him with toys, but his attention span was short. He quickly tired of things he had played with the day before and would set about exploring. Pots and pans and spoons held his interest, and Marilena couldn't count the number of times she found him lying on his back, holding some object up to his eyes, studying it as he gently turned it over and over. It never seemed to bore him. It was as if he was recording sizes and shapes and textures, feeding into his little brain all sorts of calculations. She could sit and watch this for long stretches.

Marilena had not thought much of his screaming at birth. She had read and been told that this was precisely what you wanted with a newborn. Okay, it surprised her when he had turned himself red from the effort, and the nurse had referred to him as a screamer. The doctor had said something about his lungs and his temper.

Marilena expected this to pass, but it had not. Nicky was a relatively docile child as long as everything was going his way. But a wet or dirty diaper or hunger or fatigue brought out the worst in him. His was not the pitiful whining of a typical child. As soon as he grew frustrated about anything, the screeching began. There was no buildup, no warning. If something — anything — was wrong, Nicky closed his eyes, opened his mouth, drew in a huge breath, and screamed at the top of his voice. He thrashed and swung his fists until whatever had been wrong was fixed. And then he became a sweet, peaceful child again.

Maybe it was only her imagination, but Marilena was convinced that Nicky had wisdom far beyond his years. While he was average in his progress in speech and vocabulary, as he was with learning to walk, at times she and Viv believed he was following their conversation.

He followed whoever was speaking, which she supposed was normal. But those eyes. Their blue deepness contrasted with his olive skin and yellowish hair, and in them Marilena detected a sadness, a world weariness that made her think twice about her lifelong prejudice against reincarnation. Had this little one endured a previous life of deep turmoil? Sometimes he simply gazed at her for long periods, as if trying to determine what she was thinking. And in those moments, when she tried to tickle him or play with him, he would pull away and eye her from a distance, as if he knew something she didn't.

Viv spent a lot of time with the baby, and while she did seem a bit one-dimensional, Marilena was relieved that she was so easy to get along with. The women emphasized time for themselves, not requiring constant face time with each other.

Yes, Marilena wished Viv would use that facile, if not brilliant, mind of hers for something other than her obsession with the spirit world. But that, after all, had been how they met. And Viv had recently met with Reiche Planchette and begun to advertise and teach classes in the Cluj area. She was in her element introducing new people — skeptics naturally, as Marilena had been — to the wonders of the realm beyond.

Marilena had settled into a routine of taking care of Nicky every morning through the lunch hour. Then Viv took over for the next three hours as Marilena did her reading and research, supplying information to sundry professors. While this paid nowhere near what she had made as a full professor, it proved more than enough because she paid no rent.

In the evenings, when Viv was out teaching or engaging in her own contacts with the spiritual world, Nicky was Marilena's responsibility again. When Viv returned and Nicky was asleep, the women talked. Marilena found Viv a curious sort but generally pleasant and agreeable. While Viv seemed to care about everyone she met, she was not above talking about them behind their backs. It was nice to know she wasn't perfect, but Marilena had to wonder what Viv said about her when she was not present.

Eleven

As Ray Steele neared his twelfth birthday, things began happening to his mind and body. As he became more muscular and body hair appeared, his face lost its soft smoothness and he suffered from acne, first mildly, then full force. While he remained a great athlete, a top student, and even popular, he sensed people looked at him differently.

He grew even taller, found himself clumsy — not on the field or the court, just standing or walking around. His mother's purchases couldn't keep up with his growth and often his pants left too much sock showing. Ray was suddenly self-conscious, awkward, shy. He began to avoid situations he used to revel in. He isolated himself in a small group of guys, enabling him to avoid girls. And yet it seemed all he and his friends talked about was girls, and in ways he had never dreamed he would talk.

People used to like him, to admire him. Now he was just a pimply-faced bumbler whose gangliness made him appear more clumsy than athletic. He didn't like himself and wasn't sure he liked anyone else either.

Ray had no idea what went on at Steele Tool and Die in Belvidere, Illinois, before he began working there.

Even when he started, sweeping the floors and taking out the trash twenty-four hours after his thirteenth birthday, the only machine he recognized in the shop was a drill press like the one he had seen in industrial arts class. He was fascinated with the safety precautions built into it. The operator could manually center the piece of steel beneath the huge, ugly cutter, but he could not engage the drill unless each hand was on a separate button, far from the action.

Ray pledged to attack his job the way he approached his studies and his sports — with everything that was in him. He wanted to work hard so he could keep his job, make his money, make his dad proud, and — mostly — so he could afford flying lessons when he was fourteen. If in the process he learned the machines and the business and how to interact with working people, so much the better.

The workers — four men and two women — took to him immediately. They seemed old and mature enough not to care about his out-of-control acne and his fast-growing gangliness. Two seemed to view him with quiet suspicion at first, their expressions making clear they wouldn't kowtow to him just because of who he was. Another seemed overly friendly, as if perhaps he *would* kiss up to the boy. But eventually, Ray believed he had won them all over with his deference and hard work. He believed they genuinely liked him for himself, and they were generous with their teaching and advice.

His dad had a zero-tolerance policy. "No breaks for the boss's kid. I got to answer to six full-time employees who are gonna be watching you — and me — every day, looking for favoritism." It helped that his father clarified that, while they were to teach Ray the machines, their jobs were not in jeopardy. "Anyway, legally he's too young to operate these alone. And by the time he's old enough, he plans to be on to other things."

Ray didn't know if his dad had really resigned himself to that, but it was nice to hear him acknowledge it.

Nicky Carpathia would be required to

start school when he turned six, and while that was a year away, his mother couldn't wait. Despite her prodigious academic history and doctorate, Marilena felt inadequate to keep up with a child she resisted calling *precoce,* but precocious he was. As soon as he learned to walk and talk, Nicky had soared to heights she couldn't imagine. Even with Viv and Marilena trying to keep him engaged, no amount of teaching and reading and studying proved enough to satisfy him.

After being read to every night since he was old enough to understand, by age four Nicky had insisted on trying to read by himself. He would stop Marilena and point at words, sounding them out. It seemed in no time he was reading. Marilena and Viv took to speaking in Russian or English when they wanted to discuss something in front of him. But he soon caught on to that too. Marilena experimented by buying children's books in various languages, including Chinese. Before she knew it, he understood and could speak — at least rudimentarily — nearly every language she and Viv knew.

Now, at age five, Nicky was deeply into nature. He would dig on the property, bringing roots and bugs and other creatures into the cottage, demanding to know what

they were. Marilena bought a set of encyclo-
pedias and also showed Nicky how to look
things up on the Internet. Within six
months he was as proficient as she on the
computer.

Nicky was generally even-tempered but
distant. At times he scared Marilena, seeming so old for his age. She never spanked or
disciplined him, though she often wanted
to. When he resisted going to bed, she insisted and tucked him in, turning off his
light and shutting the door. She would
check on him later and frequently find him
standing on his bed, and when she turned
on the light she could see his fierce look,
arms folded, eyes smoldering.

He was already telling Marilena and Viv
when he wanted to eat, what he wanted to
eat, and refusing anything else. His schedule
was his schedule, and nothing they did
could dissuade him. It wasn't long before
Marilena realized he was running the show.
She had wholly lost control, but fortunately,
when left alone, he was satisfied to stay out
of trouble. He read, he logged time on the
computer, he explored outside.

Then came the day he read a book of
short stories about a girl who had her own
horse. He badgered and badgered until
Marilena and Viv agreed to buy him a pony

and a saddle and a bridle. Marilena told him he would have to wait until an expert could come teach him to ride, but Nicky would have none of it. She watched in horror as he entered the makeshift corral and the animal stiffened and backed away.

Nicky stood in front of the pony and spoke to it. "Your name is Star Diamond, and I am going to ride you." Somehow he managed to get the saddle on and the bridle and reins in place, and within minutes he was walking the horse in circles. A week later Nicky was riding it about the property.

He read everything he could find about horsemanship and began to look as if he had been born in the saddle, holding the reins between his fingers just so. Still average in size for his age, he controlled Star Diamond, fully in charge of a beast eight times his weight.

Marilena had read that teenagers could be difficult, finding their parents and authority figures wrong on every issue, countering their every suggestion. It seemed Nicky was a five-year-old teenager. He argued and debated and crossed her. He refused to do anything he didn't want to, and he spoke disrespectfully to both her and Aunt Viv.

His only interaction with other children

came when Viv's spiritualist classes brought their families together for outings, sometimes at the cottage. To Marilena's amazement, Nicky somehow got along with other kids. She didn't understand it. He was so much brighter than even those older than he. And he was an only child used to getting his own way and not having to share toys or attention. But he showed qualities of a diplomat: flattering, complimenting, feigning interest, and manipulating others for his benefit. Marilena had been certain some parent would complain about her impossible child, but the opposite happened. She was bombarded with invitations for him to visit other kids in their homes.

He steadfastly refused to go. "They can come here," he said. And they did. Marilena wasn't aware of everything he did or said, but the kids were either intimidated or impressed, because they seemed to enjoy Nicky and were content to do what he wanted.

When he discovered soccer on television, Marilena could barely pull him away. He begged for a soccer ball and taught himself to dribble it with his feet and boot it around the property. He set up a goal and looked amazingly fast to Marilena. But he was wearing her out. When flat-out honest with herself, she admitted that he scared her.

What had she gotten herself into? She looked forward to letting someone else be responsible for him for the better part of each day once he started school.

Nicky's energy was exhausting. Marilena and Viv took him to the mountains for hiking and climbing. The first time he saw ski slopes he demanded to be taught to ski. In the summer they drove to the Black Sea coast, where she and Viv sunbathed and read and he swam all day.

One day, when Marilena simply needed a break, Viv agreed to watch Nicky while Marilena drove to some country art fairs. But when Nicky caught wind of where she was going, he begged until she felt obligated to take him, so all three went. The boy amazed adults with his questions and studying of their homemade crafts. He wanted to know everything that went into making blankets and carvings and knick-knacks, and soon he was asking Marilena for the tools and resources to start fashioning his own pieces.

Marilena feared the start of school in the fall. "Oh, I don't know, Viv. He's so young."

"His soul is as old as the universe, Marilena. Surely you can see that."

"All I know is that he scares the life out of me."

"That's where we differ," Viv said. "I'm already in awe of him. He thrills me to death. Reiche is eager to see him start his training."

"Well, he's not Mr. Planchette's child."

"Careful, Marilena. In a sense, he is."

Marilena would not argue that point, but she would never concede Nicky to Planchette, even if she had given her word about his spiritual training. "How do you propose to start?"

"Just by talking to him," Viv said. "With that curious mind, he'll eat up stories of the origin of the universe."

As a high school freshman, all Ray Steele had going for him was that he had finally begun to get used to his new height. He was over six feet tall, and the athleticism that had been his hallmark in elementary school began to catch up with his new size — at least on the fields and courts. He was still awkward in social situations. He didn't really fit the chairs in the classrooms, and he tripped and stumbled and bumped into things enough to elicit laughs.

On the positive side, Ray was largely an A student and stayed out of trouble. He worked more and more hours at the tool and die, mostly after school and sports, because the more money he made, the more flying lessons he could afford. His parents made him attend church and Sunday school and youth group, but Ray mostly tuned that out.

There were a couple of girls he liked to see at church, but with his acne flaring worse than ever and having never returned to his status as the attractive jock he had been in grade school, Ray couldn't bring himself to talk to them.

At school he was enamored with girls too. How he would have loved to have been able to brag to a girl about learning to fly. But the thought of conversing with one, let alone asking one out, was beyond him.

Twelve

"Fredericka, transmit this via secure e-mail to R.P., please. Then destroy it."

"Certainly, Mr. S."

He slid the handwritten note across his mahogany desk and spun in his chair to peer out over Manhattan.

R.P.:

Have the discussion posthaste. Report soonest. Your call on revealing my identity.

Regards, J.

Marilena should have known something was up. Reiche Planchette had tried to influence her raising of Nicolae from the beginning, but he had bothered to get to the cottage only once since the boy was born. All Planchette's influence had otherwise come via Viv Ivins, and Marilena had done her best to ignore it.

But now Planchette had requested an audience with her, and Marilena was already regretting acceding to it.

"I'm sure it has to do with Nicky's schooling," Viv said. "There's no sense getting defensive until you know."

"What does he think, that I don't know how old Nicky is? that I wouldn't have already preregistered him? Is he going to remind me to pack him a lunch?"

Viv smiled. "Let's give him the benefit of the doubt. He and the society have been nothing but helpful so far."

Intrusive was more like it. And as much as Marilena protested, there was a dark, inner part of her soul that felt some relief she would never acknowledge — especially to Viv. The fact was that while she still desperately loved her son, the gift of motherhood had satisfied only half her deep need. She remembered clearly that longing to have someone to love who would also love her. Sadly, Marilena had never felt loved by her son.

From infancy Nicky had treated her like a necessary evil. He needed her and wanted her only for nursing the first several months. He was not a cuddler, constantly stiffening and pulling away. Marilena had read enough parenting books to know that she should never give up, never stop showing Nicky physical love, whether he responded or not. She believed he would one day begin to turn, to change, to need and want her touch and be willing to return it.

Worse, Marilena found herself jealous of Viv. It was as if the boy didn't really understand the difference between an aunt and a mother. Besides, Viv wasn't really his aunt. Marilena had tried to tell him that she herself had carried him in her body and had delivered him. He took this in, asked questions, insisted on looking up childbirth issues in the encyclopedia and online. But it didn't change his apparent attitude toward Marilena.

The women were treated equally, and he seemed to manipulate each. When he wanted something to eat or help with his reading or the Internet, he would consult whoever happened to be closest. Marilena wanted to be his priority. She believed she had earned it. Anyway, if Nicky had the brain she thought he had, shouldn't he recognize that she was the more intelligent, more widely read of the two? Maybe someday.

If Viv got her way — and Marilena conceded that she too had Nicky's best interests at heart — she would begin educating him in spiritualism. If he took to that the way he did to most other new topics, Viv would again gain an edge. The more Marilena thought about it, the more she was tormented.

There was no way out of it. She had agreed that Nicky would be raised in spiritualism, and as things stood now, Viv was the logical choice for that. She had many years in the discipline, plus she was a true disciple, a believer, a lover of the chief spirit.

Marilena took some solace in remaining true to herself. She had no question that Lucifer was real and that Luciferianism was valid. But she had not become a devotee or a serious student of it, only because she didn't feel the emotional tug toward the personalities — specifically Lucifer himself.

Marilena regularly attended Viv's classes and considered herself a believer. But she was getting tired of the weekly warnings from the spirit world that there was someone among them — a chosen one — who still withheld full loyalty. It was her; of course it was. But if Lucifer was a true deity, would he not value honesty and transparency above all? Or was there something to the charges from the other side that Lucifer was actually Satan, the prince of darkness, the father of lies? Marilena didn't want to believe it — *didn't* believe it — but why all this badgering to get her on board against her will? She certainly wasn't an opponent or an antagonist. She simply had logged too many years revering the human mind and the material world to be able to easily surrender her emotions to a suitor from the great beyond.

Marilena, however, was considering a fresh look, a new approach. If Nicky was going to be schooled in spiritualism, she should take the lead. That would solidify her role as his mother and his true guardian. She would count on Viv for input, of course, but in no way could she cede her full responsibility for the spiritual training of her own son.

That was Marilena's mind-set when Mr. Planchette visited for dinner that evening. From the moment he arrived, she worked on her attitude. In the past she had never hidden her aversion to his style and approach. When he was the visiting dignitary at Viv's meetings, she didn't offer any cordial or emotional connection, despite their history.

They seldom had words, though she rarely hesitated to challenge him, disagree with him, or speak her mind. He was due some respect, but this night she wanted to appear a changed woman. It wasn't that Marilena was willing to take the last step toward full devotion, but she had to become more of a team player to make herself the clear choice to become Nicky's spiritual mentor. As things stood now, that made no sense.

"How do you like your *friptură*, Mr. Planchette?" she said.

"Medium rare, thank you. I *love* steak!"

"I had heard that. But I would have guessed you for well done." Marilena felt phony, small talking nonsense like this, but it was working. He appeared to devour the attention.

"Really? Why?"

She hadn't thought of that. *Why?* Because . . . he was masculine? a man's man? She could never say that. She just smiled and shrugged as he beamed.

Marilena was stunned, however, to discover that Nicky's spiritual training was not the topic of the evening. After all her worrying and ruminating, in the end it was — as Viv had predicted — Nicky's schooling Planchette had come to discuss.

"It's taken care of," Marilena said flatly, fearing that she was already off on the wrong foot. She glanced at Nicky, who seemed unusually absorbed in the small chunk of meat she had diced for him, as if ignoring the conversation. "He's registered and ready to go at the end of the summer."

"Where?" Planchette said casually.

"Where? Well, where do you think? The school is four miles from here."

"The public school?"

"Of course."

"Unacceptable."

"What does that mean? Who are you to — ?"

"It's unacceptable, *Mom*," Planchette said, infuriating Marilena. Her title dripped off his lips as if she — above anyone — ought to know better than to enroll Nicky in public school. "All I've heard from both of you since day one is that this is a brilliant child. And all the evidence points to it. The linguistics, the reading, the computer work, the curiosity. Of course, this should come as no surprise, and it certainly isn't to the sperm donors."

"Wait, wait, wait," Marilena said. "Surely you're not implying that the donors know who their child is. So much was made of confidentiality, and I signed away any right to ever even attempt to find out who they were. . . ."

"I misspoke."

"You did not."

224

"I should have said that Nicolae's brilliance comes as no surprise to the sperm *brokers*. *Înşelăciune Industrie* predicted this."

"But that's not what you said, Mr. Planchette. You're a more careful speaker than that."

"Nonsense."

"Don't talk to me as if I'm an imbecile, sir. I am not the one who said more than I intended. Now I want to know whether the sperm *donors* know who their child is."

"Well, they shouldn't, should they?"

"Is that a denial or a change of subject?"

"Really, Mrs. Carpathia. You're being impudent."

"*I* am? I asked you a question, sir, and I want an answer."

"You know well, ma'am, that there is no way I should know that. But let me tell you —"

"No way you *should* know. But you do, don't you? You know whether —"

"Really, Marilena," Viv said, "you must stop parsing every syllable."

"I'll thank you to stay out of this, Viv."

Finally, Nicky spoke up. "You should not talk to Aunt Viv that way."

It was all Marilena could do to keep from backhanding him in the mouth, but she had never struck him and wasn't about to start.

"I'll thank you to stay out of this too, young man."

Marilena felt herself flush. She was outnumbered, ganged up on, and she was not used to it. She fought to keep from lashing out. Most alarming, Nicky seemed to realize he had the upper hand. He had frustrated her, but rather than appear ready to keep badgering, he affected a smirk not unlike Mr. Planchette's.

"Let's just all take deep breaths, hm?" Planchette said, and Marilena glared at him. Nicky sucked in a huge breath and sighed, and even she had to smile as Viv and Reiche laughed. "There," Planchette added, "you do the same, Marilena."

She pressed her lips together and shook her head, no longer amused. He could change the subject all he wanted, but she was going to get back to this topic. Nothing could be more complicating than the sperm donors' knowing who their child was. How could she possibly keep them from him if he somehow became a celebrated personality? The truth was, *she* didn't even want to know who they were, let alone have her son find out. She foresaw nothing but trouble in that. On the other hand, if Planchette knew who they were, that meant Viv knew, and that was one more advantage the older woman didn't need. If Viv in fact knew, Marilena had to know too, whether she wanted to or not.

Mr. Planchette dabbed his mouth and slid back from the table. "Wonderful, thank you. Now let me tell you what we have in mind for Nicky's schooling. You'll be surprised and pleased to know that he has an unusual and more-than-generous benefactor, which allows us options we hadn't even considered."

Marilena had lost her appetite when the conversation began, and now she sat with a hardly touched steak before her. Nicky had finished his small portion and was clearly eyeing hers. "Are you going to finish that?" he said, jarring her by speaking English.

She shook her head and he stabbed the meat, drawing the slab onto his plate. Marilena thought about reprimanding him for his manners, but she felt she had surrendered the right.

When she leaned over to cut the meat for him, he reached for her steak knife. Marilena hesitated, but she felt scolded by his look and watched closely as he carved the steak for himself. She wanted to stop him from starting with a huge bite, but he smiled as he stuffed it into his mouth. She knew he was playing with her, but she had been waiting for his smile for so long, she just watched him devour the meat.

Thirteen

Planchette seemed to do everything with a flourish. He pulled out one of his business cards and an ancient fountain pen. He made a show of crossing out his information on one side and turning it over to write on the other. He tried to cover the card with one hand as he wrote, but Marilena could see it was in flowing feminine (that was all she could think to call it) script. With his trademark sly grin, he slid it across the table to her, dramatically turning it right side up at the last instant.

Marilena could tell this was not news to Viv. She was usually curious above all else, but she sat there smugly, as if she knew what was coming. " 'Jonathan Stonagal,' " Marilena read aloud.

"Jonathan Stonagal," Planchette repeatedly loudly. "Can you believe it?"

"Am I supposed to recognize this name?"

"*Gunoi,* Mrs. Carpathia, you can't bluff

me! You're better read than that. You know who Stonagal is."

It was true. She read the news magazines, watched the international news. Stonagal, an American banker and financier, was one of the wealthiest men on the planet. Rumor had it he was behind various nefarious clandestine commissions and coalitions that had as their goals control of international finance and world domination.

"What does he have to do with me? with us? Unless you're going to tell me *he* is one of the sperm donors, I don't see —"

"Oh, that would be something," Planchette said. "Imagine that. But his brilliance is hardly academic. I mean, he's brilliant, but it's more *stradă intelept.*"

Nicky perked up. *"Stradă intelept!"* he said. "Street smart!"

"Very good," Planchette said. "Mr. Stonagal has taken an interest in Nicky, Marilena. Can you conceive of a benefactor with unlimited means?"

She was speechless. What possible interest would Jonathan Stonagal have in a mental prodigy from the middle of nowhere? And how would he have found out about Nicky anyway?

"How wonderful," Viv said.

Marilena shot her a look. "I already owe

Lucifer the boy's soul. What will be left for Stonagal? Or are you trying to tell me this is wholly altruistic — he merely wants to help out of the goodness of his heart?"

Planchette apparently found that knee-slappingly funny. Late on the uptake, Viv joined the hilarity.

"I'm serious," Marilena said. "What's in it for Stonagal?"

"Shall we retire to the other room?" Planchette said. "Let the boy be excused?"

That must have sounded perfect to Nicky, as he horsed down a last big bite of steak and headed for the computer.

"Clear your place, young man," Marilena said, but he didn't so much as look at her.

"I've got it," Viv said.

Marilena found it disconcerting that Viv busied herself in the kitchen as Planchette explained the Stonagal connection. That left no doubt that Viv was already up to speed — which reminded Marilena once again that she had been just the vessel in this deal, the carrier and bearer of the chosen child.

"Jonathan Stonagal sponsors many scholarships around the world," Planchette began when they had settled onto the couch. "To my knowledge there is no requirement that recipients eventually work for one of his companies, though they could do worse. I should think the students would be left with a certain impression of Mr. Stonagal and would take advantage of any opportunities offered, but as I say, I don't know of any stipulations, any strings."

"How much *do* you know about this, Mr. Planchette?"

"I'm sorry?"

"I have many questions."

"I'm at your disposal."

"Let's start with how many scholarships or offers to finance an education have been made to children who are about to start school at age six."

Planchette looked nonplussed. He pointed at Marilena. "Excellent," he said. "Point taken. My guess is that this is unique. I believe Mr. Stonagal's other educational stipends are offered exclusively to college students."

"Not even high school students?"

"To the best of my knowledge."

"So, how many? Dozens?"

He shrugged. "Probably more."

"Hundreds?"

"Throughout the world? Yes. I would guess in the hundreds."

She nodded. "Hundreds of scholarships all over the world for college students, plus one for a six-year-old."

"Wonderful, no?"

"Suspicious," Marilena said. "I don't get it."

"Be flattered, Mrs. Carpathia! Be thrilled. Imagine the advantages for Nicky, for you."

"How is Mr. Stonagal aware of my son, anyway?"

"I'm not at liberty to —"

"No, no. Don't start with that. Don't come here with this news and think you can leave out the most important part of the equation. Is Stonagal a spiritualist? a Luciferian?"

"I can't speak for him. I —"

"You *are* speaking for him! You're offering his beneficence!"

"I believe he is sympathetic to our cause, yes."

"Sympathetic or an adherent?"

"I believe both."

"Um-hm," she said. "And so he knows about Nicky through those channels? From you or from Viv?"

"Neither."

"Come now, that would be better than what I might fear. Please tell me the news of Nicky has not covered the globe, that every spiritualist in the world is aware of him."

Planchette shifted his position. "No, I don't think so. There are rumors that a special child is a gift from beyond. But it's not like they know his name or where he was born, nor do people see him as some sort of —"

"All I'm concerned with right now is how Jonathan Stonagal views Nicky. And if he did not hear about him from you or Viv, where then?"

Planchette studied his nails.

"Come, come, Reiche," Marilena said. "I deserve to know at least that."

"Stonagal . . . ah . . . owns — in fact, you could discover this with a little research on the Internet, so if it comes up later you might want to say that's where you heard it. . . ."

"Fair enough. I'll cover for you."

"He owns *Înşelăciune Industrie*."

"Mr. Planchette, you know this has impropriety written all over it."

"I told you: He *owns* —"

"And that allows him to violate the company's own confidentiality policies?"

"What are you saying, Mrs. Carpathia? Because of a technicality, you're going to thumb your nose at the chance of a lifetime?"

"A technicality? I'd sooner call it an egregious invasion of my son's privacy."

Planchette sighed and sat back. "Marilena, you need to understand something. You are the mother of a unique son."

"You think I don't know that? That doesn't make him the property of —"

"Hear me out. Please. Let me tell you what Mr. Stonagal has in mind for Nicolae, and then you can decide whether to turn your back on it."

"I was under the impression I wouldn't have that choice. It seems you have come not to request this, but to inform me of a decision already made."

Marilena was bothered that Planchette did not dispute her. So that was it. No one had considered that a mother could do other than gratefully receive such news. But this mother was increasingly feeling left out of the equation, and she feared this eventuality would complete her alienation from her own flesh and blood.

"The public school that made so much sense to you — which frankly surprises me, given your own academic credentials —"

"Excuse me, sir, but I am a product of public schools."

"Then you know better than I that only five percent of such students are prepared for college. The private school we, er, Mr.

Stonagal has selected or would like to recommend —"

"How much time has Mr. Stonagal spent in Romania, sir?"

"I have no idea. I —"

"And he would have no idea what is available. How convenient that he knows just the right private school for my son."

"He has advisers, of course. Any good manager does."

"He does not manage me."

"No, he doesn't. He's merely making a most generous offer, ma'am, and if I may be blunt, you'd be a fool to reject it."

"All right, I'm listening. Where have you and the world's ultimate manager decided Nicky is to go to school?"

Planchette smiled as if believing that as soon as Marilena heard the news, all her doubts and fears would be eradicated. "*Intelectualitate Academie* in Blaj."

"Blaj! That's more than fifty kilometers from here!"

"Transportation will be provided."

"What are you talking about? A bus? A limo? Fifty kilometers each way to school every day?"

Planchette's expression soured. "Be grateful he is not being sent to boarding school."

"You would have to kill me first."

And for the first time, because of what she saw pass over Reiche Planchette's eyes, Marilena realized she had neared some awful truth. Eliminating her was not out of the question. She had no claim to this child. She was transported to when first the maternal instinct flooded her being. The emotion she felt now, the mother-bear instinct — fueled by fear for her own life, made that initial biological-clock trauma seem like child's play.

She wanted to rail, to challenge, to threaten, to tell this smarmy pretender that neither he nor any American billionaire would tell her what to do with her own son. And yet she couldn't back it up. They were going to do what they were going to do. Viv was in on it, and Marilena's agreement to raise Nicky as a spiritualist carried with it all these other obligations. The only way out was to, in essence, kidnap her own child and spirit him away in the night.

But where would she go? What would she do? She had no money and an income that barely met their needs even with most of their expenses already cared for. And as it was, her meager funds were dependent on her contacts with major universities. There was no way to do her work clandestinely. As she sat across from Reiche Planchette, she realized the awful truth. She had lost whatever freedom she thought she had.

Marilena quickly adapted and adjusted. If she could not think of a way to escape with her son, she would have to play the game — or appear to. She would have to accede to this "recommendation" of where to educate him. She would have to agree to teach Nicky their "religion," as she had pledged. Now it became more imperative than ever that she take the lead on this. She might even have to fake personal allegiance to Lucifer. He would know the truth, of course. She couldn't fool him. And if these people were as cosmically connected with him as they claimed — and had shown evidence of — he might warn them about her. In oblique ways, at the meetings or through Ouija or tarot or automatic writing, he already had warned Viv.

Would Marilena have to get her mind right? Would she have to open herself to an entirely different look at Luciferianism? Could she persuade herself that the prince of the power of the air was worthy of worship after all? If it made the difference regarding her relationship with her only son, her only living blood relative, she would have to do what she had to do.

But she couldn't show weakness now. "I do not want my son riding a bus or being driven to school every day by anyone but me."

"Not even Ms. Ivinisova?"

"I will do it."

"But Viviana should at least share those duties so she can begin instructing Nicolae on the ways of our faith."

"She can spell me occasionally and take over in the cases of emergency or illness. But I will do the teaching as well."

"You?"

"Of course me. Why not?"

"But I thought —"

"Sir, I have been a faithful student of spiritualism since before Nicolae was born."

"I know, but —"

"I pledged to raise him in the discipline, and I covet the privilege . . ."

"Well, that's certainly admirable. And you can easily do that during the daily round-trips between here and Blaj."

"That would be my plan. And you say a vehicle will be provided?"

"That's the best part."

Sure, whatever it is will make this all worth it.

"You'll have the use of a new SUV. And every expense related to it will be taken care of. Fuel, maintenance, you name it."

"All out of the goodness of Jonathan Stonagal's heart," Marilena said.

Planchette smiled. "Precisely."

As a sophomore Ray Steele began to come out of his shell. Besides his mother and his doctor conspiring and finally hitting upon the right medication for his face, Ray's growth spurt slowed enough that he began to feel as graceful in the hallways as he did while playing sports. He recognized that girls seemed to notice him, greet him, maintain eye contact. He had to work at keeping his mind on class and homework, as the opposite sex monopolized his thoughts.

Fourteen

"Fax for you, sir," Jonathan Stonagal's chauffeur announced.

Stonagal caught Fredericka's eye and nodded toward the machine humming in the backseat of the stretch Bentley as it waited at a light in midtown. He noticed she folded the sheet vertically without so much as a glance at it, then handed it to him.

J.S.:
   Bearer unimpressed at worst, indifferent at best.

R.P.

Stonagal slowly and precisely tore the fax into neat pieces and handed them to Fredericka. "Ask Planchette how crucial the mother is," he whispered.

The relationship between Marilena and

Viv Ivins had finally begun to chill. After years of partnership in raising Nicky, the women's rapport had begun to fray.

It began when Marilena discovered that the brand-new SUV provided by the spiritualism association — through the largess of Jonathan Stonagal, of course — had been registered in Viv's name. "Why must it belong to either of us?" Marilena said.

"It means nothing," Viv said. "It's just a convenience, a technicality. If it needs work or anything, it's good to have it in one of our names."

"Then why not mine?"

"Who cares? What's the difference?"

"It should have been at least in both our names," Marilena said.

"You're the one so disinclined to our being mistaken for lesbians," Viv said.

"Why couldn't the vehicle have been registered to Mr. Planchette or the association or to one of Stonagal's companies?"

"Honestly, Marilena, what is your problem? This seems petty, even for you."

Even for you? What did that mean? Viv thought Marilena was petty as a rule?

"I just feel like an outsider, that's all. I am part of the association too. I come to the meetings. I'm raising Nicky the way I said I would. Why am I treated like a fifth wheel?"

Viv just shook her head. Worse, she had not responded well to the idea of only spelling Marilena as Nicky's daily driver. "Why don't we trade off?" she said. "I could take every other day. Or one of us could take him and the other pick him up."

"Forgive me if I want a couple of uninterrupted hours with my own son!" Marilena said. "You have enough influence on him, and I appreciate that; I really do. But I can teach him what you want taught, and frankly, he and I need to bond more. I think the boy is confused about who's who around here."

Viv muttered under her breath.

"What?"

"Don't ask."

"I'm asking. What are you complaining about?"

"I'm just saying," Viv said, "that I always have the recourse of Reiche arbitrating this."

Marilena closed her eyes. "You don't even want to start with me on that. What am I, an employee of Nicolae Enterprises? I am his mother!"

"So you keep insisting."

"What's that supposed to mean?"

"You birthed him, Marilena. You were a receptacle, a carrier. You didn't add much to the mix then, and you certainly have not found traction as his mother since."

The truth of that hit Marilena in the solar plexus. "But whose fault is that? You're the outsider, Viv. No, I couldn't have done it without you, but shouldn't you work at maintaining boundaries? You're not his mother."

"Spiritually I am."

"Well, I intend to change that, and I'll start by being his driver."

For the next few years, Marilena and Nicky would rise early every day and were on the road before sunup. When she returned, Marilena did her research work, transmitting her results to various clients. She spent the remainder of the day studying what she wanted to convey to Nicky and, to her consternation, found she often had to consult the expert: Viv.

Maddeningly, Viv affected an air of helpfulness. Perhaps Marilena would have been even more infuriated if the older woman had proved uncooperative. But Viv was thorough, teaching Marilena not only what needed to be passed on to Nicky but also advising her on how to say it, what to emphasize, what to understand about a young boy and how he learned.

"He learns like an adult," Marilena said.

"But he's still a child, and you must not

forget that. Allow him to grow at his own pace; be sensitive to his limited emotional and spiritual capacity."

Marilena stiffened. She didn't need to be lectured about her own child. "He has shown unlimited spiritual capacity. He astounds me every day."

"Children can be amazing receptors," Viv said. "Just be careful."

Marilena wanted to slap her. Was there no way out of this? Could she not dismiss Viv from her own house? But it wasn't Marilena's house. It too was being provided.

True, Nicky was full of questions, and the spirit world captivated him like nothing else, though he had limitless interests. Even in the hoity-toity private school, he proved head and shoulders above other students his age and even older. He had been the only first-year student who could read and was now certainly the only one already fluent in three languages. His teachers, reminding Marilena of Viv, cautioned her not to push him, telling her that "children develop at their own pace. The others will catch him soon enough."

Not a chance. This boy was a born leader, and no one would ever equal him.

The day of his first solo flight at age sixteen, Ray Steele told himself he could do this. He knew he could. He'd been dreaming of it for years and training for it for months. And he had done it countless times with an instructor next to him. What would be different this time? Solo. No instructor. No safety net. The last dozen times he had flown, his instructor had done nothing, said nothing. He had merely been there, ready to help if anything went wrong.

Still, there was no denying his butterflies. But was that all these were? Could butterflies make you vomit? Ray was sick to his stomach and couldn't quit fidgeting. And the grin. If he felt so bad, why couldn't he wipe off the grin?

"Any questions before I step out?" his instructor said, unbuckling.

"Nope. Don't think so. Ready. Eager. Want to get going."

"Don't let your excitement cloud your judgment."

"I won't."

"And I don't just mean in the air."

"Sir?"

"First thing you'll forget is something on the ground. Use your checklist. You're trusting your life to this craft."

Ray checked and double-checked. Fuel was topped off, electrical systems go. Everything seemed fine.

"What if I told you, Ray, that I mis-adjusted something on purpose, just to see if you'd find it?"

"Did you?"

"I asked you first."

"Uh, I'd be confident I covered every-thing?"

"You asking me or telling me?"

"I'll check again if you want."

"If *I* want? Think, Ray. Of course I wouldn't let you take 'er up if I *knew* you had missed something. But this has to matter more to you than it does to me. I mean, I'd hate to have to break bad news to your parents, but what about you? You have a death wish? You want this to be your last flight?"

"Not a chance. I want it to be the first of many."

"Well, then, you strapping in or checking again?"

Ray studied the checklist and sped through it again in his mind. He was sure he'd verified everything. And he was also sure his instructor would not let him take up a bird that had something wrong with it. Flashing a thumbs-up, he settled in behind the controls. The instructor pointed to the runway, and Ray taxied to where he would wait for clearance to take off for a thirty-minute flight.

Fear, nervousness did not do justice to what he felt. He had to admit he was ill at ease, eager to be on the ground again, to have the maiden voyage behind him. But he had no doubt about his proficiency and knowledge. Unless something went terribly wrong with the weather or the craft — and of course he had double-checked both — he would land safely. Ray's goal was to do it smoothly, to impress his instructor, to be cleared to fly solo from this point on.

As the small prop plane hurtled down the runway, Ray saw something in his path. A small animal? Something metallic? A bolt? Should he swerve? abort? Too late. His right tire hit it hard, just as the drag over his wings lifted him gently from the earth. He fought the craft to keep it straight and wondered if his instructor had seen what happened.

His radio crackled to life. "That was a little shaky," his instructor said.

"I think I ran over a bird."

"Everything okay?"

"Perfect."

"Carry on."

It had been just a little fib. That had certainly not been a bird. It had rattled loudly against the fuselage and gone bouncing off the runway. But Ray didn't want to admit to anything that would force him to cut short his first solo. There seemed no damage to the plane, and everything was going fine now.

Half an hour later, as he circled the airstrip and maneuvered for landing, Ray regretted not telling his parents how big a day this was. No, this was best. He would tell them at dinner, and their response either way could not dampen the thrill of this accomplishment.

Ray was just ten feet from the pavement when he noticed his fuel gauge read empty. He still had thrust, so there must have been something in there. He wanted the wheels to touch simultaneously, but the left hit and chirped first. When the plane settled onto the other wheel, the craft grabbed the runway and began spinning crazily. The right tire was flat and acted as a brake.

Ray fought to hang on, praying the plane wouldn't flip. In a flash he was grateful there was not enough fuel to even register on the gauge. If the prop hit the runway and the plane pitched, the sparks could ignite the fuel.

By the time the plane finally skidded noisily to a stop, Ray could see his instructor sprinting down the tarmac, followed by a couple of guys from the tower and a vehicle with lights flashing.

His instructor was pale as he helped Ray from the plane, asking over and over if he was all right.

"I'm fine," Ray kept saying.

"He landed on a flat tire and with a severed fuel line," a man inspecting under the plane said. "You're one lucky kid. If you were a cat you'd have only eight more lives."

Ray fought to control his breathing and pulse. Why hadn't he reported the takeoff incident? How long had he gone on virtually no fuel? Was soloing worth his life?

When he and his instructor finally sat across from each other in the tiny terminal lunchroom, the man ran his hands through his hair. "Hoo, boy!" he said. "You feel as lucky as you are?"

Ray had to be honest. He shook his head. He didn't know what to say.

Nicky, as he advanced through the elementary grades, seemed most impressed by the secret nature of Luciferianism. "Others must not know," Marilena told him, "because the majority of spiritually minded people in this world have bought into the idea that Lucifer is Satan, the enemy of

God. We know better. He merely made the mistake of wanting to excel, to be wise, and to know the truth."

"What is wrong with that?" Nicky said.

"Exactly. Who put God in charge? Why should one of His chief angels have to do His will and obey His orders? Lucifer's ambition was called pride and sin. But he is, as we are, divine. Why would we adore and blindly obey a god other than ourselves?"

"And why is this a secret?" Nicky said.

"Religious people have the mistaken idea that God is good and Lucifer is bad. But we know better. If anything, the opposite is true. If God is in charge, why does He let such horrible things happen? And why is He threatened by a spiritual being who merely wants to be more? God is jealous, selfish, self-serving. But say that in public, and you will be vilified. Know what that means?"

"Of course, Mom. 'Ridiculed. Put down.' "

How she loved it when he called her Mom.

"Lucifer's so-called sin was self-awareness," she said. "Why should that be such a threat if God is almighty? If He is really the creator of all things, would He worry that His creatures love or obey Him? Of course not, unless the whole point of creating them was to make for Himself a legion of slaves.

Who is He to say what is right or wrong? We are all individuals, captains of our own destinies. We are unique, and life tells us all we need to know."

Marilena stole a glance at her son. His eyes were bright. "So this is our secret," he said.

"Right."

"And there are others who know, but we are keeping it to ourselves."

"Yes."

"How do we get more people?" he said.

"We have to be careful. If someone is dead set against this, there's little hope of their moving to the side of truth. It's the people who are undecided or who have come to no conclusions who are the best candidates." Marilena told Nicky how she herself had worshiped at the altar of knowledge and scholarship. "Even there, the spiritual life, both sides of it, was suspect."

"But you learned different," he said.

"I did. Especially when I longed for a child and you were the promised gift."

How Nicky loved that story. He asked to hear it again and again, and Marilena may have been kidding herself, but she believed the truth of it gave him a new view of her. She had wanted him, hoped for him, prayed for him, pledged to raise him in devotion to the one who promised him. He never articulated his love and devotion to her, but she was convinced they were there.

It struck her that her relationship with Lucifer was the same. She was treating him the way her son treated her. She was his child, his daughter, one he had courted by giving her the greatest desire of her heart. While she didn't shake her fist in his face, she withheld herself, holding him emotionally hostage. Marilena suddenly felt childish, unworthy, drunk with the power to manipulate the feelings of one so powerful. Maybe now that she saw the error of her ways, Nicky would see his.

"So we know the truth," Nicky said, "right, Mom? And most other people do not?"

"Not only do they not, they believe a lie."

"But we are right."

"Yes." She truly believed it. And she could see he did too. At least it was clear he wanted to. This appeared to be delicious to him, the clandestine nature of it, being set apart from the crowd.

"Some kids go to church to worship God," he said. "What do we do?"

"We go to our own kind of church to worship Lucifer. They are just classes, but he and his spirits speak to us."

"Like he did to you about me."

"Exactly."

"Wow."

After schooling Nicky as much as she could during their daily rides, Marilena found he had questions. "So what did God think was so wrong about Lucifer wanting to be like Him?"

"That's the whole point, Nicky. Only a weak-minded and threatened God would find that a problem. Know what I mean?"

"Sure, yes. Maybe He did not want to lose His followers. Most of them were probably afraid of Him, but Lucifer was more curious."

Marilena never ceased to be amazed at how adult Nicky's mind was. "Yes," she said. "His beauty refers to his mind and his aura."

"But you said God offered him forgiveness."

"That's taught in our tradition. God wanted Lucifer back, along with the angels who agreed with him. So He offered to forgive them. But only a few accepted."

"And not Lucifer."

"Of course not. He was noble, an idealist, and he would never stray from his beliefs, no matter what."

"That makes him a hero, right?"

"It sure does."

"Why do so many people think he is bad then?"

"That's the question of the ages, Son. He's beautiful, he's a shining light, he's called the morning star. And yet so many choose to believe he's the devil! It makes no sense. And there are more of them all the time. People aren't looking for enlightenment. They are wallowing in ignorance."

"But not us."

"Not us."

"We know the truth, the real truth."

"We do, Nicky. And there's power in the truth. The truth can set you free."

"Free from what?"

"From prejudice, ignorance, from blindly following a jealous God just because everyone else does."

"I would not."

"I know."

"But I will not tell anybody, Mom. They would not understand."

As a junior Ray Steele had had another off year, shooting up two more inches and actually playing worse football, basketball, and baseball than he had the year before. All the hype and promise of his being a three-sport starter and a standout on the varsity teams proved wrong as he had tough seasons in all sports. He started as the varsity quarter-back, but after winning the first two games against weak teams, he lost the last eight, throwing more interceptions than touch-downs. The only reason he didn't lose the job was because no one else had his size or potential. His coach, Fuzzy Bellman, also the high school athletics director, encouraged him. "You've got all the tools, Ray. We'll have a good season next year."

"Yeah, but you don't get a scholarship based on just a good senior season."

"You could. You never know."

In basketball Ray was expected to be a starter, but he wound up riding the bench most of the season as backup to a good power forward a year younger. Ray played a lot of scrub, cleanup minutes and found himself actually hoping his sophomore teammate would get hurt.

What's the matter with me? he wondered late at night. He didn't remember being jealous and petty when he was younger. But he hadn't had cause either. The worse the basketball season grew — his team finished even — the harder Ray worked at his studies. It was gratifying to be on his way to a high grade point average, especially in math and science, but he had to admit he would rather be revered as a great athlete than a great student. He had a better chance at a scholarship as a student than as a jock, but that wasn't as much fun.

At least his flying lessons were going well. He was able to get to the airstrip only infrequently, due to all his other activities, but Ray's instructor assured him he would be able to get his private license by the time he was eighteen and a senior.

Baseball during the spring of Ray's junior year proved disappointing as well. He was to be the ace pitcher and play first base. He could throw ninety miles an hour — which would guarantee attracting big-league scouts — until he hurt his arm. Then he merely played first, batted eighth, and didn't hit .300. So much for an athletic scholarship.

Worse, Ray became less popular, even among the guys. In elementary school he had been the leader, the go-to guy, the one everybody wanted to hang with. Now they had all caught and passed him in ability and achievement, and he became the butt of teasing instead of being the one dishing it out. At least that showed him how it felt to be on the receiving end. Rather than laughing it off the way the other guys did, Ray found himself defensive and obnoxious. He was humiliated, and his anger made him try to play beyond his ability, only rendering him less effective.

At home Ray had learned to get along with his parents by going along with them. But every day he drifted further from them. They didn't understand him, tried to counsel him, but he didn't want to hear it. He knew they didn't have anything to worry about. He was a good citizen, if nothing else. He wasn't into smoking or drugs or sex, though the latter wasn't due to lack of wishing and hoping. And he did sneak the occasional beer, which he loved, mostly because he knew it was illegal.

During Ray's senior year everything fell together for him. His sore arm healed, he reached six foot four, and he developed more speed and finesse. He impressed Coach Bellman at preseason football workouts and was named captain of the varsity team and starting quarterback again.

Ray's face was fully clear now, and he had stumbled upon the right style for his thick, dark hair. He was elected student council president over a popular cheerleader, then homecoming king (she was queen), and seemingly overnight became big man on campus. Even with everything he had going at school, Ray still squeezed in as many hours in the cockpit as possible, pointing toward that private license.

Ray's passing and play calling kept Belvidere in the race for the conference championship until two close losses at the end of the season. Unfortunately, he also just missed making all-conference, because the league was loaded with good quarterbacks.

"Okay, Coach," Ray said at the end of the season. "How many letters did you get about me?"

"None."

"C'mon, I know how you lobby colleges for your players. And I know you hold all this stuff until the season is over."

"I don't understand it myself, Ray. I pitched you to several Division I programs, and when I didn't hear back, I started with the second tier. I got form letters from three small schools where I wouldn't even recommend you go, unless all you want is to play football."

"You've got to be kidding."

"I wish I was. It's getting tougher all the time to catch the interest of college and university programs, Ray. There's a lot of big kids and talent out there. Fortunately, with your grades and extracurricular stuff, you'll land somewhere."

"But not as an athlete."

"Well, not as a quarterback anyway."

Fifteen

"Get Planchette on the secure line for me, Fredericka. And remind him to remain obtuse regardless."

Stonagal read reverence, if not fear, in Reiche Planchette's tone. Maybe he needed to call the man personally more often. "I just want to know whether the entity in question has outlived its usefulness."

"Oh . . . ah . . . uh-huh . . . yeah. I'd say —"

"Is all that hemming and hawing a yes, R.P.?"

"Ah . . . no. No! Viv, ah, our contact tells us that she, that . . . um . . . it is or has been okay for a while. Not fully on board, but teaching the . . . the target, and okay."

"You seen what's been happening to the markets, R.P.?"

"Sir?"

"The markets! The markets!"

"I'm not up to speed on that, sir, no."

"Ach! Listen; things are coming together. Things are happening. You follow?"

"Um, okay."

"You follow or not?"

"Clarify for me, sir."

"I just want to streamline this is all. If something is in the way, if it impedes progress, it must be eliminated. Clear?"

"I think so."

"Is that where we are? Are we at that point, R.P.?"

"I'm not sure we are yet, sir, but you know the signs better than I, certainly."

"Consider this a provisional green light. Anytime you think we're ready and this is necessary, you're free to trigger whatever action is necessary. And keep me posted."

Marilena watched as Nicky bounded from the SUV with his book bag and sprinted across the schoolyard toward his nine-year-old classmates. She always got him there in time to play before school. But as he headed away from her, his teacher was coming her way, waving. Short, stout Mrs. Szabo knelt and said something to Nicky as he flew by, but it appeared he didn't even acknowledge her.

Marilena rolled down her window.

"Mrs. Carpathia," the teacher said, "I

wondered if you'd have time to meet with me at the end of the day."

"Happy to," Marilena said, "but Nicky's Aunt Viv will be picking him up this afternoon. Is there a problem?"

"Just some things we should discuss. I've already talked to Ms. Ivins."

"Then I will make it work," Marilena said, barely able to hide her pique. "I would appreciate it if you would not talk to Viv about Nicky without my knowledge."

"Oh!" Mrs. Szabo said, as if truly surprised. "But I thought . . ." She trailed off.

Marilena didn't want to pursue it. "I'll see you this afternoon then."

Marilena worried she would be unable to concentrate on her work for worrying what might be the problem with Nicky. Had he been talking about Luciferianism to his classmates? It was one thing that he was brilliant enough to have a grasp of spiritualism and the cosmic conflict between God and the other angelic beings. But to actually expect a boy his age to keep all this to himself was unrealistic. He may have the mind of an adult, but he still had the emotions of a child.

At home she confronted Viv. "Please don't discuss my child with his teacher without my knowledge."

"It wasn't my idea," Viv said.

"You should have told her you would be more comfortable with her talking to me."

"But that wouldn't be true, Marilena."

"What does that mean?"

"I am *not* more comfortable with that. I don't trust your judgment related to Nicky."

"How can you say that?"

"The irony is that while you are his mother, you are not close to him."

"That's not true! I —"

"Not as close as you think you are or would like to be. Admit it, Marilena. You're *a sătura.*"

"Cloying? He's my son! I won't lose him to you or to the association or even to Luciferianism."

"What are you saying? You're reneging on —"

"Hardly, Viv, and you know it. I'm raising him in the tradition I promised. And I've become more devout myself. But I don't know how many times I have to say this: I will not have outsiders interfering with a blood relationship."

"Interfering? Outsiders? That's what you think of me? I have given the last ten years of my life to you and this boy, and I've been glad to do it. I thought we had become family. I am not his aunt in name only. I consider you a sister."

Viv looked truly hurt, and that had not been Marilena's intention. "Well, but, but — how would you feel if you were me? Say you bore a child and . . ."

"And pledged to cooperate because he was the fulfillment of a promise from the spirits?"

"Well, yes, but —"

"You see, Marilena," Viv said, tearing up, "I can't have a child. You once asked why not me? I said I was too old and couldn't imagine giving birth. The truth is, I have another assignment. I have been bestowed gifts of clairvoyance that the spirits believe are crucial to the association. I feel honored and blessed and useful, but —" she began to sob — "I would have given anything to be in your shoes, to trade roles with you. Please don't shut me out."

Marilena found herself filled with remorse and compassion. She wanted to be careful not to be taken in. What was this sudden change of attitude? It had seemed for years as if Viv had reveled in her superiority, her station, her place as spokesperson for those who held sway over Nicky. She had insinuated that she could pull rank, could have Reiche Planchette arbitrate differences, that she was in a privileged position that made Marilena feel like a mere means to an end.

But now this. It was as if Viv were pleading to have a place at the table. In spite of herself, Marilena felt empowered and emboldened by Viv's apparent neediness and weakness. She embraced the older woman, realizing that they had seldom touched in all these years and hardly ever embraced.

Viv seemed to lose control, weeping loudly as she buried her face in Marilena's shoulder.

"Can we not come to some sort of an agreement?" Marilena said.

"I'd like that."

"I don't want to leave you out. I know your influence on Nicky has been positive, and he loves you. How he loves you. I guess that's what's bothering me. He loves you more than he loves me."

"That's not true!"

"Of course it is. I'm trying to change that, because it's not right and proper, but I need you to agree and help me."

"Help you turn his affection away from me?" Viv said.

"No! I don't want him to quit loving you. But I want him to treat you like an aunt, not like a mother. I mean, let's face it; you're not really his aunt either."

"I'm closer than an aunt!"

"That may be, but yours is a place of assumed privilege, not earned by blood."

"Earned by more than blood," Viv said. "I've invested in you both, sacrificed."

"Come, come. There's nothing you'd rather have done."

Viv chuckled, seemingly in spite of herself. "Well, that's certainly true."

"Now sit down," Marilena said. "Tell me what Mrs. Szabo is going to talk to me about."

"I'm not at liberty —"

"Need I remind you that we are talking about *my* son? How many times do we have to go over the same ground?"

Viv wiped her face and appeared to regain control. "Listen, you've made your point, and I will work hard on helping maintain your appropriate place in Nicky's life. And I will urge Mrs. Szabo to consult you first on all matters relating to him. But in this case I do not want to make the mistake of trying to speak for his teacher. She deserves the right to be heard without any shading from my viewpoint."

"My goodness, Viv. How bad is this?"

"It's not horrible. It's just a concern."

"We're clear then that I will pick him up

this afternoon so I can talk with her?"

Viv nodded. "I could ride along. Keep him occupied while you're meeting."

That made sense. It wouldn't do to have another teacher watch him, and the other students weren't likely to stay long after school. She agreed.

And as Marilena feared, she was unable to concentrate on anything else for the rest of the day.

In basketball as a senior Ray Steele had redeemed himself by winning the starting position as weakside forward and wound up leading the team in scoring. Belvidere finished third in their conference, however, and again Ray was overlooked by college recruiters.

His play did make him the most popular guy at the school. Suddenly Ray was anything but short of dates. And despite the fun, that left him frustrated. The girls who showed the most interest were the ones he had pined after for years, but he had been invisible when he was suffering from acne. He now enjoyed the attention, sure, but it all seemed so shallow. He was the same person he had always been; he merely looked different. Maybe he exuded more confidence and his athletic prowess had matured, but if that and his looks were all the girls were interested in, what did that say about them?

Ray found himself more friendly and cordial, but inside he had learned not to trust people. Everyone was so surfacy. Was he too? He hoped not. He obsessed about the phoniness of his new relationships to the point that he couldn't maintain a relationship — let alone develop a long-term girlfriend — for more than a few weeks.

Being popular was better than the alternative, but Ray's distrust of everyone and their motives gained a toehold in his mind. His one solace was flying. Flying solo thousands of feet in the air on his way to getting his private license, he felt a freedom and power he couldn't put into words. No one would understand why it gave him such a sense of satisfaction. There was sure nothing phony about it. Flying was the perfect picture of cause and effect. It was his job to check every function of the aircraft, and once satisfied, he knew it would do what he instructed it to do with all the various maneuvers he had been taught. If he flipped the right switches and pushed and pulled the control yoke with the right pressure, the plane responded — and it didn't care about Ray's looks, athletic ability, grades, or popularity.

His dad wasn't going to want to hear it, but flying was going to be Ray's life.

Marilena and Viv conversed as they had in years past on the way to Nicky's school that afternoon. It was actually pleasant, Marilena thought, and she chastised herself for becoming possessive and defensive and jealous. She had been drawn to Viv from the beginning because the woman seemed to care so much for others. That hadn't changed.

Viv wasn't perfect, but who was? Marilena should have expected some disappointments, living in the same house with someone all this time. She herself had been no prize; why should she expect otherwise from Viv? Well, because Viv was basically a better person, Marilena decided. More social, more people-oriented. Nicer, that was all.

Despite the sisterly fun and laughter they enjoyed on the way, it was not lost on Marilena that neither even mentioned Nicky. She knew Viv didn't want her to push, to pry, to try to get out of her what Mrs. Szabo's problem was. And when they arrived it quickly became obvious that the teacher had told Nicky she would be talking with his mother while his aunt watched him, for he came racing out of the school ready to play. As Viv opened the door, he leaped into her arms. In spite of herself, Marilena felt a fresh, sharp pang of jealousy. The boy did not even acknowledge his mother's presence.

It didn't help that Mrs. Szabo arranged their meeting so that Marilena sat facing the windows in full view of Viv's cavorting with Nicky. They played catch, played tag, pushed each other in the swings, climbed after each other on the monkey bars. Marilena could have done that — would do it — if just given the chance.

"Nicolae is the brightest nine-year-old I have ever taught," the teacher began.

That was clearly intended as an icebreaker, but Marilena couldn't even force a smile. She had not been invited here to be complimented. "Um-hm."

"Surely you must have heard that before."

"From every teacher. Yes, I'm very proud of him."

"Even though this is a school for advanced children, he is unique. There are days when I wonder where I will find more to challenge him, days when I feel like his student rather than his teacher."

"Welcome to my world," Marilena said.

"I am concerned about his behavior, however."

"He doesn't obey you?"

"Generally he does. But I am in a unique position to observe how he interacts with the other children. Let me not beat around the bush. He is what I would call pathologically manipulative."

This was not news to Marilena, of course. She had seen it at home. But part of her had hoped it wasn't obvious at school. "How does it manifest itself?" she said.

"He's *every*one's friend," Mrs. Szabo said. "And yet it's clear he plays the children off each other. They all seem to like him and appear oblivious to what he's up to, but everybody always does what he wants. He wins all the games, his team always wins, everything revolves around him."

"He's selfish then?"

"That would be understating it. The world belongs to him. He gets himself elected team leader for every project. When we had a mock election for president of the class, I felt it was someone else's turn to enjoy the spotlight, so I arbitrarily nominated another boy and a girl to run against each other. They were to campaign, give speeches, choose teams to help them win, display posters, everything. Nicolae volunteered to be Victoria's campaign manager, and she quickly became the favorite. Now get this. Not only did she win, but she won unanimously. Even her opponent voted for her."

"Nicky threatened him?"

"No! I believe Nicky promised him something."

"What?"

"The vice presidency."

"But, how — ?"

"When Victoria won, she announced that as president, she could choose the vice president."

"And she chose the loser?"

"No, she chose Nicolae. Then she resigned as president, saying she realized she would be better as a helper than a leader. Nicolae became president, and he chose the loser as his VP. All this at nine years old."

"I don't know what to say. What did Victoria get out of it?"

"She gets to be his girlfriend. They hang around together."

"Girlfriend!"

The teacher nodded. "You know, he tries the same techniques with me. He tells me everything that goes on, anything bad he can think of about the other children. And when he senses I have heard enough, he assures me he can handle it and not to worry about it. A couple of days later he'll tell me he has fixed whatever was wrong. I have actually been tempted to enlist him to help me control the class. But I have resisted, because I think he controls the others enough."

"What can I do about this?"

"Teach him, Mrs. Carpathia. He has astounding gifts, but they must be channeled. He's a diplomat, a politician, a genius, a social gadfly, a divider, a uniter. He must learn humility. He must learn the consequences of power. He could sell a legless man a pair of shoes."

If that was intended to be funny, it didn't hit Marilena that way. This was worse than she feared. "I'll try," she said. "Thank you for letting me know."

"There's more. We had a competition between the boys and the girls for a homework project. The respective sides were to assign different students to memorize the functions and positions in the national government, who held each one, that sort of thing. As you know, Romania has a complicated form of rule, two houses of parliament, all that. Nicolae memorized everything, his assignment and everyone else's, but I didn't want his team to win only because of that. I insisted that each team member recite a different set of facts. The boys won hands down, and I found out that Nicolae had taught them how to remember their individual parts through pneumonics. He used acrostics and acronyms so that if they learned a simple word, the letters represented the first letter of what they had to remember."

"Ingenious. Surely you couldn't have had a problem with that."

"Except that it was almost maniacal. Nicolae was so obsessed with winning that it became no fun for his team. He encouraged and cajoled, but he also badgered and belittled. These boys had no choice but to learn this stuff and win, because of the sheer force of his personality."

"A gift that could be good or bad," Marilena said.

"Certainly. His strengths are his weaknesses, as is true with so many of us. Help me teach him team play, to value others and their feelings. It's as if there's a disconnect in his mind, as if he really believes that this world and everyone in it are here for his benefit."

"I'll try," Marilena managed.

"I will keep you informed," Mrs. Szabo said.

I'm sure you will.

Ray Steele lay in his bedroom, unable to

concentrate on his homework. Nothing held his interest — not TV or music or magazines or the Internet — after the way the conversation had gone at dinner.

Ray had no idea how strongly his father felt about his future. He should have known, of course. His dad had never made a secret of it. Ray just thought the old man would have to be impressed that he had gotten his private license at eighteen and the fact that he had a concrete plan. Ray knew what he was doing, what he wanted, and how to achieve it.

"I've been signed up for Reserve Officer Training Corps since late last year, and Coach Bellman says getting my license before I'm even out of high school assures me of enough other scholarships to pay my way through college."

"Well, that's fine," his father said, "but what does Fuzzy know about it?"

"He knows I'm not going to get any help going to school as an athlete. Unless I want some small college."

"But why? You were the best —"

"Dad, come on. Times have changed. Even ten years ago I might have gotten a deal somewhere, but no more. You have to be the best in your sport in the whole conference now to get any kind of ride."

"Baseball's still your best chance."

"And it's my favorite, Dad, but it's not going to happen."

"How can you say that?"

"I can't throw ninety anymore, and I'll be surprised if I hit over .400. The last guy from our conference who got a full ride to a D-1 school hit nearly .600 with lots of bombs."

"That's not out of the realm of possibility for you."

"You're a little biased, Dad, don't you think?"

"I don't know what I'm talking about? You don't think I know the game?"

" 'Course you do, and you taught me everything I know. But you also taught me to be realistic about my ability. I'd have given anything to stay healthy and be able to throw hard enough to attract the scouts. But that's over, Dad. I'm going to have to pitch anyway, because too many other guys aren't playing this year. There's something about cars and girlfriends and how few people come to baseball games that makes guys want to quit unless they're superstars. If I didn't love it so much, I'd think about that too."

"So you're going to have a lousy team?"

"Likely. A lot of young guys, and nobody

to draw the scouts unless we put together some kind of a win streak. I don't see it."

The fireworks came when Mr. Steele tried to outline a scenario for Ray's future that still included the tool and die. He talked about college and ROTC and military duty, at least minoring in business or manufacturing, and then coming back to take over the business.

Ray had hoped that by outlining his own plans — and pointedly not including the tool and die — his father would finally resign himself to reality. Ray sat silent.

"Huh? What do you think, Ray? Good education. More hours in the planes. A little military training. Job waiting for you. Future secure, huh?"

Ray glanced at his mother, who forced a smile. She was a lot of things but dense wasn't one of them. She had that dreading-this-moment look, obviously knowing her husband wasn't going to hear what he wanted.

"I'm not coming back to the tool and die, Dad."

"What, you know that already? You hate me and my business so much that —"

"C'mon, Dad! You know that's not true. I admire what you've done with it, but you can't force me to —"

"If I was paying for your education I could, couldn't I? But you made sure you didn't need that."

"You *told* me you couldn't put me through college! That's why I've tried all these different ways to get help!"

"Yeah, but since I'm not financin' the deal, you feel free to —"

"I just want you to know now so you can make other arrangements. Groom someone else."

"My people are too old. And none of them has what it takes."

"So hire an heir apparent."

"*You're* the heir, Ray! You! It's been my dream all my life."

"But not mine, Dad. You wouldn't want me in the saddle if I didn't want it, would you? What kind of a job would I do then?"

His dad stood, face red. "I can't eat anymore."

"Please, honey," his wife said.

"I just don't see how you can decide now how you're going to feel in four to six years. That's a long time. Time to get your mind right. At least keep your options open and plan a little for this possibility."

"No! Then we'll have this discussion again, Dad, and you'll have wasted all that time without finding someone else. I'm going to be a pilot and that's that. I —"

"What if it doesn't work out?"

"Why wouldn't it? I'm made for it. I'm a pilot now. I'll start working my way up to the heavy jets, and —"

"And you'll come back to the tool and die only if all your dreams are shattered somehow."

"I wouldn't come back anyway, Dad. If for some reason I couldn't fly, I'd want to teach aviation. Or coach. Or both."

His dad left the room, throwing over his shoulder, "You *do* hate me."

Sixteen

Marilena Carpathia had never felt further out of her element. In nine years as a mother she had somehow adapted, learned, gone on instinct. But this was new territory. How would she broach such a touchy subject with her brilliant son? This would have to be an adult conversation, and while he had many of the worst characteristics of an adult — and some of the best — Marilena was ever conscious that he was emotionally still a child.

On the drive back from Blaj, she urged him to read while she chatted softly with Viv in Hungarian. "What will we do?" she began.

Viv smiled and patted her hand. "We? Now it's *we?* Now it's not so bad someone else has been drawn into this crisis?"

Marilena took it well. That was funny. Yes, her jealousy seemed misplaced now. She didn't want to be alone in this. "I know I must bear the brunt of it," she said, "but believe me, I am receptive to any advice. In my heart of hearts I long for, ah —" she struggled to find the right foreign word for her son without mentioning his name — "my progeny to use his incredibly gifted mind for the betterment of mankind."

"He will, Marilena. He will."

Suddenly Nicky draped his arms over the back of the front seat and perched his head atop them, putting himself between the women. Marilena felt him there and saw him in her peripheral vision. She kept her eyes on the road, peeking at him in the rearview mirror. He appeared amused.

"You should be buckled in, young man," she said, back to Romanian now.

"I am all right," he said in Hungarian, astounding her. "My prince would not let anything happen."

Marilena shuddered. He understood Hungarian, had heard their conversation. Was nothing hidden from him? Her fear turned to anger in an instant. She resolved not to lose control of this boy, wondering to her core whether she ever had any control over him. "Sit back and get your belt on!" she said. "Now!"

Marilena saw Viv jerk, apparently in surprise at her tone.

Nicky was silent, but in the mirror he showed no emotion. He wasn't surprised or cowed. Neither was he obeying.

"Don't make me pull over, young man," she said.

"Do what you want," he said flatly. "You do not dare hurt me. And you do not want to talk to me like that again either."

Marilena swerved the SUV off the pavement and slid to a stop. She turned in her seat to face Nicky, her face inches from his. "Sit down and buckle up!" she shouted. He didn't move. She lifted her elbow and pressed it to his face, pushing with all her might.

"Marilena!" Viv screamed.

Marilena dug in her heels and straightened her legs, putting all her weight into trying to drive Nicky back. But he held fiercely to the back of the seat, and it was as if she were pressing against granite. Seething now, Marilena released her seat belt and wrenched herself completely around until she was on her knees facing him. She grabbed his shoulders and shook him, trying to drive him back.

Viv grabbed Marilena's arm and tried to pull her away.

"Viv! Don't fight me! Help me!"

"We're not going to fight!" Viv said. "Stop!"

"Yes!" Nicky yelled. "Stop!"

"I'm not driving this car until he's buckled in."

"I am protected!" Nicky said.

"What?"

"I will not be hurt."

"What are you saying?"

"You will get hurt before I will."

Exasperated, Marilena turned to Viv.

"Let's just go, Marilena. We'll talk this through at home."

"You don't care that he's not buckled in?"

"I agree he's protected."

Marilena swore. "I don't know what either of you is talking about!"

"That's the problem," Viv said. "We're in communication with the spirits every day. He *is* protected. He's immune to danger from which others might suffer."

"I'm not driving."

"Then I will," Viv said.

Nicky pointed at Marilena. "She is not sitting back here with me."

Marilena wished she had a weapon. She'd test the so-called protection of this brat.

"Get out and switch places with me," Viv said softly.

Marilena left the car, trembling; the last thing she wanted was to get back in. But what was she going to do, hitchhike? She

282

didn't want to go home either. She was without options. As she passed Viv in front of the car, the older woman said, "Breathe, Marilena. Calm yourself."

Viv slid behind the wheel, but Marilena stood with her hand on the open passenger-side door, trying to relax. Nicky had settled into the backseat again, and Viv was talking softly to him, though Marilena could not hear. Finally she got in, slammed the door, and buckled up. She resolved not to even look at her son. Her son. He seemed like an animal.

"*Căţea,*" Nicky whispered.

Marilena whirled in spite of herself. "What did you call me?"

"You heard me."

As Viv pulled back onto the road, Marilena again unbuckled and turned, swinging wildly. The boy dodged and weaved, laughing. Finally she reached his wrist and yanked, but he grabbed with his other hand, pulled her forearm to his mouth, and bit fiercely, drawing blood.

Marilena shrieked and pulled back.

Viv yelled, "Marilena! Stop!"

"He bit me!"

"You deserved it!" Viv said.

Marilena slid back into her seat, covering the wound with her free hand. "What?!"

283

"Yes," Nicky said, "you deserved it. *Căţea*."

Marilena screamed at Nicky, calling him a name worse than the one he had called her.

"This has to stop!" Viv said. "Marilena, you're acting his age."

That was the problem. He was acting older than his age.

"I need an emergency room," Marilena said, blood oozing through her fingers. "The little monster probably has rabies." She pulled her hand away and thrust her forearm toward Viv. Top and bottom teeth had sunk deep into her flesh.

"Oh, *Dumnezeu!*" Viv cried and pulled into the passing lane, the accelerator to the floor.

Marilena glared back at Nicky and held up her bleeding arm so he could see. "Look what you've done, *copil nelegitim*."

He lifted his eyes from his book and smiled. He stuck his tongue out at her, and she burst into tears. Shaken to her soul, Marilena realized she was furious enough to kill him if she had the chance.

Twenty minutes later Viv wheeled into the hospital where Nicky had been born. She told Nicky to stay in the car and rushed Marilena in. It was almost as if a doctor had been waiting for them.

"There was an accident," Viv said as he examined Marilena.

"An accident?" the doctor said. "This is a bite. A human bite. Too small for an adult. A child bit you?"

Marilena wanted to tell all, but Viv said, "I had to slam on the brakes to keep from hitting an animal, and she tried to protect my son. But he was thrown forward, causing this injury."

Her son! For once Marilena was glad not to claim him. She squinted at the doctor, trying to read whether he was buying the account.

"Perhaps I should look him over," he said.

"He's fine," Viv said. "Isn't he, Marilena?"

"Yes," she said, still trying to keep from trembling. "He's just perfect."

The wound from his upper teeth took eight stitches. The lower took six. Between the tetanus shot, the anesthetic, and the pain prescription, Marilena had mellowed by the time she returned to the SUV. That she found Nicky stretched out on the backseat, sleeping like a baby, renewed her fury.

"You'd better keep him away from me tonight, Viv," she said.

"He won't harm you," Viv said. "I'll see to that."

"I'm not worried about *him* hurting *me*," she said.

"Actually I think I will take him for a week's vacation," Viv said.

"Really? Where?"

"Do you care?"

"No, I guess I don't."

Marilena's head felt so heavy she had to rest it on the back of the seat. That wasn't comfortable, so she lowered the seat until it angled into the backseat. She was grateful Viv was driving slower now, because though Marilena's arm was numb, the rest of her body ached. She felt vulnerable, her seat extending back to near where Nicky sat reading. At least she thought he was reading. She peeked left and found him staring at her.

"Read," she whispered, hoping her tone would be the first step in a healing process. She did not want to be on the outs with her own son. It was his fault, she was certain, but she had overreacted, escalated things, not acted maturely. But who could have? Who would put up with a nine-year-old acting like that?

He flashed an obscene gesture, which made her sit up in spite of her fatigue and pain. "Nicky!" she said.

"Aunt Viv!" he called out. "She just flipped me off!"

"Marilena! Honestly!"

The fight had gone out of her. She wasn't going to defend herself against lies. Viv would take his side anyway. Marilena turned and faced the passenger window. The scenery drifting by made her dizzy, so she shut her eyes while drowsiness overtook her. A sob rose in her throat, but she would not give in.

What had happened? What had become of her? Was it possible she had fallen so short of ever connecting with her own flesh and blood? She had wondered what could be worse than deeply loving a son with all of your being and having him act as if you didn't exist. Now she knew: having him hate you enough to cause you to question your love for him.

Marilena didn't want to hate him, and yet she had a feeling he was still looking daggers at her, scowling, prepared to call her names, give her the finger, falsely accuse. Why had she wanted a child in the first place? The gift that was to have brought her love and companionship as she grew old had become a curse that made anything good in her life pale to insignificance. What was there to live for? Her reading? Her study? Her research? They held no appeal if her own son hated her.

She heard Viv on her cell phone; it was clear she was talking with Mrs. Szabo. "Yes, ma'am, Mrs. Carpathia and I have made some progress with Nicky already and believe you will see a changed boy when he returns to class. . . . We would like to get him out of that environment, take him on a vacation where we can work with him. . . . Thanks for understanding. If you don't hear from us, expect him back a week from today."

Marilena heard Nicky move forward. "Good one, Aunt Viv," he said. He still wasn't buckled in. Marilena almost wished Viv would lose control of the SUV to see if he really was protected.

"Marilena, can you drive?"

"What? No, I'm —"

"It's less than ten kilometers, and I need to e-mail Reiche."

"I'm out of it, Viv. Can't it wait?"

"No, now — oh, never mind. I'll just pull over."

"I really need to get home, Viv."

"Well, you can't have it both ways. You'll get home quicker by driving, because I need to do this."

"Just call him."

"I will, but not in the car, Marilena. Because this message is private."

Great. She's going to tell him what has gone on.

Viv pulled over, got out, and slammed the door. Marilena surreptitiously lowered her window an inch, hoping to catch the conversation. Whenever Viv glanced her way, Marilena shut her eyes, but when she had the chance, she kept them open, trying to read the older woman's lips.

At one point, Viv turned her back to the car and talked as she moseyed away.

Marilena said, "I love you, Nicky."

Nothing.

She said it again. Still no response. She turned and found him stretched out, hands behind his head, asleep. Marilena envied him. How she would love to be able to close her eyes to the world, to the mess her life had become. She only hoped she could stretch out on her bed at home and drift off. Right now she couldn't imagine it.

Marilena curled back into her least painful position, facing the side window.

Viv was striding back toward the car, talking earnestly. "Yes, yes, of course. You may tell him the deed is done. . . . I have no idea how long. . . . At least twenty-four hours, I suspect. . . . Tonight then for dinner. We'll expect you at seven."

Oh no. Please, no. Marilena fully expected the anesthetic to wear off by six, and she wouldn't feel like preparing a meal for a guest.

"Reiche wants to talk to us," Viv said as she got back in.

"He's coming tonight."

"I'm not cooking," Marilena said. "And I don't know how sociable I'll feel."

Viv was immediately sarcastic. "Well, it's all about you, Marilena. Don't you worry. He's bringing the food. And you don't have to be sociable. My guess is you had better be prepared to listen."

"What, *I'm* in trouble now? If Mr. Planchette has to know what went on today, why can't he come help us with our child?"

"The child is not the problem, Marilena."

Seventeen

Marilena had long loved the Cluj cottage. It was cozy and warm, and she could conjure up the smell of the smoke from the fireplace even when she was away. Now it beckoned as an oasis, but she dreaded sharing the space with the boy she no longer knew. Had she ever known him? He had always been so distant, resistant to cuddling and affection.

As Viv pulled in and the gravel crunched, Marilena groggily raised her seat, her limbs leaden. How she wished that either her son or her longtime friend would be thoughtful enough to help her from the car, into the cottage, into her bed so she could relax before Planchette arrived.

It was way too much to expect from Nicky, who had never proven thoughtful. But Viv? What had happened to her trademark selflessness, her sensitivity? Had she really turned against Marilena? Actually believed she had been in the wrong here? Certainly Marilena should not have attacked a little boy. But he hadn't acted like a child. His meanness was deep and adult and nasty. Who could have or should have taken that kind of abuse, especially from one's own child?

Nicky bounded out of the car before Marilena could open her door. Viv asked him to help set the table because "Uncle Reiche" was coming. So now he was an uncle the way Viv was an aunt? Shouldn't that title be bestowed by the mother, if and when she so chose?

Nicky had better not agree to help Viv after he had been so vile toward Marilena. But he remained consistent. In a chipper tone he said, "No thanks!" He flung his book bag inside the cottage, then raced out to play with Star Diamond.

That was a relief. Though no one was helping her, Marilena would at least be able to retire to bed for a while. She felt way older than her years as she sleepwalked inside.

"I suppose preparing for Reiche is all on me," Viv said.

Marilena didn't answer. Being uncivil, even under these circumstances, nagged at her sensibilities, but she was not about to cave. If she ever deserved consideration, it was now. And if no one else was going to provide it, she herself would. She kicked off her shoes and gingerly stretched out atop the down quilt she so loved. Within seconds she was asleep.

Pain woke her, and Marilena was shaken to see that it was now dark out. She smelled Asian food and heard voices. Had it been Viv's thoughtfulness that allowed her to sleep through dinner, or Viv's and Mr. Planchette's rudeness? No doubt they had exploited her absence to talk about her.

Marilena splashed water on her face, downed a couple of pain pills, and padded out. Nicky was at the computer in the next room.

Planchette rose, a bit too gallantly, Marilena thought, and greeted her warmly. She tried to force a smile.

"There's a little left," Viv said. "I didn't know whether you'd be hungry, but I —"

"Famished," Marilena said.

"— knew you'd want to sleep."

"Thank you," Marilena said, sitting heavily and eating directly out of one of the boxes. Hunger, she had always said, was the best seasoning, but the pungent tanginess of the food hit her strangely, probably due to her medication. Her arm throbbed.

"We need to talk," Planchette said. "When you're ready."

Marilena was already tired of being treated like an invalid. "I'm ready."

"Child abuse is a very serious matter," Planchette said.

"*Child abuse?* I —"

"One word to the authorities, and you could easily lose your son."

That didn't sound so bad right then, but child abuse?

"Mr. Planchette, the boy —"

"Please don't try to justify it, Mrs. Carpathia. Kids will be kids and boys will be boys. Regardless of his fault in this matter, you are the adult, the parent, and your actions are without excuse."

"But —"

"Without excuse!"

"Fine! I heard you. I assume you are leaving the authorities out of this."

"Of course. Civil authorities anyway. The association is most concerned. Frankly, your role as Nicolae's mother has been compromised."

"Nothing changes that I *am* his mother," Marilena said.

"Let me be clear," Planchette said. "You are on probation. I'd like to say that if there are no similar incidents for a year, you would be off probation, but I have been reminded by my human and spiritual superiors that there is zero *toleranţa*. One more physical attack on the chosen one — ever — and you lose your rights as his mother."

Marilena could barely breathe. Her voice came timid and weak, and she hated herself for it. "And what about his attack on me?" She raised her bandaged arm, wincing at a fresh dagger of pain.

"Self defense!" Planchette and Viv crowed in unison. "What else could he do?"

"Oh, I see," Marilena said, and she felt as she had in elementary school when kids ganged up and falsely accused her, jealous of the smartest kid in the class. When it was her word against several — true or not — her position was hopeless. She'd had to resign herself to her fate then, and she would have to now.

"So you will pledge that no similar outbursts will ever again occur?" Planchette said.

"If it happens, my punishment has already been determined. If I do it in spite of a pledge, does that change anything? I would simply be double guilty, guilty of the attack and guilty of breaking my word."

"So you *can't* assure me this won't happen again?"

"That depends on whether I am again provoked."

"Wrong answer," Planchette said, forcing a smile.

"Wrong answer," Viv parroted, and Marilena hated her.

"If I cannot walk away from here tonight with your assurance that this will never happen again, I can't promise you'll ever see your son again."

And for all Marilena's frustration with and revulsion for her own man-child, that cut deeply. They would actually attempt to separate her from Nicky? They would have to kill her first. And if they were able to effect it without killing her, she would have to kill herself. Surely nothing else was worth living for.

Could they really do this? Had she ceded such rights to the association by pledging to raise Nicky in spiritualism? She couldn't imagine.

"I will do my best," she managed.

"That is hardly a pledge."

"What do you want to hear?"

"That you were wrong. That you lost your head. That you realize you sought to do physical harm to a chosen envoy of the spirit realm. That you promise on your life to never again let anger and emotion rule you."

Marilena set her jaw, her teeth grinding. "I acknowledge all that and accede to your wishes."

"I'd like to hear it in your own words," Planchette said.

I'll just bet you would.

"I am sick. I am in pain. I feel incoherent. I would ask that you give me the benefit of the doubt on this, based on my spotless history, and accept that I have heard you and concur."

Planchette seemed to study her. "Very well," he said finally. "But I must say that your record is not as pristine as you may think. No, you have never before attacked the boy, but neither have you bonded with him in a healthy way. Our records indicate he is largely passive toward you."

"How would you know that?"

"Why do you think Ms. Ivinisova is here? Just to help out? Surely you must know she is our eyes and ears."

Marilena nodded. So she had been under scrutiny every day. And Viv had been funneling information to the powers that be. Terrific. Just terrific.

Did no one control Nicolae then? Was his status as a spiritual chosen one such that, regardless of what he did, he was untouchable? If he was some sort of a god, by definition even his odious actions were divine. Marilena's only hope was to become his follower, his devotee. There had never been any mothering past his infancy, and there never would be. And she should never expect any acknowledgment from her son that she held any place of honor or prominence or even that she mattered to him.

She had borne him, suckled him, rocked him, changed him. But no child remembered such details, not even mortal ones. She had been merely a role player, a means to an end. Now she was to live at his mercy.

And what would happen if he leveled a false charge at her? claimed she attacked him when they were alone? Or worse, if Viv *was* there and yet sided with him anyway? End of story. End of relationship. Marilena came to the awful conclusion that she remained Nicky's mother only at his whim. Probation, indeed. If she wanted to retain any position in his life, she had to become a *linguşitor,* a *parazit,* a sycophant.

"Here's what happens next," Planchette said. "Ms. Ivinisova will remove Nicolae for a week, giving them a chance to regroup, bond, solidify their relationship."

Their relationship! They were fine. Better than fine. Marilena was the one who needed time alone with Nicky.

"Will she be counseling him on his school behavior?"

Planchette smiled and looked at Viv, who grinned back. "Frankly, Mrs. Carpathia, we are not concerned about that. In fact, we couldn't be more encouraged. Nicky is showing leadership skills far beyond his age. No wonder an elementary school teacher cannot keep up with him. Who could? He's displaying political skills that bode well for his future."

"I see." Did she ever see. Nicky had everyone's number; they were all in his corner. Planchette himself was apparently prepared to ride Nicky's coattails for years.

Planchette stood. "I feel we have made some progress. Viviana and the boy will leave in the morning, and you are not to be in contact with them until they return. Understood?"

"Where will they be?"

"That is confidential."

"Then how would I contact them anyway?"

"Precisely."

Marilena shook her head. Surely they couldn't expect her to like or accept this, but what choice did she have? This appeared designed to put her in her place and keep her there. She had no options, no power. One false move and she lost her child. Her mind raced with images of kidnapping her own son. Marilena and Nicky would be on the lam, and with no income or prospects — especially with an unwilling son — she would be lucky to last twenty-four hours. And then she would lose him for certain.

Marilena had never spent a week outside the presence of her son. She couldn't imagine it, but something deep within her actually looked forward to it.

Marilena was jolted from a fitful, pain-racked sleep at dawn by the sounds of Viv and Nicky knocking around. Marilena threw on a robe and rushed out, only to find Viv shooing Nicky out the door, his backpack stuffed. "Hurry," she whispered. "Go!"

"Wait!" Marilena said. "I need a good-bye."

"No, you don't," Viv said. "This is best."

"Best for whom? Best for what? Why do this?"

"Marilena, be rational. You traumatized him yesterday. He doesn't know what to think. A phony compassionate good-bye will only confuse him. Now let him be. We'll see you next week."

"I hate you," Marilena said.

Viv sighed. "I know. But I don't hate you. I pity you. You need time to get your mind right, Marilena. Work on yourself this week, will you?"

"Viv, what am I to do for transportation?"

"Where do you need to go?"

"Back to the doctor."

"For?"

"To get stitches removed."

Viv hesitated. "That can wait."

"No, it can't."

"Then call a cab. Be resourceful. You're a grown woman."

Marilena stomped back to her room and slammed the door, collapsing onto the bed in tears. When she heard the SUV, she moved to the window and watched the taillights fade into the distance. Was it possible she would never see Nicky again? Had she fallen for a monstrous ruse? Had they decided she was unfit and simply spirited him away?

She called Planchette, and a groggy woman answered. "No, ma'am," Marilena was told. "He's already left for Bucharest."

Bucharest? "Please have him call me as soon as you hear from him. It's an emergency."

There was a long pause. "I will do that if you will promise me something."

Marilena sat on the edge of her bed, thoroughly puzzled. She didn't even know this woman. Mrs. Planchette? A daughter? A mistress? And yet she was asking Marilena for a favor? "What?"

"Promise you won't mention that I told you where he was."

"Why?"

"I was not supposed to."

"Is he with Ms. Ivinisova and my son?"

A longer pause. "I know nothing more."

"Be sure he calls me."

"I'll tell him if you promise." The woman sounded almost as distraught as Marilena felt.

"Wait. I'll agree on one condition."

"I have already set the condition, Mrs. Carpathia. You know your end of the bargain."

"Ma'am, I must know. Just tell me whether they're planning to return with my son."

Silence was the last thing she wanted to hear. Anything but that.

"I have no idea," the woman said at last, but she had paused too long.

"*A face un jurămînt;* swear to me."

"Please," the woman said, "I know nothing."

"Do you have children?" Marilena said. "Are you a mother?"

"Yes."

"I beg you, tell me."

"Really," she said, "I don't know."

"Have him call me," Marilena said. "I will protect you."

Marilena was convinced she was going mad. How had she allowed this? Nicky was all she cared about, all she had to live for. If she could have just a few moments alone with him she could make things right, get back on track, convince him she loved him as dearly as her own life.

In her robe and barefoot, Marilena caught a glimpse of herself as she passed the mirror on her bureau. She *was* a crazy woman, her hair Medusa-like, coiling in every direction. Her face was pale, her eyes bloodshot with dark circles and bags. She wore a mask of panic and desperation; she was trapped and helpless. She could call a cab, but where would she go? To whom would she run? Who could help?

How does one tell the authorities that her own child has been kidnapped by his ersatz aunt? What would spur them to intercept the SUV? The wrong move could cost Marilena any prayer of seeing Nicky again.

Prayer.

The last port in this storm. To whom should she pray? If Lucifer was behind all this, what kind of god was he? How worthy was he of her allegiance? And yet if she sought help from the other side, might she so enrage Lucifer that she would regret it forever?

Listen to yourself. You're mad. Mad.

"God," she prayed, "is it too late? Can You help me? I know I am unworthy. I know I am a sinner. I know I have no grounds on which to come to You. But I'm desperate. I need Your help, even though I chose the other path. Help me. Show me what to do. Protect my son."

It was as if heaven was silent.

Marilena marched from room to room, each piercing her with reminders of Nicky. She hyperventilated and had to calm herself. As the pinks and oranges of the rising sun peeked through the curtains, she trembled from the pain in her arm. She downed another pill and considered, for the first time in her life, gulping the rest and floating into nothingness.

Marilena threw back the draperies with her good arm and groaned in frustration, falling to her knees and crying out. She slammed her fists on the hardwood floor until her hands pulsed as painfully as her forearm. She had been a fool! How had she let things unravel this far?

"God, help me!" she cried. "Save me!"

Marilena was aware she had shifted focus. That last desperate call had not been for the return of her son but for the salvation of her soul. Could the true God, a God of love, ignore that request? She felt herself calm ever so slightly, rocking back painfully on her knees. How she longed for peace of mind. But would she recognize it if it came? Would it not be clouded by the desperate longing for her child?

A faint picture came to mind. A memory. A flash. What was it? *Biserică Cristos.* Christ Church. Where had she seen that? A sign. With an arrow, pointing off the highway somewhere between the cottage and Nicky's school. How far away? Too far to walk? And was she in any condition to try?

Marilena was no mystic. Never had been. It had taken tangible proof to get her to acknowledge that the spiritual realm even existed. But could she attribute this — this whatever it was — to her frantic prayer? Her learned mind fought it, but she was without recourse. She wanted to believe with all of her being that this was an answer from God.

Marilena hurried to the phone and called for the listing, her hands shaking. An answering machine picked up, informing her of the times of Sunday services and that other questions might be answered by church staff anytime after noon, Monday through Friday. She left her first name, her number, and a message. "I need to talk with someone. About God. I don't know what I need, really, but I would appreciate a call."

Having connected with only a machine, Marilena still felt better. She was able to drag herself to the shower and then dress. Hoping someone got that message, she also prayed that the woman at Planchette's could persuade him to call. She was prepared to say whatever was necessary, promise anything, accede to any condition. Marilena determined to keep her wits about her and get something accomplished in the meantime.

By ten o'clock, she had forced herself to take another pain pill and have breakfast. Unable to stop herself, Marilena called Planchette's home again. No answer. Not even a machine. Half an hour later, she called again. A mechanical voice informed her the number was no longer in service.

Marilena dialed Nicky's school and asked to speak with Mrs. Szabo.

"Oh, Mrs. Carpathia, we were just about to call you, but we understood you were on vacation. Mrs. Szabo has had a crisis arise in her family and had to leave us virtually without notice. Her mother died suddenly, and her father is unable to care for himself. Apparently she was the only sibling available. Anyway, we will be announcing a replacement for her as soon as we find one."

Panic rising, Marilena resorted to something she had told herself she would never do. She called the university and asked for Sorin. In the years since she had left him, he had never once connected with her without her initiating the contact. She had sent notes, pictures of Nicky, even school reports. When she did hear back, she got cordial notes, thanking her and wishing her the best. Each contained bromides about what a handsome son she had produced and how Sorin hoped she was happy and productive. He even said occasionally that he had heard good reports about her research work.

Not once, however, had he written or called unbidden. He apparently had no real interest in her or her son's well-being. Marilena had to face that she had been merely a roadside stop on the highway of his life. She was convinced that if she had not intermittently kept him up to date, he would have forgotten her in no time.

"I'm sorry, ma'am," she was told, "but Dr. Carpathia is no longer associated here."

"Excuse me?"

"It's been nearly two years, ma'am."

"Well, where is he?"

"Retired, I believe."

She was reeling. "Connect me with Dr. Baduna Marius then, please."

"Oh, they left at the same time."

Marilena, shaken, asked for one of her former colleagues. But she was in class. "I'm sorry to be such a pest," Marilena said, but she asked for a woman professor she had known from the psychology department. The woman had always been good for the latest gossip, but they hadn't spoken in years.

After the usual how-good-it-is-to-hear-from-you, Marilena got to the point. "Whatever became of my former husband and his lover?"

"Well, they married, as you know."

"Yes, but they left the university?"

"More than eighteen months ago. Of course, it was only a matter of time. They must have won the lottery, Marilena. Had it been a known prize, we all would have been aware, but —"

"What are you saying?"

"Well, not long after you left, right around the time of their marriage actually, Sorin and — what was his name . . . ?"

"Baduna."

"Yes, they started living high on the hog.

Oh, I remember when it was. Not long after Mrs. Marius's funeral. You heard about that."

"I was there."

"Oh, certainly. Anyway, Sorin and Baduna were suddenly living in the lap of luxury. We speculated that his wife had left him a ton of money or —"

"I don't believe she came from money," Marilena said.

"— or that he had taken out a massive insurance policy on her."

"Unlikely. And don't companies hesitate to pay for suicides?"

"Well, he and Sorin somehow came into serious money, because they sold Sorin's apartment, sold Baduna's house, and bought a multimillion-leu penthouse condominium in downtown Bucharest."

"Impossible."

"But true. We all knew it would be only a matter of time before they left here. I'm surprised they stayed so long. They clearly didn't need the income."

"What are they doing now?"

"Writing, lecturing. Their books don't sell and their lectures can't pay much. For all anyone can tell, they've virtually retired."

Marilena thanked her old associate and became maniacal to find out what Viv Ivins had kept protected behind lock and key for so many years. The woman had never allowed Marilena into her bedroom. Marilena pulled a fork from the kitchen drawer and bent back all the tines but one, fashioning it into a rudimentary pick. Within minutes she had tripped the simple doorknob lock and swung the door open.

Eighteen

The baseball season had proved as dismal as Ray Steele feared. The seniors he had played with the previous three years mostly found reasons to not come out or to drop off the team early. That left Ray as the senior statesman, captain, pitcher, and first baseman.

He was healthy, but he had lost a few miles an hour off his fastball. Ironically, that made him a smarter pitcher — he had to be — and he led the team in wins. Unfortunately there weren't enough of those to give Belvidere even a winning season. While he was named MVP, it was Ray's least fun sports experience in four years. In fact, it soured him on playing over the summer. He would concentrate on his flying and finishing up at the tool and die.

His father would make that difficult, but Ray decided that was not his problem. At graduation Ray received more accolades than anyone else — scholar-athlete, athlete of the year, and a couple of peer-voted honors: best-looking male and most popular.

Again such things left Ray feeling empty, though he enjoyed congratulations from many friends, classmates, and parents. Any time someone congratulated his parents, however, Ray heard his dad mutter, "Of course I'm proud of him, but a lot of good it does me."

In the fall Ray would attend Purdue University on academic and ROTC scholarships and keep his options open for admittance to the Air Force Academy in Colorado Springs. He didn't want to mislead the air force into thinking he wanted a military career. This was all a means to an end. He planned to be a commercial pilot and make enough money to have the kind of house and cars — and wife — he wanted.

Viv's room proved tidy — no surprise to Marilena. But the individual locks on the closet door and several dresser drawers puzzled her. What was so important that Viv felt the need to protect it so securely?

Marilena tried picking the locks, but they were not so simple as the one on the door had been, and she didn't want to leave evidence.

She soon repented of that as her angst rose. Why no phone call from Reiche Planchette or from Christ Church? Her heart galloped as again she felt isolated and helpless.

She went outside to the shed near the tiny corral, and as the horse snuffled at her, Marilena found a hammer and long screwdriver. Was the horse now her responsibility? She hadn't thought of that. She had never mucked out a stall and wondered how cruel it would be to leave Star Diamond wallowing in his own waste for a week. But why should he have it any easier than she? And what made her think it would be only a week? If her son had been stolen, she would be alone the rest of her life. Would the association, Planchette, and his minions allow her to stay here at all?

Well, this wasn't the innocent horse's fault. Later she would find the shovel and do her duty, but Star Diamond had better know to move out when she entered. Marilena had no idea how to maneuver a horse.

Back in the house she tried to gently pop the lock on Viv's closet, but the more she worked, the more she scratched the lock and left nicks in the wood. Finally she realized there was no choice but to do what she had to. Marilena threaded the blade of the screwdriver through the C-bolt of the pad-lock and pressed the blade against the closet doorframe. She pushed with all her weight, and the screwdriver sank into the soft wood, finally splitting it and reaching the wall beneath.

The lock was not about to pop off, but the frame and wall were slowly giving way. By now she didn't care what kind of a mess she made. Soon the framing broke free, the wall crumbled at the point of entry, and the lock, still secure to itself, hung from the door.

Unless Marilena could find a handyman with skill and speed, there would be no hiding this invasion of Viv's privacy. Marilena didn't care. Anything this secretive likely pertained to her and her son, and she felt entitled to it.

Once the door had been forced open, she was confronted with a safe. Fortunately, it was not state-of-the-art and hardly top-of-the-line. It too had a combination lock, but she believed she could break into it with the tools she had. A few minutes later she had bent the door and popped it open. Consequences be hanged. She was in way too deep to turn back now.

Inside the safe lay an overstuffed accordion file. Not surprisingly, Viv had precisely organized the documents chronologically. They were labeled by year, starting several years before Marilena had met Viv, then skipping ahead to a year or so before they met, containing several pages per year since then.

Marilena was on to something. She removed and stacked the papers on Viv's bed. Her heart nearly stopped when she realized what she was looking at — from her own pre–Sorin Carpathia days: correspondence between Viviana Ivinisova and Marilena's future husband.

Sorin had known Viv? He had never said a word, not even years later when Marilena had dragged him to Viv's meetings.

One of the early letters from Viv:

The carrier of the chosen child must be bright, well-read, and at least agnostic, if not one of us. According to the spirits, the looks may come from your lover, but the intellect must come from you and whomever you select to bear the child.

Mr. Stonagal sends his greetings and best wishes and asks that I thank you again for your many kindnesses to his now late son, who told him more than once that Zurich was among the happiest seasons of his short life.

In the bonds of the spirit,
Viviana Ivinisova

Could these documents be forged? Had Viv hoped Marilena would one day discover them? Were they meant to torment her? Was it possible Sorin had been in on this from the beginning? from before the beginning? And Baduna too? *They* were the sperm donors? Marilena could not make it compute. Sorin *had* attended a private high school in Zurich, his prodigious mind earning him shoulder-rubbing privileges with the children of international wealth.

She riffled through the documents, coming to one from Sorin referring to his first wife:

Ms. Ivinisova:
My wife, of course, has proved unfit, as have two promising students. But I am still diligently searching. How much easier this would be, were I allowed to use our own association as a pool. But I see the value of an outsider as a vessel, provided she is not an enemy of the cause. Still searching and humbled to be of use.
Sorin C.

Marilena could barely breathe. Subsequent letters told of Sorin's discovering Marilena and slowly, carefully determining her suitability. It stabbed to see his references to being *grateful she would not be contributing to the boy's appearance.* Later he spoke highly of her intellect and academic capacity.

Viv urged him to be cautious but expeditious. *We are being urged to make this a priority. Don't rush, but don't dawdle either.*

Later Sorin sought advice on how to broach the subject with Marilena, his live-in lover, who had quickly become merely a live-in colleague: *pleasant enough, but not romantic material.*

Viv had responded:

The desire for a child can be prayed into her, Sorin, if you know what I mean. It's crucial that she thoroughly believes this is her idea.

Sorin wrote disparagingly of Marilena as a target:

I married her, per your suggestion and with the long-term financial benefit in mind, so please assure me I am not wasting the best years of my life.

Viv assured him of just that.

Then came the strategizing of how to plant within Marilena the longing for a child and expose her to the diversion of a weekly meeting that would introduce her to the spirit world. Sorin had been attending private meetings for years with Baduna. Marilena shook her head at her naïveté. Not only had she assumed Sorin had been seeing another woman, but she also never suspected he was anywhere but in someone else's bed all those lonely evenings.

The maternal instinct merely a construct? Marilena had never felt anything so deeply, wanted it so badly. She could not be persuaded, despite this evidence, that it had been anything but real. Planted by Lucifer? Could that explain the driverless car? It couldn't be. Marilena's fingers shook as she flipped through the pages, her wasted life documented in computer printouts.

A major issue proved to have been her reluctance to buy into Luciferianism with the gusto they had hoped. Viv had written to Reiche Planchette:

That would have solved everything, but she is a tough case. Even my moving in with her, which does not seem to have made her suspicious, has not seemed to move her closer. She's a dilettante, but I am beginning to fear she will never be a disciple.

Expendable, per J.S., Planchette had replied.

Marilena's eyes began to swim. Her life had been a sham, someone else's idea. She tore through the rest of the documents, catching snatches of details she thought had made up the vicissitudes of her existence. She had merely been a pawn, her life choreographed by others for their purposes and their gain. Her own husband had used her to win a fortune and to seed a cause in which he claimed not even to believe!

Was it possible her own son had never connected with her, never returned her affection, because he was not hers at all? Was he merely a product of the spirit world — a pseudo cheap imitation of the Christians' incarnation — and not flesh of her own flesh? She could not accept it, not abide it. She was bonded to Nicky as if he were part of her — an organ, a limb, an extension of herself.

Marilena's forearm throbbed, and she was horrified to notice that redness and swelling had spread from all four sides of the bandage. Infection. And a fast one. She could consult online medical resources, but she knew she was in trouble. The hand on her bitten arm quivered as if she had Parkinson's, and her vision began to cloud. She must not let her anguish make her physical injury worse.

The phone rang and she ran to it, light-headedness forcing her to grab at the wall and then slump to the floor once she answered.

The male voice sounded middle-aged. "Yes, ma'am, is this Marilena?"

"Speaking."

"Are you all right? You sound shaken."

"Who's calling please?"

"This is the *protopop* at *Biserică Cristos.*"

"Yes, Vicar, thanks for calling. I must come see you, but I fear I need medical attention first."

"What's wrong? How can I help?"

She told him but said it had been a dog bite.

"I'm afraid I must recommend you take a cab to your doctor," he said. "I have obligations this afternoon and was going to suggest that you drop in to see me around five o'clock."

"I can do that," she managed.

"Are you sure? Should I call someone for you?"

"No, please. Thank you. I can make it to the doctor, and I will get to the church by five."

Marilena had to call three taxi companies

before she found one in Cluj-Napoca that would send a car that far, and they demanded a hefty premium. They were to pick her up in an hour.

Perhaps it was her imagination, but Marilena was convinced the redness around her bandage had deepened in the past few minutes. She fought panic when she felt pressure beneath it and something oozing. She staggered back into Viv's room and quickly spread out the final few pages of the file, speed-reading them to be sure she missed nothing.

Marilena froze when she noticed Mrs. Szabo's name. They knew her? had known her before? planted her? Was the whole school issue part of the ruse, a setup to pit Marilena against Nicky? And the doctor! Even he, "Doctor Luzie," and the medical facility were named. But there the file ended. There had to be more!

Marilena moved to Viv's computer, but it was password protected. She tried every combination of words and numbers she could think of, using Viv's birth date, addresses, names of friends and associates, words associated with spiritualism. When nothing worked after more than half an hour, Marilena started entering the numbers backward. Viv had been born June 12.

Marilena had tried and failed with 612. She tried 216.

As she heard tires in the gravel outside and a horn, the home page opened and welcomed "Viviana" to the Internet. Marilena quickly scanned the lists of folders and files, spotting one titled "SC." If that stood for Sorin Carpathia, it might have the latest information.

Marilena stood to ask the cabdriver to wait, but dizziness struck and she had to sit on the bed a moment. Finally she slowly rose and made her way out. She held up a finger to inform the driver she would be another few minutes, but he angrily pointed at his watch.

"I'll hurry," she said.

"Two minutes!" he shouted.

Nineteen

Had Marilena not had enough to eat? Something pierced her gut. If anything, she had, in her panic, eaten too much. So why was she light-headed and nauseated? She stayed close to the wall, extending her good hand for balance, and found her way back to the computer.

The SC folder demanded a password as well, and 216 worked again. Viv was apparently, fortunately, not terribly computer literate. The folder contained a list of files arranged by dates, and Marilena quickly deciphered that they matched the documents she had found in the safe. She could have saved so much time and mess by starting at the computer, but how could she have known?

With her vision fast deteriorating, Marilena fought to concentrate. At the end of the detailed list she found documents dated later than what she had read. Why had Viv printed out all this stuff? It made no sense. If she wanted Marilena to find it, why had she not just shown it to her?

Blinking, eyes swollen and dry, she leaned forward to read an entry from just three days before. It was to Planchette.

Nicky has devised an ingenious way to provoke Marilena. He amazes me afresh every day.

Marilena was no physician, but she had read enough in the medical field to know the signs of shock. And that's where she believed she was headed. Racing against the clock, she squinted at a sentence she feared her own wounded mind had conjured up:

If we can effect this before we reach Cluj-Napoca, your man will be in place.

Your man? The doctor? Marilena racked her brain to recall the hospital visit. They had not had to wait for a physician; that was rare. And had they gone through the usual red tape — the registering, the insurance check, all that? She couldn't recall. But the doctor had seemed sympathetic, mentioned that the bite was human, offered to examine the child who had inflicted it. How did that fit? Or was it all part of the plot?

Marilena was paranoid and reminded herself not to chase irrational trails. She heard the horn outside and reached past the computer to pull back the curtain. She gestured, pleading for more time, but she couldn't tell whether the taxi driver was looking.

When she sat back down she noticed she had brushed the keyboard, and her page had disappeared. She had to refresh it to get back to the list of files, but now she heard the cab moving. He couldn't leave. Maybe he was just repositioning. But another two short bursts on the horn made her realize she had exhausted his patience.

Marilena leaped off the chair and staggered to the front door. She opened it to a cloud of dust as the taxi pulled out onto the highway. "No!" she wailed. "I'm sorry! I'm ready! Come back!"

But he was gone. As Marilena shut the door, her knees buckled and she dropped to the floor. She landed on her right hip, and a sharp pain shot through her pelvis. As she tried to rise, dizziness forced her down again, and there she lay, panting.

The room swam and she tried to pray. "God, I have given myself to You, admitting

I am a sinner and pleading for Your forgiveness, for salvation. Do You not care? Can You not help me? I'm dying."

Marilena forced herself up to all fours, her knees tender on the wood. She crawled to the phone, noticing dark purple tracks extending from all sides of her bandaged forearm. Her mind kaleidoscoped with conflicting images. She imagined herself on the phone, talking to the hospital and their telling her they needed the name of her doctor. She couldn't remember it, though she had just seen it in the computer file. In her mind she recounted the treatment, told them it had just been the day before, the time, the injury. No record. No record. No record.

But I need help. Need an ambulance.

We have no ambulances. Call the authorities.

I don't know the numbers and can't get to the phone book. Could you call them for me?

That is your responsibility, ma'am.

But I am going into shock.

Call Planchette. Call Viv. Call Nicky.

You know my son?

He is not your son. He is the son of Lucifer.

You know this? Everyone knows this?

Ma'am, you are dreaming. Call the vicar.

You know the vicar? Can you call him for me?

The vicar is Lucifer.

No! No, he's not! He's kind, but he's busy. He'll see me at five.

The phone was ringing. Marilena shook her head, trying to return to sanity, to real consciousness. Was the ringing real? Or was this also part of her hallucination? She wanted to get to it before the machine picked up.

She reached, but it seemed to drift farther from her the closer she got. She whimpered as the fourth ring ended and the machine kicked in: "You have reached the home of Viv, Marilena, and Nicky. Please leave a message after the tone, and we will get back to you as soon as possible."

"Ah yes, this is Dr. Luzie, checking on our patient. If she or one of you could call me —"

This was real! But dare she talk to him? She had to take the chance. Luzie? What kind of a name was that? As he droned on about wanting to know if there were any signs of infection or whether she had any questions, she wondered if there was anything to the fact that his name was close to *iluzie,* "illusion." Was her mind still playing tricks?

With a desperate reach, Marilena grabbed

the phone. "Doctor! I'm here!"

"Ms. Ivins?"

"No! Marilena."

He hesitated. "Just checking to see how you are, ma'am."

"Thank you, thank you. I'm in trouble, maybe going into shock, delirious."

"Have Ms. Ivins get you to the hospital as soon as possible. I'll meet you —"

"She's gone! I'm alone. No car."

"Can you call a taxi?"

"Takes too long . . ."

Marilena was fading, angry. Why couldn't he understand she needed an ambulance? Her tongue was thick, her mind whirling again. Was this real? Was he real? Could he be trusted? Of course not! He had been planted, all part of the Înșelăciune.

"Sir, if you have any decency . . ."

Marilena heard the phone hit the floor just before she did. She was drifting . . . drifting . . . and while she fought to remain conscious, the lure of sweet peace overwhelmed her. Sleep would quiet the cacophony in her brain. She could do nothing for herself anyway. Had she been close enough to the pain pills, she would have taken them all, no question.

"God, grant me peace. And if I am dying, receive me."

Marilena had no idea how long she had lain here. Her watch read four thirty, if she could trust her eyes and her mind. Nearly twenty-four hours since her own son had bit her. She was cold, shuddering. Hungry. Dare she eat? She still felt nauseated. She carefully rolled to where she could get back up on all fours, then kneel, and finally stand. Woozy.

Marilena sat on the couch. The phone lay on the floor ten feet from her now, and she heard the annoying tones and intermittent recorded message asking whether she was trying to make a call. She should pick it up, hang it up, try Planchette again, leave a message for the vicar, call the hospital. Do something — anything. But the ten feet looked like ten kilometers, and so she just sat.

Was this how it was to end? Had her foolish, selfish choices led to losing everything, including her son and her life? Waste. What a waste. But Marilena was a fighter. She wouldn't simply sit and take it. She forced herself to stand, stumbling to the wall for support until her head cleared. She hung up the phone, then picked it up to dial.

She would try Planchette's home first. Demand to know whether the woman — whoever she was — had heard from him, given him the message. Marilena would yell, cry, threaten, whatever she had to do to get answers. Maybe she would reveal that she knew everything and that she would go to the press, the authorities, expose the association.

But what about the fact that that number was no longer in service? Had that been an illusion too? a dream? She dialed. Same message. She slammed the phone down and picked it up again. The church line was answered by machine again too. The hospital. She would call for an ambulance. But before she could dial she heard a car.

Marilena made her way to the front window and peeked out to see a late-model black sedan. When the driver emerged, the car still running, she saw it was the doctor! Was this salvation or death? It made no sense. Why would he come himself? Why not send an ambulance? He had to be part of the conspiracy.

Oh, if she could only believe he had a sense of decency, a modicum of humanity! But she couldn't risk it. Marilena headed through the kitchen to the back door. As she slipped out, she heard him knock quickly and open the front door. How long would it take him to realize she was not there? He would discover the mess, the file, the computer.

Her survival instinct masked her myriad ailments. She had to get away, but where would she go? She could hide in the woods only so long. The barn might shield her, but he would think of that. She had to get to his car. How delicious was the thought of leaving him in a cloud of dust. But where could she drive? If not straight to the emergency room, she might die. But she would be easily found there too.

Regardless, it was her only chance. She began a wide circle around the cottage, staying far enough from the windows that she could dart from behind one tree to another. She heard slamming and banging inside, the back door opening, footsteps. She waited. He cursed and returned inside through the back door.

Marilena crouched behind a tree about twenty feet from the idling car. It represented sweet freedom, at least temporarily. But he would report it stolen and she would soon be apprehended. At least that would put her with the authorities, who — if they didn't write her off as a fantasist — might at least provide sanctuary.

Marilena was about to bolt for the car when she heard the front door swing open with a bang and saw the doctor stride onto the porch, hands on his hips, jaw set. Luzie scanned right and left, clearly seething. Then, as if realizing his carelessness, he all but slapped himself on the head, bounded down to the car, turned it off, and removed the key.

Marilena's last option had expired.

Or had it? She would not just crouch here, waiting to be discovered. She could not outrun him, but she had to somehow elude him. He returned to the porch, looked around some more, turned his back to her, and flipped open his cell phone.

Marilena hurried back the way she had come, keeping the cottage between her and him. She peered around the side to see if he was coming her way. From behind a hedge she saw him searching the other side of the place, near where she had watched the car. That left her free to head the other way, toward the barn.

Star Diamond faced into the stall. The stench overwhelmed her, but she was not about to swoon now. Keeping her distance from the murderous back hooves, she talked soothingly and moved in beside him toward his head. "Easy, Star Diamond," she said. "It's just me, boy."

He was calm, seeming to eye her warily. She didn't know how much horses knew or remembered, but he should recognize her.

Marilena pulled the bridle from a hook on the wall and was grateful the horse didn't resist as she clumsily got the bit in his mouth and pulled the rest over his nose. The saddle was another matter. It straddled the side of the stall, but with only one good arm, she couldn't heft it. Was there any way in the world she could ride this horse bareback?

Thoroughly unsure of herself, Marilena gently tugged the reins, trying to lead the horse. To her immense relief, he turned around. "Good boy," she said, wondering how to climb aboard. And if she did, what then? If he spooked, there was no way she could stay on, and if he went fast at all, she would surely be thrown. Well, at least she would die trying.

Marilena knew nothing about horses, but to her, Star Diamond looked curious, anticipating he didn't know what. She climbed the railing next to him, reins still in her hand. He was close enough that she could have easily hopped atop him had it not been for her injury. Now she had to work up her courage and refire her determination. Finally, knowing she was without options, Marilena pulled at the reins again until the horse was as close to her as he could be without pinning her.

She reached as far as she could toward his

neck and swung her foot over his back. As she settled onto him, his coarse, smelly hair repulsing her, he snuffled and pranced. "Whoa! Easy there, boy. Easy."

Marilena tried to hold the reins in both hands but had no idea how to thread them through her fingers as Nicky did. One thing she remembered was that Nicky acted gentle and firm at the same time, taking charge but not alarming the animal.

Sitting there in the stall, Marilena could see the cottage. And here came the doctor, if that's what he was. He would have to come all the way into the dark barn to see her. She prayed he wouldn't, but she was prepared if he did. As soon as he got within range of the horse, she would press her heels in, rock forward, and yell to get the steed to move. If there was a God in heaven, Star Diamond would trample Luzie, and she would somehow get the horse stopped, get Luzie's car keys, and get as far away from here as possible.

From her perch she could see the doctor following her tracks in the dust. There went her hope that he would save the barn till last. She leaned forward and spoke quietly. "Ready, boy. Let's get ready to move." If she hadn't feared for her life, Marilena would have laughed at herself, having zero idea whether she could get that horse to do a thing.

As the doctor blocked the light and entered the barn, the horse's ears pricked and he stiffened. Marilena pulled the reins and pressed her knees against the horse. She tried to make a noise, but that only drew Luzie's attention. Marilena rocked violently and shook the reins, shouting, "Go! Go now!"

The horse stamped and stepped forward, but the man moved directly in front of him. "Whoa, *Stea Diamant!*" he said, and the horse stopped. How did he know its name? How tied in to Viv could he be?

"Get down, Mrs. Carpathia," he said.

But she yanked again at the reins, trying to get the horse to move, to rear, to buck, to do anything. She would rather die being thrown against the barn wall than be captured by this pretender. The horse was clearly spooked but seemed to look to the man for instruction.

Luzie reached for the reins and dragged them from Marilena's hands. "Down. Now."

Marilena forced herself to slide off the other side and attempt to run. She felt like a fool, lurching, limping, staggering. She whimpered as she hurried to the exit at the other end of the stable, hearing the determined footfall of the man behind her. He wasn't even running, just striding purposefully, patiently, as if knowing she had nowhere to go and would soon spend herself.

He was mistaken, she thought, to not stay close, because if nothing else, she might be able to lock herself in his car. It would not be an escape, but it would frustrate him. If he meant to kill her, she was certainly not going to make that easy. Mustering her ebbing reserves, Marilena first tried to fool him by tumbling in the dust. She looked back, and sure enough, he slowed and smiled.

Marilena scrambled painfully to her feet and made a mad dash for the car. As she dived into the passenger side and shut and locked the door, he pulled the keys from his pocket and dangled them. She hit the door lock and folded her arms, staring at him. He shook his head and popped the locks with the remote.

How could she have been so stupid? For a few seconds they traded jabs with her relocking the doors every time he hit the button. All the while he was coming closer. "Just get out," he said. "You're embarrassing yourself."

She flashed him the same gesture Nicky

had used the day before, but it gave her no satisfaction and only made him laugh. He was looking down at her through the window now, holding the remote before her eyes. He hit the button. She locked the doors again. The next time he pushed the button, she was ready with her good hand on the handle. As soon as the lock popped, she pulled the handle and drove the door into him with her feet.

She yelped with satisfaction as he fell, and she quickly pulled the door shut again and locked it.

He bounced up, face red, eyes smoldering. With a karate kick he drove his heel through the window, showering her with glass.

Marilena grabbed the steering wheel and slid across the seat and out the driver's-side door. She bounded up the steps onto the porch, raced inside the cottage, slammed the door, and locked it. As she hurried to the back door to do the same, she could see Luzie running beside the cottage. They reached the back door at the same time and he burst in, pushing her to the floor.

So this was it. She had lost. He stood over her, shaking his head. "Foolish *căţea*," he said.

That was all she needed to hear. Whatever

he planned to do to her or with her, she was going to make it difficult. He would pay for every offense. She would not surrender, not go easy. She acted as if she had given up, letting her shoulders slump. But as he reached for her, she drove her foot into his shin and pushed him back. She got up and rushed to the phone.

Before she could dial he tore the phone from her hand and threw a forearm into her that knocked her onto the couch. She slammed against the back and tumbled to the floor. Marilena wasn't sure how much more she could take, but she knew all this was only making her injuries worse.

"Listen," he said, "I *am* a doctor, and I *can* make you feel better if you'd just let me."

"Oh, certainly, Doctor," she said, panting. "What reason would I have not to trust you?"

He pulled a syringe from his pocket.

"No way in *iad*," she said. "Get anywhere near me with that and you'll regret it."

He shook his head and sighed, sitting across from her. "You're going to wish you'd accepted this the easy way."

"I don't think so. What kind of woman would I be? What kind of mother?"

"You're no kind of mother," he said. "We've already established that."

That made her want to attack, but she felt herself fading. The longer she sat, the stiffer she grew. Her bad hand was swollen to where she couldn't bend her fingers.

"You're full of poison, you know," he said. "Your emergency-room treatment was lethal. I'm surprised it hasn't felled you already. You're on borrowed time."

"I suspected as much."

He waved the syringe. "This will put you out of your misery. No pain. You'll just drift off."

"You'd like that, wouldn't you?" she said.

"I would indeed. This has already been too much work. I have a mess to clean up in Ms. Ivinisova's room, not to mention the rest of this place. Don't make me shoot you." He pulled back his suit jacket to reveal a snub-nosed revolver on his belt. "Blood takes so long to bleach and cover."

Strangely, that gave Marilena hope. She wasn't going to survive this, but if she could somehow stave off the injection, he would be forced to shoot her and make a mess. The satisfaction of making his task so much more complicated was a small consolation, but she had not yet surrendered her will to live. That instinct burned brightly deep inside her, and she wondered if there was a chance she could in any way turn the tide.

"I'm done," she said. "Just shoot me."

"I don't want to do that," he said. "Believe it or not, I respect your *hotarâre*."

Determination? She had that all right.

"Just resign yourself to the inevitable, ma'am, and take the injection. It will be so much easier for both of us."

She nodded. "I don't want an ugly death."

"That's the spirit," he said. He pulled a small vial from his pocket and from it filled the syringe.

"Will you do me a favor?" she said. "Would you give it to me in the bad arm? It's numb and I won't feel it. And I so hate needles."

"I can do that," he said, sounding as relieved as she hoped. He slid forward on his chair.

She lowered her head and extended her bad arm.

He left his chair and knelt before her, taking her wrist in his hand. "I hope you know this is anything but personal."

"This is," she said, swiping the gun from his belt with her good hand and firing it point-blank into his face. It blew a hole in his cheek, and a spray of blood and gore splashed the wall behind him. His face went ashen, his eyes wide as he dropped to his seat, the syringe rolling away.

Marilena held the gun on him, wondering how it was possible she had missed his brain. He was clearly still alive, struggling, gasping, incongruously reaching for tooth fragments on the floor. He moaned, then lurched, fisting the syringe and diving toward her.

As Marilena fired again and again, hitting him in the neck and shoulder, he fell full force upon her, driving the needle deep into her chest. It hung there as she stood and he crumpled, and she emptied the revolver into him.

She dropped the weapon and reached for the empty syringe, slowly pulling it from her body, knowing all the while that she was too late. Too late.

As she dropped back onto the couch, the phone rang. Was there still hope? Could she get to it and talk whoever it was into getting to her in time to counteract the deadly dose? Marilena tried to rock forward but she could move only an inch. Both arms were paralyzed now and her vision was going black.

Her throat constricted and she fought for air, feeling her body go rigid. Her feet shot out, as if to catch her as her brain told her she was falling. But she had not moved, could not move, desperate as she was.

The machine finally picked up, and Marilena fought to remain conscious through the cheery greeting and tone. Finally . . . finally, "Yes, this is the vicar again, eager to chat with you. I'll be at the church as promised."

"Help!" she rasped, as if some miracle could make him hear her without the phone. "Help me!"

"Very good then; I'll look for you soon, ma'am."

Click.

"God," Marilena said silently, feeling her soul spiraling. "God. God. Receive me. Please. God."

Twenty

Nicky Carpathia awoke in a private room, part of a palatial suite on the top floor of the InterContinental Hotel in Bucharest. The sun streamed through the window.

He heard a faint knock. "Aunt Viv?" he called out.

"Yes. Are you awake?"

He hurried to the door. "Can we order breakfast like you promised?"

"I need to talk to you first."

"I am hungry."

"You need to hear this, Nicky."

"What?"

"It's about your mom. You'd better sit down."

He sighed. "First, I do not need to sit down. Second, I want you to call me Nick from now on. I am not a baby."

"Of course you're not. I —"

"And third, you said I would not be seeing

343

my mother again. Is that still true or not?"

"It's true."

"Good. Then I do not care what else. Let us eat."

"No, now you must hear this."

"All right! What?"

"She died yesterday."

"Died? How? You said that doctor guy was going to take her somewhere, and I would never have to worry about her again. Did he kill her?"

"Yes."

"Hmm. Guess we do not have to hide from her or worry about her anymore then, right?"

Aunt Viv nodded. "How does it make you feel?"

"Hungry. I told you."

"But she was your mother."

"And now she is dead. What is the difference if I was not going to see her again anyway?"

"Well, just because someone has been a problem doesn't mean we won't miss them."

He began dressing. "You are going to miss her?"

"Of course."

"Good. At least someone will."

"You won't miss her, Nicky? Nick."

He pursed his lips and shook his head. "What is to miss?"

"She loved you."

He shrugged. "Everybody does."

Viv told Nicky that she would be his legal guardian from then on and that they would be moving to Bucharest.

He was having none of it. "What about Star Diamond?"

"You can get another horse someday."

"No, I want *him*."

"There's nowhere for him here in the city."

"Then let us move back to Cluj."

"The association doesn't want us to return to the cottage. Your mother died there."

He stared at her. "It is what I want, Aunt Viv."

She sighed and went to make a phone call. When she returned she told him his teacher would not still be at the school either. "You might as well get a fresh start here."

But he knew better. Not everything was clear in his mind, but of some things he was certain. He was special. He was somebody. For some reason, people did what he wanted. When he locked eyes with Viv and spoke in his serious tone, she didn't argue.

"I want to live in the cottage, and I want to

go to my school. I do not care who the teacher is."

"That's final then?" she said.

He nodded, and she returned to the phone. He tiptoed behind her and waited by the door. She was arguing. "Then you tell him, Reiche. . . . No, of course I didn't say that. He wouldn't understand. *Crime scene* would be just words to him. . . . The place doesn't have to be destroyed. Why can't it just be cleaned up? . . . I'll be here by the phone."

Nick moved away from the door, and when she returned, Viv said, "We're seeing what can be done."

He smiled. He knew what would happen. What always happened. Things were taken care of. Anything to keep him from becoming upset. "I have been reading about humanism," he said.

"You have?"

He nodded. "It would be a great cover."

"How so?" she said.

"We do not want people to know what we are really all about, right?"

"Right, Nick. Because they wouldn't understand."

"And would not agree and would worry about us."

"Right."

"But they understand humanism, even if most people do not like it. There is a Young Humanists group in Luxembourg. I want to join."

"I'm sure that could be arranged. You know what they believe?"

"I told you, Aunt Viv. I have been reading about it."

"Yes, but I didn't know how much you were able to glean from —"

"When I say I have read about something, that means I understand it. You should know that by now. I read it in two languages."

"That does not surprise me."

"Then stop asking such stupid questions."

"I'm sorry," she said.

He liked when she was sorry. And when people said that, or when they asked forgiveness, he knew it was customary to say, "It is okay." But he never did. There was power in not giving people everything they wanted.

When Mr. Planchette called back, Nick didn't eavesdrop. He knew what was coming, and he was right. Viv reported: "It may take a couple of weeks, but we think the cottage will be ready for us. And you can return to your school."

Nick just looked out the window and nodded.

Two weeks later, when Viv unlocked the cottage, Nick walked in and held up a hand. The place was different. It smelled of bleach and disinfectant and fresh wood.

"My mother was not the only person to die in here," he said.

Viv seemed to freeze.

Nick shut his eyes. "The doctor is dead too, am I right?"

"Yes."

"They killed each other."

"Yes."

"Excellent," he said.

Ray Steele might as well have been on one of the coasts, as far as he felt from Illinois. But he was only one state away. The sprawling Purdue campus had opened his eyes and his mind to all sorts of possibilities and potential. The best part was that when he looked in the mirror, he saw a man. Not a work in progress, not an overgrown kid on his way to maturity. A man. Six foot four and two hundred and twenty pounds of muscled, in-shape, square-jawed man.

It used to be, when he imagined how he might look someday, that he sucked in his gut and thrust out his chin as he tried to affect a look. Now it came naturally. Ray had always thought it was guys who ogled girls. Now that his face and body had matured, he realized the looking went both ways. He drew stares and glances, double takes. And he worked hard at exuding a quiet confidence, a diffident air. He wasn't always sure he was pulling it off, because he was too aware of the effort, but he was clearly the most attractive and popular guy outside the scholarship athletes and frat brothers.

He wasn't a fraternity type of guy, much as he wanted to be. Frat boys came from money, and they sure weren't part of ROTC. Ray had been stunned to find that the military component of his education — for as wise as it seemed and as strategic to his future — was met with scorn by people who seemed to matter.

Within a month of arriving on campus, he had learned to fulfill his ROTC obligations — excel at them actually — but not talk about them. That had taken some adjustment. He worked at being friendly, getting to know the men and women — as the administration referred to all students — of his dorm and in his classes. That traditionally entailed trading family stories, backgrounds, where you grew up, your major, your plans, your emphases.

Ray's, of course, were Belvidere, Illinois;

only child; son of self-made, hardworking parents; high school sports star (resigned to intramurals now); studying liberal arts with some mechanical subjects thrown in; aiming to be a commercial pilot; and active in ROTC.

That last had an unusual effect on people. Even if they expressed intrigue or interest, Ray was astute enough to recognize that it was not because they were impressed. It was because they couldn't believe it. Anything connected with the military, with discipline and uniformity and the establishment, was viewed with suspicion by the modern collegian. Some couldn't hide their views. Their expressions and tone said it all, and for others, their comments boldly drove the point home.

"Why in the world would you want to be in ROTC?" some said. "Thought that was for nerds, AV techies, Boy Scouts."

Ray defended his choice at first, trying to sell doubters on the advantages. There was the scholarship, the discipline, the future. But no one was buying. No one but other ROTCs, as they were known. Soon ROTC was Rayford Steele's dirty little secret. Inside he didn't feel ashamed. He was surprised more people didn't take advantage of it. It was the perfect vehicle to help secure his future. But he learned quickly to quit talking about it.

Ray had also developed a riff to explain why he was not in a fraternity. While he wasn't a rich kid, he wanted to be. In fact, besides the freedom and sense of power flying gave him, that was the reason he wanted to be a commercial pilot. Bad-mouthing frat brothers for being materialistic only spotlighted his own socioeconomic shortcomings, so he instead became dismissive. "I was rushed by all the houses," he'd say. "Couldn't decide. Anyway, I'm the type of person who gives his all once he's committed, and I don't have the time to be the kind of fraternity brother I would want to be."

"Well, aren't we impressed with ourself?" Katherine-call-me-Kitty Wyley had responded with a smile. She had giggled at his name. "You'll forgive me if I just call you Ray."

He shrugged. He thought Rayford — which he had kept a secret until college — made him sound older, but whatever.

Kitty, a freshman, had been a cheer-leader — blonde and perky — in a northern Indiana high school and was majoring in business. They met at a mixer the third week of his junior year. Ray had been un-impressed at first. She had that stereotypical cheerleader look, accessorized by impeccable style. From her shoes to her socks to her jeans to her tops, hair, nose, makeup, everything — here was a girl who apparently invested in me-time. She reminded him too much of the high school girls who had ignored him as an underclassman and angled for dates when he was a senior and big man on campus. How long must it take for someone to be so put-together? Well, he supposed it was better than the alternative. The New York wannabes wore severe shoes and all-black outfits, cut their hair blunt and short, and disdained makeup. Katherine-call-me-Kitty was at least easier to abide than those.

Ray had initially shrugged at her barb. "I don't mean to sound impressed with myself," he said. "I guess it's a golden rule kind of thing. I wouldn't want to be a frat brother unless I could be the type I would want to have in the house."

"Well," she said, bringing him a drink, despite that she was still three years from the legal drinking age and he a year away, "if you're not impressed with yourself, I am."

Ray couldn't deny he enjoyed her attention, not to mention being seen with the cutest girl in the place. But something, he feared, was damaged inside him. He couldn't trust anyone, especially someone trying to compliment him. If Kitty saw a picture of him from before his face had cleared up, before his jaw had become defined, before his musculature had caught up with his height, what would she think? She'd be on to someone else, he was sure.

"Does it bother you that I'm in a sorority?" Kitty said.

"Hardly. It's admirable. I can only assume you're committed to it."

"But we traditionally date only frat guys."

If only Ray had the courage to speak his mind. What did that have to do with him? They had just met! What was she saying, that he would have to join a fraternity to qualify to see her? What made her think he had an iota of interest?

"Well, there you go," he said, wondering where he had dredged up that gem. What else was there to say except what he was thinking? There was no call for rudeness, despite her impudence. *Must be nice to assume every guy is dying to take you out.* Kitty looked like something special, but she sure came across shallow.

It took Ray almost a month to realize that he had stumbled upon an irresistible formula. He hadn't meant to do it. The whole thing had been a product of his deep distrust, spawned by the way he had been treated in high school. As a good-looking senior leader he had been the same person inside that he had been when he was an acne-plagued underclassman. But how he was viewed and treated had been as different as chess and tiddlywinks.

Somehow his disdain for Kitty Wyley's manipulative approach made him come across mysterious, aloof. Despite his appearance and carriage and presence, Ray was still just twenty years old. It took him a while to recognize that the very reason Kitty was pursuing him was because he didn't seem to care. He wasn't going to join a fraternity just to qualify for her attention. Inside he loathed the thin-sliced depth of her character, but somehow his disdain had merely made him appear unattainable to her.

Kitty made that plain when they ran into each other again a little over three weeks later. She broke away from a cadre of guys and girls who looked like her, and Ray felt their stares as she approached.

"Ray Steele!" she said. Kitty set her books down and reached for him with both hands. At first he didn't know what to do. He set down his own bag, and she took his hands in hers. "Our house is having a cookout Friday night, and I'd love for you to come."

He cocked his head. "Sure I can get in

without a frat pin?"

"Don't be silly. If I invite you, you'll be welcome."

"I'd have to come a little late. There's a ROTC dance that night."

"And you have to go?"

"I have a date."

"Oh!" she whined. "You'd rather be with me, wouldn't you, Ray?"

Actually, no. Irene, the ROTC freshman with the archaic name, might not turn heads like Kitty, but she didn't put on airs either. She had been an army brat, living in bases all over the world before her dad was killed in combat. She wasn't even in ROTC for a military career. Irene was just comfortable with the type of people who joined because she had been raised around them.

"I'll try to come, if I can come late," Ray said.

"Promise me," Kitty said.

"I'll be there."

"And your date is not invited."

That seemed to go without saying.

"And while everyone will know you're not in a house," Kitty added, "let's not talk about ROTC, hm?"

In spite of himself, Ray nodded. He should have just told her off, ended the relationship — if anyone could even call it that — right there. He was anything but phony. She was inviting Rayford (but she wouldn't call him that), a non-frat guy (which everyone would know so there was no reason to dwell on it) and a ROTC plebe (which neither he nor Kitty would mention), and he was to dump his previous date as soon as he could.

That all added up to why Rayford should run from this girl, but he stood there like a dolt, agreeing to every caveat. Was she that special? Hardly. Talk about skin-deep. Maybe he enjoyed the power, but he wasn't being true to himself, at least not to the man he wanted to be.

Over the next few days, not only did he try to talk himself out of going, but he also discussed it with — of all people — Irene. She was a smallish brunette, pleasant-enough looking, and fun. Her history allowed her to talk easily with all the other men and women in ROTC. Rayford was not attracted to her in even a preliminarily romantic way. They had simply been chatting about how there were so many more men than women in ROTC that girls from outside the corps would have to be invited to the dance.

"I don't really know anyone I'd want to bring," he had said.

"Me either."

"We could go together," he said. "Not worry about it."

"Yeah, okay."

And that was it. That was why Ray didn't feel so committed and why he felt he could even talk to her about making it an early evening.

They sat in the ROTC lounge Thursday afternoon, slouching on the couch, feet on the coffee table. "Sorority cookout," Irene said. "It doesn't sound like you."

"It's not. But I've been ignoring this girl almost to the point of rudeness, and she did ask."

"That's big of you, but you don't want to lead her on."

Ray chuckled. "She's not going to worry about my letting her down. There's plenty of fish in her sea. Listen, you're not offended, are you? That I want to cut out early, I mean."

She smiled. "Of course not. I don't like to stay to the end of these things anyway. And it's not like it's a date. We're just showing up together. I mean, I wasn't going to dance with only you."

Ray studied her. If she was only covering, she was good at it. He was convinced she meant every word. Impressive, wholesome woman. Nice.

Ray did not even pick up Irene for the dance. He didn't know where she lived, didn't ask, and she didn't offer. They had merely agreed to meet at the event. She was waiting for him, and they greeted awkwardly. It wasn't a date, but it had the trappings, and he attributed his discomfort to the fact that they didn't know each other well enough to know how to act.

They hung around together for about ninety minutes, and though Irene had said she was not going to limit her dances to Ray, that's exactly what she did. Maybe because he was so physically imposing and they appeared to be together, none of the other guys dared ask or try to cut in.

Ray was not much of a dancer, especially on the slow songs. There was no sense of connection with Irene when they embraced, and that seemed as much his fault as hers. This was an arrangement of convenience, so he was not looking for sparks. And she may have been on edge, worrying, or at least wondering, about his intentions. They touched each other the way Ray had allowed his ugly old aunt to hug him. And after each slow dance, their conversation was more awkward and stilted.

Ray delayed the begging off as long as he

could, and to his relief, Irene brought it up. She looked at her watch and said, "You'd better get going, huh?"

"Yeah, I should. You want me to walk you home or are you going to stay or what?"

"I'm okay," she said. "You go."

"Well, thanks."

"No, thank you."

He hurried off, but when he got to the other side of the quad he had second thoughts and actually considered going back, standing up Kitty and her silly social cookout. Ray was intrigued that Irene was still at the dance, and despite how fractured the evening had seemed, he found it disconcerting that she might be dancing with others right now.

He turned to head back, only to see Irene leaving alone. Ray snorted with the realization that she had been there only with him and for him. He turned toward Kitty's sorority house.

The cookout was unlike any he had ever attended. To Ray a cookout was an amateur like his dad or uncle or he himself throwing a bunch of meat on a too-hot or too-cool fire and trying to guess when it was done. People drank too much and frolicked in the pool and didn't care if the burgers and dogs were over- or underdone. It was about being together and having fun and gorging on carbs.

Not so this night.

Ray hated situations like this. Besides going against his better judgment, he had to enter a gathering where he knew only one person, and if he couldn't find Kitty immediately, he would have to ask for her . . . ask a person who probably doubted he had really been invited. Everyone at this bash would know one another, except him.

He heard music coming from the backyard of the huge mansion, but to get there he had to go through the house. No one answered his ring or his knock, so he carefully ventured in. He passed rooms occupied by couples in various stages of physical activity, from making out to more. Any one of them could have heard him knocking, but apparently such houses were always open and people were expected to just walk in.

He passed through the kitchen and was greeted by a couple of girls rummaging through the refrigerator. Both said hello as if they were pleased and surprised to see him. They each thrust out a hand and introduced themselves.

"Ray," he said.

They tried to guess what frat house he represented, and he kept shaking his head.

"Just looking for Kitty," he said.

The girls looked at each other and smiled. "Who isn't?"

Ray was largely ignored in the backyard but hadn't felt so conspicuous in years. It was obvious this was no standard cookout. For one thing, it was catered. White-clad chefs in tall hats huddled around top-of-the-line cookers, and there wasn't a dog, a brat, or a burger in sight. No paper plates either.

Lights were strung about a large patio, illuminating linen-clothed tables laden with silver and china. Though no one was dressed up, those who were not dancing to the raucous music — with the requisite DJ — sat enjoying shish kebabs of beef, shrimp, pork, and fruit. There were also steaks and chops. And waiters everywhere.

Finally Kitty spied Ray and came squealing. She hugged him and kissed his cheek, thanking him for coming.

"Wouldn't have missed it," he said.

She introduced him to a dozen people, always mentioning that he was from Illinois, studying to be a pilot, and not a fraternity brother. That usually ended the conversations. Kitty had been right, he decided, to leave out the ROTC mention. He might have been bounced over that.

When the blaring music finally changed to a slow love song, Kitty pulled him to a makeshift dance floor and snuggled against him. Her embrace felt entirely different from Irene's. He gathered her in gently, and they seemed to fit. She was warm and soft. She laid her head on his shoulder and hummed with the music as they moved together, and she was on key.

When he pulled her closer, she reached up and wrapped her arms around his neck. It was as if they had been made for this. And in spite of everything — every red flag, every warning bell — Ray breathed in her essence and fell in love.

Twenty-One

The year Ray Steele spent in love with Katherine Wyley proved the worst of his life, even worse than the early high school years when he had lost his coordination and his looks. He learned what addiction was.

Everything about the woman clouded his judgment, but the puzzle of it was always with him. He loved the idea of being in love. He enjoyed being seen in the company of one of the most dramatic lookers on campus. And when he was away from her, she made it clear he was her one and only lifetime choice.

That should have felt good, except that when they were together he couldn't shake the idea that he didn't even like her. How could that be? What did he see in her? His grades suffered. His other relationships, with guys in his dorm and the men and women in ROTC, faded to nothingness.

The only other person he really talked with was Irene. "Dowdy Irene," as Kitty referred to her. "A nice girl with no sense of fashion," Kitty decided. "Bet she winds up with one of the ag students. She'll make a nice farm-wife."

That was a rotten thing to say, Ray thought. He knew several ag students, and some of them had gorgeous girlfriends.

Every day he spent with Kitty, Ray felt he was losing the core of himself. Was she that strong a personality? He hated her values, the things she said, the issues that seemed important to her. He asked himself over and over why he continued with her, why he didn't simply confront her and end this. He practiced speeches before the mirror, wrote long treatises with it's-not-you-it's-me themes.

Was the entire relationship physical? They had quickly fallen into that routine, and there was no denying she was fun to sleep with. Could he have become as shallow as she, putting up with values and attitudes that violated every sensibility he had been raised with, all because he enjoyed the sex?

He had taken her to Belvidere, introduced her to his parents. There Ray and Kitty slept in separate bedrooms and pretended to have a chaste relationship. Ray's mother doted on

Kitty, seeming to love everything about her. His father was formal and distant, perhaps because Kitty hadn't hidden her boredom with the tour of the tool and die, and because he didn't have the right answers when she asked what clubs he belonged to and how he spent his leisure time.

"Not sure I know what leisure time is," Mr. Steele had said. "Sounds like wasted time, if you ask me."

All the way back to Indiana, Kitty had made fun of Ray's parents. He laughed and took it, and to his own disgust, added stories to make it worse.

Then, of course, came the visit to her parents in northern Indiana. Her father and mother were divorced and both remarried, remaining in much the same social circles as when they had been together. So there were two formal dinners, two visits to the country club, a round of golf each with the real dad and the stepdad . . . and for all Ray's size and strength and athleticism, he was spectacularly bad at the game.

Everything about the milieu disgusted him. He was not and would not be a club kind of a guy. The casual wear that cost more than a tuxedo; the inside jokes and the banter; the camaraderie that seemed so easy and friendly but always managed to work in how guys' businesses were going, how their new luxury cars were working out, and how they were manipulating their handicaps to score better in the next tournament.

Ray and Kitty spent two nights each at her respective parents' homes, and both put them up in one bedroom without question or mention that it should be any different. In spite of himself, Ray was embarrassed. It was an adult thing, he tried to tell himself. Good. Mature. Why pretend things were other than they were? These sophisticated, worldly-wise people wouldn't have even considered that a modern college couple who had been together a while would save sex for marriage. And why should that surprise him? They were right.

The drive back to campus was different than the one from Illinois. There was no making fun, no criticizing of her parents or stepparents. Kitty was proud of how both her mom and dad had remained major influences in her life and had not let their personal acrimony spill onto her. "Sure, they had unkind things to say about each other for a while, but they eventually came to a truce so my sisters and I wouldn't suffer." She giggled. "And of course we learned to play them off each other and trade on their guilt over what they had put us through.

We've all always had everything we wanted whether we need it or not. And it's nice they both remarried well, because we get double everything. Imagine our wedding, Ray."

He could imagine it, all right. He had not formally proposed, but after six months of dating they talked about the future as a foregone conclusion. They discussed his career, the fastest route to becoming a commercial pilot, where they would live, whether she would work — Kitty had no illusions about needing to. "Me-time can be a full-time job. I want to stay gorgeous for you, Ray. That takes a lot of time and a lot of money."

It was meant as a compliment, and he pretended to take it that way. He felt as if he were sliding down a mountain on his rear end with nothing to stop him but jagged rocks. What was it about Kitty's personality that had such a hold on him? Part of it, he knew, was that he also wanted many of the trappings required to keep a woman like her happy. He wanted a trophy house and trophy cars. And while perhaps he would never be a country clubber, who knew? Maybe he would someday. And didn't houses and cars like that come with trophy wives? He could sure do worse than a beautiful woman like Kitty.

They hardly ever fought, but it wasn't because he didn't want to. There were days when everything about Kitty and her lifestyle and her opinions and priorities offended him to his soul. And they always did what she wanted to do, fulfilled her priorities, went where she wanted to go. She whined and cajoled and begged and played to him, acting as if he was the sweetest thing she had ever known because he treated her so well. Ray felt as if he had disappeared. He was her arm candy, and while she had more resources than he did, that would change. They discussed this often. He was on a path to a comfortable life, and she was excited to be along for the ride.

One afternoon at the ROTC center, Ray and Irene sat in their usual spot in a corner on an overstuffed couch, feet up. That day's activities had been exhausting but ended with a training film, and now plebes were milling about, heading back to dorms, or playing games and snacking in the lounge.

Irene, it seemed, had become Ray's only friend besides Kitty — and of course *friend* was not the right term for his almost fiancée. In some ways, the provincial Irene reminded Ray of his own mother. For one thing, because he was always called by his real first name in ROTC activities, Irene called him Rayford. And lately she had taken to shortening that to Rafe. He liked her. She had depth. Because she had lived in so many different places, she had learned about people and knew how to interact. And because of the loss of her father, a soberness deep within her seemed to give her earthy values.

"You don't even like the girl you love, Rafe," she said.

He had to smile. That hit the nail on the head. "Let's face it," he said. "I'm not going to do better than Kitty Wyley. I don't even know what she sees in me."

"Maybe she's smarter than you think. She's got all those frat boys mooning over her, but you're better looking, have more potential. You're more of a self-made man."

"Not yet," Ray said. "Potentially, maybe, but not yet."

"C'mon, Rafe. You flew solo at sixteen and got your private license before you got out of high school. You worked an actual job. You were a great student and active in extracurriculars. Don't sell yourself short."

"I must brag a lot too."

"Well, someone had to tell me. Might as well have been you."

"You want to hear something funny, Irene? I actually pray about Kitty."

That seemed to get her attention. "For her or about her?"

"I don't pray for anybody but me. Don't believe in it."

"So what're you praying about?"

"Whether I should marry her."

"You're asking God? What's He telling you?"

Ray laughed. "I'm getting nothin'! Shouldn't be surprised. Last time I was in church was when Kitty and I were at my parents'. They just assumed we would go. First time in almost two years for me. Kitty said it was her first time since junior high, when some Holy Roller girlfriend talked her into going." He affected a high-pitched voice and mimicked Kitty: " 'Never again, I swear!' "

Irene fell silent for a moment. "I don't pray anymore," she said. "I miss it."

"You used to go to church?"

She nodded. "Raised that way. Never seemed to work for me though. I prayed and prayed for stuff that never happened. I don't know. Maybe they were selfish prayers. My little brother was born with spina bifida cystica. The bad kind. Myelomeningocele. That wasn't fair. What'd he ever do to deserve that? I prayed — and I mean prayed hard — that he would be healed. Some victims live to young adulthood. He died before he was ten."

"I'm sorry, Irene."

She shrugged. "Guess I should have prayed harder for my dad too. When he went into combat it seemed we prayed all the time. At the base church they prayed for all the people who were over there, but nobody seemed to mention that it worked for some and not for others. When moms and dads and sons and daughters came back, people would say their prayers were answered. But when soldiers came back in boxes, nobody said their prayers *weren't* answered. That's how I felt. My mom couldn't drag me back to church after my dad's funeral. And I haven't prayed since."

"But you miss it?"

She nodded. "Don't know why. I never got any answers, but I have to say it seemed like when I prayed I was sort of communicating with God. I couldn't hear Him, and nothing ever worked out the way I asked, but sometimes it felt like He was there and listening."

"That's how I feel!" Ray said. "I mean, as I said, it's not like I'm getting any answers, but when I ask whether I should marry Kitty, it seems I should at least be getting some feeling one way or the other."

"And are you?"

"I just feel rotten, like it's the wrong thing to do and I know better."

"So God's telling you what I've been trying to tell you. And what your conscience has been telling you. Maybe that's what God is. Our conscience."

"You're probably right," Ray said. "I do know better about Kitty. I shouldn't have to ask."

Irene asked if Ray wanted a cookie. Somehow it seemed like the best idea he'd heard in a long time. What was the matter with him? Irene moved to the snack table and returned with not only his favorite — chocolate chip with a big chocolate kiss baked in — but also a Styrofoam cup with coffee just the way he liked it.

He thanked her. "You're not having anything?"

She shook her head. "Not hungry. Just thought you might be."

Ray was struck not only by Irene's thoughtfulness and selflessness but also by the realization that this was something Kitty had never done and — he believed — never would. She baby-talked him, manipulated him to get what she wanted — always rewarding him with squeals of delight. But cater to him and his needs, show sensitivity or even awareness of his preferences? Simply not part of the equation.

"Whatcha thinking about, Rafe?" Irene said.

He cocked his head. "So you don't believe in God anymore, or what?"

She seemed to think a long time. "I still believe in Him, I think. Of course I do. I'm just not sure I like Him much. I sure don't trust Him."

That was all Ray could think of that night when he and Kitty went out for pizza. Both were still too young to drink, but he was never carded, and she had a phony ID. As they chased their slices with mugs of beer, Ray leaned in and shouted over the din, "Kitty, do you believe in God?"

"What? Sure. I guess. Supreme being. Made the world. Bails me out now and then."

"You talk to Him?"

"Him? Not sure God's a Him, but yeah, occasionally."

"Like for what?"

She looked at him strangely, as if she had already lost interest in this subject and wondered what was on his mind. "Uh . . . for stuff. You know. Like if I really, really want something. Or if I've screwed up, like I didn't study for a test."

"And He comes through?"

"She, you mean?" she said, smiling. "Or

it? Nah. Just makes me feel better. Makes me cram more. God helps those who help themselves."

That was Ray's dad's line.

"You ever pray about me?" Ray said.

She actually blushed. "How did you know that?"

"Just wondering."

"Actually, I did. I wanted you from the minute I laid eyes on you. I promised God a lot if I could have you."

"No kidding?"

She nodded. "And she came through." Kitty had made herself laugh, but Ray chalked it up to too much alcohol for her little body.

"So what was your end of the bargain?"

"That I would keep myself in shape, never get fat, never embarrass you by being sloppy or dressing bad."

Ray couldn't even force himself to smile. He sat back and stared into the distance, barely aware of the raucous activity all around. No promise to go to church, be a better person, do something for the poor or the handicapped? Nothing like that? If God gave Kitty what she wanted — Ray himself — she promised to be more of what she already was, basically a self-possessed nothing.

She reached across the table and grasped his forearm. "So, how'm I doing?"

"Hm?"

"You think I'm keeping my end of the bargain?"

He nodded.

"What?" she said. "What?"

Maybe it was the booze, though he'd only had two beers and could usually handle that. But after all the worrying and praying and talking to himself over the last year, Ray had come to zero hour. He was about to tell the truth, and he dreaded how it was going to come out. Worse, he could imagine the fallout. Kitty would be hysterical.

Was this the place to do it, to say it?

"What's going on in that beautiful head of yours?" she said. "You proud of me? proud to be with me, to be seen with me? Am I doing what I promised God I would do? What do you think?"

Ray imagined himself saying, "Frankly, my dear, that may be the dumbest thing I have ever heard."

But he would regret it the next day. He would blame it on the beer, apologize, convince her he didn't mean it, take it back, and ask her to marry him. That made him sick to his stomach.

"Talk to me, Ray," she said. "You're scaring me."

"What?"

"I need you to tell me how I'm doing."

"How you're doing?" he said, loathing himself. "Who could do better than you?"

It was a nonanswer, a skate, but of course she had heard what she wanted to hear. "You love me, don't you," she said, telling rather than asking.

And feeling like the world's greatest liar, Ray reached for her and pulled her toward him across the table. "With all my heart," he said.

When Irene showed up at ROTC drills one afternoon wearing makeup, Ray was thrown. She actually looked cute in her own way. She had to know she would take abuse from the commander — which she did, but mostly in the form of teasing about having a date or a boyfriend. She ignored it all with a smirk. *Strong,* Ray thought.

That day he turned the tables on her. As they chatted in the lounge, without asking he delivered her favorite refreshment: coffee, black with extra sugar. "So what's this all about?" he said, circling his own face with a finger.

"You like it?"

"Quit sounding like Kitty. It looks nice."

"Good. I'm trying to impress someone."

Ray caught his breath in spite of himself. Was it possible she was referring to him? And why did he care? He didn't see her in that light. Anyway, he was deeply committed to Kitty. At least he was supposed to be. If anyone knew better, it was Irene.

"I'll bite," he said, not sounding as casual as he had hoped. "Who's the lucky fella?"

"You know him," she said.

"Do I?"

She nodded.

"I have to guess?" he said.

"Twenty questions."

"Here on campus?"

"Yes."

"ROTC?"

"Uh-huh."

"How well do I know him?"

"That's not a yes or no question," she said.

"Do I know him well?"

She smiled, shrugging. "Well enough. His name will be immediately recognizable."

"I'm drawing a blank."

"No you're not. This isn't that big of a ROTC. You know everybody."

"Janie?" he said.

She laughed. "Right, I'm gay."

"I know better than that," he said.

"Do you? How?"

"I danced with you, remember?"

She squinted at him. "That didn't persuade me *you* were straight. What did I do to convince you?"

Well, she *had* been awkward, and they hadn't seemed to connect. Nah. She was pulling his leg.

"So I was right? Janie? She's got a bit of a masculine thing going."

"Don't all female ROTCs? I get that all the time. No, it's not Janie. So you don't have to waste a question — I'm not gay and you know it."

He knew what would get a laugh out of her. "Commander Olsson!" he said. "You've got a thing for the Swede. Am I right or am I right? It's you and Bodil steppin' out tonight."

"How'd you know?"

Very funny. He had to be twice her age, but it was known he was single. For the third time. To Ray's shock, however, the color in Irene's cheeks said he was at least close.

"But he teased you about the makeup!"

"Pretty good cover, don't you think?"

"Is it Olsson really?"

She nodded. "He asked and I accepted."

"Where are you going? What are you doing?"

"What are you, my mother? A movie and dinner."

Ray shook his head. That rascal Olsson. Who would have guessed? There had to be some regulation against this.

"You're seriously interested in him?" he said.

"How would I know? He's apparently interested in me."

Twenty-Two

Ray told himself that his obsession with Irene's date with ROTC Commander Bodil Olsson was purely because he felt protective of a friend. Irene was like a sister, and he didn't want to see her hurt. Olsson was an upstanding guy, though he had a history of bad marriages — two Ray knew about. And he was, literally, twice Irene's age. He had no business with her, and vice versa.

Compared to Kitty Wyley and her ilk, Irene was plain. Ray had to admit she looked good with makeup, and she was trim and athletic. Smart. Funny. Warm. She did not, as far as he could tell, date as a rule. She had never mentioned anyone else, not even from high school, and he had never seen her with a guy in a formal situation. Good grief, she was probably a virgin. No wonder the poor thing was susceptible to an older man's attention.

But what did Ray care? Couldn't he just be happy for her? She was too smart to get serious with a man old enough to be her father. Anyway, what if she did? She was an adult. She could make her own decisions.

It didn't sound like her, for one thing. In all their talks and all the counsel she had offered him, he had not detected a proclivity for making a mistake like this. On the other hand, why did he have to assume it was such a mistake? Maybe both those wives of Olsson's had been shrews, and he had just been unlucky. Maybe he deserved a quality woman like Irene.

What was Ray thinking? That one date was going to lead to marriage? He was driving himself nuts with this, and he didn't even know why. Ray had an hour before he was supposed to pick up Kitty, so he surfed the Internet until he found regulations for dating between ROTC commanders and plebes. There was a technicality. Irene was not officially signed up as a scholarship student, committed to going on to military school. That made her a civilian and provided the loophole. Apparently the military could not tell Olsson — and especially Irene — what they could do on their own time.

The whole thing preoccupied Ray and

later apparently made him seem distant to Kitty. She kept asking what was wrong, so he finally told her.

"Dowdy Irene?" she said. "Well, hey, good for her, you know?"

"No, I don't. How do we know it's good for her to be seeing an old guy like that?"

"Who else is she going to see, Ray? I mean, come on. Her name alone would turn most guys off."

"Like she had any control over that. It's some kind of family name, and she doesn't seem bothered by it."

"Please," Kitty said. "If I was stuck with a moniker like that, I'd have changed it in the driveway before I left for college."

"Apparently so, Katherine."

"Well, I changed that long ago. *Katherine* was old-fashioned the day I was born, but *Irene?* That's been out since my grandparents' days. A woman can decide what she wants to be called."

"She must be okay with *Irene*," Ray said.

"Well, like I say, good for her."

Ray still wasn't so sure, precisely because Kitty was on the other side of this. Anything that looked good from her perspective had problems written all over it.

Kitty rushed ahead of him as they walked and turned to face him, walking backward.

"You know what I want to do tonight, Ray?"

"Pray tell."

"Look at rings."

"You do?"

"Can we, please?"

He shrugged. "Why not?"

Actually, Ray could think of a lot of reasons why not. He had not asked her to marry him yet, and with each passing day he was less sure he wanted to. Kitty had a habit of getting her way, and here was the first step on another slippery slope.

"Oh, thank you!" she said, rejoining him and wrapping one of his arms in hers. "I have several you can choose from, and they all match my dress."

"Your dress? You have a dress already?"

"Well, no, but ordered."

"You've ordered your wedding dress?"

"I didn't want to lose it. I saw it in a magazine and knew I had to have it. All my bridesmaids agree it's perfect."

"Your bridesmaids?"

"Well, I know who they'll be. I haven't told them all yet, but —"

"And do you have a date picked out too?"

"Well, we're thinking about next summer, aren't we?"

"Apparently you are."

"Oh, Ray, don't be this way! Let's enjoy

this. It's the most special time of our lives."

Yours maybe.

They got to a small, exclusive jewelry store in West Lafayette, and the assistant manager — who insisted Ray call him Billy — greeted Kitty by name. That couldn't be good.

"You're right that marquises are making a comeback," Billy said, sliding out a case of selections. "Notice how these complement the picture you showed me."

Ray glared at her. This stranger had seen the picture of her wedding dress? Kitty quickly pulled a folded picture from her purse and spread it on the counter for Ray. He had to admit it was gorgeous and would look perfect on her. He could not believe the price, and she must have sensed it. "My dads are splitting the costs," she said.

The marquise selections were monstrous, with prices to match. The least expensive ring was more than three times what Ray expected to pay, if and when he ever made such a commitment. He tried to hide his discomfort, but Kitty could apparently read his quietness. "Nothing would make me happier than this one," she said, slipping on a two-and-a-half-carat stone.

It was all Ray could do to keep from swearing. "That's half my starting salary if I got a job flying jumbo jets tomorrow," he said. "And we both know I'm a few years from that."

"Oh, Ray! We can make it work. This is important to me. Please, sugar bear?"

Sugar bear? Sugar daddy was more like it. There was not a chance.

"Let me see something in more of this price range," Ray said, surreptitiously jotting down a figure and handing it to Billy.

Kitty leaned to see it, but Ray pulled her away. "You're not supposed to know," he said.

The assistant manager raised his eyebrows and quickly scanned the display cases. "I may have something in the back. But probably not in a marquise."

"Make sure it's a marquise," Ray said. "Even if you have to order it."

Kitty was already turning colors. She pulled her hand from Ray's arm and jammed it in her pocket, moving toward the watch case and busying herself there. "I'm not going to be happy with something other than what I showed you," she said.

"Something less, you mean."

"Well, yeah. You wouldn't want to embarrass me, would you?"

Embarrassing her was sounding better all the time.

Billy took so long in the back that Ray took it as a statement. No way it would take that much time to find a more reasonably priced ring.

Billy finally emerged with one ring to show. It still looked large to Ray, but it was slightly less than a carat. Billy seemed to be trying to put the best face on it, but he was clearly repulsed. "It's actually a high-quality stone," he said, "for its size."

"It's beautiful," Ray said. "Kitty, look."

"In a minute," she said.

Billy filled time by polishing the ring until Kitty moseyed over, obviously wary. He held it under the light, but she did not reach for it. "The band isn't the right color anyway," she said.

"We could easily reset it," Billy said.

"No doubt. It's cute; I'll say that. But it won't do."

Ray couldn't control himself. This time he did swear. Kitty turned her back and pretended to study another display case.

"All right then," Billy said. "Why don't you two talk it over and tell me what you'd like. I can order other pieces, design something just for you, match something you see in a catalog, whatever."

"You have the ring I want," Kitty said, "and Ray knows what it is."

"I sure do."

"We do have creative payment plans," Billy said, "and we can find ways to work with virtually any budget. Let me show you, with no obligation."

"No, I don't think —"

"No obligation, Ray!" Kitty said. "What could be the harm? At least hear him out. Maybe he can make it easy for you to make me happy."

That'll be the day. But Ray didn't want to appear unreasonable.

"This'll just take a moment," Billy said, and he pointed Ray to a chair. As they sat, Kitty stood behind Ray and massaged his shoulders. No pressure there. Billy produced a laminated chart and ran his finger along a column, stopping at the retail price of the ring. "If you can see your way clear to putting 10 percent down, which we can take via credit card — but we would have to tack on a fee, so you might want to do that by check — here would be your monthly payments for six years."

Ray shook his head and heard Kitty sigh.

"A larger down payment," Billy said, "say 20 percent, would result in this monthly figure."

"Still beyond me," Ray said.

"You don't know that!" Kitty said. "You

can come up with that. Your dad would lend it to you. *My* dad would. Even my stepdad, if necessary. And then with a little sacrifice, cutting out a few things every month —"

"Yeah, like a car payment."

"— and this would be hard only until you got the job you wanted."

"Even 5 percent down would let you take the ring with you tonight," Billy said.

"No, I —"

"Really?! Oh, Ray! If I could show this to the girls tonight, it would be the happiest moment of my life!"

Billy smiled. "Write me a check for 5 percent. We run your card through and set it up to trigger another 15 percent sixty days from now — you'd have no payments until thirty days after that — and then you begin paying monthly. Doesn't get any easier than that."

"Oh, Ray! I can't tell you how much this would mean to me!" She leaned close and whispered in his ear, "But I'll try to show you later."

I know exactly how much it would mean to me, Ray thought. And it was way too much.

It was nine o'clock and incongruously, Ray found himself thinking about Irene and her date. "I'm not prepared to make this transaction tonight," he said.

Kitty's hands went limp on his shoulders, and he felt them slide off as she pulled away. *Terrific.*

Billy put the chart in a drawer and said, "Certainly, sir. Just know we're here to serve your needs whenever you are ready."

"How late are you open?" Kitty said.

"I'll be here until ten. Listen, if knocking the down payment to 4 percent would help get it done, I could make that happen. The card would then be dinged for 16 percent in two months."

"That's not it," Ray began. "I'll —"

"Ray, 4 percent! That's nothing."

"Not tonight."

Kitty stormed out.

"Sorry," Ray said.

"Not a problem," Billy said. "At least you know the price of making her happy." Truer words were never spoken. "I suspect you'll be back."

Don't count on it.

When Ray got outside, Kitty was halfway down the block. He thought about calling after her, running to catch up, but why? She was dramatic, if nothing else. In spite of himself, he began to feel like a heel. He didn't want to hurt her, to disappoint her. She plopped onto a bench at the corner and buried her face in her hands. Ray told himself not to cater to her.

When he arrived, she was weeping quietly. He sat next to her and thought he heard her hold her breath, as if to hear whether he had anything to say for himself. He didn't. He put a hand on her shoulder until she wrenched away.

"So the only thing that's going to make you happy is that ring; is that it?" he said. He wanted to add, "Not me? Not knowing that I would be choosing you for my wife?" But he hadn't even proposed yet. The ring would make that moot.

"Yes," she said.

He shook his head. *Unbelievable.*

"Is it so much to ask, Ray? Did you not bring your checkbook, or what?"

"Of course I didn't. I don't carry it with me."

"Well, I have mine."

"You want to buy your own ring?"

"You could pay me back! It's only 4 percent."

"It's 4 percent of a lot."

"Apparently I'm not worth it."

He was beginning to think so.

"Let me write the check, Ray. Then you can pay me back and not have any payments for three months. And if you need me to ask my dad or my stepdad —"

"No! If we do this, I'll handle it."

"Oh, Ray! I love you! I love you!"

Yeah, it sounds like it.

"It'll be the greatest thing that ever happened to me!"

Ray couldn't believe he was considering this. What was it about this girl that held such sway over him? She had put him in a position where what he did made all the difference in the world to her. He could make her happy with one, albeit expensive, word.

"Please, Ray! I'll never ask for another thing — ever. I'll check every purchase with you for the rest of our lives, and I'll go without whatever we need until we're on our feet. Please, sweetie?"

"And you just happened to bring your checkbook."

"I always do, Ray."

"You're sure this is what you really want . . . ?"

She leaped off the bench, bouncing and squealing. He so wished she had said, "I don't want to badger you into it. I want this only when you're ready and excited about it." But that wasn't on her mind in the least, as far as he could tell. She *had* badgered him into it, and she didn't care what he thought about it now. It was a done deal. She grabbed his hand and yanked him off the bench, running back to the store with him in tow.

Ray knew he looked sheepish when they burst in, but Billy — who had apparently seen all this before — was already polishing Kitty's ring. "I had a feeling," he said. "You want it boxed and bagged, or — ?"

"I'll be wearing it," Kitty said. And she reached for it. Not only did she not ask Ray to put it on her, she had not required him to kneel or even propose, let alone ask one of her dads for her hand.

Ray felt on the brink of an abyss, and he came very close to simply ending the whole deal, not just the ring transaction but also the entire relationship. Despite her promises, this was what his life was going to be if he stayed with this woman. "Changed my mind," he imagined himself saying. "I don't want to do this. Not tonight. Not ever. It's over."

But Kitty stood there admiring her ring, turning it under the spotlight so the diamond flashed and radiated.

"Did you want to handle the down payment with a check, sir, so we wouldn't have to tack on a surcharge, or . . . ?"

Ray pulled out his credit card and looked to Kitty, expecting her to explain that she would be writing the check for the down payment. But she said nothing. And he was not about to ask her. "Put it all on here," he said.

"You realize we add a —"

"Yes, it's all right," Ray said. "No problem."

The biggest lie he had ever told.

Ray didn't say a word all the way back to Kitty's sorority house. He didn't have to. She was in a zone, unable to stand still, unable to keep her hands off him. She stopped him at every corner and planted a wet one on him, continually reminding him that she was prepared to make good on her promise to reward him — that very night. All Ray could think of was that he had taken pride in never before having paid for sex. So what, now he was engaged to a high-priced . . . There was nothing he wanted less than to sleep with her tonight.

At the corner with her house in view, he stopped. "I'll see you tomorrow."

"Are you sure? But —"

"I'm sure, Kitty. You enjoy your sisters' reactions and say nice things about me." *It may be the last time.*

"Oh, I will!" she said. "Bet on that! You're going to be the hit of the place. And I'll show it to everybody tomorrow too."

What's the matter with me? Ray thought. *I'm such a coward.*

He walked back to his dorm, and all he wanted was to talk with Irene. He called her room and was surprised she was already home. "Didn't go well?" he said.

"Actually no, it didn't," she said.

"Olsson behaved himself, I hope."

"Oh, yeah. Perfect gentleman."

Ray laughed. "That's why it didn't go well? You were hoping to be ravished?"

"Hardly. I'll tell you about it sometime."

"How about tonight?"

"I'm game if you are, Rafe. Sure you're up to it?"

"I've got a story for you too."

"You do?"

"Yup. I'm engaged."

"You're kidding."

"Ring and all. But I might not be by tomorrow."

"This I've got to hear."

"Listen, Irene, tell me you'll never go out with the commander again and I'll break up with Kitty for you. Deal?"

There was silence just long enough for Ray to worry he had insulted her. "Yeah," she said finally, chuckling. "That's all I need. You on the rebound. Tell you what; you come to your senses and dump Rich

Girl, prove you mean it by staying single a couple of months, and I'll consider your application."

"Promise?"

"But first I've got a story for you, and it sounds like you have one for me."

"Meet you at ROTC headquarters?"

"Twenty minutes," she said.

Twenty-Three

Though it was late, a few other ROTCs hung around the HQ lounge, watching TV, playing games, and talking. Irene had changed into a sweater and jeans. She embraced Ray. "Are congratulations in order?" she said.

"Hardly. I'll tell you about it, but you first."

They sat in easy chairs in a corner and drank coffee. "It wasn't at all what I expected," she said. "Bottom line, it was like church."

"What? Start at the beginning."

"Well, we left from here, but we started in his office. Commander Olsson — he kept telling me to call him Bodil, but I just couldn't — started with ground rules. He kind of grossed me out, really. First he said I should not be alarmed because even though this was a real date, he wasn't looking for a wife."

"He said that?"

She nodded. "I told him that was good because I frankly saw him more as a father figure. Rafe, he looked crestfallen."

"So he really *was* looking for a wife?"

"Oh, I don't think so. I think he was hurt that I raised the issue of his age, indirectly. I mean, I see him more as a father figure because he's old enough to be my dad."

"Ouch."

"Yeah, I felt bad. But anyway, he did everything short of having me sign a paper, stipulating that our evening was going to be totally civilian in nature and that nothing he did or said should be construed as ROTC or military related."

"That had to scare you. What did he have in mind?"

"It did scare me. And I said so. I said, 'Why should I be worried about that?' And he said, 'You don't need to be worried. *I* do. I just wouldn't want you saying that I used my position to give more weight to my words.' I told him I would be more concerned about his actions than his words. He said, 'I told you. This is not about even a potential relationship. The fact is, I don't believe I'm free to marry again as long as my former wives are still alive.' "

"That would have sent me running," Ray said.

"It almost did. I told him, 'Commander, maybe this isn't such a good idea. You're creeping me out.' Well, he apologized all over the place, laughed, said he hadn't thought how that was going to sound, and assured me he had no inappropriate plans for me or for his former wives."

"So you went to dinner and a movie?"

"Dinner but no movie. I thought the conversation would never end. Truthfully though, Rafe, it was really, really interesting."

"I'm all ears."

"He drives me to *Julio's* and —"

"Wow. Nice."

"Tell me about it. He's chivalrous, opening doors, pulling out my chair, the whole bit. But he's got his Bible with him."

"You're not serious. He's got a Bible?"

"Believe it or not. And it looks well used."

Ray shook his head. "He didn't read to you, did he? In public?"

"No, not that I wasn't afraid he might. He did ask if I minded if he asked the blessing when the food came. I never felt so conspicuous in my life."

"Why didn't you tell him no?"

"I didn't really mind. It was quaint. Reminded me of old movies where a family prays before they eat."

"Your family do that?"

She shook her head. "If the chaplain was visiting. We just sort of got out of the habit."

"Olsson's not a chaplain, right? I mean, he has no divinity school training or anything like that?"

"Not that I know of. But he wants to be. That's his next goal."

"I didn't even know he was a church kind of guy."

"He wasn't. That's just it. He had quite a story. He got himself saved last year."

"Saved?"

"That's what he called it. He was depressed about his divorces and was drinking too much, having a bunch of one-night stands with women he never wanted to see again, especially sober. Anyway, some guy on the street was passing out leaflets about how to find a new life with God, and Olsson took one. He said the guy tried to talk to him right there, but he was too embarrassed and just kept moving. Said he got home, read it, found a Bible, looked up the verses, and got saved."

"Saved from what?"

"His horrible life, I guess. It sounded a little severe compared to how I grew up. I mean, we went to the base churches, but we weren't Baptists or anything. Isn't getting saved what they always talk about?"

"Baptized, I thought," Ray said. "But, yeah, maybe saved too."

"Well, saved or whatever, the commander got saved. Prayed some kind of prayer and went out looking for the guy with the leaflets. Didn't find him again until a few days later, and the guy got him connected with some church. I'm invited, by the way."

"You don't say."

"Oh, yeah, and so will everybody else in ROTC, not to mention everybody else he knows. You know, Rafe, I'm not going — and I told him that and told him why — but I have to say, this is good for him. He really seems happy and persuaded, and he's earnest about telling other people about it. He's careful, and it finally came to me why he was so specific about how the conversation was personal and not official. I suppose he could get in trouble if he was doing this in his official capacity."

"No doubt. So was he trying to get you saved?"

"Oh, sure. I told him I might get back to church one day, but that God and I had some deep problems because of my brother and my dad. He tried to tell me that God knew what it meant to have a family member die. That was kind of creative. But I always thought if that whole Jesus-on-the-cross thing was true, that was God's choice, right? And He raised His Son from the dead after that. No such luck for me with my dad.

"The commander told me I should talk to God about it. I told him I had done that till I was sick of it. He said God could take it and that I should be honest with Him, tell Him I disagreed with Him, hated Him, whatever I felt. Have to admit I hadn't heard that one before. I told him maybe I would consider religion again if I ever got married and had kids. I mean, I can't imagine raising kids without church in their lives. It at least makes you think about being a better person."

Ray nodded. "Can't say I'm eager to go back though. My parents think Kitty and I go to the little church just off campus here."

"Wayside Chapel? Why do they think that?"

"I wouldn't lie to them. Well, maybe sometimes, a little white lie. But my mother asked me what I was doing about church. I told her Wayside was the nearest church, and she asked how I like it. I didn't really say. I just told her, 'Well, it's not Central.' That's where they go and where I went growing up. That made her feel good about Central —"

"And about you."

"I suppose. I just have to make sure they

don't visit on a Sunday and expect us to take them. They'd realize that no one recognizes us."

"Why can't you be honest with them?"

"Tell them the only time I've been in church was when Kitty and I were visiting them? Yeah, that'd go over big."

Irene went to get more coffee and brought back another for Ray. "Don't you believe honesty is the best policy?" she said.

"Is that a Bible verse?"

"Probably. I should ask Olsson."

Ray laughed. "Honesty can get you in trouble."

"So can dishonesty," Irene said. "I'm getting the impression you weren't honest with yourself tonight."

He sat back. "Well, I wasn't honest with Kitty; I'll tell you that."

"You're seriously engaged, ring and all?"

He nodded. "Not quite sure we're engaged, but she thinks so, and everyone else is going to. That ring'll convince 'em."

"You didn't ask her, set a date, anything?"

He told the whole story.

"I kinda wondered," she said, "what you were doing here if you just got engaged."

"Kitty would probably wonder the same thing."

Irene pressed her fingers to her temples.

"Oh, Rafe," she said, "you're in deep."

"I know."

"Why?" she said.

"Why what?"

"Why did you let that happen? You're clearly not ready for her. You may never be. I've said it before; it's obvious you don't even like her. Is the sex that good?"

He laughed. "It's awful good."

"That's not funny. That's not you. Well, maybe it is if you can't even tell your parents the truth."

"Touché," he said.

"I'm not sparring with you, Rafe. What are you doing? I care about you as a friend, and you're on the brink of ruining your life. How are you going to get out of this?"

"You're recommending the truth?"

"What else? You going to make up a terminal illness? run away? commit suicide? What?"

"Those options aren't all bad."

Irene stood and moved to look out the window. Ray knew she could see nothing with the lights on in the center. She had to be staring at her own reflection.

"Don't bail on me now, Irene," he said. "I'm listening."

"All right," she said. "Are we friends?"

"Of course."

"Can friends tell each other the truth?"

"You can."

"Then listen up. Rafe, you're an impressive guy. You're big and athletic and good-looking and smart. You have ambition, know what you want, and know how to set about getting it. What scares you so much about telling the truth? You don't like Kitty, and you don't love her either. She may be a scoundrel — I don't know her; that's not for me to say — but regardless, she deserves to know what you think."

"That would be ugly."

"Of course it would, but that's your fault! You've led her along! She thinks you worship her, and now she thinks you're committed to her for life. You shouldn't let another day go by without her knowing the truth."

"Oh, boy."

"You know I'm right."

He nodded miserably. "I do."

"What're you going to do, Rafe?"

"Marry you, I hope."

She laughed. "I told you; I'm not taking you on the rebound."

"I'll wait, do whatever I have to do."

"Be serious."

"I am, Irene. I really am. We'd be perfect together. You'd tell me the truth and make me do the same."

"Talk about threatening a beautiful friendship."

She returned and sat, and they were silent for several minutes. What was the matter with him? She was right. He had to end things with Kitty, and fast. Could he really be falling in love with Irene at the same time? Maybe that wasn't what this was. Maybe she was just a port in a very bad storm, someone he could sail to when he did what he had to do and his life started to sink. Ray couldn't imagine the wreckage when this all went down. Kitty would hate him. Her friends would hate him. Her families would hate him.

"It won't be easy," Irene said at last.

Ray sighed. "Don't s'pose I can do this by e-mail."

"Very funny. Not by phone either. Be a man, Rafe. You owe her that. You owe yourself that."

"You've lost respect for me," he said.

She didn't say anything.

"You're supposed to deny that, Irene. And tell me you still admire me."

"Yeah, I know. I respect that you told me that whole ugly story, because you were honest then, even though it cast you in a pretty bad light. Fact is, you never should have let that happen tonight, and you know it."

He reached for her hand. "I'm going to need you — as a friend — when this happens."

"I'll be here," she said, but she dropped his hand. "But I'm not kidding about your waiting to start pursuing me."

"You think I was serious about that?"

"I know you were. But I need to see some real growth, Rafe. I can't preach honesty without being honest myself. I might love taking our friendship to another level, but not now, not with you this way. To hear you tell it, you haven't been wholeheartedly into Kitty since you first danced with her. Everything she said or did turned you off except the way she felt when you held her on the dance floor."

"Pretty shallow, eh?"

"You said it. And then it only got worse. She was everything you'd been raised to despise, and you just deepened the relationship, took her home, went home with her. That makes you an animal."

"Okay, I think that's enough truth for one night, Irene."

"Sorry."

"No, I deserved it."

"So, what're you going to do and when are you going to do it?"

He stared at the floor. "I have to allow her to save some face, don't I?"

"If you can while still being honest."

"I can't tell her I hate everything about her and her values."

"I agree. Maybe you need to tell her you've been deceitful though, that you've been faking your deepest feelings."

"Wouldn't it be easier for her if I could say it's not her, it's me? I mean, that's true, Irene. She hasn't been phony. She's been what she is and always has been and will always be. I may not like it, but it's not like she has hidden it."

"True."

"So why don't I tell her that yes, I've been dishonest and that I've found someone else?"

"Honesty, Rayford. Honesty above all."

"But it's true."

"Rafe!"

"I'm in love with you, Irene. Don't look at me that way. I am. And Kitty deserves to know it."

"Leave me out of it. You know where I stand. And how's it going to look if you tell her you're breaking your engagement — or whatever it is; you're dumping her anyway — for me, and then no one sees us as a couple for a while?"

"How long are you going to make me wait?"

"A couple of months at least. And listen — I'm not interested in being your mother. I wouldn't want a relationship where I was in charge, holding you to my standards. I want to see you become who you really are. Bold, confident, honest, knowing yourself. Not acting in ways that disappoint even you."

"You've thought this through," Ray said.

"Actually, I haven't."

"You're brilliant then."

"Well," she said, "there is that, yes."

He laughed. "Let me walk you to your dorm."

She looked at her watch. "Oh, good grief, yes. Let's get going."

"You going to let me kiss you good night?"

"Yeah, right, while your fiancée sleeps with your ring on her finger. What do you think?"

Ray had trouble sleeping — not that it surprised him. What a fool he had been! And for so long. About three in the morning he rolled out of bed, tired of fighting swirling thoughts and eyes that wouldn't stay shut. He sat on the edge of his bed, staring out the window into a darkness dotted by streetlights. He rested his elbows on his knees, his chin in his hands.

Dreading the confrontation with Kitty was one thing. He might have even been able to formulate a plan of attack and then settle into a fitful sleep. But his mind and heart were plagued by the other issue. He was in love. And not with Kitty.

When had Ray come to this conclusion? And was it real? Or was he only rebounding, as Irene had said? No, it was real. In fact, he told himself, he had not really known what love was before. He had never felt toward a woman what he felt for Irene now.

What but love could make him see her in his mind's eye as prettier even than Kitty? No one else would likely share that view, but he didn't care. He longed to hold her and kiss her and proclaim his love. The thought that he might even be obligated to give Kitty a farewell kiss repulsed him.

How could he have gotten himself into this mess? Had he ever truly believed he was going to spend the rest of his life with someone as shallow as Kitty Wyley? This was as much her fault though, wasn't it? What had she seen in him in the first place? He could tell from the lean and hungry looks of the frat boys who hung around her sorority house that they were all wondering the same thing: how had this flyboy from Podunk even landed a date with a prize like her? She would land on her feet. He would tell her that.

Ray would have to leave all that out of the confrontation, whatever form it took. There could be none of the cowardly blame-me-not-you, no pretending this was about Irene. Her name couldn't even come up. He had been a fool. Dishonest. Shallow. He had loved all the wrong things about Kitty, and she deserved better.

Some of it he had to lay on Kitty, to be wholly honest. She had jumped the gun, ordering a wedding dress, begging for a ring before he had even proposed. The question was, how much could he emphasize that their values didn't even align? Whose fault was that? If he had a problem with her emphasis on the material, he should have raised it a long time ago. As he had told Irene, Kitty had not hidden where her values lay.

Anyway, Ray wasn't much better. Though his affections had shifted to Irene and he loved her character, he was still consumed with becoming somebody, having things, giving her (all right, giving himself, because Irene didn't seem to care as much) a nice house in a great neighborhood, a trophy car, and an income to afford it all. He was determined to be transparent with Irene, however, if she was serious about considering him. No more games. No more pretending. He would be more of a man of character, but he wanted what he wanted and she might as well know that up front.

Ray finally collapsed and dozed for a couple of hours at dawn. He was awakened by his phone. "What think ye of me now?" Kitty purred.

"I think we need to talk."

"What?"

"You heard me, Kitty."

"Don't tell me you're having second thoughts."

"I wouldn't call them *second* thoughts. But we do need to talk."

"Don't do this, Ray. We're engaged."

"What makes us engaged? I never even proposed."

"You bought me a ring!"

"*You* bought you a ring. Listen, Kitty, let's not do this by phone. I'll come get you."

The line went dead.

By the time he had walked all the way to Kitty Wyley's sorority house, wishing the whole way he could somehow justify having someone with him — Irene, of course — he had at least talked himself into being strong. It wouldn't be easy. He had to own the blame for almost all of this mess, but he could not give in, would not back down. He wouldn't be able to live with himself if he left Kitty with anything less than a complete severance of the relationship. Otherwise, Irene would never allow him in her future. Ray had to keep all that in the forefront of his mind, no matter how Kitty responded.

She might bargain, beg, plead. The easiest course would be to let her promise to change and give her that chance. But that wasn't fair. Why should *she* change? Her values were conventional and acceptable to most. Why should he be the arbiter of her life?

Ray entered the sorority house, and it was clear the word had already spread. More girls than usual were up and around, and all were giving him the cold shoulder and the evil eye. He could read their thoughts. *How dare you show your face? How could you have done this? You'd better come to your senses.*

"I'll tell her you're here," one said. "Wait in there." She pointed to a TV room, where he and Kitty had spent a lot of time. He couldn't help casing the place, looking for an easy exit. This was worse than waiting for a punishment from his father.

He sat, tempted to flip on the TV for something to take his mind off the tension, but that would project the wrong image. It was only fair that this at least appear as traumatic for him as for her.

But he could not match her look. In a floor-length robe, hair piled atop her head, no makeup, Kitty shut the door against the eyes of several girls just happening by. Ray had to admit she looked good in spite of it all. Of course, she had looked better. But this was what he could have awakened to for the rest of his life: someone who didn't need an hour before the mirror to look presentable and yet would likely be prepared to invest the time.

"Hey," he said.

Kitty nodded and sat across from him, her face streaked with tears, nose red, hands balled into fists with a raggedy tissue showing. She was not wearing the diamond.

"Okay, what?" she said.

"I'm not ready," he said.

"Ready for what? This? I'm not going another minute without you telling me what's going on."

"Not ready to get married."

"We're not getting married, Ray. Not today. Not this month. Not next month. You've got a long time to prepare yourself for the wedding."

"There's not going to be a wedding."

"Oh," she whined, "don't do this! Why? What changed your mind?"

"I never had a chance to make up my mind in the first place, Kitty. You jumped the gun. You made assumptions. You pushed me way past my comfort level."

"You didn't want to get married? Where did you think this relationship was going? You think I was sleeping with you for fun? Why did we talk about where we'd like to live, what kind of cars we wanted, how many kids we wanted? You can't tell me you were thinking of a future without me in it."

"Granted. But you got way ahead of me."

"Fine, my bad. I'll reel it back in. I'll return the ring and we can slow down. I'm sorry. I didn't mean to scare you. I just thought we were on the same page."

"We're not."

"But we can be, right? You just want to concentrate on your studies and your flying. We don't have to get serious about the wedding until the end of the school year."

"No, Kitty. I'm done."

"Done with what? With me?"

"Done with us. I'm telling you I'm not ready, and I don't think I'm — no, let me be clear. I owe you that."

"You sure do."

"I am not ever going to be ready. I don't

414

want to marry you."

Her face twisted into a grimace, and she had to fight to be understood through her tears. "Why? What have I done that was so awful? I got ahead of you? Forgive me for loving you that much! I'm sorry I didn't notice you weren't on board. I can learn from this, Ray. Don't dump me."

"I just did."

"Ray!"

"I don't mean to sound so cruel, Kitty, but I've been pretending far too long, and I've been wrong."

"Pretending to love me?"

"Yes. I mean, I thought I loved you; I really did. But I don't. I don't see us together in the future, and you need to know that. I know it's my fault. If I hadn't been sending the wrong signals, we wouldn't be sitting here right now."

"Ray, I'm begging you. Just step back a little. Give it some time. Think it through. We're perfect for each other. I've never loved anyone the way I love you."

"Kitty, stop. You must stop. I'm so sorry; I really am. But it's over. I don't mean to be harsh, but you have to hear me. The easiest thing in the world would be to keep trying, but that would just prolong the inevitable."

"You hate me that much?"

"I don't hate you at all. I'll miss you. I will. But I can't pretend anymore."

"Is this the let's-be-friends pitch now? Because I can't —"

"Neither can I, Kitty. We've been way too close for that to ever work. This has to be it, and we have to become a memory of something that almost worked."

She buried her face in her hands. "I just don't understand," she said, shoulders heaving. Ray wanted to put an arm around her, to hold her. But he must not. "What will I tell people?" she said. "Dumped the day after I showed off my ring?"

"Tell them I was a scoundrel, not what you thought I was. I didn't want to say this, but you can do better. Guys will be lined up around the block."

"Well, I may not be here," Kitty said, wiping her nose. She pulled the ring from her pocket and handed it to him. "There's nothing I can do?"

He shook his head. "I'm sorry. I really am."

"I wish I could say I hate you."

"I wish you could too. I take all the blame, Kitty."

"That makes no sense. Something made you fall out of love with me."

"It's-not-you-it's-me is such a cliché, but —"

"Yeah, it is," she said. "So please, Ray, spare me that."

He nodded. "We don't have to be friends, but let's not be mean, okay?"

"Why would I be mean?"

"Because you're angry, and you have a right to be. I'd understand. But I won't be bad-mouthing you. And we will likely run into each other. I'd like to think we could be cordial."

She forced a smile. "I can't promise I won't be bad-mouthing you, Ray. But, yes, if we ever see each other again, you can expect me to be cordial."

Twenty-Four

By the time Nick Carpathia was twelve years old he was president of the international Young Humanists, despite being the youngest member by two years. He chaired meetings in Luxembourg (where he learned enough Luxembourgian to add a smattering of it to his fluency in French and German) and spoke at two international conventions — one in the United States, where he spoke English, and one in Hong Kong, where he spoke Chinese.

He was featured in *Time* magazine, where it was noted that he wore stylish suits and tied his own neckties. He was also asked about his plans.

"I want to serve mankind," he said. "I will support myself in some kind of business, because I am entrepreneurial by nature, but I expect I will wind up in some sort of public service."

"*Entrepreneurial*," the reporter said.

"Where does a young man learn a word like that?"

"The same place an old man like you does," Nick said without a smile. "By reading with a dictionary handy."

The story made him a hit in Cluj-Napoca and at his school, but when Viv Ivins tried to make a big deal of it, he sniffed. "It means nothing if it is not the cover story."

Irene was true to her word. She made Ray Steele wait exactly two months before she agreed even to go out with him. In the meantime, Kitty Wyley had become the talk of the campus, at least in sorority and frat circles. She quit showing up to class, and within a week she had left the university and moved back home.

Ray reluctantly accepted calls from both her dad and her mother, as well as her stepdad, having to rehearse for each the incidents that led to his decision. "I accept the blame," he said. "I handled it all wrong. She's a wonderful girl, and I wish her only the best."

Her father was the only one who seemed to understand. But then he was the one who had had an affair and left Kitty's mother, probably inflicting upon himself many of the same travails Ray faced. Both her mother and her stepdad tried to shame Ray and tell him what a scoundrel he was.

Word soon came from northern Indiana that Kitty Wyley was engaged.

Though not officially dating yet, Rayford and Irene spent time together as they had before, only more now because he didn't have the other "obligation," which was how they came to refer to Kitty. To her credit, Irene did not allow Rayford to bad-mouth his former girlfriend.

"She never hid who she was," Irene would remind him. "You knew what you were getting into, and you contributed as much to that mismatch as she did."

The truth was, Irene drove Rayford crazy with the waiting. The most she allowed were occasional embraces, a peck on the cheek. She wouldn't even hold his hand.

He couldn't take his eyes off her, and his attention seemed to have a positive impact on her. She appeared to have an extra spring in her step, and she always looked her best. The closer the time came to their first real date, the more anxious Rayford became. He wanted it to be perfect, but she kept reminding him that just being with him was all she cared about.

That first date went off without a hitch, and they were soon deeply in love, but Irene made it clear she didn't plan to sleep with him until they were married — and they weren't planning that until the end of his senior year. He accepted this at first, but the more time they spent together and the more amorous he felt, the more he became convinced he could wear her down, weaken her defenses, make her succumb to her own love and desires.

When she didn't, he grew sullen. Finally she told him, "If this is going to become an issue, I'm going to quit looking forward to being with you."

"Because I want to love you?"

"There are all kinds of ways to show your love for me, Rayford. Including waiting. We're going to talk about this, because it's important to me. And what I care about, you need to care about, or this will never work."

"Since when did you become a virgin, Irene? I mean, in this day and age? You're not telling me . . ."

"I didn't say I was a virgin. But I can't say I was ever really in love before either. I just want us to wait. And if you love me —"

"Got it," he said. At times he still tried to push her, but he soon realized she was resolute.

Rayford had long been embarrassed by

his cumbersome name. But Irene liked it and never called him Ray. When she shortened it, it became Rafe. And so he began introducing himself as Rayford, signing that way, having it sewn onto his shirts and printed on his name badges.

When Irene's mother endured a rough patch with her new husband — a career military man like Irene's late father — Rayford decided he would spend as little time in the air force as possible. He couldn't be sure it was the milieu that made some men hard to live with, but he didn't want to risk it. Anyway, the real money was in commercial piloting, and that was where his heart lay.

Because Irene had been a military brat and had never sunk roots anywhere else, she was content to be married in Indiana. They had the wedding in the spring of Rayford's final year of school, so the crowd at Wayside Chapel was made up mostly of school and ROTC friends.

Rayford was alarmed to detect the first stages of dementia in his father. He kept getting lost in the tiny church, and he told his son the same stories over and over. When Rayford got his mother alone, she burst into tears. "I'm losing him," she said. Rayford feared she had become fragile too. Having parents older than his friends' parents had been an embarrassment when he was young. Now it was a real problem.

"I suppose it would be too much to ask," she said, "that you help your father sell the tool and die."

Of all things to bring up on his wedding day. "Yes, it would be too much to ask," he said. "I know nothing about the business end. And with me there he would get it into his head that he didn't have to sell. He would be on me every day to just take it over, and that's the last thing I want. Mom, if his mind is fading as fast as it appears, you're going to need me making as much money as I can to help take care of him."

Rayford could have had no idea how prophetic that was. Within six months of their wedding Irene was pregnant. Rayford was logging as many hours in the air as he could every day at a small air force installation near O'Hare Airport in Chicago.

And then he and Irene were invited to his parents' thirtieth wedding anniversary. What a sad event that turned out to be. Distant family members unable to attend his wedding somehow made the effort to get to Belvidere for this, some curious about Rayford's wife but most — he was sure — believing they were seeing the last of the elder Mr. Steele as they knew him.

Saddest for Rayford was watching his parents sit for their formal photo. He read panic on his mother's face, as she was already burdened with not letting her husband out of her sight. He had deteriorated even since the wedding. Having married late and waiting to have Rayford, his parents were already pushing seventy and looked older than that — nothing like the youngish parents of Rayford's contemporaries. The best photo showed Mr. Steele with a childlike smile of wonder, and Rayford knew he would not likely remember posing for it.

If Rayford heard it once, he heard dozens of times that day his father asking lifetime friends and relatives, "Tell me your name again." Mr. Steele greeted his own younger sister three times as if she had just walked through the door. "I know you!" he said. "So glad you could come."

The anniversary cake had thirty candles, of course, and Rayford's father watched with curious glee as his wife blew them out in three great puffs. "How old are you?" he asked. "Aren't we going to sing the birthday song?"

The party was almost over. Rayford's father had gone to take a nap even before some of the guests began leaving. Rayford's mother pulled her son into a corner.

"There's something I want you to pray with me about, Son," she said.

His eyes darted. This was not like her. Surely she wasn't going to ask him to pray right then and there.

"You still pray, don't you, Rayford?"

"Uh, yeah. Sure. 'Course I do." He couldn't remember the last time. And what God was allowing to happen to his father wasn't likely to change that. Irene resented God for allowing her father to be killed. Well, this was worse. It would have been easier to hear that his father had been hit by a car or died in his sleep. "Just don't ask me to pray for Dad's healing, because that's not going to hap—"

"That's not it," she said, fighting to keep her composure. "It's just that Daddy and I had a goal. The odds were against us because of how old we were when we married, but we've talked about it since the day we fell in love."

Rayford was already uncomfortable with this, whatever it was. He had never heard his parents talk about being in love. They were nice enough to each other, didn't argue or fight much, but neither had they ever been terribly affectionate.

Rayford and his mother kept being interrupted by people saying their good-byes.

"Mom, we're being rude. Can this wait?"

"I shouldn't burden you with it anyway," she said.

"You're the hostess. You should —"

"Fine," she said, abruptly moving toward the door.

Rayford couldn't deny he was relieved, but he felt guilty watching her do her duty with a tight-lipped smile, her face red and her eyes full.

Irene slipped her hand into his. "What was that all about?" When he told her, she said, "Rafe, you must pursue it. She won't get back to it. Convince her it's your top priority. You're all she has left. She has to know she can unburden herself to you."

"Irene, whatever it is is going to require something I don't have to give. You and I are trying to get established. I want a house, a decent car or two, a good job . . ."

"Don't you believe in karma?"

"Karma? Hardly."

"Sure you do. We agree that what goes around comes around, don't we?"

He backed away and squinted at her.

"Don't look at me that way, Rafe. I'm just saying that if you don't do right by your parents, the same thing is bound to happen to you someday."

When everyone else had left, Rayford noticed his mother pointedly ignoring him. He approached her and said, "Mom, I want to get back to that conversation."

"No, you don't."

He looked at Irene, who nodded at him and pointed to the other room.

"Yes, I do. Now come sit down. You were telling me what was so important to you and Dad."

He could see in her eyes that his lie had convinced her. He wanted to have this conversation the way he wanted to spend an afternoon at the mall when the Bears were on television.

She took his hands in hers and led him to the couch in the living room. "Here's what I want you to pray about, Rayford. Though it's clear Daddy's mind is going and it's likely Alzheimer's, the doctor says he is otherwise healthy as a horse. I don't know why they always say it that way, like horses are healthier than other animals. They aren't, are they? I never heard that they were."

"I don't know, Mom. Back to your story."

"Sorry. Anyway, Daddy and I always said we wanted to celebrate fifty years together."

"Fifty years?"

She nodded.

"He probably can't even remember wanting that," Rayford said, regretting it as soon as it was out of his mouth.

"Don't be cruel."

"No, I'm just saying . . . if there's a benefit to this malady, it's that he will not likely be disappointed by missing those things he can't even remember hoping for."

"Well, *I'm* hoping for it, okay?"

That was so like her. And it made Rayford feel bad.

"The doctor says it's possible he will live another twenty years," she said. "We'll have to institutionalize him eventually, which should make it easier for *me* to last twenty more years."

"Why is that so important, Mom? I'm not disparaging it. I really want to know."

She dabbed at her eyes. "Besides raising a fine son and wishing for all the best for you, being married fifty years was our life's goal. I'd still like to make it, whether he's aware of it or not."

Rayford could only imagine their fiftieth anniversary photograph.

"So will you pray with me about that?" she said. "Maybe when you go to bed at night."

He nodded, not wanting to put this lie into words.

"You still pray when you go to bed, don't you, Rayford?"

"Sometimes."

"I believe in prayer," she said.

I don't.

Rayford's impatience for the good life grew into frustration as he and Irene slogged through their days in a tiny apartment. He was excited about the impending child, of course, but though he loved all the flight time he was logging, life seemed to drag. Irene became more tired and irritable while the baby grew within her. Rayford's mother became needier when his father was sent to a facility that required as much of Rayford's monthly income as he could afford to bridge the gap between the cost and his parents' insurance.

It wasn't that Rayford begrudged helping. But his own dreams were on hold. How would he ever afford a house, cars, all the things that made life worth living?

As thrilling as the birth of their daughter, Chloe, was, Rayford had to admit that even that glow didn't last. He was flooded with love for her, but he had envisioned more fatherly things than just helping Irene with chores, changing the baby, and fetching her in the night so Irene could nurse her.

Rayford hated himself for feeling that way. He still loved his daughter and his wife, of course, but the fact was that his life was not yet what he dreamed it would be.

Then there was Irene's eagerness to start going to church again.

"I thought you had learned your lesson about all that," Rayford said.

"All I've learned is that I don't know so much," she said. "I miss the best things about it, and I told you years ago I didn't want to raise a child without religion in her life."

And so they began attending a big church where Rayford could easily get lost in the crowd and slip out as soon as it was over.

Irene seemed pleased enough. She appeared to enjoy being a wife and mother, spending time with Rayford and helping him in his career. But that wasn't enough for him. Rayford applied to all the major airlines and devoted himself to qualifying on bigger and bigger jets.

The bottom line was that life was not as fun as he thought it would be. Money, he was convinced, would change that. Prestige, which went with captaining an airliner, would too.

The happiest day of Rayford Steele's

life — though he didn't admit to Irene that it superseded even their wedding day, their honeymoon night, or the birth of their daughter — came when he got the offer from Pan-Continental Airlines to become a flight engineer in the cockpit for flying 747-200s. He had trained on the monsters in the air force and impressed the Pan-Con brass.

Standing before the mirror in his new dress blues with Irene and Chloe, then four, admiring him and cooing over him, Rayford could not stop grinning. At six-four and two hundred and twenty pounds, his gold braid and buttons gleaming, all he could think of was a house in the suburbs and a great new car. Within a month he was dreamily, satis-fyingly, as deep in debt as he could afford.

Irene cautioned that they had bought more house than they needed, but Rayford could see in her eyes that she loved the place. She had been a fastidious house-keeper in their dingy apartment, but now she was a woman on a mission. Creative and precise, she made their new home neat and gorgeous — a haven.

Complicating Rayford's life, however, was the fact that his father was now altogether incapacitated. He was in the full-care unit, nearly twice as expensive as the normal resi-dence had been. Rayford's mother had deteriorated as well. She seemed older and more fragile than ever. That her husband did not recognize or even acknowledge her seemed to crush her spirit.

Worse, though Rayford tried to convince himself otherwise, he detected symptoms in his mother he had noticed in his dad before he was diagnosed. "Tell me it's just normal aging, Irene," he said.

"I wish I could."

For the next few years, the Steeles lived on the edge of solvency. When his mother was also institutionalized, Rayford drowned in the many details of selling off the family home, trying to salvage something from the sale of the tool and die, and attempting to stay afloat financially. Despite what he called "too much month at the end of the money" every paycheck, his income allowed him more credit than he could afford. He would not deny himself a BMW convertible and a sedan for his wife.

"I don't need this," Irene said. "Can we afford it?"

"Of course," he said. "Don't deny me the privilege of buying you something nice."

Though it racked him with guilt, Rayford began wishing his parents would die. He told himself it would be better for them. His father had long since been virtually gone, unaware of his surroundings, enjoying hardly anything resembling quality of life. And his mother was hard on his heels. They would be better off, and so would Rayford and his family.

Nick Carpathia somehow avoided the typical travails of preadolescence. He never went through a gangly or awkward stage. His glowing skin never broke out. By the time he was sixteen he was so far ahead of his peers that he could have tested out of high school. But he wanted to be valedictorian first. Once that was accomplished, he enrolled at the University of Romania at Bucharest, determined to graduate in two years.

"I want to stay at the InterContinental," he told Aunt Viv.

"That would be exorbitant," she said.

"And I want Star Diamond boarded as close by as possible."

"I'll see what I can do."

Of course she would. She had apparently been put on earth to do Nick's bidding. He found her amusing. He loved going to her classes and beating her to the punch. The netherworld seemed to communicate with him first, and it was not beyond him to clarify messages for her or even shout them out before they reached her.

Irene Steele had talked of having another child, but Rayford wouldn't hear of it. He didn't want to tell her how delicate their financial situation had become, but she had to have an idea. When Chloe was seven years old, Irene carefully broke the news to Rayford: another baby was on the way.

He tried to act excited, but he couldn't muster the requisite enthusiasm. That threw Irene into a funk that lasted until she was able to announce that it was a boy and that she hoped Rayford would agree to name him after himself. Rayford's ego was stroked, and he even looked into moving to a better neighborhood — until Irene put the kibosh on that. "You think I can't read our bank statements?" she said. "I admire what you're doing for your parents, but as long as that continues, this is going to be our lot."

Rayford enjoyed striding through the corridors of the country's major airports. He was already graying, but he liked the new look, and Irene said it only made him more distinguished.

When he was nineteen Nick Carpathia demanded a meeting with Reiche Planchette. "It is time for me to know my natural history," he said.

"Meaning?"

"You know what I mean, Reiche." He could tell Planchette didn't like to be referred to by his first name, especially by a teenager. "I want to know who my father is."

"Impossible. Thoroughly confidential."

"By tomorrow," Nick said.

"I'll see what I can do."

The next day Planchette arrived at Nick's suite with a thick folder. "I need not remind you how highly classified this information is."

"Then why remind me, Reiche? Just let me see it."

"I can't leave it with you. It is not to leave my —"

"You have copies."

"Of course, but —"

"I will return these to you tomorrow."

"Very well."

The next day Nick showed up at Planchette's tiny office in a dingy building in downtown Bucharest. "This place is an embarrassment to the association," Nick said.

"All our money goes to your lodging and whims, Nick."

Young Carpathia stared at him. "Do I detect resentment, Reiche?"

"Maybe. Are you familiar with the phrase *high maintenance?*"

Nick rubbed his eyes and let his head roll back. "Oh, Reiche. Are you familiar with the term *unemployment?*"

Planchette stood. "I've been a loyal employee of the association long enough to not have to be subjected —"

"Oh, sit down. I have questions about this file."

"I can't imagine, Nick. Everything is there."

"So I am a freak. I have two fathers."

"Correct. Well, not the freak part, but yes."

"And they have been given all this money?"

"By Mr. Stonagal, yes."

"And you complain about *my* expenses?"

"Well —"

"Stonagal has a sea of money, Reiche. I would say that, so far, I am a bargain. I want two things: a stake in an international import/export business. Say ten million euros to start."

"Ten *million!*"

"And I want these two opportunists off the payroll."

"Impossible."

"Not if they are eliminated."

"They are your fathers. We can't just —"

"Am I having trouble making myself understood, Reiche?"

"I'll pass the word along, Nick."

Carpathia tossed the folder onto Planchette's desk, and it pushed other papers onto the floor as it slid to him. "That reminds me. I guess I want a third thing: to be referred to by my given name."

"Nicolae? You seem —"

"Good guess, Reiche."

"You seem so young —"

"To be making more money than you? Was that what you were going to say?"

"No. I just —"

"Because that will be true soon; will it not?"

"Well, I — I mean, the powers that be will have to decide whether your being a businessman is in the best interest of —"

Nicolae stood. "Please, Reiche, spare me the time, would you?"

Planchette sighed and hefted the folder, scowling.

"You are going to resent working for me; are you not, Reiche?"

Planchette cocked his head. "Am I?"

"Going to resent it or going to work for me? Because there is no question of the latter. The only question is the former."

"I am a loyal soldier, Nick . . . olae. Nicolae. I will do what I am called upon to do."

"I know you will. Tell me something. When does one get the privilege of talking to the big guy, the leader, the boss?"

"Stonagal?"

Nicolae laughed. "You think *he* is in charge? Maybe that is why you will be working for me before long. You know who I am talking about."

"The chief spirit? That is a privilege. A rare privilege."

"How about you, Reiche? Have you had the privilege?"

"Two different times, now many years ago. Ms. Ivinisova too. Just once for her. But I can tell you this: it isn't like you talk to him; he talks to you."

"But you can then respond, right?"

"Of course."

"I cannot wait."

Twenty-Five

When he finally became a captain, Rayford believed he had arrived. He got his finances under some modicum of control, and he looked forward to the birth of Rayford Jr., whom Irene was already referring to as Raymie.

"That makes no sense if he's a Rayford Jr.," Rayford said, but the name stuck.

He loved flying, being in charge, supervising a crew, chatting up the passengers; and he took satisfaction in his perfect safety record. But when Rayford allowed himself the luxury of assessing his life, he had to admit he was living for himself, not for anyone else. Oh, he did things for Irene and Chloe and soon Raymie. But everything revolved around him.

Rayford was proud he had never allowed his love for alcohol to impede his work. One December afternoon, just after he arrived for a flight, O'Hare had been shut down due to heavy snow. The forecast looked bleak, and he assumed he would be sent home soon. So he and a few colleagues enjoyed a couple of martinis each, then hung around in the pilots' lounge, waiting to be released.

But suddenly the snow stopped, the plows gained purchase on the runways, and the announcement came that takeoffs would begin again in half an hour. Rayford asked his teammates if they were up to flying after drinking. To a person, each said he had had only a couple and felt fine about proceeding.

Rayford felt the same but also believed he shouldn't risk it. He called his supervisor, Earl Halliday. "I'll take whatever dock in pay you have to mete out, Earl," he said, "but I had a couple of martinis when I was sure we'd be grounded, and now I'm afraid I had better ground myself."

"Where'm I gonna get a replacement at this hour, Steele?" Halliday said. "You sure two martinis are going to have an effect on a big guy like you?"

"I'm sorry, Earl. But I'm not going to drive a fully loaded heavy tonight."

Halliday slammed down the phone, but on Rayford's way home — confident to drive himself but not to be responsible for hundreds of passengers — he took a call from Earl. "Got somebody, in case you're interested."

"That's a relief. Sorry about that, Chief. I won't let it happen again. What's it going to cost me?"

"Nothing."

"Say again?"

"You did the right thing, Steele, and I'm proud of you. You gave me a headache, but the alternative could have been a nightmare. Good man."

Irene seemed to love to tell that story. Rayford had to ask her to quit referring to him as her "straight-arrow captain," though secretly he was thrilled that she was proud of him. That's why his brush with infidelity would have flattened her. He could never tell Irene, and he lived with the guilt of it — even though, thankfully, it stopped short of actual adultery — for years.

It happened just two weeks after he had grounded himself. He and Irene were about to head to Earl Halliday's staff Christmas party when at the last minute Irene announced she couldn't make it. She was two weeks from delivery and not feeling well, but she insisted he go and enjoy himself and greet everyone for her.

He wasn't scheduled to fly that night, of

course, and knowing he could get a cab home, Rayford did not temper his thirst. He was not the type to dance on tables, but he sensed himself getting louder and friendlier as the night wore on. Trish, a beautiful young intern in Earl's office — the one who always smiled when he dropped by — flirted with him all evening. Her boyfriend was out of town, and when she said one too many times that she would love to get Rayford alone, he said, "You'd better quit advertising if you're not selling."

"Oh, I'm selling," she said, "if you're buying."

While some were holding forth at the top of their lungs around the piano and others were dancing, Trish grabbed Rayford's hand and pulled him into a secluded closet.

Five minutes later, after some heavy necking, Rayford pulled away. "I'm not going to do this," he said.

"Oh, come on, Captain. I won't tell."

"Neither would I, but I would know. And I'd like to be able to face myself tomorrow. Irene is —"

"I know," she said. "Go home to your pregnant wife. There are more where you came from."

Two days later, racked by a guilt he would never fully shed, Rayford dreaded a visit to

Earl's office. The boss just had routine business with him, but Rayford didn't want to face Trish. No such luck. She greeted him on his way in and asked if he had a minute later.

On his way out she beckoned him to a corner where they could be seen but not heard. "I want to apologize for the other night," she said.

"Don't give it another thought," he said. "We were both drunk."

"Not as drunk as I got later, thinking about my boyfriend. He's about to pop the question, and I feel terrible."

"Imagine how I feel, Trish."

"Forgive me," she said.

"It never happened," he said.

But it happened over and over in his mind for the next several years. The pangs hit him at the strangest times. It might be when he was frolicking with Raymie or playing with Chloe or just talking with Irene. At times he felt such a compulsion to confess to his wife that he had to find other things to distract himself. Nothing had really happened, and while it had been stupid and would have infuriated him if it had been Irene with some guy, he knew telling her would only hurt her and that nothing positive could come of it besides getting it off his conscience. Trish had long since left the airline, married, and moved away.

So what was the guilt all about? It certainly hadn't come from their church, something he had feared when first they began to attend. He actually liked the generic flavor of the services. No one was made to feel like a worthless sinner. There was just lots of inspiration and friendliness. No wonder people enjoyed going there.

Strangely, in the last several months, Irene had seemed to grow restless. "There has to be more," she said more than once. "Don't you ever feel like you'd like to reconnect with God, Rayford? Personally, I mean."

He had to think about that one. "That implies we were once connected."

"Weren't you, ever? I feel like I was. Until He didn't answer my prayers."

Rayford shook his head. "I was never really into it. I mean, I'm okay with church. And I believe in God; don't get me wrong. But I don't want to become some fundamentalist or literalist or whatever they call those people who talk to God every day and think He talks to them too."

"I don't want to be a weirdo either, Rafe," Irene said. "But feeling like you're actually talking with God and He's communicating with you? What could be better than that?"

By age twenty-one, Nicolae Carpathia was nearly finished with graduate school and ran an import/export empire with Reiche Planchette low on his payroll. Carpathia was on the cover of every business magazine in Europe, and while he had not yet made the cover of *Time* or *Global Weekly*, that couldn't be far off.

He lived in a mansion on the outskirts of Bucharest, not a half mile from where his biological fathers had been assassinated a few years before. Viv Ivins enjoyed quarters on the top floor and managed his personal affairs. She supervised his valets, his drivers, his household and garden staff. His every need was cared for.

Nicolae was in the middle of two projects: clandestinely hiring an off-the-books cadre of professional facilitators who would make sure his least cooperative competitors met the same fate his fathers and his mother had, and surrounding himself with the politically astute. His next horizon was government. First he would get himself elected to the Romanian parliament. Then he would angle for the presidency. Next step Europe. Ultimate goal: the world.

There was no such position yet, of course,

leader of the world. But by the time he ascended, there would be. He just knew it.

The day would come when Rayford Steele tried desperately to communicate with God. He and Irene had been married a dozen years. Chloe was eleven, Raymie three.

Rayford had just been named captain on a Pan-Con Boeing 747-400 and was about to fly from O'Hare to LAX with a first officer who introduced himself as Christopher Smith. "I go by Chris." A couple of years younger than Rayford, Chris said he was married and had two elementary-school–age boys. He seemed a seasoned, no-nonsense guy — the type Rayford appreciated. Having only two men in the cockpit of a heavy was going to take some getting used to.

The only other newbie on the crew was a young flight attendant named Hattie Durham, who looked enough like the infamous Trish that Rayford had to once again slug it out with his conscience over the Christmas party fiasco a few years before. Hattie was introduced to him by his favorite senior flight attendant, Janet Allen. When she sent Hattie back to her chores, Janet whispered, "Just between you and me, Captain, she's a little ditzy. Ambitious, though, I'll give her that. Wants my job on an international route."

"Think she'll make it?"

"I'm not sure she knows when we're in the air or on the ground just yet."

As he and Chris Smith settled into the cockpit, Rayford said, "I love flying these. They handle nice and solid on final because of the weight."

"Tell me about it," Smith said. "Wind doesn't affect 'em much, does it?"

"Got to love a stable approach," Rayford said. "The downside is you can't maneuver quickly. It's no fighter jet."

Rayford reached behind his seat for the maintenance logbook. He was to read all the past write-ups before pushing back from the gate. He was about halfway through when Janet interrupted with the credentials of a jump-seater — a pilot from another airline catching a free ride. By the time Rayford studied the document and signed off on it, it was time to go.

Once in the air, First Officer Smith split his time between reading the *Chicago Tribune*, monitoring the instruments, and answering all radio calls from traffic control. Rayford was a stickler for rules and would not have read recreationally while in the air, but since Smith seemed an old hand and didn't miss a thing, he didn't say anything.

The sun hung just below Rayford's glare shield, making him squint even behind his dark gray lenses. The next time Chris Smith looked up, he said, "Oops, how long has that been there?"

"What?"

"That message," Smith said, pointing. He tossed his paper on the jump seat and sat up straighter.

Rayford shielded his eyes and found the message screen reading "ENGINE #1 OIL FILT."

His lower monitor, normally blank, now displayed engine readings. Oil pressure was normal, even on the engine in question, the one farthest to his left. "Engine number one oil-filter checklist, please," he said.

"Roger," Chris said, digging into the right side pocket for the emergency manual. Rayford did not recall this procedure on his last simulator ride and so assumed it was not a big deal. On the other hand, neither had he finished checking the maintenance log.

While Chris was finding the right section, Rayford grabbed the log and speed-read. Sure enough, engine number one had required an oil-filter change in Miami before the leg to O'Hare, and metal chips had been detected on the used filter. They must have been within acceptable limits, however, as the mechanic had signed off on the note. And the plane had made it to Chicago without incident.

" 'Retard thrust level slowly until message no longer displayed,' " Chris read.

Rayford followed the procedure and watched the message screen. The throttle reached idle, but the message still shone. After a minute he said, "It's not going out. What next?"

" 'If ENG OIL FILT message remains displayed with thrust lever closed: FUEL CONTROL SWITCH . . . CUTOFF.' "

Rayford grabbed the control cutoff switch and said, "Confirm number one cutoff switch?"

"Confirmed."

Rayford pulled out and down in one smooth motion while increasing pressure on the right rudder pedal. Engine number one shut down and the auto throttle increased power on the other three. Airspeed slowly decreased, and Rayford doubted anyone but Janet would even notice. And she knew enough not to bother the pilots right then.

He and Chris determined a new altitude, and he instructed Chris to call air-traffic control at Albuquerque to get clearance to descend to 32,000 feet. They then positioned a transponder to warn other traffic that they might be unable to climb or maneuver properly if there was a conflict.

Rayford had no question they could reach Los Angeles without incident now. He called Janet. "You probably noticed we descended awhile back."

"I did. Seemed a little early for step-down into LAX."

"Right. I shut down number one due to a minor oil problem. I'll make an announcement shortly."

Rayford became aware of the strain on his right foot and remembered he had to increase pressure to compensate for the uneven thrust of the remaining engines. *C'mon, Rayford. Fly the airplane.*

"Mind taking the controls for a minute, Chris? I should call the company."

"I have the airplane," Chris said.

Following protocol, Rayford confirmed, "You have the airplane."

After Rayford informed Pan-Con of the situation, the dispatcher told him of low visibility at LAX. "You'll want to check weather as you get closer."

"We have plenty of fuel if we have to divert," Rayford said. "In fact, I wish we had less. We're going to land a little heavy."

"Roger."

Rayford made his announcement, telling passengers he had shut down the number one engine but that he didn't expect anything but a routine landing at LAX. The lower the plane flew, however, the more he could tell that the power margin had increased. He did not want to have to go around, because going from near idle to full power on three engines would require a lot of rudder to counteract the thrust differential.

LAX tower was informed of the engine issue and cleared the Pan-Con heavy for initial landing sequence. At 10,000 feet Rayford began checking descent figures. Chris said, "Auto brakes."

Rayford responded, "Three set."

That configured the plane to brake itself at a medium rate unless Rayford intervened manually. LAX approach control turned Rayford and Chris over to the tower, which cleared them to land on runway 25 left and informed them of wind speed and RVR (runway visual range).

Rayford flipped on the taxi lights and directed Chris to zero the rudder trim. Rayford felt the pressure increase under his foot. He would have to keep up with the auto throttles as the power changed and adjust the rudder pressure to match. He was as busy as he had ever been on a landing, and the weather was not cooperating. Low cloud cover blocked his view of the runway.

"Glide slope's alive," Chris said.

"Gear down," Rayford said. "Flaps 20."

Rayford worked with Chris, setting the speed to match the flap settings and feeling the auto throttles respond by reducing power to slow the plane. "Glide slope intercept," he said, "flaps 30, landing check." He set the speed indicator at 148, final speed for a flaps-30 approach with that much weight.

Chris followed orders and grabbed the checklist from the glare shield. "Landing gear," he said.

"Down," Rayford said.

"Flaps."

"Thirty."

"Speed brakes."

"Armed."

"Landing check complete," Chris said.

The plane could land itself, but Rayford wanted to be in control just in case. It was a lot easier to be flying than to have to take over if the autopilot had to be suddenly switched off.

"Final approach fix," Chris said.

A loud horn sounded when Rayford clicked off both the autopilot and throttles. "Autopilot disengaged," he said.

"One thousand feet," Chris said.

"Roger."

They were in the middle of clouds and would not likely see the ground until just before touchdown.

A mechanical voice announced, "Five hundred feet." It would announce again at fifty, thirty, twenty, and ten feet. They were ninety seconds from touchdown.

Suddenly Rayford overheard a transmission. "Negative, US Air 21," the tower said, "you are not cleared for takeoff."

"Roger, tower," came the answer. "You were broken. Understand US Air 21 is cleared for takeoff."

"Negative!" the tower responded. "Negative, US Air 21! You are *not* cleared to take the runway!"

"Fifty feet," the auto announcer called out. "Thirty."

Rayford broke through the clouds.

"Go around, Cap!" Chris shouted. "A '57 is pulling onto the runway! Go around! Go around!"

Rayford could not imagine missing the 757. Time slowed, and he saw Irene, Chloe, and Raymie clearly in his mind, imagined them grieving, felt guilty about leaving them. And all the people on the plane. The crew. The passengers. And those on the US Air.

In slow motion he noticed a red dot on the center screen of the instrument console with a minus 2 next to it. The auto announcer was sounding, Chris screaming, the tower shouting on the radio, "Pull up! Pull up! Pull up!"

Rayford mashed the go-around buttons on the throttles twice for maximum power and called out, "God, help me!"

Chris Smith whined, "Amen! Now fly!"

Rayford felt the descent arresting, but it didn't appear it would be enough. Rayford imagined the wide eyes of the US Air passengers on the ground. "Flaps 20!" he barked. "Positive rate. Gear up." Smith's hands were flying, but the gap was closing. *I'll never miss another Sunday at church as long as I live. And I'll pray every day.*

The plane suddenly dipped left, the three good engines causing the slight roll. Rayford had not added enough rudder to counteract them. If he didn't adjust, the wingtip would hit the ground. They were a split second from the 757's tail — standing nearly four stories — and about to bottom out. Rayford closed his eyes and braced for impact. He heard swearing in the tower and from Chris. What a way to go.

The Pan-Con heavy could not have missed the US Air by more than inches, and the left wingtip missed the ground by less than that. Climbing slowly now, Rayford was drenched and, he was sure, ashen. "How did we miss them, Chris?"

"Your prayer musta been answered, Cap. Praise the Lord and pass the diapers."

The tower was still shouting, interrupted by the US Air cockpit. Rayford's knuckles were white, and, finally persuaded he was alive, he set about getting control of the plane. All he wanted was for the flight to be over. When the tower gave a final vector, Rayford announced an auto land.

"I second that!" Chris said.

The pilots configured the plane again and ran the landing checklist. The screen read LAND 3, indicating that all three autopilots were functioning normally. They touched down without incident.

Rayford heard applause from the cabin, but no one was as relieved as he was. He knew messages would be waiting from the ground agent to call operations and the tower. That was all he needed, to rehash the nightmare.

Had God answered his prayer by making

him err on the rudder and cause the slight turn that allowed the right wing to miss the US Air? Strange kind of intervention, Rayford thought, but he had made a bargain. This time he might just have to make good on it.

Twenty-Six

Nicolae Carpathia was awakened from a sound sleep. At least he thought he was awakened. Maybe he was still dreaming. There had been no noise, no light. His eyes had simply popped open.

As was his custom when a dream seemed too real, he reached under his silk pajamas and pinched himself. Hard. He was awake. Just like that, on full alert. He sat up in the dark bedroom and peered out the window.

What was that? A figure sitting on the roof? There was no way up there without a serious ladder. Another ten feet and the figure would have reached Aunt Viv's level. Nicolae was tempted to direct it that way. If the figure had an ill motive, better her than him, and he would have time to escape.

But the figure wasn't moving. Holding his breath, Nicolae slipped slowly out of bed, quietly drew open the drawer of his bedside stand, and pulled out a massive Glock handgun. As he crept toward the window, the figure turned to look at him, and Nicolae froze, though there was no light in the room, no way for the figure to see him.

He lifted the Glock to eye level, hands shaking. But before he could pull back the firing mechanism, the figure lifted a finger and shook its head, as if to say he wouldn't need that. "I am not here to harm you," Nicolae heard, though not audibly. "Put down your weapon."

Nicolae set the Glock on the bureau and stared. His heart rate slowed, but he didn't know what to do. Unlock and raise the window? Invite the figure in? In the next instant he was transported outside, still in his pajamas, and now he and the figure, a male, stood in a desolate wasteland. Nicolae tensed at the growls and howls and whines of animals. He pinched himself again. This was real.

The figure was draped head to toe in a hooded black robe, his face and hands and feet hidden. "Wait here," the man said. "I shall return for you in forty days."

"I cannot survive here! What will I eat?"

"You shall not eat."

"Where will I stay? There is no shelter!"

"Forty days."

"Wait! My people —"

"Your people will be informed." And with that the figure was gone.

Nicolae wished the time would speed as it had when he had moved from the bedroom to this place. But it did not. He was aware of every crawling second, the heat of the day, the bone chill of the night. Nicolae had grown accustomed to creature comforts. He was not used to hunger, to fear, to darkness. He might have tried to walk home, had he any idea which direction it was. All he saw was nothingness on every side.

Irene Steele tried to fight off a niggling restlessness by telling herself that hers was the lot of many young mothers. She had a daughter in school and a prekindergarten son, not to mention a traveling husband. Her days were long and hard and anything but boring. Money was an issue, of course, but she couldn't deny she had been fully aware of Rayford's materialistic bent from the beginning. Maybe he was trying to fill some hole too. Nothing ever seemed enough. The luster of a new gadget or toy seemed to quickly fade.

Irene fought to inject deeper meaning into their lives. But Rayford seemed restless at family picnics, bored with walks that ended with keeping the kids from fighting or running too far ahead. Rayford was good enough with Chloe and Raymie, but his days off were filled with golf and television.

Just about the time Irene contented herself with a diagnosis of sleep deprivation, one of the other young mothers in the neighborhood raised a curtain for her that Irene hadn't even realized existed. She and Jackie — a cute, athletic brunette — sat chatting while their preschoolers played in the park. They had met nearly a year before but had never been to each other's home or socialized outside the park.

That's why Irene was taken aback when Jackie seemed nervous. "I want to ask you something, Eye," she said, using her unique nickname for Irene.

Raymie was at the top of the monkey bars, so Irene couldn't look away. "Sure, shoot."

"You happy with your church?"

My church? Irene didn't know what to say. She shrugged. "I guess. Yeah. It's big. Lots of stuff for the kids."

"You and your husband real involved?"

"No. We just go Sunday mornings. Rafe has been on some outings with the men. Fishing. A Bears game. A golf tournament."

"And you?"

"The women have a circle something-or-other," Irene said. "We collect stuff for inner-city moms." Raymie was on the ground now, so Irene stole a glance at Jackie, who still seemed self-conscious. "Why, Jackie?"

"Oh, nothing. I just thought if you weren't happy at your church, if you were looking for something more or different, you might want to try ours. It's called New Hope."

Interesting name, Irene thought.

"It's smallish," Jackie said. "Just a couple of hundred people is all. Nondenominational. Just a bunch of born-again Christians trying to get other people to heaven."

Aha, there it was. No wonder Jackie had been ill at ease. She said her church was nondenominational, but she was sure sounding like a Baptist.

"Nope," Irene said. "We're happy. But I'm glad you like your church."

Jackie seemed to relax, as if she had fulfilled an obligation and could get back to being a friend. Oh, she was still on a religious riff, but she must have been in more of a comfort zone now. She went on and on about how she had finally found peace of mind, a reason for living, knew why she had been "put on this earth. I know why I'm here, what my purpose is, and where I'm going."

Irene didn't want to pursue it, despite the

fact that she was dying for her own answers to those very questions.

After several days Nicolae thought he would go mad. He tried to mark the time by gouging the ground with a stick every sunrise. His hair and beard grew; his pajamas became tattered. He feared he was wasting away. Time and again he called out for the figure, finally screaming maniacally for hours, "I will die of hunger!"

Nicolae lost all track of time, not sure whether he had missed a day or two or added marks too often. At the end of a month he lay in a fetal position, his bones protruding, his teeth filmy. He rocked and wept, willing himself to die.

Hours and days passed long after he believed the forty days were up, until he despaired of ever being rescued. He slept for long periods, waking miserable, filthy, trembling, utterly surrendered to his fate. He had had a good run, he told himself. At twenty-four he was already one of the most promising, revered men in the world. He didn't deserve this.

Irene had to admit that her relationship with Jackie — limited as it was to the park, anyway — had begun to fray. Jackie was nice enough, and there was no question she was earnest. But she was now raising spiritual issues every day, and it was only Irene's politeness that seemed to encourage Jackie and convince her this was okay.

But it wasn't okay. She was meddling now, invading Irene's comfort zone. Yes, some of the things Jackie said nearly reached Irene's core. But mostly she felt threatened, insulted. That was the trouble with people who took this stuff too seriously. It was as if their way was the only way. It wasn't good enough for them that you were a Christian and a churchgoer. You had to be their kind of believer. Next thing you knew, you'd be rolling in the aisles, speaking in tongues, and getting healed.

Irene began to clam up when Jackie broached the subject, and finally — finally — Jackie must have noticed. "You don't have to come to my church, Eye," she said. "Just know you're welcome. Our pastor preaches and teaches straight out of the Bible. Your church teaches salvation, doesn't it?"

Irene shrugged, not hiding her pique. "We're going to church because we believe in God and want to go to heaven."

"But that's not how you qualify for heaven," Jackie said. "It's not something you earn. It's a gift."

Here we go again. Irene changed the subject. And Jackie backed off, at least temporarily. At home though, during those few minutes she had to herself, Irene could think of nothing else. Could it be? Heaven as a gift and not something you earned? It made no sense, but if it was true . . .

Irene knew her body language and tone had reached Jackie when her friend talked about everything but the issue the next couple of days. Irene determined not to raise it, despite her curiosity. No, it was more than that. It had become a hunger, a thirst. While she could have lectured Jackie on friendship and manners and diplomacy, Irene set that aside and thought only of the potential truth of her friend's point.

The fact was that Irene's church did *not* emphasize salvation. It was assumed they were all Christians, all on their way to heaven, all doing the best they could in a modern world. That there was something more, something deeper, something more personal, a way to connect with God . . . Irene could only pray that Jackie would get back to that subject. If Irene brought it up, she could imagine the floodgate of earnest sermonizing to which she would be subjected.

From somewhere, Jackie must have developed some sensitivity. For when she did get back to the issue, she rightly assessed where Irene stood. "I care about you, Eye," she said. "And the last thing I want to do is to insult you or push you away. If I promise to never bring this up again unless you ask me to, can I just give you a piece of literature and leave it at that?"

Irene was moved. She was so taken by Jackie's new approach that she had to be careful not to let the pendulum swing too far the other way. She was tempted to assure her friend that she wasn't offended, that she appreciated her concern, and that yes, she had a thousand questions.

Was it pride that got in her way? She didn't know. Irene affected an air of caution. "Okay," she said quietly. "That's fair." And she accepted the brochure. In truth, she couldn't wait to get home and read it.

Finally, at long last, the robed man re-appeared. Nicolae tried to muster the strength to attack, to harangue, but the spirit again lifted a finger and shook his head. "Are you the chosen one?" the figure said.

Nicolae nodded, still believing he was.

"Look around you. Bread."

"Nothing but stones," Nicolae rasped, cursing the man.

"If you are who you say you are, tell these stones to become bread."

"You mock me," Nicolae said.

The spirit did not move or speak.

"All right!" Nicolae shouted. "Stones, become bread!"

Immediately the rocks all around him became golden brown and steaming. He fell to his knees and lifted one to his nose with both hands. He thrust it into his mouth and began to devour it. "I am a god!" he said, his mouth full.

Rayford was on an overnight flight. Chloe was sleeping over at a friend's. Raymie had been asleep for a couple of hours already. Irene sat before the TV, her favorite program holding no interest for her as she fingered the tract Jackie had given her. It was short, simply written. Religious sounding. Full of Bible verses. And yet she sensed it contained answers. Was she kidding herself, playing mind games?

The thing promised a personal relationship with God through His Son. She had heard those words all her life and had run from them. They sounded weird, made no sense. But now, for some reason, they seemed to beckon her. She did not feel close to God.

Irene felt unworthy. The idea that she had been born in sin, was a sinner, had always repulsed her. Now it seemed to reach her. Something deep within told her it was unfair to hold against God what had become of her brother and her dad. If what the Bible said about her was true, did she deserve any better? In fact, she deserved worse. She deserved death herself.

The Bible verses reached her. She turned off the TV and read over and over the ones from the first chapter of John: "He came into the very world he created, but the world didn't recognize him. He came to his own people, and even they rejected him. But to all who believed him and accepted him, he gave the right to become children of God. They are reborn — not with a physical birth resulting from human passion or plan, but a birth that comes from God."

The tract urged the reader to receive this rebirth and be saved from sin. Irene suddenly wanted this more than she had ever wanted anything in her life. Acts 16:31 told her, "Believe in the Lord Jesus and you will be saved."

"Are you god?" the spirit said.

Suddenly Nicolae stood at the top of the temple in Jerusalem, warm bread still in his hand. "I am," he said. "I am that I am."

"If you are, throw yourself down and you will be rescued."

Shuddering, wasted, standing barefoot in tattered silk, Nicolae felt full of bread and full of himself. He smiled. And threw himself off the tower of the temple. Hurtling toward the rocky Temple Mount, he never once lost faith in himself or the promise of the spirit. Twenty feet from impact he began to float, landing on his feet like a cat.

Irene could not stem the tears. *How do I do this?* She read the brochure again and again. Could it be this easy? Confess to God that you are a sinner. Ask Him to forgive you. Receive His gift of salvation through the death of Christ on the cross. And then you are saved?

She shuddered, pushing conflicting thoughts and doubts from her mind. Irene was smart enough not to be swayed solely by emotion, but something was happening to her. She was thoroughly convinced that God was reaching out to her. She slid off the chair onto the floor and knelt, something she had never done in her whole life.

Suddenly Nicolae and the spirit were at the top of a mountain, barefoot in the snow.

The air was frigid and thin, and Nicolae felt his chest heaving, fighting for enough oxygen to keep him alive.

"From here you can see all the kingdoms of the world."

"Yes," Nicolae said. "I see them all."

"They are yours if you but kneel and worship me, your master."

Nicolae dropped to his knees before the spirit. "My lord and my god," he said.

Irene was aware only of the ticking clock on the mantel over the fireplace. She imagined Rayford walking in on her or one of her kids seeing her like this. She didn't care. "God," she said aloud, "I know I'm a sinner and need Your forgiveness and Your salvation. I receive Christ."

When Nicolae opened his eyes, he was back in his bed. That the experience had been real was borne out by his own stench and filth and ratty garments. He staggered from his bed and noticed a sheet of paper under the door. It was in Viv Ivins's flowing script:

Shower, change, and come down, beloved. Barber, manicurist, masseuse, and cook are here and at your service.

About the Authors

Jerry B. Jenkins (www.jerryjenkins.com) is the writer of the Left Behind series. He owns the Jerry B. Jenkins Christian Writers Guild (www.ChristianWritersGuild.com), an organization dedicated to mentoring aspiring authors, as well as Jenkins Entertainment, a filmmaking company (www.Jenkins-Entertainment.com). Former vice president of publishing for the Moody Bible Institute of Chicago, he also served many years as editor of *Moody* magazine and is now Moody's writer-at-large.

His writing has appeared in publications as varied as *Time* magazine, *Reader's Digest*, *Parade*, *Guideposts*, in-flight magazines, and dozens of other periodicals. Jenkins's biographies include books with Billy Graham, Hank Aaron, Bill Gaither, Luis Palau, Walter Payton, Orel Hershiser, and Nolan Ryan, among many others. His books appear regularly on the *New York Times*, *USA Today*, *Wall Street Journal*, and *Publishers Weekly* best-seller lists.

He holds two honorary doctorates, one from Bethel College (Indiana) and one from Trinity International University. Jerry and his wife, Dianna, live in Colorado and have three grown sons and three grandchildren.

Dr. Tim LaHaye (www.timlahaye.com), who conceived the idea of fictionalizing an account of the Rapture and the Tribulation, is a noted author, minister, and nationally recognized speaker on Bible prophecy. He is the founder of both Tim LaHaye Ministries and the Pre-Trib Research Center.

He also recently cofounded the Tim LaHaye School of Prophecy at Liberty University. Dr. LaHaye speaks at many of the major Bible prophecy conferences in the U.S. and Canada, where his prophecy books are very popular.

Dr. LaHaye earned a doctor of ministry degree from Western Theological Seminary and an honorary doctor of literature degree from Liberty University. For twenty-five years he pastored one of the nation's outstanding churches in San Diego, which grew to three locations. During that time he founded two accredited Christian high schools, a Christian school system of ten schools, and Christian Heritage College.

There are almost 13 million copies of Dr. LaHaye's fifty nonfiction books that have been published in over thirty-seven foreign languages. He has written books on a wide variety of subjects, such as family life, temperaments, and Bible prophecy. His current fiction works, the Left Behind series, written with Jerry B. Jenkins, continue to appear on the best-seller lists of the Christian Booksellers Association, *Publishers Weekly*, *Wall Street Journal*, *USA Today*, and the *New York Times*. LaHaye's second fiction series of prophetic novels consists of *Babylon Rising* and *The Secret on Ararat*, both of which hit the *New York Times* best-seller list and will soon be followed by *Europa Challenge*. This series of four action thrillers, unlike *Left Behind*, does not start with the Rapture but could take place today and goes up to the Rapture.

He is the father of four grown children and grandfather of nine. Snow skiing, waterskiing, motorcycling, golfing, vacationing with family, and jogging are among his leisure activities.